From These Hills, From These Valleys

This book was commissioned by
Mellon Bank, N.A.,
for the people of western Pennsylvania

From These Hills, From These Valleys

Selected Fiction About Western Pennsylvania

David P. Demarest, Jr., Editor

Anthony Spataro, Research Associate

University of Pittsburgh Press

Library of Congress Cataloguing in Publication Data

Main entry under title:
From these hills, from these valleys.

1. American fiction — 20th century. 2. Pennsyl-
vania — History — Fiction. I. Demarest, David P.
PZ1.F93 [PS648.P45] 813'.5'0932   75-15088
ISBN 0-8229-1123-X

Picture Credits

P. vi. Portion of oil-on-canvas mural by H. Moore on walls of forty-first floor of Mellon Bank Building, 525 William Penn Way, Pittsburgh.

P. xvi. Early view of Fort Pitt. Courtesy of Carnegie Library of Pittsburgh.

P. 5. *The Evening of Braddock's Defeat, July 9, 1755,* by William Coventry Wall. From collection of Historical Society of Western Pennsylvania.

P. 11. Replica of the *New Orleans,* manufactured for one hundredth birthday of boat, from *The Story of the New Orleans.* Courtesy of Historical Society of Western Pennsylvania.

P. 21. *Portrait of Jenny Lind,* by William Etty, R.A.

P. 23. From *Pittsburgh Post-Gazette,* November 12, 1851. Courtesy of Carnegie Library of Pittsburgh.

Pp. 34, 35, 36. Photographs by John O. Mather. Originals in Mather Collection, Drake Museum, Titusville. Courtesy of Carnegie Library of Pittsburgh.

Pp. 42, 51. Photographs by Frank E. Bingaman. Courtesy of Carnegie Library of Pittsburgh.

P. 45. Photograph by Charles Bax, Curator, Schellsburg Union.

Pp. 50, 63, 104, 107, 155. Courtesy of Carnegie Library of Pittsburgh.

P. 57. Photograph by Charles Lilley. From collection of David L. Polechko.

P. 64. Courtesy of Curtis Collection, Hillman Library, University of Pittsburgh.

P. 65. Courtesy of Carnegie Library of Pittsburgh and Agnes L. Starrett.

Pp. 71, 77. Photographs by Thomas Bell. Courtesy of Mrs. Marie Bell.

Pp. 73, 177. Photographs by Abram M. Brown. Courtesy of Carnegie Library of Pittsburgh.

P. 74. Photograph by Chautauqua Photograph Co. From *The Steel Workers,* by John A. Fitch. Russell Sage Foundation, 1910. Courtesy of Carnegie Library of Pittsburgh.

P. 75. Courtesy of Mrs. Marie Bell.

P. 86. *American Iron Works, Pittsburgh, Pa.* Courtesy of Frederick A. Hetzel.

P. 91. From *History of Allegheny County, Pennsylvania.* L. H. Everts & Co., 1876. Courtesy of Carnegie Library of Pittsburgh.

P. 92. Photograph by R. W. Johnston. Courtesy of Carnegie Library of Pittsburgh.

P. 99. Monongahela House. Courtesy of Carnegie Library of Pittsburgh.

P. 105. *The Flood at Pittsburgh, Pennsylvania, View from Allegheny City Looking Toward Herr's Island,* sketch by Alexander Y. Lee. From collection of Historical Society of Western Pennsylvania.

P. 119. Courtesy of Westmoreland Historical Society.

P. 125. *Making Bessemer Steel at Pittsburgh,* by Charles Graham. From *Harper's Weekly,* April 10, 1886. Courtesy of Frederick A. Hetzel.

Pp. 126, 135, 136, 137. Courtesy of United Steelworkers of America.

P. 159. Courtesy of Samuel A. McClung.

Pp. 168, 169. Courtesy of Mary K. Armstrong.

P. 179. Courtesy of Kaufmann's.

P. 193. Courtesy of Chester Aaron.

P. 194. Courtesy of Michael Weber.

P. 203. Photograph by Dale Gleason. From *Pittsburgh Press.*

P. 210. Courtesy of Kennywood Park.

P. 223. Courtesy of Robert J. Gangewere, Carnegie Institute.

P. 231. Photograph by Harry Coughanour. From *Pittsburgh Post-Gazette,* Dec. 29, 1969.

P. 232. Photograph by David P. Demarest, Jr.

Acknowledgments to publishers and individuals for permission to reprint stories are found on page xi.

For
Liz, Vic, and Jamie

Contents

Preface

The work that led to this anthology was begun out of innocent curiosity. In 1973, I became Anthony Spataro's adviser in a section of his graduate program at Carnegie-Mellon University, and together we decided that it might be interesting if he tried to compile a complete bibliography of published fiction about western Pennsylvania. Our assumption was that not much fiction about the region existed; certainly no one seemed to have heard of much. Beyond a few authors — Willa Cather, Mary Roberts Rinehart, Marcia Davenport — who had ever written about Pittsburgh and the immediate area? But we were curious.

Our assumption that there was not much material proved wrong. Mr. Spataro's list grew from twenty-five to fifty novel titles, from fifty to one hundred, then to one hundred and fifty. As the months went by, no end was in sight. Not only was there a lot of fiction, but some of it was excellent, and from a regional point of view, a great deal of it was very interesting.

The idea for an anthology developed naturally enough. Why not share the riches? In a collection that sampled the best of this fiction, why not try to tell the story of western Pennsylvania itself?

I discussed this idea with Frederick Hetzel of the University of Pittsburgh Press and with Hax McCullough and Mary Brignano of McCullough Communications. They were all encouraging. Mr. McCullough in turn presented the idea to Mellon Bank as a possible service to the people of western Pennsylvania in the Bicentennial year. Mellon Bank was interested, and commissioned me to compile a manuscript. Without Mellon Bank's support,

From These Hills, From These Valleys would not exist.

When the manuscript was complete, Mr. Hetzel proposed to the Bank that the book be published under the imprint of the University of Pittsburgh Press — if it were favorably evaluated by the advisory committee of Pitt faculty that must approve every University Press publication. The Bank agreed, and the Press committee supported Mr. Hetzel's recommendation.

Researching — "discovering" — local literature has special problems and pleasures. The joy of recognizing familiar regional locales in a novel is often counterbalanced by the problem of acquiring a given book. Sometimes the rule seems to be "the closer to home the subject, the harder to get a copy."

Pittsburgh's major libraries can supply many of the titles in a regional bibliography — the Pennsylvania Room at the Carnegie Library is a particularly good source, although its copies do not circulate. Even so, more than fifty novels about western Pennsylvania seem available only from libraries outside the region. (For example, Lucien Hubbard's *Rivers to the Sea* had to be obtained from Seattle, Washington.)

Sometimes local inaccessibility results from a book's being "used to death" by area readers. When that happens a second problem arises: Most regional books, because their primary audience is limited, go out of print and stay out of print; they are no longer on the market and are not easily replaced. Almost all the novels represented in this anthology are, in fact, out of print.

The joy of recognizing local scenes and people in fiction is good compensation for these frustrations. And there are many novels, beyond those represented here, that are rich in local color. A person who knows the Oakland and Squirrel Hill areas of Pittsburgh may be delighted by Aleen Leslie's *The Scent of the Roses* (a murder mystery set on Wilkins Avenue, circa 1910), Al Hine's *An Unfound Door* (a family chronicle set on Denniston Avenue during the first half of the twentieth century), or Elinor Stone's *Fear Rides the Fog* (a kidnapping in Point Breeze some thirty years ago). In the full body of fiction about western Pennsylvania there is probably a novel, somewhere, about almost any sector of the region.

Many people contributed, in a variety of ways, to the development of this anthology.

Anthony Spataro's work on a bibliography of fiction about western Pennsylvania laid the groundwork.

Marlene Demarest did research that made timely completion of the project possible.

Hax McCullough and Mary Brignano managed the book through production and played an important role in the selection of illustrations; Jeannette Brian also gave significant assistance.

In addition to Fred Hetzel at the University of Pittsburgh Press, Louise Craft and Beth Luey played various editorial roles.

Maria Zini and Ann Loyd, of the Carnegie Library's Pennsylvania Room, were always helpful in making materials available.

Many people read the manuscript as it evolved and supplied critical reactions; some suggested novels that had not yet turned up in the bibliographic search. Even a partial list of such people should include Joe Baim, Russ Brignano, Vicki Demarest, Paul Garver, Ruth Kunkle, Jim and Judy Korn, and Kathleen Sashin. In particular, Bob Gangewere was a reader and rereader.

Special thanks go to Mellon Bank, not only for their interest and support, but for the completely free hand they gave me in developing the manuscript. The selections in *From These Hills, From These Valleys* and the accompanying commentaries are solely my responsibility.

David P. Demarest, Jr.

Acknowledgments

This is a continuation of the copyright page. Grateful acknowledgment is made to the following publishers and individuals for permission to reprint the stories in this book:

"Militia of Babel." From *The Forest and the Fort* by Hervey Allen. Copyright 1943 by Hervey Allen. Copyright © 1971 by Ann Andrews Allen. Reprinted by permission of Holt, Rinehart and Winston, Publishers.

"Figure Eight." From *Rivers to the Sea: An American Story* by Lucien Hubbard. Copyright © 1942, by Lucien Hubbard; copyright renewed © 1969, by Lucien Hubbard. Reprinted by permission of Simon and Schuster.

"Jenny Lind." From *Where the Red Volleys Poured* by Charles W. Dahlinger. Published in 1907 by G. W. Dillingham Co. Out of copyright.

"The Odor of Raw Black Oil." Excerpts from *Captains and the Kings* by Taylor Caldwell. Copyright © 1972 by Janet Rabeck. Reprinted by permission of Doubleday & Company, Inc.

"Brothers of No Kin." Short story by Conrad Richter. Originally published in April 1914 in *Forum* magazine. Out of copyright.

"Undergoing a Caesarian." From *The Cinder Buggy* by Garet Garrett. Copyright 1923 by E. P. Dutton & Co., renewal, 1951, by Garet Garrett. Reprinted by permission of the publishers, E. P. Dutton & Co., Inc.

"Oh My Darling." Chapter VI in *The Iron Woman* by Margaret Deland. Copyright, 1910, 1911 by Harper & Row, Publishers, Inc., renewed, 1939 by Margaret Wade Campbell Deland. By permission of Harper & Row, Publishers, Inc.

"A Grand Sight." From *Clouded Hills* by Elizabeth Moorhead, copyright 1929, R. 1957 by Elizabeth Moorhead Vermorcken, reprinted by permission of the publisher, The Bobbs-Merrill Company, Inc.

"A Laborer Named Mihal." From *Out of This Furnace* by Thomas Bell. Published by Little, Brown and Company. Copyright 1941 by Thomas Bell. Copyright © 1968 by Marie Bell. Reprinted by permission of Marie Bell and Collins-Knowlton-Wing, Inc.

"The Old Man's Presence." Reprinted by permission of Charles Scribner's Sons from *The Valley of Decision* by Marcia Davenport (1942).

"Conscience in Art." Short story by O. Henry, copyright 1907 by Doubleday & Company, Inc., from *The Gentle Grafter* by O. Henry. Reprinted by permission of Doubleday & Company, Inc.

"Another Flood." From *The Case of Jennie Brice* by Mary Roberts Rinehart. Copyright 1913 by Mary Roberts Rinehart. Copyright 1941 by Stanley M. Rinehart, Jr., Frederick R. Rinehart and Alan G. Rinehart. Reprinted by permission of Holt, Rinehart and Winston, Publishers.

"A Beau at Institute." Reprinted with permission of Macmillan Publishing Co., Inc., from *The Rolling Years* by Agnes Sligh Turnbull. Copyright 1936 by Macmillan Publishing Co., Inc., renewed 1964 by Agnes Sligh Turnbull.

"Crazy-Mad Steel." From *Blood on the Forge* by William Attaway. Published in 1941 by Doubleday, Doran & Co. Reprinted by permission of William A. Attaway.

"Very Young and Very Sweet." From *The Big Money* by John Dos Passos. Published in 1936 by Harcourt, Brace and Company. Copyright by Elizabeth H. Dos Passos. Reprinted by permission of Elizabeth H. Dos Passos.

"Double Birthday." Short story by Willa Cather. Originally published in February, 1929 in *Forum* magazine. Reprinted by permission of Charles E. Cather, trustee of estate of Willa Cather.

"The Young Violinist." From *Black Fury* by Michael A. Musmanno. Published in 1966 by Fountainhead Publishers, Inc. Reprinted by permission of the publishers.

"The Great World of Timothy Francis Brennan." From *Duffy's Rocks* by Edward Fenton. Copyright © 1974 by Edward Fenton. Reprinted by permission of the publishers, E. P. Dutton & Co., Inc.

"That Polack Anti-Semite Toadstool Expert." From *About Us* by Chester Aaron. Published in 1967 by McGraw-Hill Book Company. Reprinted by permission of the author.

"The Story of My Life." From *Maria Light* by Lester Goran. Copyright © 1962 by Lester Goran. Reprinted by permission of the Houghton Mifflin Company.

"Irish Picnic." From *Miners Hill* by Michael O'Malley. Published by Harper & Row, Publishers, Inc. Copyright © 1962 by Michael O'Malley. Reprinted by permission of the author.

"The Persistent Image." Excerpted from *The Persistent Image* by Gladys Schmitt. Copyright © 1955 by Gladys Schmitt. Reprinted by arrangement with The Dial Press.

"Confirming the Obvious." From *The Rocksburg Railroad Murders* by K. C. Constantine. Copyright © 1972 by K. C. Constantine. Reprinted by permission of the publishers, Saturday Review Press/E. P. Dutton & Co., Inc.

"How Pittsburgh Returned to the Jungle." Short story by Haniel Long. Originally published on June 20, 1923, in *The Nation*. Out of copyright.

Introduction

Arranged chronologically, by subject, to span the past two hundred years, *From These Hills, From These Valleys* is a record — a commemoration — of work and life-styles in western Pennsylvania as they have been experienced and interpreted by writers of fiction. This volume is a sample of the surprising number of novels and stories that have been written about the area.

From These Hills, From These Valleys attempts to give a realistic picture of the region, to illustrate problems as well as pleasures. During its two-century development by the white man, western Pennsylvania has never been touted for bland, conventional prettiness. Its fascination derives from tension and contrast, from energy and potential conflict, from the mix of various nationalities, of workers and giant industry, of mills and mines and natural landscape. Even in a "nation of immigrants," western Pennsylvania is distinctive in the number and variety of its ethnic groups.

If this anthology has any preeminent theme, it is to commemorate the diversity of peoples who have come to call western Pennsylvania home.

The twenty-four selections in *From These Hills, From These Valleys* (mostly excerpts from novels) were chosen with several guidelines in mind.

To appeal as good, readable fiction. A rule of thumb in making selections for the anthology was that a good fictional episode allows a reader to see the action through the eyes of believable characters, in some fashion "to be there." The facts about historical events can be learned from reading history books. It is the achievement of good fiction to let a person relive an event.

Of course, the commemorative and historical purposes of *From These Hills, From These Valleys* complicated selection. Many episodes call for commemoration because they are dramatic moments in the area's history — in the eighteenth century, the defeat of Braddock and the Whiskey Rebellion, or the railroad and the Homestead strikes of the nineteenth. Some important chapters in western Pennsylvania history have been omitted because there seemed to be no selections of appropriate length with the special quality of good fiction.

The standard of readability has created another pattern in selection: All of the pieces in *From These Hills, From These Valleys* come from works written in the last seventy-five years.

It would be possible to put together an anthology suggesting the development of western Pennsylvania by going to "historic" writers. An on-the-scene sense of the eighteenth century could come from Hugh Henry Brackenridge's *Modern Chivalry*, one of the first novels written in the United States, parts of which were published in Pittsburgh in the 1790s; or the mid-nineteenth century could be represented by Jane Swisshelm and Rebecca Harding Davis, both of whom wrote about western Pennsylvania from the point of view of feminist social critics. Unfortunately, while a book produced by this method of selection might be scholarly, it would not be very readable. From the vantage of the 1970s, the further back in time one reads, the more curious and mannered the styles of many fiction writers look. Such writers may be extremely interesting once they become familiar;

in short excerpts, they are hard to adjust to.

If the test of readability is taken seriously, the bias of selection is inevitably toward modern writers, for their style appeals immediately. Even with historical subjects, the readable work more often than not is of relatively recent vintage.

To suggest the historical evolution of western Pennsylvania. The emphasis here has to be on *suggest.* Twenty-four selections can at best suggest historical movements over a two-hundred-year span: Gaps and discontinuities are inevitable. Above all, an editor is constrained by the subjects authors have chosen. For instance, a "head count" of novels about western Pennsylvania shows that roughly two-thirds of them are set during the past one hundred years. That distribution — plus the difficulty of adapting some of the earlier materials — is reflected in the contents of this volume.

It is also the case that authors have written time and again about certain subjects while apparently ignoring others. For example, steel magnates, coke kings, and oil men abound in the fiction, but no one seems to have taken the Pittsburgh area during the Civil War for a central subject, although the mobilization of industry, the war panic, and the arsenal explosion at Lawrenceville made it a dramatic time. No fiction has been uncovered that focuses much on sports, although professional and club sports have been part of the regional scene for at least a century. Here an anthologizer simply remains frustrated.

Despite such limitations, *From These Hills, From These Valleys* is arranged chronologically by subject matter and thus provides a selective account of the changing quality of life in various parts of the region during the past two hundred years.

To illustrate a variety of the region's ethnic and work styles. A volume commemorating western Pennsylvania could hardly be accurate or complete without an ethnic emphasis, and therefore an early intention was that the anthology be something of an "ethnic reader."

Such an emphasis may redress an imbalance that can develop in literary or historical studies. By definition, "famous" people are most often celebrated. Generals, presidents, and industrial magnates are memorialized in statues; after all, "success" makes fame. It follows that it is easier, and may even seem more important, to study the career of Andrew Carnegie than the lives of individual workers in his mills. Similarly, "successful" ethnic groups publicize themselves and enjoy lifestyles that invite attention. Such bias always needs correcting. A region that prides itself on the variety of its people appropriately commemorates ethnic groups, as well as individuals, whose success is unpublicized but whose daily work may in reality define the fiber and flavor of a community.

Fortunately, the fiction that has been written about western Pennsylvania is rich in its emphasis on a range of ethnic and work styles. Probably the basic theme connecting the whole body of fiction about the region is the tension and hoped-for reconciliation between various nationality groups, between blue-collar workers and managerial classes. The theme is sounded from the start in the fictional accounts of the polyglot European mercenaries who originally trekked into the region — the English, Scots, and Irish, the French and Germans. Will they create a viable relationship with the ethnic group they encounter — the Indians? Will they be able to work together to realize the potential of the new land?

Most of the selections in *From These Hills, From These Valleys* turn to some degree on issues of ethnic or class difference. Such problems, the fiction writers seem to say cumulatively, are what the history of western Pennsylvania is really about.

To include at least some of the famous or "favorite" authors who have written about the area. Although one intention of *From These Hills, From These Valleys* is to introduce readers to a sample of relatively little-known fiction about western Pennsylvania, some authors are included who have written a good deal about the area and who are, or have been, widely read. In a com-

memorative volume, it seems altogether fitting and proper to acknowledge the work of writers like Agnes Sligh Turnbull, Margaret Deland, Gladys Schmitt, and Hervey Allen.

Overall, of course, the purpose of *From These Hills, From These Valleys* is to stimulate interest in the heritage of western Pennsylvania and to encourage readers to make their own explorations into the fiction.

Except for occasional omissions (indicated by ellipsis marks), the authors' original texts have been reproduced verbatim, with no attempt to correct such minor factual errors as may occur.

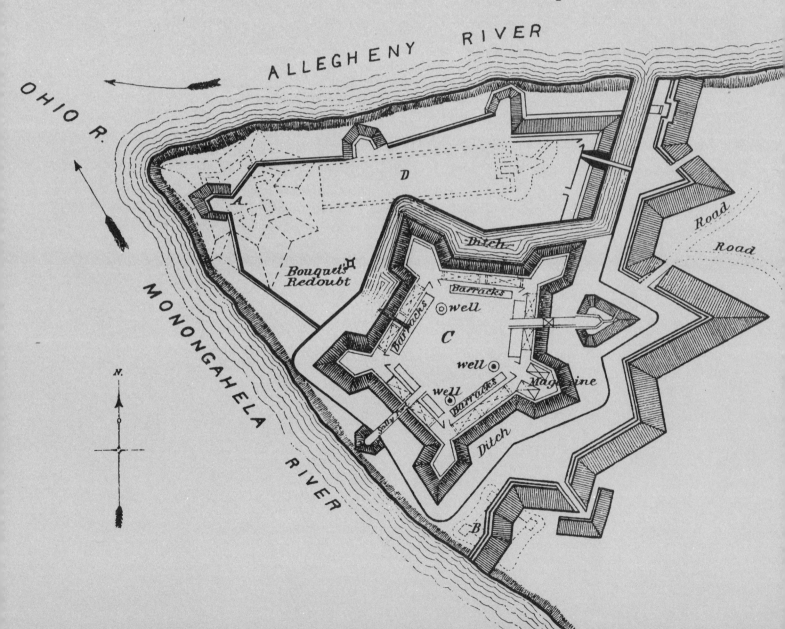

PLAN OF
FORT PITT

A. *Fort Duquesne.*   C. *Fort Pitt – Built 1759–60.*
B. *Stockade Fort 1753.*   D. *Stockade, covering French Barrack*

ALLEGHENY   RIVER

OHIO R.

MONONGAHELA   RIVER

D

A

Bouquet's Redoubt

Ditch

Barracks

well

Barracks

C

well

well

Barracks

Magazine

Sally

Ditch

Road

Road

B

N.

HERVEY ALLEN
"Militia of Babel"

Simeon Ecuyer ponders
life west of the Alleghenies

Time: 1763

Setting: The Forks

A surprising number of eighteenth-century names have descended into modern times in the Pittsburgh area. Thanks to street signs and township names, Forbes, Grant, O'Hara, Bouquet, St. Clair, Halket, and Braddock (to name a few) are still part of the public record. But while Braddock and Grant achieved their fame through spectacular military failure (the former in the Turtle Creek massacre of 1755, the latter in a suicidal foray on Fort Duquesne in 1758), it has been the fate of Simeon Ecuyer to illustrate the belief that "old soldiers fade away."

Ecuyer commanded Fort Pitt for about a year, in 1763-1764. As it happened, 1763 was the year of the Pontiac War, the only concerted Indian resistance ever encountered by whites as they occupied what is now the Pittsburgh area. Through disciplined defensive measures, Ecuyer held the Indians off at the Point until Colonel Bouquet, advancing from the east, met and defeated their forces at Bushy Run.

For the most part, events by-passed Fort Duquesne/Fort Pitt. During the struggle between the French and the British for control of the Forks, General Braddock's army had approached from the south in 1755, crossed the Monongahela near the present-day Kennywood Park, and been ambushed and slaughtered by the French and Indians just west of where the Edgar Thomson plant now stands. In 1758, General Forbes had cut a new road through from the east, marching with several thousand men toward Fort Duquesne; in September, Major James Grant was sent ahead to reconnoiter, and he and his men were cut down in the vicinity of what is now Pittsburgh's Grant Street. When Forbes himself approached the fort, the French abandoned it without a fight. It remained for Ecuyer to direct the only real siege action that involved the fort itself, though even then the main engagement was finally fought at Bushy Run, some fifteen miles to the east.

This passage from Hervey Allen's The Forest and the Fort *sums up much of what is known about Ecuyer as a person — his disciplined intellectual quality of mind, his sense of tradition and the past. What comes down historically (through logbooks and correspondence) are the attitudes Allen portrays, Ecuyer's vigorous response to the challenge of opening a new land, yet his European longing for the cultured life back on the shores of Lake Geneva.*

This selection introduces the fundamental, recurring theme of fiction about western Pennsylvania, the region's multinational (or multiethnic) composition. As Ecuyer surveys his "Militia of Babel," the Swiss, Welsh, Pennsylvania Dutch, Irish, Scotch-Irish, Germans, and Quakers, he duly notes that the solution to the Indian problem may be genocide.

Hervey Allen (1888-1949) was born in Pittsburgh, went to Shady Side Academy (as well as Sterrett and Linden public schools), and was a graduate of the University of Pittsburgh. He moved East during the First World War.

The Forest and the Fort *is the first volume of a trilogy about western Pennsylvania; the succeeding volumes are* Bedford Village *(1944) and* Toward the Morning *(1948).*

"Militia of Babel"

Beyond the mountains lay the Valleys of Eden. But to go there was to slip one's finger out of the handclasp of mankind. To go there was to go lonely; to defy the forest, the Indians, and the lawful king. To go there was to move westward without the baggage or the impedimenta of the past. It was to drop everything, except God, language itself, and the memory of simple numbers. It was to begin all over again, to become a something new and unique in time.

But that was the fascination of it. That was the lure. That was at once the refuge, the opportunity, and the goal.

The American did not begin by overthrowing society, by reorganizing an old civilization. He left all that completely behind him. He disinherited himself. He reinvented and reincarnated society. For the first time in memorized history man was free to act entirely on his own responsibility. He was back in the forest again. He had nothing but himself, the animals, and the trees to contend with. There liberty was not a dream and an idea to die for; it was a state of nature to be successfully lived in. In the Valleys of Eden, west of the Alleghenies, that was where and how new America began. The seeds of it were scattered in lonely cabins, lost apparently in an ocean of trees.

Out of them genesis. . . .

Simeon Ecuyer, gentleman, captain in his Britannic Majesty's 60th Regiment of foot, the Royal Americans, and commandant of Fort Pitt, sat near the door of his quarters and contemplated, not without military interest and a Gallic eye for the picturesque, the scene in the interior of the fort that lay before him.

He had moved that day into the "Governor's Quarters," as it was called. It was the new brick building near the southwest bastion, which Colonel Bouquet had occupied some months ago, and reserved for his use, if and when he should return. The colonel had even left his camp bed behind, with a good mattress. But, as there seemed small chance that Colonel Bouquet would be able to return from the eastern settlements and lead the remnants of his sickly West Indian regiments over the Alleghenies to the relief of Fort Pitt for some time to come, Captain Ecuyer had taken advantage of a state of siege, and the excuse of necessity, to move into his colonel's quarters.

The captain was a professional soldier and therefore an adept at judging when such necessities arose. But he was also careful, and to salve his nice military conscience he had dispatched the colonel's lame mare, now nearly well, fattened and newly shod, back to the colonel's farm in Maryland, with nothing but a burden of her own oats and a letter. God alone knew whether she and the messenger who went with her would ever arrive at Fort Bedford. Between the prowling Indians and the wild Scotch-Irish on the frontiers, the king's property and that of his officers in western Pennsylvania was ever of uncertain tenure. Even the dispatches were frequently stopped and opened.

The good captain was tired of America. He was a native of Geneva. His mother had been a Frenchwoman of the impoverished Huguenot nobility, who had married a Swiss advocate, and Simeon,

3

their only son, had been brought up on law, theology, the classics, and military history. As a curious consequence, he had become a soldier of fortune, a sceptic, and an officer whose native abilities could be appreciated only by brilliant superiors. They being few, his fortunes had languished. In the course of years and several services, he had grown patiently tired of unremarked success and unrewarded energy.

Now he would have liked nothing better than to sell out his commission in the Royal Americans and retire to spend the remainder of his days enjoying the excellent wines and the no less cultivated and elegant conversation for which the shores of Lake Geneva and his native city were so noted.

But he was still a mere captain, and as yet too young to retire. Only thirty-six, in fact, although he looked much older. And there was small chance of his being able to sell out. No one with money, and the influence that went with it, wanted to buy a commission in the Royal American regiment. It was all work and small pay in that service, and ungrateful work at that.

Colonel Henri Bouquet, whom the captain had first met when in the service of the king of Sardinia, had lured his friend Ecuyer from a minor but promising post in the electoral household troops at Munich, by tales of the opportunities for active service and swift promotion to be had with the Royal Americans. They were to be a new corps with new blood and new tactics suited to warfare in the New World. Ecuyer had finally succumbed. He trusted and admired the genius of his friend Bouquet. They had been together at the battle of Coni, and besides that, the colonel was a Swiss himself, a native of Rolle in the canton of Vaud.

Only part of the colonel's great expectations for America had come true, however. There had been a great deal of active service in the bitter school of Indian warfare, and little more. Promotion, apparently pay itself, had all but ceased. Nevertheless, it was still a distinction and a joy to serve under Colonel Bouquet. He succeeded where "great generals" had awfully failed. Indeed, he was the prime reason why Ecuyer still employed his own not inconsiderable talents in the service of King George, despite wounds, hope deferred, and growing poverty. One was constantly learning from the colonel. There at least one advanced in one's own mind and profession, one grew. And what a rare sensation was that in any army!

For the rest of the officers in the Royal Americans the captain did not care — particularly. They were well enough. Some were professional soldiers like himself, foreigners in a foreign service. They at least obeyed orders carefully for the sake of professional reputation. But it was not always so with the bulk of the English officers who had come out to America with visions of easy garrison duty on a colonial post, only to find an Indian war on their hands. That was the worst kind of war in the world; little honour, savage and merciless fighting, incredible hardships, and fearful personal risk. A certain lack of enthusiasm among the older English officers was therefore understandable, but to Ecuyer's professional mind none the less exasperating. The subalterns alone he regarded as the grand hope of the regiment. They came from good families both in England and in America. They were the most promising material for soldiers the captain had ever seen. And in his time Ecuyer had seen a good deal of promising young material from East Prussia to Sicily.

As for the rank and file, they had been raised as the act of Parliament forming the regiment had required — in America. As it so happened, mostly in the province of Pennsylvania. They were made up mainly of immigrant Swiss, Welsh, Pennsylvania "Dutch," Irish, Scotch-Irish, Germans, renegade Quakers, a few frontier riflemen, escaped servants, and quite a number of mariners picked up along the water front at Philadelphia, men who would rather fight Indians and be scalped than linger to be flogged to death in the king's floating hells.

In this "Militia of Babel," as the captain called it, the orders were given in English, and all by enlistment were made subjects of the British

5

crown. That, the Mutiny Act, the hope of some-time being paid, and fear of the officers and the enemy, kept the regiment together — and one thing more. Something which it amused the captain to think all the historians he had read, except Caesar, had contrived completely to overlook. Yet it was one of the strongest and most patent characteristics of man: loyalty to one's own military legion, *esprit de corps.* It was the only principle, so far as the captain could see, that was stronger even than self-preservation, religion, or patriotism. . . .

To the mind of Captain Ecuyer, a thoroughly cultivated and European mind, the Indians constituted a ponderous problem in extermination.

Personally, they annoyed him. Their manners were bad. Also they were the enemies of the sovereign he served, and, as a good soldier, he was being thoroughly practical about doing away with them, individually or in such numbers as might from time to time try to fall upon him. In this policy General Amherst himself concurred. In fact, he had already written Colonel Bouquet suggesting the use of Cuban bloodhounds, if they could be obtained, and the introduction of smallpox-infected clothing amongst the tribes.

In any event, Fort Pitt was not going to be surprised or easily taken by the savages. Captain Ecuyer was the warrant for that assumption. Even with a mathematical mind, a military education, and a longing to return to Geneva, a keen and obstinate sense of the importance of his command was constantly present in the captain's thoughts.

Should Fort Pitt fall, the English might well be rolled back to the eastern seaboard. The post at the DeTroit, already in desperate straits, would be cut off beyond hope, and the country west of the mountains lost, perhaps permanently. It would lapse back into the wandering keep of devil hordes with stone axes. The captain was taking several stone axes home, along with a collection of arrowheads and scalps. . . .

Leave out the presence of firearms, and the scene of the captain's cogitations might almost have been taken from a page in the *Germania* of Tacitus. In fact, the Germanic peoples *were* back in the forest again and the Celts were still with them. The five-sided enclosure of the fort resounded with a cacophony of English, Welsh, German, and Irish. The captain thought in French.

There was really nothing so unique about America, he told himself. The frontier of Western civilization had moved from the Rhine to the Ohio in about two thousand years. Meanwhile, to be sure, Europeans had forgotten what primeval forests and a barbarous frontier were like. Yet they plunged back into them as though they had an ancestral memory of what were the original conditions of their home. It must have been something like this once along the *limes* between the Rhine and the Vistula. . . .

Here in Pennsylvania or Virginia, no one yet knew which, one could again read *Caesar* with a genuine understanding. The man was full of excellent hints for Indian warfare. The captain, for instance, had just filled the ditch of Fort Pitt with small caltrops and beaver traps. They were excellent things for a moccasined foot to step on, or into. All the howls that rose from the ditch now at night were not ones of defiance. The fort was surprising its would-be surprisers.

A Rhine bridge across the Ohio glimmered in the captain's mind. There was plenty of timber to make one. He was going to suggest it to Colonel Bouquet.

LUCIEN HUBBARD
"Figure Eight"

The first steamboat on
the "Western waters" is launched

Time: 1811   Setting: Pittsburgh

In the first decade of the nineteenth century, the "Age of Steam Power" (a label good for the next hundred years) was in its infancy. The innovations of Isaac Watts, an Englishman, were only a generation old, and people on both sides of the Atlantic were experimenting with steam for rail and water transportation.

In 1807 Robert Fulton successfully launched the *Clermont*, a steamer with twin side paddle wheels, on the Hudson River. Now one of the challenges was to apply steam to the Ohio and Mississippi rivers, the route connecting Pittsburgh and New Orleans.

In 1810 Pittsburgh already had a thriving shipping industry which built oceangoing ships that were floated down to New Orleans for worldwide use. It also built keelboats for river haulage. Powered by the current (poled when necessary by sailors), the keelboats were part of an inflexible system. Though they could be as long as one hundred feet and were thus able to carry sizable amounts of freight or numbers of settlers, they could only move their cargo in one direction.

As Lucien Hubbard sums up, "What good was a country where supplies came in at one end and products went out at the other? . . . Due to the tremendous . . . difficulty of upriver transport, practically all the products of the growing West must be floated down to New Orleans, to bring whatever price the canny merchants there wished to pay for them. There was no other market." The doom of the keelboat industry seemed forecast in the downstream fate of the boats: Usually they were broken up at ports of arrival and sold for lumber.

In 1810 Nicholas Roosevelt, an East Coast entre-preneur and steamboat innovator (partner of Fulton and Robert Livingston), arrived in Pittsburgh with plans to change all this. *Rivers to the Sea* is a fictional account of the year and a half it took to build, test, and then successfully maneuver the steamship *New Orleans* through its first trip downriver. For the most part, Hubbard follows closely the historical outlines of the episode. Launched in March 1811, the *New Orleans* was given its test run in mid-October and set sail on the twentieth of that month; it arrived in New Orleans on January 10, 1812, having encountered en route the historic December earthquake.

The main character of *Rivers to the Sea* is Davie Thomas, a young man who comes west seeking new opportunities and is hired on by Roosevelt as an all-purpose mechanic. Natchez, who figures centrally in this selection, has spent his life as a keelboatman; his inclusion allows Hubbard (in other sections of the novel) to dramatize the conflict between the old and new technologies and the keelboat sailors' fear of losing their jobs. Katie, who becomes Davie's romantic interest, here provides a glimpse of the busy rowboat scene on Pittsburgh riverfronts.

Lucien Hubbard (1888?-1971) was both a journalist and a Hollywood producer, but, born in Cincinnati, he apparently had a lifelong ambition to write a novel about riverboating. He once commented, "The very oldest memory I have . . . is of standing tiptoe at the sill of a window in my father's home at night, and looking across at the lights of Mt. Adams, in Cincinnati, reflected in the water, with the packets passing up and down in a blaze of glory."

"Figure Eight"

No bell tolled, but all Pittsburgh was afoot and on its way to the water front. The brawling wind of a spring day whipped around corners, laying an unruly hand on skirts and mufflers. Overhead, fleecy clouds scudded past, their shadows racing along the ground. The surface of the Monongahela was ruffled with whitecaps.

The eager crowd gathering about Berthone's shipyards feared that the launching might be postponed because of the wind, but the word quickly spread that the builders, fighting for every day of grace, had decided to stick to their program. Promptly at two o'clock, the *New Orleans* would, God willing, slide down the ways and out upon her unpredictable career.

There had been much discussion whether to install the engine before launching, or afterward. The weight of the machinery and the difficulty of getting it aboard once the hull was afloat were balanced against the risk of accident during the launch. Over and over again, Roosevelt and Willison and Davie, Dirk Hoogstraeten and the experts summoned from New York had tested the firmness of the ground under the ways, had figured and computed, gesticulated and illustrated with blocks of wood held up to represent the position of a hull at launching.

The net result was a decision to risk all at one hazard and launch with the engine aboard.

The gravest danger was that the ship, sliding sternward into the stream, would pivot before the bow left the breast of the runway. The arms projecting over the stern, designed to hold the paddle wheel, were bound to dip beneath the surface.

Would they snap at the impact, or would their buoyancy, aided by the current of the stream, turn the hull from its course before it was completely launched, rending the bow against the breast of the runway?

The uncertainty among the experts communicated itself to the crowd. Bets were freely made that the arms would break, that the hull would hang up on the ways, that it would be swept around against the bank, that it would be carried out into the stream and away to destruction.

To prevent the last possibility, four cables had been laid to drags on the river bottom. The slack in these cables was to be taken up successively as the vessel shot out into the water. It was hoped that the combined weight of the four drags, moving more and more slowly along the sandy bottom of the launching lagoon would bring the hull to a stop before it could be drawn out into the open river. Two keelboats, with double crews, stood by to pick up the vessel, run cables ashore, and help warp her back to the Berthone landing slip. There the paddle wheel would be swung into place.

And now all was ready. The punch had been drunk, the ladies had fluttered gaily to their points of vantage, making a great to-do of their whipping skirts. The brave souls who were to make the descent with the hull had taken their places on board. The murmur of voices, the various busy sounds of the shipyard, died away. The men at the mauls stood ready, waiting the signal to strike. Every eye was turned.

Thereafter, as long as he lived, Davie could not see another such day of rough wind and brilliant,

9

patchy sunshine without again living through those breathless moments. The damp, cold scent of the river stung his nostrils. His heart thumped so hard against his ribs he could almost hear it. He closed his eyes and prayed for the ship.

"Launch!"

Roosevelt's voice sounded calm and clear in the hush.

"Blocks out!" roared Jeb Willison.

There was a din of mauls driving against the keel blocks, the notes rising in the scale as the tension mounted. As the last blows were struck, and the blocks slid out, the ship settled into the sliding ways with a scarcely perceptible creaking of timber. The blocks were carried away, each gang vying with the rest to be the first done.

"Shores away!" called Willison.

Again a fusillade of blows, and the shores dropped from the sides of the hull. Now she lay cradled only in the sliding ways, one fore, one aft, held to the runway by lashings of stout rope. At each rope an axman stood tensely, his blade glinting in the sun. The ropes must be cut at the same moment, else the hull might slew around and stick fast on the ways.

Jeb looked slowly around, enjoying his moment. He raised his arm, held it poised.

"Cut lashings!" he shouted, and his arm fell.

The four blows sounded as one. The taut ropes snapped, the ends whipping away like live things.

All eyes fastened on the bow of the *New Orleans.* She started downward so slowly that at first the movement could not be seen. Gradually she gathered speed, a cannon boomed, and a great shout went up, re-echoed up and down the bank. Faster and faster the hull slipped down the greased runway, until her stern hit the water and sent a sheet of spray out along the surface, shearing off the tops of the whitecaps. She hit fairly, dipped her wheel arms and brought them up awash. She bounced buoyantly in the lapping water of the lagoon, sending out diminishing concentric waves, and then came docilely to rest, like a captive swan, at the end of her four cables.

Davie, yelling soundlessly in the general din, wiped the tears from his cheeks.

If the launching had drawn its crowd, the trial trip of the *New Orleans* literally drained the Monongahela country of its population. Old grandpappies were hoisted into wagons, babies were taken from their cradles to gaze blankly at a sight of which they would still talk in their dotage. Every man, woman, or child who could walk or command means of transport betook himself to the water front.

The word had been published in Zadoc Cramer's *Navigator* that the test run would be made October 10. The river had risen enough to ensure sufficient water, and when the day came, crowds lined the banks of the river.

Grant's Hill, the town's highest eminence, held a group who preferred a panoramic, rather than a detailed, view of the spectacle. Coal Hill, on the opposite bank of the Monongahela, was dotted with black specks, countrymen who had left their plows and dropped their axes to gape.

The workmen in General O'Hara's glassworks, just below Coal Hill, had proved so negligent of their work that the foreman finally declared a half holiday, and the roof of the factory provided a vantage point for them and their families. Every building facing the levee on the Pittsburgh side, every craft on the water front, bore its quota of sightseers.

The steamboat lay at Berthone's wharf and was headed up the Monongahela. Steam had been raised daily for a week, and the engine had been run at idling speed. It functioned smoothly, with a reassuring "oom-pah-ker-*chug*," "oom-pah-ker-*chug*." There was a valve, hand operated, by which the engineer, Dirk, could release steam whenever he guessed the pressure was getting above the danger point.

Davie had listened so long to the engine that he, too, could detect the faint tremor, the "oom-pah-*ah*-ker-chug-*AH*," which indicated the pistons were slapping from too much pressure. Then a slight release of steam would bring the voice of the monster back to its smooth "oom-pah-ker-*chug*."

Half in joke, Davie affixed a foreman's whistle to the release valve, and thereafter, whenever the steam got too high, a shrieking blast informed the citizens of the town, who soon grew used to the sound. Once, in his enthusiasm, Dirk blew the whistle too long and the engine stopped running.

Now everything was ready. Each running part had been tightened and lubricated. Fuel of seasoned pine and oak lay piled on the deck before the furnace mouth. Extra casks of water for the boiler, extra drums of whale oil for lubricating, had been laid by.

Meanwhile the deck and wheelhouse crew had made all shipshape. The hull had proved sound and

11

tight. Not a drop of bilge seeped in, so men were set to work inside the hold, sluicing down the seams with pails of water, to swell them tightly. The wheels and rudder chains were tightened. Fresh paint, new cordage, chandlerage of the very best, made the *New Orleans* a model craft of her tonnage.

In all this work, Natchez had taken the lead, smiling, alert, and untiring. Davie blessed the day he had taken on this able seaman.

On the day of the run, dinner was served on board to a list of guests—town dignitaries, the principal merchants, and even, magnanimously, the more important keelboat factors. The galley in which meals were to be cooked on the long voyage to New Orleans received literally its baptism of fire. Punch flowed and toasts were given.

When the meal was over, most of the guests lost no time getting ashore to watch the trip from a distance. Some remained on board, among them Sam Penny and several other factors, determined to see the thing through to the bitter end.

There was a stir of excitement and protest when Mrs. Roosevelt calmly declined the arm of General O'Hara, who offered to see her safely ashore. She intended to stay and prove, she said, that steamboats were safe for any passenger. Lucy, who had prepared to go ashore, announced she would stay, too.

Roosevelt, busy with his departing guests, hastened to his wife.

"I really wish you'd go ashore, dear," he whispered. "There's a certain amount of risk, trying anything for the first time. Later—"

She shook her head, smiling as she squeezed his arm.

"I'm sure, darling, it would do me more harm to stay on shore and worry," she whispered back. "I won't worry—with you."

There was a buzz of excited comment among the ladies making their way toward the gangplank, for it had been known for some time in their private circles that Mrs. Roosevelt was in "an interesting condition," as it was called.

Now the guests who had gone ashore clustered on the wharf. Steam was up, as the whistle announced at short intervals. All was ready for the test.

The *New Orleans* lay headed upstream, and it was intended to hold her so until she had cleared the wharf. Then she would describe a wide circle to starboard, heading downstream and passing Coal Hill on the opposite shore. After crossing the mouth of Sawmill Run, the steamboat would head back across the river, shaving the Point of Pittsburgh and proceeding on into the Allegheny River. Then she would make a wide circle to port, which would carry her down into the Ohio. Continuing the circle would bring her back into the Monongahela again, and so to her home dock, having completed a giant figure eight. It was believed this course would demonstrate her complete maneuverability.

A hundred times, Roosevelt, Dirk, Natchez, and Davie had traced this course upon a map of the rivers. Roosevelt himself was to serve as Captain, Natchez would be pilot, Davie first mate, Dirk engineer. The crew had been carefully hand-picked.

Captain Roosevelt took his place in the wheelhouse. Natchez grasped the wheel. Davie took up his post just outside the wheelhouse, ready to relay orders to the crew. A fresh belch of wood smoke told of a good head of steam, and the piping of the whistle confirmed it.

"Ready at the bowline," ordered Roosevelt, quietly.

"Ready at the bowline!" roared Davie to the men ashore.

"Ready at the stern line."

"Ready at the stern line!"

Roosevelt glanced down at the wharf, up at the sky, out upon the river and the distant shore.

"Hold her two points to starboard — just enough to keep her off the wharf," he said, and Natchez nodded. The captain reached for the bell rope and pulled it twice.

There was the sound of clanking gears. The steady throb of the engine slowed a beat and took on a deeper, laboring tone. The ship started to quiver in every plank. The high crash and slap of the paddle wheel astern added to the symphony of sound; then all else was drowned in a mighty cheer as the craft began perceptibly to move against the current.

"Cast off the stern line!" shouted Roosevelt over the din.

Davie had stepped into the wheelhouse, trembling with eagerness, to catch the order. He tripped as he stepped over the sill in his haste to get back to the rail, and almost fell.

"Cast off—" he gasped. "Cast off the stern line! Cast off the stern line!"

The rope had tightened as the ship gathered momentum, and the hemp was smoking, while the bitt creaked ominously before the hitch was thrown off. The bowline, still fast, bellied down into the water as the way of the ship slacked it off. But Roosevelt, careful and methodical, delayed casting it off until he was sure the ship was really under way and that the engine had shouldered its load successfully.

"Bowline," he said at last, and Davie leaped back to the rail.

As he relayed the command, the heavy cable plopped into the water and trailed alongside as it was being hauled in by the deck crew.

Now the cheering re-echoed up and down the river, as the *New Orleans* quartered out from the bank and into general view, trailing her banner of wood smoke, and treading a white "bone in her teeth," as she gained speed. Bells rang. The ship-yard cannon barked again.

The first steamboat on the Western waters was on its way.

It seemed a great day to those on board—a great day to those assembled on the water front and on the hills of Pittsburgh.

But not the wildest dreamer of them all could imagine *how* great. Not one of them could guess that within a quarter of a century, the steamboats of the Ohio and Mississippi Rivers would become the greatest commercial fleet in the world, surpassing the entire merchant navy of Great Britain by 125,000 gross tons to 80,000. Not one of them could guess that steamboats would make a broad and sure highway from Pittsburgh to the Gulf, from New Orleans to St. Louis; that more than any other factor, they would weld together and unify, through swift and easy commerce, New England farmer and Virginian "long knife," creole and fur trapper, Canuck and Texan, into one stout mongrel breed— American.

That first steam voyage was a thing of sheer magic to Davie.

From his post on the upper deck, with the sounds of the engine and the paddle wheel sof-

13

tened by distance, it appeared that the banks of the river, and not the *New Orleans,* were moving.

As the ship maintained her initial turn to starboard, the hills on the distant shore seemed fairly to race upstream. Now Coal Hill, which he had not seen at close range since the day of his rescue by Katie, lay dead ahead. The steamboat bore down upon it with a speed terrifying to one used to the slow progress of canoe and keelboat.

Davie was afraid something had gone wrong with the steering, but even as he looked, Natchez was spinning the wheel to starboard again. When he turned to look ahead, Coal Hill was sliding easily off the port bow.

Then the glassworks loomed ahead, and the faces of the people on the roof grew momentarily more distinguishable. He could make out their excited talk and gesticulation—could almost read their expressions of awe and elation. Then they, too, raced off to port as the steamboat veered to starboard.

Now Pittsburgh lay dead ahead, strangely silent and motionless in the bright sun. Not a wagon moved. Not a person stirred. From across the river it seemed like a city of the dead, or one deserted in fear of pestilence. Then one noticed the black clusters on the hills and rooftops, lining the levee and dotting the boats in the harbor. Soon shouts of excitement and jubilation came thin and faint across the water as the steamboat drew nearer.

Bobbing on the water were small boats of every description, coming out to meet the *New Orleans.* Many of them narrowly escaped being crushed under the forefoot of the steamboat. Its speed of six miles an hour without the current caught most of the rowers unaware. It was ludicrous to see them, as they loitered full in the course, gawking

14

open-mouthed, and then, when their danger suddenly became apparent to them, began flailing the water with their oars.

In the wheelhouse, Natchez held grimly to the course Captain Roosevelt had set him. Let them get out of the way, or take the consequences.

The force of the current on her beam carried the *New Orleans* below the town, as Captain Roosevelt had estimated it would. As she passed the Point and forged into the Allegheny, a pebble could have been tossed upon her deck, and the cheers of the crowd on shore rang loudly. As he cleared the Point, Captain Roosevelt ordered the wheel hard aport. He needed all the open water there was, what with the swifter flow of the Allegheny, to bring the craft about in a great circle at full steam ahead, and so point up the Monongahela again to Berthone's.

A few small craft were caught unawares by this maneuver, and were hard put to get clear. One skiff in particular was caught in the inside of the circle. It was too late for it to cross directly in the path of the steamboat. There was nothing to do but row might and main farther toward the inside.

The skiff was heavily laden and made slow progress. Davie held his breath as he saw women aboard, and then he noticed that one of them was rowing, along with a man.

As the steamboat passed, missing it by a boat's length, he recognized Katie at the stroke oar. At the other was a stout young fellow Davie had never seen before, and in the other seats were the full company of the laundry — the girls, the giant Negress, even down to the old squaw and Aunt Ellen who, at the nearness of the escape, clamped her whisky bottle to her lips and hung on despite the pitching of the boat.

"Katie!" Davie shouted. But if she heard him she gave no sign, and soon the bobbing rowboat was left astern.

Now the *New Orleans* pointed down the Ohio, but her steady swing to port soon turned her in to the south bank, then slowly began heading her upstream again. Brunot's Island, the beautifully kept country estate of General Lafayette's foster brother, Dr. Felix Brunot, lay on the starboard beam. Glancing toward it, Davie noticed the drive and promenade circling the island, and the stately house peeping through the trees. He noted, too, the line of white water breaking over the rocks at the tip of the island.

Suddenly he realized the *New Orleans* was not moving. At first he thought the engine had stopped. Then he noted that the steady throb of the engine continued; in fact, it grew more labored as a dense cloud of smoke rolled from the single smokestack abaft the wheelhouse. Davie remembered now that he had just heard the signal for more speed. He dashed into the wheelhouse.

The predicament of the ship was at once apparent. As she swung upstream in the Ohio, she turned broadside to the full current of the river. This had slowed up her turning movement. She was now headed quartering in toward the shore, and making more progress shoreward than upstream.

Continuing the course she was on, she could not clear, but must run aground on the south bank. If she slackened speed, on the other hand, she would be powerless in the current running at millrace speed toward Brunot's Island.

The sweat stood out on Natchez' brow. Captain Roosevelt instinctively grasped the nearest spoke of the wheel, as if to take over. But there was nothing to do but hold her on her course, as the soft mud flat ahead was infinitely preferable to the rocky tip of the island.

Davie brought up short, stared from one tense face to the other. There was no need of words.

On the deck below, in their comfortable chairs, Shedd Claiborne, Lucy, and Lydia chatted idly.

"We don't seem to be moving," Lucy observed without alarm.

"Well, it's a nice spot to stop," Lydia said. "Isn't Doctor Brunot's house lovely? Remember the last time we were there?"

"On the Fourth," Shedd nodded. "We had real ice for the punch! In July!"

In the wheelhouse the three men seemed frozen into inaction.

"If it was a keelboat, now—even a hundred footer—I'd know what to do," muttered Natchez, watching the shore creep closer.

"What?" asked Roosevelt, grasping at a straw.

"Why, I'd back her—off to starboard, not to port. That'd keep her bow from swingin' round against the island. We'd miss the tip by inches, but we'd miss. When I got clear—"

"This isn't a keelboat," Roosevelt interrupted, dryly. "We can't back. We never thought we'd want to. You don't back a sailing ship."

"No, sir," agreed Natchez, humbly.

"But, Mr. Roosevelt!"

Davie's excited voice cut in.

"If we—if we stopped the engine—slipped the chain off the cogwheel—reversed it—figure eight! Wouldn't that turn the wheel backward?"

Before Davie finished speaking, Captain Roosevelt shouted: "Do it!" He grabbed the wheel, pushing slowwitted Natchez after Davie. "I'll hold this course!" he cried as they ran to the stairs. "As long as the paddle wheel turns! Make the change and

15

tell Dirk to give you full steam-*astern!*"

Their footsteps were clattering down the stairs before he finished.

"Idle the engine, Dirk!" yelled Davie as he darted into the engine room. The invited guests, who had just begun to notice something was amiss, and had deserted the punch bowl to cluster at the rail, turned as the two men disappeared into the pit.

"Idle the engine!" Davie repeated as Dirk stared.

"What for?" demanded Dirk, but Davie leaped past him to the lever. Freed of its load, the engine raced madly under its full head of steam. Over the din, Dirk yelled something angrily, but Davie sprang to the chain. As he seized it, he let go with a howl of pain. Cogwheel and chain were hot beyond handling.

He reached again and, despite the searing pain, seized the chain beyond the flywheel. All his tugging, however, only tightened the chain in the cogs.

"Let *me* have it!" roared Natchez and brushed Davie aside, almost upsetting him.

By now a ring of white faces peered down into the engine pit. Natchez bent over the wheel, seized a section of the chain in either hand. There was a smell like that which rises when a hot shoe is clamped on a horse's hoof, and the same smoke wreathed upward from the calluses on the riverman's hands as they clung to the hot chain. Then, as the calluses burned through, the smell of cooking flesh fought with the fumes of whale oil.

Natchez' huge shoulders quivered in agony, but he held on. Between his knees and his pawlike hands he whipped the chain into a figure eight. Then, with all his huge strength, he clasped it to his breast and started working it back on the cogs.

The cords stood out on his temples. His face streamed with the sweat of struggle and of agony. The cotton stuff of his shirt seared brown wherever the hot chain brushed against it. But he kept on, and by some miracle of effort at last the links slipped home. Natchez staggered drunkenly away and collapsed into a shuddering heap on the pit floor.

Davie shoved the lever back and the engine picked up its load again, now in reverse.

In the wheelhouse, Roosevelt had watched the *New Orleans* lose way, hang motionless a moment, then start running swiftly downstream with the current. The wheel was a lifeless thing in his hands. If the craft began to revolve end for end, he could not prevent it.

But luckily she kept her position in the channel as the white water at the tip of the island seemed to race toward her. The captain fought an impulse to drop the wheel and run to his wife, to get her safely away in a boat. The seconds ticked by on the wheelhouse clock. He gave himself thirty more, and began to count them off aloud. Thirty more, and then he would give up, and make sure at least his wife and Lucy were saved.

Eight, nine—ten—and good-by to all his hopes—

He had reached sixteen when the timbers began to quiver under his feet. He knew the wheel was turning. Backward—for the *New Orleans* began to outrace even the swift current. She gained steerage way. Once more master of his craft, he set her course barely to clear the tip of the island.

Soon Davie joined him, and together they watched breathlessly as the *New Orleans* cleared the white water with a scant fifty feet to spare and shot out into the deep channel.

Down in the pit, Dirk threw a pail of water over Natchez, and he came to with a shuddering groan.

16

CHARLES W. DAHLINGER
"Jenny Lind"

An international singing star
causes a riot

Time: 1851   Setting: Pittsburgh

When Paul Didier invites Mr. and Mrs. O'Neill to the Jenny Lind concert, it takes no convincing (even though old Mr. O'Neill, Daniel's father, objects to the theater on religious grounds). After all, Jenny Lind, "the Swedish Nightingale," was the most internationally famous performer of the mid-nineteenth century, and when she stopped in Pittsburgh in 1851, she had already been touring the States to great acclaim for some months. At the theater, Didier, the O'Neills, and their young daughter are joined by Dr. Goos, the editor of a German-language newspaper in Allegheny City.

The ensuing violent events of the evening are a matter of public record. A biographer of Jenny Lind sums up one theory of their cause:

Pittsburgh was a mining community, and someone should have warned Barnum [the promoter] that Friday, the day set for the first concert, was also payday for the miners. According to immemorial custom, a considerable portion of the men made immediately for the saloons, and by evening were going from one tavern to another in uproarious spirits. [Gladys Denny Schultz, *Jenny Lind, the Swedish Nightingale*]

In any event, it is clear that the evening's mayhem was much as Dahlinger describes it in this selection, down to the details of the back-alley escape, the broken fence, and Jenny Lind's vow never to visit Pittsburgh again.

Dahlinger's Where the Red Volleys Poured *is a Civil War novel, with much of its action taking place on and about battlefields below the Mason-Dixon Line. But for the first hundred pages, it is very much a book about Pittsburgh. The main character, Paul Didier, is a German who migrates to America after the failure of revolutionary causes with which he had aligned himself in 1848. After landing in New York, he proceeds to Pittsburgh via the rail and canal route, settles in the primarily German community of Allegheny City, and goes to work as a railway construction engineer for Daniel O'Neill. As background to the later Civil War action, Dahlinger sketches the democratic fervor among the German immigrants — an abolitionist sermon at Economy, the singing of revolutionary songs in the German "beergardens flourishing on the Butler turnpike at the eastern edge of the city, or with the members of the new Gesang-verein in their hall on East Lane." Later Dahlinger describes the mobilization of troops in Pittsburgh: "The members of the Gesang-verein . . . formed themselves into a military company immediately after South Carolina had passed its ordinance of secession."*

Charles W. Dahlinger (1858-1935) was a practicing attorney in the Pittsburgh area, but he was also a historian who wrote about western Pennsylvania and for five years edited the Western Pennsylvania Historical Society magazine.

"Jenny Lind"

All day long during that memorable Friday on the evening of which the concert was to be given, there had been excitement in the city. In the morning the steamer *Messenger* had arrived from Cincinnati, bringing the famous singer and her company, after having stopped at Wheeling for a few hours the evening before in order that a concert might be given in that place. The crowds at the Pittsburgh wharf had been enormous, but orderly. They had then melted away, only to reappear again in the evening. Curiosity seemed to be mingled with a certain degree of antagonism. There were two diametrically opposite opinions of Jenny Lind's ability as a singer held by the more unthinking portion of the people of the United States: the one, that she was the greatest singer of modern times; the other that she was an imposter who owed her reputation to the liberal manner in which she had been advertised; that her much-lauded charities were merely part of a clever advertising scheme. The latter opinion seemed to be held by many persons in Pittsburgh, at least among those who did not patronize the concerts. But whether the antagonism arose because the people believed that they were being humbugged, or because the prices of admission were so high that they could not afford to purchase tickets, or whether it was because so many of the tickets were in the hands of speculators who held them for another profit, and with whom Barnum, Jenny Lind's manager, was said to be in league, or because the singing was to be mainly in foreign languages, or . . . because the ministers had preached against the holding of the concerts, or whether it was for all of these causes combined, is uncertain, but true it is that the mob which as early as five o'clock in the afternoon, began gathering on Fifth Street in front of the hall where the concert was to be given, was bent on mischief.

Daniel and his wife had enthusiastically promised Paul to accept his invitation before he left them on Sunday. Paul had engaged a carriage to call for him, and afterward take him and his guests to the concert. The driver was the first person to inform him of the fact that a mob had collected on Fifth Street, and that it had been impossible for the carriage to come down that thoroughfare. Mrs. O'Neill received this news from Paul with pleasurable anticipation; it must portend a magnificent reception for Miss Lind, or the people would not be so clamorous to be near the hall, she opined. Doctor Goos had given Paul an extra ticket, and he asked Mrs. O'Neill what to do with it. Turning to her husband, she said with a mischievous smile, "How would it be if we asked your father to come with us, Daniel?" Her husband laughed. "Will you invite him, Alice?" he inquired, and when she nodded added soberly, "Better not make father angry unnecessarily. He holds certain set views which you and I do not share in; but he really interferes very little in what we do. Let us take Eleanor instead."

"Eleanor!" exclaimed his wife deprecatingly; "she is entirely too young, and would be obliged to stay up too late for her; she would hardly appreciate the music either."

"What's the difference?" protested Daniel; "she will think she does; she will perhaps understand as much about the music as half the people who are there; then tomorrow is Saturday and there will be no school for her to attend, and she can sleep as long into the morning as you allow her." He laughed, and took Eleanor, who had just come into the room, in his arms.

Eleanor was immensely pleased. She had heard scarcely anything else spoken of for nearly a week past but Jenny Lind's concert. Now to be taken there herself fairly set her wild, and it did not take any urging from her mother to induce her to go up to Paul, and climb on his knee and impetuously throw her arms around his neck and kiss him, declaring as she did so, "I'm awful glad I can go, Mr. Didier. I want to hear Jenny Lind sing the 'Casta Diva.' I don't know what that is, but mother says it's very fine. I wonder whether it's funny like 'Billy Boy,' " she concluded interrogatively. Then she danced out of the room to inform her brother Jack of her good fortune, causing that young gentleman to bound immediately into the parlor, and with eyes brimming with tears ask that he also be taken to the concert. But on his mother promising to get him two white rabbits to take the place of the pair that had died during the winter, he at once turned to his sister and told her triumphantly that he would far rather have the rabbits — concerts were only for girls, anyhow.

When they left the house, an hour later, all clad in evening dress, Paul could not help admiring the handsome appearance of his guests, not the least interesting being little Eleanor, with her reddish curls, stepping along so proudly at his side on the way to the carriage. At the corner of Wood and Fifth Streets the driver was compelled to stop the horses, the crush in Fifth Street being impenetrable for vehicles. After waiting for fully fifteen minutes,

they decided to get out of the carriage and walk to the hall. The crowds were boisterous, but good-natured; they seemed to know the performers who were beginning to arrive, and made running comments as they recognized them. As Paul and his friends were nearing the entrance, two dark-faced foreign-looking gentlemen were struggling to get in. The men crowding about the door at once began yelling: "Look at the frog-eating Frenchmen; the taller fellow is Belletti, the barytone; the other one's Salvi, the tenor." Another voice corrected, "They're not French — them's Iyetalians — Iyetalians is macaroni-eaters." A wild laugh greeted the last sally. Now the members of the orchestra arrived with their instruments in their hands. This started more chaffing. "Here comes the fiddlers," yelled a tall fellow standing near the curb. "They all look like Dutchmen. Three cheers for the Dutch!" And three hearty cheers were given, although the people a little distance away from the speaker did not know what they were cheering about.

By this time Daniel and his wife, followed by Paul and Eleanor, had gained the interior of the hall and were shown to the seats for which their tickets called. A lugubrious expression had come over Daniel's face, and as another cheer rose in the street, he whispered to his wife, "Alice, I wonder whether the concert is going to take place here or outside." Mrs. O'Neill looked uneasy, but Eleanor was happy and her eyes were sparkling with excitement. Paul's gaze had been wandering about the hall, admiring the handsomely gowned women, and their well-dressed male escorts, when he espied Doctor Goos. Doctor Goos also saw the O'Neills and Paul at the same instant, and came up to them. After having shaken hands with his acquaintances,

including Eleanor, whom he treated with exaggerated politeness, much to that small person's gratification, Doctor Goos declared agitatedly, "Diss iss apominable. What can de rabble mean py greating diss disturbence? — ant Fräulein Lind de greatest cantatrice in de whole world. I am disgoosted."

"Oh, never mind, doctor," was Daniel's cheerful reply. "They will soon get tired and stop their noise, and then the concert can begin."

The German shook his head. Seating himself between Daniel and Eleanor he said, "I know dat crowd. Dey intend to make drouble, ant will not stop until de conzert iss ofer. I am reminded off de boys ant de frogs in de fable."

Eleanor's forehead became puckered up with thought. A moment later she whispered to Paul, asking him what Doctor Goos meant. Doctor Goos divined the question, and hastened to tell her of the bad little boys who were watching the frogs by the side of a pond, and as fast as a frog lifted its head, pelted it with stones, driving it back again into the water. "Den, my little fräulein," the doctor went on, "one off de frogs spoke to de boys, ant said, 'boys, you forget dat dough diss may be fun for you, it iss deat' to us.' De beople outsite are de boys," he concluded, "ant we are de frogs."

Eleanor was deeply interested, but still puzzled. Her face was very grave, and when Doctor Goos had turned away and was talking with her mother, she inquired anxiously of Paul, "Mr. Didier, do you think they'll kill us and then rob us? — for if they do, I'd like you to take my new bracelet and my two rings and my earrings and put them away in your pocket. I wouldn't like to lose them." Paul's laughter reassured her, and she made no effort to take off her precious jewelry.

The seats were all occupied now by a brilliant audience; and many persons were standing in the rear of the hall and in the gallery; the mayor of the city, tall and stately, was there, talking and laughing with several male companions as if there was no trouble in the street, and as if he had no connection whatever with the maintenance of the good order and peace of the city. The judges of the courts looked pompously toward the stage, those unlearned in the law being equally dignified with those who were supposed to know the law. The wealthy manufacturers and the wholesale grocers, and the wholesale liquor dealers were there with their wives and daughters, who kept severely aloof from the wives and daughters of the retail grocers, and the merchant tailors, and the other smaller tradesmen scattered through the audience. Freely intermingling with the fashionables were the professional men — the lawyers, the physicians, the journalists — and the few other persons capable of appreciating good music. In the less expensive seats in the gallery, were more persons who would recognize good music when they heard it — music teachers, organists at the few churches possessing organs, singers in the church choirs. Doctor Henrici, quiet-mannered and quaint of dress, with a brother Harmonist, was there to indulge the only passion of which he was guilty. Mr. Droste and several members of the Allegheny City Gesangverein occupied some of the cheapest seats in the last row.

The orchestra was in its place, and Herr Benedict, the conductor, arose with his baton in his hand, ready to begin the concert. With a crashing sound the first notes of the overture to "Oberon" fell on the ears of the audience. Almost at the same moment from without came the shouts: "The

22

Dutch are at it! The Dutch are at it!" the shouters attempting to yell in unison with the music. "De swine!" was Doctor Goos' terse comment, as the ushers went to the Fifth Street end of the hall and lowered the windows, which had been raised on account of the warmth of the interior.

The noise was less noticeable now, and the orchestra played on with a good deal of vigor, although Herr Benedict was plainly annoyed. Herr Benedict was himself a musical genius of the first order, his compositions even at that time having an international fame, and it hurt him to have the splendid work of Weber marred by the unseemly disturbance. Suddenly the noise broke out again so loud that the finer notes of the composition were entirely lost on the audience, and they began paying but scant attention to the performers, and commenced talking animatedly to one another. Paul was deeply disappointed. In addition to being passionately fond of music himself, he had intended that his friends should spend an evening of unalloyed pleasure, and now they were merely wasting time. Turning to Mrs. O'Neill, he said in a voice in which he hardly attempted to hide his chagrin, "I suppose we must be a little patient; the police will surely be here soon."

Mrs. O'Neill saw his distress and replied smiling, "No doubt the crowd will get tired some time, then they'll keep quiet. I do not care a great deal for orchestral music, anyway, and am only anxious to hear Miss Lind."

Her husband joined in the conversation. "Alice," he said, "even if we don't hear all the selections on the program, we will at least have had the satisfaction of being able to say that we saw the greatest singer of the day."

"Yes, ant you shall talk to her, ant see what a

GRAND FAREWELL CONCERT.
M'LLE
JENNY LIND
Has the honor to announce that she will give
ONE GRAND CONCERT
IN MASONIC HALL,
On Thursday Evening, November 13, 1851,
ASSISTED BY
SIGNOR SALVI,
MR. OTTO GOLDSCHMIDT,
SIGNOR R. BELLETTI,
MR. JOS. BURKE.
PROGRAMME.

23

gracious lady she iss," interposed Doctor Goos. "When on my way to America I spent several monds in London, ant often met Fräulein Lind in de circles in which I moved. I called on her at her hotel diss afternoon, ant have received her permission to bring you all into her dressing room after de performance — all except de youngest member of de pardy." He looked humorously at Eleanor, and added, "I did not know dat we would be honored with de little fräulein's presence. But maybe we can smuggle her into de room unobserved — she iss pretty small."

Eleanor got quite close to Paul, and asked confidentially, "Will she talk to me — do you think, Mr. Didier? Can I talk to her? Mother says in the countries where Miss Lind has been she has friends among the kings. Won't I have lots to tell at school on Monday!" she concluded with a happy smile.

The overture was finished, and Belletti and Salvi stepped forward. The buzz of conversation stopped suddenly. Of Belletti the audience had read many accounts, as he had come with Miss Lind from England, and had been with her on the whole of her American tour. But of Salvi they knew scarcely anything, he having been only singing with the company for a week. The two were to sing a duet together from Donizetti's "L'Elsire d'Amore." The noise of the fluttering of the fans was the only sound now to disturb the stillness. Scarcely had the first notes sounded through the hall, the listeners had hardly settled themselves back in their seats in order to enjoy the music fully, when from without came the noises again. Shrill whistles, catcalls, howls blended with cries of all descriptions, penetrated through the closed doors and windows. The singers struggled bravely on, and, although the audience was so distracted by the noise in the

street that they could not appreciate half the beauties of the selection or perceive the masterliness of the singing, yet at the conclusion of the duet, they rewarded the performers with a liberal amount of applause.

Jenny Lind came next on the program; now the people were to hear her in the "Casta Diva," from Rossini's "Norma," the selection in which she had made much of her American reputation. Every eye was turned expectantly toward the side of the stage from which she was expected to enter. Doctor Goos had been in deep thought for some moments. Suddenly he turned to Daniel. "Something must be done to stop de noise outside," he declared. "Fräulein Lind must not be allowed to be treated de same as de other performers. I have a plan." Without further explanation he arose and walking up the aisle, went out of the hall. A minute or two later, the well-known figure of the star of the evening, clad in a simple gown of white, accompanied by Herr Benedict, came forward to the front of the stage.

Hardly a sound came from the outside now Doctor Goos or some other potent agency had evidently been successful. For a second the hall was still as death, then a wild wave of applause broke forth. The audience intended to show that they at least had no connection with the disturbing element in the street. Men and women rose to their feet; they clapped their hands; they waved their handkerchiefs; they shouted and yelled — only less loudly and more decorously than the mob outside. The applause was almost continuous; several times it died down, only to be renewed time after time. Once, twice, three times, the orchestra started up preparatory to the singer beginning her part, only to be each time drowned in the sounds of the applause. All the time Jenny Lind stood there motionless, calm, smiling, serenely confident. Finally the notes of the orchestra rose louder than the tumult in the hall, and the time arrived for the singer to begin her part. She did not merely take the part, she was the part. The audience were in raptures. A soprano so pure, so sweet, so fine, yet so strong and penetrating had never been heard before; it was a voice without a fault, without a blemish. Behind all this was the frank, kindly soul of the singer, which went out to the audience in every tone, in every trill.

Deafening was the applause which greeted her when she sat down. If there had been any noise on the outside now, it would have made no ripple in the hall. Four or five large bouquets were handed up to the diva. Again and again she rose and came forward and bowed and smiled. But the audience would not be satisfied with bows and smiles; they wanted another song. She shook her head and smiled again. Another wave of applause rolled through the interior; she said a word to Herr Benedict, and he sat down before the piano, while she came forward, still smiling. Herr Benedict ran his fingers over the keys, and she began singing the Swedish "Herdman's Song." It was wild, quaint, entrancing, with the aroma of the field and forest in every note; the audience almost imagined that they could hear the calls of the cows, the joyful laugh of the herdsman, the echo as it vibrated from hill to hill. The audience were on their feet again, waving handkerchiefs, clapping hands, laughing, yelling, calling on the songstress for another song. Miss Lind attempted to get away without complying with the last request, but her attempt was vain. The tumult would not be stilled, and for the third time she came to the footlights and prepared to sing. Now it was something in their own language; something that every one knew, "The Last Rose of Summer," sung as none in that audience had ever heard it sung before. They were bewitched with the feeling conveyed in that superb rendering. But they had some consideration for the singer, and realized that she must be fatigued from the continued pressure to which she had just been subjected. They allowed her to retire to her dressing room with only a faint echo of the former applause.

Doctor Goos had reentered the hall during the singing of "The Last Rose of Summer," and had taken his seat. When quiet again reigned, Daniel observed to him gaily, "I see, doctor, that you succeeded in bringing about order in the street. We owe you a vote of thanks."

The doctor smiled, but did not volunteer any information, except to say that he was afraid that the noise would start up again. "Dose swine have no reason," he observed moodily, "but you have now heard de divine fräulein at her best, and should be satisfied." As if in corroboration of his prediction the uproar in the street broke out again, more violently than at any time during the evening, and he observed resignedly, "De swine are at it again; I am ready to go home — after we have talked a few moments with de most brilliant musical star in de firmament."

The noise hardly slackened again during the remainder of the concert. There were other fine selections yet to be given. Herr Benedict and Herr Hoffman played a duet on the piano. Belletti and Salvi each sang several numbers very capably in Italian. Miss Lind herself sang again in English, but no more enjoyment was to be obtained there that evening. The performance was shortened. With

25

tears in her eyes Miss Lind retired to her dressing room. And with feelings about evenly balanced between the pleasure they had enjoyed, and resentment at the manner in which the evening's entertainment had been interfered with, the audience moved silently out of the hall and down the stairs, only to rub elbows with the mob outside, waiting patiently for a chance to stare at Miss Lind as she came into the street.

Paul's party had remained in their seats until the hall was empty, and the janitor began turning out the lights, when Doctor Goos led the way to the door at the side of the stage from which the dressing rooms were reached. Miss Lind, who was alone with two members of the orchestra, was greatly agitated at the treatment which she and her company had received from the people in the street. There was a depth of sorrow in her voice as she greeted Doctor Goos. "Can you guess the meaning of this disturbance?" she asked plaintively in her precise English, after having been presented to the others. "I am really terrified. Look at the broken windows, and observe the stones which came crashing through the glass." She pointed to three or four good sized stones lying on the floor. "I feel truly glad that a few friends remain with me," she continued; "I have decided to wait until the mob leaves before going to my hotel."

Daniel attempted to treat the matter lightly. He laughed at Miss Lind's fears. "The stones and the broken glass are probably the work of a few thoughtless boys," he observed. "I do not believe a serious attempt has been made to do you an injury."

Doctor Goos also attempted to make merry of the affair. "Fräulein Lind," he declared, "notwithstanding your fears, you would have laughed your-

self had you seen dese swine when I was among them, telling them lies in order to get them to keep quiet while you sang. To some who didn't know me I said I was de mayor of de city — I was ashamed of myself for saying so," he interjected drolly, "because de mayor iss such an incompetent ass, who has entirely lost his het. I saw him at de conzert a while ago ant he was making no effort whatever to quell de riot. To others I stated that I was de representative of de mayor — again I felt ashamed, for de same reason that I have just mentioned — and threatened them with dire punishment. To one group I declared that de President of de United States had been telegraphed to, you being de subject off a friendly foreign power, ant that troops would soon arrive from de arsenal, with cannon to be used against de crowd. Two policemen who had been standing about calmly smoking cigars, paying no attention whatever to what was going on around them, hurried away when I mentioned troops."

By this time Miss Lind was much relieved. "If you can only get me safely away from this building, I will think you are a greater man still," she laughed. "But why should I feel such trepidation?" she added abruptly. "This little girl here is not as much afraid as I am, are you, dear?" She reached out and drew Eleanor toward her, holding her close and repeating, "Are you, dear?"

Eleanor had been startled when Miss Lind took hold of her so suddenly; now she was perfectly at home, and answered confidently, "Not as long as father is here, and mother and Mr. Didier."

"And Doctor Goos," added Miss Lind. "Do not forget Doctor Goos."

"And Doctor Goos," repeated Eleanor, glancing at that individual in a manner indicating that she had some doubts as to his prowess in case of an emergency. A moment later she explained, "I haven't known Doctor Goos as long as I have my father and mother; Mr. Didier I know nearly as well as I do my parents."

The interior of the hall had been in darkness for some time. The door leading to the street had been closed, and nothing could be heard inside of any further disturbance down below, so Paul volunteered to reconnoiter. As soon as he showed his face outside, a roar arose from the crowd still lingering in front of the building. "Now she'll come out," they cried. "Now we'll see Jenny Lind." Paul hastily retraced his steps, closing and locking the door after him. Without making his intention known to those in the dressing room, he had the janitor direct him how to get down by the back stairs, his intention being to find a way of getting Miss Lind out through the rear of the building.

A small dark yard enclosed on three sides by high board fences met his view; he climbed one of the fences and was soon in the adjoining yard. A few feet away were the outlines of a dingy brick house, with no light anywhere, as if the occupants were all asleep. Alongside of this ran a brick-paved walk, leading apparently to Virgin Alley. This was what he was looking for. A minute's walk brought him to the narrow alley. Everything was quiet here; not a person was in sight. He was soon back again in the hall detailing his plan to Miss Lind.

"But how am I to climb over the fence?" she asked, laughing. "I was never very good in athletics." She was satisfied when told that a board or two could be easily knocked off, then there would be no further hindrance in the way. Telling the two musicians, who had stood silently by, to go out by the front door, and if any one asked for her to say

she had gone to her hotel long ago, Miss Lind reached for her cloak lying on the table. She smiled her assent when Paul stepped forward and asked to be permitted to place it on her shoulders.

In the yard all was darkness and silence as before. It was harder work to loosen the boards than Paul had anticipated, and it was not until he and Doctor Goos had taken up a heavy post which they found on the ground, and pounded vigorously against the boards, that they gave way. Just as they had all crawled through the opening, a light appeared in the two rear windows of the brick house, and an instant later, the door opened and the burly figure of a man stood in the opening. In a harsh voice he demanded to know what they were doing in his premises.

Daniel attempted to explain, but the man would hardly listen, and his eyes lighting on the opening in the fence, he glared savagely as he yelled, "And you have broken down my fence, too. You've likely been robbing some store. I'll have the police here in a few minutes, and arrest the whole pack of you."

There was a loud hum of voices in Virgin Alley now; delay was inconvenient and might lead to embarrassing consequences, and Paul concluded that they must not be hindered; bold measures must be adopted. "You know we are telling the truth and are not thieves," he declared. "What will it cost to repair your fence? — we will pay you now. If you do not accept our money we will go away, anyhow." The man's eyes glittered when money was mentioned, but he stated that he was a law-abiding citizen and would not settle with night-prowlers, about whom he knew nothing. In the same breath he added that if he were paid ten dollars he would allow them to proceed.

27

"Ten dollars!" echoed Doctor Goos derisively. "Do you want to sell us de whole property? We will give you twenty-five cents. Five cents' worth of nails iss all that it will take to fasten on de two boards again." Paul quickly compromised the matter for a dollar, and in another moment they were in Virgin Alley. A crowd of men and half-grown boys was there. "There she is," they all yelled, pressing forward, and staring rudely at Miss Lind as she came out.

Paul was walking with her toward Wood Street. Eleanor trying hard to suppress her sleepy yawns, but without a trace of fear on her face, was holding confidently to Miss Lind's hand. Daniel and his wife followed with Doctor Goos. The crowd was all about them, but beyond their free comments on the songstress' appearance, they offered no indignity. At Wood Street they were joined by more men coming from Fifth Street. Some of them had evidently become tired of waiting for Miss Lind's appearance in the street, and had beguiled the weary hours by drinking in some of the taverns; their talk was loud and coarse, and they staggered in their walk, and they came closer to Miss Lind than any of the others had yet come. One lean fellow attempted to shake hands with her, but was brushed aside by Paul, the suddenness of the movement causing the man to pitch forward into the gutter.

An angry growl went up from half a dozen of the nearest men, but they seemed undecided what to do, while Miss Lind moved swiftly on in the direction of Fifth Street. Paul's carriage was in sight, only a few feet away, when three or four rough-looking men made a rush forward, their object being, apparently, to get at Paul. The most daring of them received a sledge-hammer blow in the face from Paul's fist, while Miss Lind and the rest of the party pushed on a few feet still nearer to the carriage. Another wild rush was made by the mob, and Paul and Doctor Goos again aimed blows at them, neither, however, coming away unhurt this time, the former receiving a cut on the forehead, and the other a blow on his nose, which started the blood to flowing freely; both also lost their hats. In the meantime Daniel had hurried the two women and Eleanor, who were pale and trembling, closer to the carriage. Paul and the doctor, their backs to their friends and facing the mob, were slowly backing in the same direction. They heard the noise of the carriage door being opened and waited a moment longer, and then also rushed forward. The others were already in the carriage. "Get in, doctor," almost commanded Paul, pushing the editor violently into the vehicle and slamming the door after him. A moment more and Paul was on the seat beside the driver, yelling at him to drive like the devil.

And drive like the devil he did, and the cobblestones came flying after the carriage almost as fast, but fortunately only one struck the carriage and this did no harm. Along Wood Street the driver went to Fourth Street — there being too many people in Fifth Street to turn into that thoroughfare — then down Fourth Street to Market Street, and on across the bridge into Allegheny City to Daniel O'Neill's home. Miss Lind was still pale with fright when they alighted, and she warmly thanked the three men for their efforts in her behalf. As she accepted Mrs. O'Neill's invitation to remain overnight, she vowed that her concert engagement for the following Monday evening should be canceled and she would never sing in Pittsburgh again. And she never did.

TAYLOR CALDWELL
"The Odor of Raw Black Oil"

Joseph Armagh sets out
to seek his fortune

Time: Early 1860s   Setting: Titusville

Taylor Caldwell's Captains and the Kings *is a long and complex novel that follows the fortunes of an Irish family from their mid-nineteenth-century migration to Pennsylvania until the First World War. Joseph Armagh, whose mother dies en route to the United States, begins his American career as an impoverished orphan, heads for Titusville when news of the "oil rush" becomes current, and in a few years has made a fortune and become the founding father of a powerful Irish-American family. The fact that his son is assassinated during his campaign to become the first Catholic president prompts the reader to identify the fictional Armaghs with the Kennedys.*

The chapters of the novel that deal with Titusville are among the most specifically visualized scenes in the book. The passage printed here portrays the almost epidemic "fever" of the rush, the hurly-burly mix of various national groups ("foreigners"), and the general indifference among these fortune seekers to the Civil War and the government's call for recruits.

Historically, the oil boom in the Titusville area was set off in 1859, when "Colonel" Edward L. Drake constructed the world's first successful oil well (Drake was a railway conductor who had been hired by some businessmen to build the well). For the next several years, as rumors of instant jobs and instant fortunes circulated, the area was the target for an influx of fortune seekers. Pithole City was the most famous of the boom towns; its rise and fall are quickly summed up:

The owners of the Holmden farm had laid out 500 lots for a town, which came to be called Pithole City. On May 24th [1865], there was one building under construction. By September Pithole City had two banks, two telegraph offices, a post office which was said to be the third largest in Pennsylvania, a daily newspaper, a theater, a waterworks system, a fire company, two churches, and a score of boarding houses, grocery stores, machine shops, and other businesses. There were over fifty hotels and some, like the *Morey, Chase,* and *Bonta,* were large, elegant, and comfortable, furnishing their guests with all the conveniences of a metropolitan hotel. Ninety days before, Pithole City had been a spot in the wilderness. Now it was a city with about 15,000 inhabitants. . . .

The rise of Pithole City had been swift and amazing, but its decline was even more breathtaking. When some of the wells stopped flowing in August and dry holes were drilled, operators, speculators, and businessmen lost faith in the territory and quickly departed. The eager throng of fortune seekers had disappeared by January 1866, and Pithole was a deserted village. Today a solemn silence reigns over the grassy land which once provided oildom's greatest excitement. [Paul H. Giddens, "The American Petroleum Industry — Its Beginning in Pennsylvania"]

Taylor Caldwell (1900–) is one of the most prolific historical novelists currently writing, having published upwards of thirty books in the last thirty-five years.

"The Odor of Raw Black Oil"

The train for Titusville had not yet arrived when Joseph's train reached the little town of Wheatfield. So, with others, he left his train, pulled his cap down lower on his forehead and tried to appear as inconspicuous as possible as he entered the hot little depot, which was well lighted and crowded to its walls. Joseph had never seen such a bewildering gathering of men as he saw now, to his astonishment. There were men in silk and tall beaver hats, rich greatcoats and florid waistcoats and splendidly pinned cravats and fawn pantaloons, men fat and red and sweating of face and with flowing hair and sideburns and exquisitely trimmed beards and mustaches, and carrying Malacca canes with gold or carved silver heads and with fat fingers loaded with sparkling rings and with watch chains embellished with jeweled charms, and conversing with each other with jovial laughter and hoarse joking voices, their avid eyes glittering over strangers. They all smoked thick cigars or cheroots and they smelled of bay rum or racier perfumes, and their boots shone daintily. A considerable number of their faces were pockmarked, but they exuded excitement and confidence and money. Among them milled workmen in cloth caps and patched coats and blue shirts stained with sweat and oil and dirt, and ebullient men in shirtsleeves and with loud hectoring voices demanding and commanding, their fat legs moving constantly. There were also the quiet and deadly men in subdued but rich clothing along the walls, watching all newcomers closely, their rings shining, their shirts ruffled and fluted, their cravats and pantaloons and waistcoats elegant. These were the hunters and gamblers.

Posters imploring enlistments covered the dirty stained walls of the little depot and in one corner stood a young lieutenant in blue with his forage cap smartly over his forehead, a little table before him and two soldiers soliciting the younger men to join "the patriotic service of your choice." Several youths jested with them lewdly; the young lieutenant sweated in the hot rank air but he remained composed and serious though his aides grinned and spat. His eyes glowed with the fervor of the dedicated soldier, and it was obvious that he was a graduate of West Point and not a mere enlisted man. His shoulder patch read, *The Army of the United States.* He was proud of it.

All the narrow benches were occupied, though men, as if overcome with impatience, would rise and join the milling crowd, their seats immediately confiscated. The uproar was appalling with the constant crescendos of masculine voices arguing, wheedling, boasting, promising, and raucous. Spittoons were ignored. The floor was almost covered with blackish-brown slime. The stench and the heat overpowered Joseph and he kept near the door in spite of the jostling he received. Men raced out onto the wooden platform with papers in their hands, or carpetbags, cursing the tardy train to Titusville, then raced back inside, their eyes goggling as they sought out friends they had just abandoned. Another smell rose above the smell of bay rum and chewing tobacco and smoke and sweat, the smell of money-lust and greed, and it was insistent. The lamps overhead stank and flamed brightly; a wind blew in cinders and hot dust and chaff. Somewhere a telegraph chattered like an insane woman. Men shouldered others aside, were cursed or clapped on the back. There was an odor of raw whiskey as men tilted bottles to their mouths. The depot was like an enormous monkey house, seething with heat and movement and restiveness and vehement roars and impassioned shouts and great belly-laughter and good-humored imprecations. The old stationmaster crouched like an animal trainer behind his counter, his mouth working silently, his spectacles glimmering, as he tried to placate constant besiegers who demanded an explanation for the delay. He shrugged, he shook his head, he threw up his hands, and looked about him helplessly. Men fell over luggage on the dirty floor, cursed, laughed or kicked aside the portmanteaus and bags. The young Army lieutenant, momentarily discouraged, surveyed the dazing movement in genteel bafflement, for it was apparent that he was a gentleman among men who were certainly not gentlemen. He had been taught good-will by his mother and his mentors, and he struggled to maintain it, keeping a reserved but friendly half-smile fixed on his boyish mustached face. But his expression was becoming haunted. The flag at his right hung limply in the suffocating and noxious air. The two windows of the depot were open but no cool breeze entered.

After a little Joseph could endure it no longer and he went out on the platform and looked down the tracks which were silvered by the moonlight. Here, at least, there was the cleaner smell of steel and cinders and dust and warmed wood and rock. The lights of Wheatfield glimmered dimly in the distance. The moon rode in a black sky seemingly without stars. Occasionally the platform vibrated as clots of men exploded from the depot to look down the tracks also, to speak to each other in loud excited voices, to joke, to brag, and then to rush back inside as if something of stupendous import was going on in there.

At last Joseph became aware that someone had been standing silently beside him for several minutes and would not move away. He ignored the presence, continuing to stare glumly down the tracks. He was very tired after his long day, and he knew he would have a miserable ride to Titusville, and he was becoming afraid that if he were not vigilant there would be no room on the train for him. He was thirsty. He had seen a pail of water on a bench and a chained tin cup attached to it but he shuddered at the thought of drinking from it. Light spilled through the window nearby onto the platform. Joseph kept just to the rim.

"Got a lucifer, mister?" the presence asked at last in a very young voice.

Joseph did not turn. "No," he said in his usual short fashion when approached by strangers. A small fear came to him. Had he been followed after all? It was this fear and not mere curiosity which made him cautiously move his head a little and glance sideways through the corner of his eyes. But what he saw reassured him. The presence was smaller than he, and infinitely more shabby, even ragged, and it was only a boy about fifteen years old, a boy without a cap or hat or coat, and very thin. He had a starveling appearance but not one of degradation nor had he spoken with the sniveling importunity such as the very poor affected.

His whole appearance and manner were astonishingly lively, even gay and lighthearted, as if he were perpetually happy and interested and cheerful. Joseph, accustomed to the bland anonymity of the Anglo-Saxon appearance in Winfield, was surprised at the elfish face which hardly rose to his shoulder, a dark face, almost brown, the great black eyes gleaming through thickets of girlishly long lashes silken and glimmering, and the electric mop of vital black curls and the prominent "hooked" nose. The undisciplined and obviously uncombed hair spilled over the low brown forehead, over the ears and rioted over the scrawny nape and straggled in vibrant tendrils against the thin flat cheeks. A pointed chin with a dimple, and a smiling red mouth, added reckless gaiety to the impudent face, and white teeth shone eagerly between moist lips.

"I don't even have a cheroot or a stub," said the boy, with actual glee. "I just wanted to talk." His voice was light, almost as light as a girl's, and faintly and exotically accented. He laughed at himself. But when he saw Joseph's truculent expression and his cold, half-averted ironic eyes, he stopped laughing though he continued to smile hopefully. "I just wanted to talk," he repeated.

"I just don't want to talk," said Joseph, and turned aside and studied the rails again.

There was a little silence. Then the boy said, "My name's Haroun. You goin' to Titusville, too?"

Joseph's mouth tightened. He debated a lie. But this strange boy might be on the same train and he would appear foolish or a suspicious runaway or a criminal in flight. So he nodded his head.

"Me, too," said Haroun. Joseph permitted himself to glance swiftly at that remarkable young face again. The boy was encouraged. He gave Joseph a very large smile. "You can make lots of money in Titusville," he said. "If you've got a mind to, and I don't have nothin' else to put my mind to so I am goin' to make money!" He laughed joyously and Joseph, to his own amazement, felt his face move into a smile.

"I can say that, too," he said, and was again amazed at himself.

"All I got in this world is six bits," said Haroun. "All I make is two dollars a week in the blacksmith shop, and a bed in the hayloft and some bread and bacon in the mornin'. It wasn't bad, though. Learnt how to shoe horses and that's a good trade, yes sir, and you can always make a livin' at it. I'd'a saved money from that two dollars but I had my old granny to take care of, and she was sick and there was medicine, and then she died. God rest her soul," added Haroun with no melancholy in his voice but only affection. "Took care of me after my people died, here in Wheatfield, when I was a little shaver, washin' clothes for the quality folk when she could get work. Anyway, she died, and she's buried in potter's field, but I think like this: Where does it matter where you're buried? You're dead, ain't you? And your soul's gone off someplace but I don't believe up in any heaven as my granny told it to me. Anyway, after I bought my ticket today I've got six bits until I can find work in Titusville, or maybe Corland."

The recital was so artless yet so explicit and so full of confidence and inner surety that Joseph was reluctantly intrigued. Here was one who totally loved life and believed in it and found it blithe, and even Joseph in his youth could recognize the soul which was not only indomitable but lighthearted.

Haroun permitted himself, without resentment or uneasiness, to be inspected thoroughly by Joseph's small eyes which were like bright blue stone between the auburn lashes. He even seemed amused.

Joseph said, "How far do you think you can go on six bits?"

Haroun listened acutely to his voice. "Hey,

33

you're a foreigner, too, like me, ain't you?" He stuck out his small brown hand frankly and Joseph found himself taking it. It was like hard warm wood in his fingers. "Where you from?"

Joseph hesitated. His associates at work in Winfield had known him as a Scotsman. Now he said, "Ireland. A long time ago. And you?"

The boy answered, shrugging eloquently. "Don't know where it is, but I heard it was Lebanon. A funny place, near Egypt or maybe it was China. One of them places. What does it matter where you're born?"

Joseph, the proud, looked at him coldly then decided that one so ignorant deserved no rebuke but only indifference. He was about to turn finally away and into the depot to escape the boy when Haroun said, "Hey, I'll share my six bits with you if you want to."

Joseph was freshly amazed. He looked over his shoulder and halted and said, "Why should you do

that? You don't even know me."

Haroun grinned whitely and the great black eyes laughed. "It'd be Christian, wouldn't it?" and his voice rippled with mischief.

"I'm not a Christian," said Joseph. "Are you?"

"Greek Orthodox. That's what my folks were, from Lebanon. That's where I was baptised. Haroun Zieff. I was only a year old when they come here, to Wheatfield. My Pa was a weaver, but he and my Ma got sick here and died, and so there was just me and granny."

Joseph considered him again, half-turning. "Why are you telling me all this?" he asked. "Do you tell every stranger your whole history? It's dangerous, that it is."

Haroun stopped smiling, and though a deep dimple appeared in each cheek his antic face became grave. He, now, studied Joseph. His full red lips pursed a little and his long eyelashes flickered. Then he said, "Why? Why's it dangerous? Who'd hurt me?"

"Best to keep your own counsel," said Joseph. "The less people know about you the less harm they can do you."

"You talk like an old man," said Haroun, kindly and with no rancor. "You can't sit around all the time and wait for someone to knife you, can you?"

"No. Just be prepared, that's all." Joseph could not help smiling a little.

Haroun shook his head violently and all his curls fluttered over his head. "I'd hate to live like that," he said. Then he laughed. "Maybe nobody ever hurt me bad because I didn't have anything they wanted."

One of the young soldiers sauntered out on the platform, taking off his forage cap to wipe his wet forehead. He saw Joseph and Haroun and bright-

ened. He said, "You men want to join up? Looks like we're going to have a war."

"No, sir," said Haroun with much politeness, but Joseph showed only contempt.

"Pay's good," said the soldier mendaciously.

"No, sir," repeated Haroun. The soldier peered at him with suspicion, at the dark face and the mass of black curls. "If you're a foreigner, you can get to be a 'Merican citizen quick," he suggested after he had decided that Haroun, though obviously dark, was not a Negro.

"I'm already American," said Haroun. "My granny made me one, couple of years ago, and I went to American schools, too, in this here town, Wheatfield."

The soldier was doubtful. Haroun's appearance made him namelessly uneasy. He turned to Joseph who had listened to this exchange with harsh amusement. Joseph's face and manner appeased the soldier. "How about you, sir?"

"I'm not interested in wars," said Joseph.

The young soldier flushed deeply. "This country's not good enough for you to fight for, is that so?"

Joseph had not fought since he had been a young lad in Ireland, but the memory of combat made his fists clench in his pockets and the hair at the back of his head bristle.

"See here," he said, keeping his voice quiet, "I'm not looking for a quarrel. Please let us alone."

"Another foreigner!" said the soldier with disgust. "Whole country's getting overrun with 'em! The hell with you," and he went back into the depot. Haroun looked after him, shaking his head merrily. "Only doin' his duty," he said. "No call to make him mad. D'you think there'll be a war?"

"Who knows?" said Joseph. "Why should it

matter to us?"

Haroun stopped smiling again, and his young face was suddenly enigmatic.

"Don't anything matter to you?" he asked.

Joseph was startled at the perceptiveness of one so young and he retreated in himself. "Why do you ask that?" he said. "That's impertinent, I'm thinking."

"Now, I didn't mean anything," said Haroun, spreading out his hands in a gesture Joseph had never seen before. "You just don't seem to care, that's all."

"You are quite right. I don't care," said Joseph. A group of bellowing men erupted onto the platform and they glared up the tracks and cursed futilely. They were very drunk. "Won't get in 'til noon, now!" one bawled. "And got a derrick to deliver 'fore that! Ought to sue the railroad!"

They returned in a sweaty rout to the depot. Joseph followed them with his eyes. He said, as if to himself, "Who are all these people?"

"Why, they're prospectors — oil," said Haroun. "They're going to Titusville to stake out a claim or buy land around there and start to drill. That's what you're going there to work for, ain't you?"

"Yes." Joseph looked at Haroun fully for the first time. "Do you know anything about it?"

"Well, I heard a lot. There's not much work in Wheatfield, with the Panic, and people don't even keep their horses shod right, and I'd like to make more than two dollars a week," said Haroun, cheerful again. "I aim to be a millionaire, like everybody else who goes to Titusville. I'm going to drive one of them wagons with nitroglycerin, and when I get a stake I'm going to buy a drill myself or go into partnership with somebody, and take options on the land. You can do that, if you can't buy the

37

land, and be sure nobody around Titusville or even Corland is selling out his land right now! You take options, and if you strike oil then you give the owner of the land royalties. I heard all about it in Wheatfield. Lots of men going there now, to work in the oil fields. Some of the men in the depot already struck it rich, real rich, and they're here to buy more machinery cheap, and hire help. I'm already hired," he added, with pride. "Seven dollars a week and board to work in the fields, but I'm going to drive the hot wagons. That's what they call 'em."

"They let a young lad like you drive those wagons?"

Haroun stood up as tall as he could, which was not very tall. The top of his head reached only to Joseph's nostrils. "I am almost fifteen," he said, very impressively. He is not even as tall as Sean, thought Joseph. "I been workin' since I was nine, but I've had five years of schoolin' and can do my letters and figures right well. I'm no greenhorn." Now, to Joseph's surprise, the black eyes were wise and shrewd as well as straight in their regard, but they were not hard or malicious. There was a deep maturity in them, and an awareness without wariness, a pride without mistrust. . . .

Suddenly there was a howling and clanging and ringing and grinding on the rails, a clamoring like an outbreak of furious metallic madness. A huge and blinding white eye roared out of the darkness around the bend and the rails trembled and so did the platform. Joseph could hear the rattling of coaches, the hiss of escaping steam as brakes were applied, and there was the train to Titusville screaming towards the depot, the squat black engine dwarfed by the gigantic smokestack which was retching smoke and fire into the night. The

engineer, in his striped cap, vigorously pulled the whistle, and the unbearable sound pierced Joseph's ears and he put up his hands to protect them. . . .

Joseph was awakened by brilliant sunshine lying on his eyes and face. Stiff and aching and weary, he moved on the rattan seat where he and Haroun had spent the night in heavy slumber. The younger boy's head lay on Joseph's right shoulder, as a child's head lies. . . . His thick curling hair, black as coal and as shining, spilled on Joseph's arm and neck. One of his hands had fallen on Joseph's knee. . . .

The air was chill and bright outside the train, and the new rough depot platform milled with excited men carrying their wicker luggage and portmanteaus. Carryalls, surreys, carts, wagons, buggies, and a handsome carriage or two, horses and mules, awaited them, and a number of buxom women dressed gaudily and wrapped in beautiful shawls, their bonnets gay with flowers and ribbons and silk and velvet, their skirts elaborately hooped and embroidered. Everything dinned with ebullience and loud fast voices. If there was any thought of the fratricidal war gathering force in the country there was no sign of it here, no sober voice, no fearful word. A golden dust shimmered everywhere in the sunlight, adding a carnival aura to the scene. It was as if the insensate length of the train, itself, was quivering with excitement also, for it snorted, steam shrilly screamed, bells rang wildly. Everyone was in constant motion; there were no leisurely groups or easy attitudes. The scent of dust, smoke, warmed wood, hot iron, and coal was pervaded by an acrid odor Joseph had never encountered before, but which he was to learn was the odor of raw black oil.

CONRAD RICHTER
"Brothers of No Kin"

A church-deacon farmer
bargains to save a soul

Time: 1870s?   Setting: Bedford

No internal evidence in "Brothers of No Kin" precisely establishes when the action of the story takes place; a good guess seems to be the latter part of the nineteenth century. But the story's timelessness is relevant to its subject, the Bible Belt culture of western Pennsylvania (and adjacent regions) that was there in the eighteenth century and that still exists today.

The timelessness contributes to the tone of the story, to establishing what Richter is saying about his subject. The life of Ebenezer Straint, deacon, is dominated by the regular, repetitive simplicity of farm work that is defined more by the seasonal rotations than the niceties of clock time. In a sense, there is not much to say about his life, and the fact that Richter can treat forty years in quick summary suggests the steady but undramatic devotion to duty that characterizes this man's career. At still another level, the timelessness relates to the religious theme, for in Ebenezer Straint's scheme of values mere wordly time is subordinate to the final meaning of his life, his salvation. His daily work is no more than background to the proper cultivation of his soul.

Finally, the timeless quality stimulates a certain feeling of awe and reverence that Richter invites his readers to take toward his provincial folk hero. Ebenezer Straint is seen almost as a natural phenomenon, a rock, a tree, a spirit grown from the land itself, expressive of simple verities and strengths that are part of a primitive and continuous human heritage. The point of view of the story underscores this effect, as the narrator seems to shake his head while sharing with the reader his amazed admiration: "It was a steep and sandy Allegheny road, a stony, endless road, that has never been traveled by you or me."

Conrad Richter (1890-1968) was born in Pine Grove, Pennsylvania, and in his early career worked as a journalist in various Pennsylvania towns (Johnstown, Patton, Pittsburgh) before moving to Cleveland in 1912 and then in 1928 to the Far West.

"Brothers of No Kin," published in 1914, was one of his first stories. Though it was selected by the Boston Transcript as the best short story of that year, the meager twenty-five dollars Richter was paid for it apparently disillusioned him, souring him on "serious" writing for the next fifteen years.

Richter eventually became a voluminous writer of serious fiction who is probably best remembered for his stories of frontier days in western Pennsylvania and especially Ohio. He won a Pulitzer Prize for his novel The Town (1950), the third book in his trilogy The Awakening Land (1966).

"Brothers of No Kin"

Ebenezer Straint, deacon, was not a man like you or I. In either your town or in mine, a hard-headed, shallow-minded religious crank he would have been, a church fool and stiff pedestrian in the strait and narrow path. Youth would have laughed and cynic would have sneered. There would have been many to point to his red head as a shaft example of miserhood and base hypocrisy. Any urban congregation would have been numerically better off without his name upon its roll. Even a doubtful Christian as you or I would have called him an obstinate, bigoted, old illiberal, and shaken our heads sadly over his good in this world of yours and mine.

But chance was kind to Straint and bore him among his own sort, down in a hemmed-in valley of Pennsylvania, south-west, among spurs of the Alleghenies, upon the hard red soil that yields such kind of being as he.

Then in Bedford County was another man, a man perhaps like you or I, a man whom fate, in a fit of perversity, must have transplanted from the deck of some old-time African-coast trader. Wild, adventurous, exotic, he failed to be tamed by the triad of school, stern church and stony, hilly farm.

To you and me, it doesn't matter why; but he and Ebenezer were friends. There are friends in business, friends in pleasure, and friends who are friends only because they are. Such latter were Ebenezer and Ritter—that was his name—Jeremiah Ritter. But even the stiff-backed fathers of Bedford's coves learned to forget and call him Jerry.

All this happened, and at twenty-three Jerry Ritter had left the hills of Southern Pennsylvania behind him.

There is a good book which somewhere declares that a genuine friend sticketh closer than a brother. Anyhow Ritter remembered and it didn't matter to him that Ebenezer was a hard-necked, puritanical Christian, even more, an obsolete, hell-believing, country deacon.

During thirty-five long years the post office at Heisler Cove delivered small packages and letters with queer foreign stamps. Once in twelve months is often during thirty-five years. Sometimes the stamps bore heads of queens, sometimes tigers, or waterfalls, sometimes the faces of curious-looking men. There were scrawls of a year's wanderings and adventures, much of pleasures, hints of toil and hardships, all crowded into the unprinted back of some floating poster or dissected envelope. Transposed into cool, wet type, they would have made literature. But Ebenezer read the letters over and put them away in a seasoned old chest with a lock like a wine room door's. There was no trunk in Ebenezer Straint's possession. Never had he felt the need of one. Then, too, Bedford County was settled early and in several generations a few heirlooms can be far divided.

Ebenezer never at any time re-read the letters. He remembered. Occasionally, for the sake of modest curiosity, he referred to the school geography of his youngest offspring. The pictures of strange scenes and peoples that came in sporadic packages were reserved for future patrimony among his children.

There had not been a letter now for several years. Ebenezer thought often about it as he

41

turned a moist furrow or steadily cradled yellow wheat. Never had he even mentioned receipt of news from the vanished Ritter to neighbors or parents of the absent boy. The night before Jerry Ritter disappeared, he had left behind him an empty whiskey jug gotten God knows where, and two battered sons of the cove's church trustees. And four days later there was red Bedford shale between one of the youths and daylight.

Regularly year after year, Ebenezer stole up to the cemetery evenings before Ascension day. The first letter had asked that. And farmers in Heisler Cove often watched a ghostly, yellow spark that glimmered from the church hill a night or two in May. When the moon came full, there was no light: which convinced the neighborhood that spirits fear the moon. But it was not logically explained why the grave of a murdered young man should be always trimmed of grass and flower-bedded long before the remainder of the family lot.

Things went on until Ebenezer Straint grew old, and was ready for his grave and what reward lay beyond. Then it was that one night in February a tall, gaunt figure, bent with the clutch of a disease that kills, crawled into Heisler Cove and lay down outside the big Straint barn. Ebenezer found him there in the morning, and stopped short with two dull-tinned milk buckets on his arm. Nomads were rare in Bedford County.

"Get up, stranger, or you'll freeze," said Ebenezer, shaking the figure with a canvas-gloved hand.

The man stirred, then got stiffly to his feet. For a minute he stood staring full at the stern old farmer.

"You don't know me, Red?" he asked.

Red! No one had called him so for forty years.

Why, he was a deacon and everywhere had respect. To Straint the stranger's face seemed horrible,— sallow, hollow and worse. Besides, he was old, and when age is unkempt, dirty and ill, very ill, it is not pleasing to look at.

The man laughed, mirthless, shortly. Ebenezer still stared. But only for a moment. He knew that upward tilt of the head the second it happened.

"Come into the house, Jerry," he said; you and I might have thought harshly. But Ritter would have sworn it was soft and low.

The good family of Ebenezer Straint stood back in astonishment as, without a word, the old father entered and helped the disreputable-looking stranger to a chair between the oil-clothed breakfast table and the wood-burning kitchen stove. Silently Jerry Ritter was given three or four cups of hot, uncreamed coffee. Silently Jerry Ritter drank them. Then the two went upstairs. The family below heard heavy footsteps on the heavy white-pine flooring of the front spare room, then creakings of unused ropes. In the parlor underneath, the worthy Mrs. Straint looked dazed. No one had slept in her spare room bed for several years.

There was no remonstrance, question or word, when the father alone returned downstairs, and left the back door for milk pails and the barn. Ebenezer ruled his own house.

That was the immediate all the family of Ebenezer knew. It watched the old Heisler Cove doctor go up the winding stairs and putter down again with wonder in his face and white, shaking head. It saw Ebenezer three times a day carry upstairs victuals and deep, wide cups of coffee. The food nearly always came down untouched, but the coffee never. Ebenezer also performed various nurse's duties at which his family marveled. Finally

43

it was April.

One Sunday morning, Ebenezer found his patient cowering against the wall.

"Nice and sunny out to-day, Jerry," began Ebenezer.

There was no answer from the bed.

"Jerry!" said the deacon sharply.

The long frame stirred under Ebenezer's washed-out flannel night-shirt.

"I'm going to die before night, Red. To-day's the last sunshine. I want another doctor. I'm a wreck. I'm old. I'm afraid." The skin-clothed skeleton shook convulsively in bed.

Ebenezer sat down on the heavy linen coverlet.

"It isn't a doctor you need, Jerry," he said gently. "This morning we'll go to church."

"Church!" The decrepit man turned face about.

"The old stone church, Jerry. You haven't been there for many a day. The house of God will do you good."

The man on the bed began to curse in a long abusive strain of raped English and foreign blasphemy.

"Don't do that, Jerry," sternly reproved the deacon. "Thou knowest thou shalt not take His name in vain."

The anathema stopped, but the voice went on.

"Little a church can help me, Red. You found Billy Houser, when I went. That wasn't all. On the *Belle Marie* the second engineer and I never could hit it together. Coming into Rio, in the night, I found him taking air. The grog in me pushed him off the stern, into the Niagara Falls behind the propeller. A week after in the harbor, the old man found the back of a head floating on the water. And it was him, with his face and his nostrils full of mud. They never guessed it was me. But if there's a Somebody watching, IT saw me."

"Thou shalt not kill," said the deacon severely.

"I deserted my mother and father, Red, and me the only son they had."

"Honor thy parents," came sternly from Ebenezer.

"In London, in Paris, in Cape Town, in Sydney, in Melbourne, in Halifax, I've worked my countrymen for money when I had money. It's the dirtiest trick of all."

"Thou shalt not lie," repeated the deacon.

"I've gone through the pockets of dead men that fought for their country, which I never did. And I've done it to men that walked."

"Thou shalt not steal, thou shalt not covet, thou shalt not bow down to graven images."

The derelict was silent. Then, slowly: "And thou shalt not commit adultery."

White and gaunt, in a green-black suit of Ebenezer's Jerry Ritter managed up into the indestructible Straint spring wagon. And later, parishioners stared as their venerable deacon assisted the helpless, aged stranger up the aisle to the Straint front pew.

There was no opening anthem, only an old familiar hymn, sung for the most part untunefully. All the while the worshipers watched the white-haired deacon up in front support his companion to stand. Jerry Ritter made no protest. Well he knew that with Ebenezer no custom of church, not even for a dying man, could be bowed.

There was Bible reading, another hymn and a prayer, and the wayward son of Heisler Cove nearly died during the physical agonies on his knees. To regain the bench, he had to let Ebenezer lift him.

The strings of life were now so loosely let that

Ritter, who had seen many a fellow being flicker out before, knew well his proximity to the Stone of the Stepping Off. The unshaven preacher had just, for the third time, repeated his text, when a high, awful voice, freighted with fright and despair, hushed the Biblical words.

"Red! It's getting dark! I'm dying! I'm going to Hell! Help me, Red! Where are you, Red!" In his sudden blindness the old derelict was reaching about with bony hands.

"Here, humble thyself, Jerry," the startled congregation heard its deacon say. "Get down and pray—pray for thyself—no matter how weak. He will give thee strength."

"Pray, Red! Here! I couldn't. I don't know—"

"Thou dost not pray to the people here," rebuked Ebenezer. "Humble thyself and pray."

Falling stiffly upon his knees, Jeremiah Ritter forthwith prayed a prayer, a sequenced, incoherent, agonized prayer, of astounding confession and strange phrases, such as never in the old stone church of Heisler Cove had been heard. He cried as he prayed, but the thing that sapped the congregation was the terrible note of despair in it all. Suddenly the pleadings to an unseen Maker broke off abruptly with a cry of agony that quavered down the vertebrae of strong-backed Bedford worshipers.

"Red, no use! I can't find Him. The door is shut. It's blacker than night. Oh, Red, you pray for me! Tell everybody to pray for me!"

Deacon Straint rose to his feet, unshrinkingly.

"Brethren, sisters," earnestly he began. "Let us pray." Then he bent his own bony knees in a deep-toned beseechment of cant form and ecclesiastical phrase. Others rapidly took up the cause

Conrad Richter

and soon the church was a mingling of fervid supplication that would have sounded bedlam to you or me.

After a half hour the heavy emotionless voice of Deacon Straint alone continued. Finally it, too, had stopped.

When Ebenezer raised his eyes, he found his old friend crouched in the corner of the pew.

"No use, Red, no use," he whispered hoarsely. "I'm going to Hell—no use." There was little lurid terror now in the cry, just dumb, hopeless despair. Desperate but helpless, Ebenezer watched the twitching face.

"Red!" the other called of a sudden, "You're slipping off! I can't hold you back. A couple of seconds and it'll be too late! You never can be happy in Heaven and see me in eternal torment down below! Can't you do something quick, Red, quick!" There was a hopeless appeal in the agonized tones that made even the strongest young farmer shudder. Then the congregation saw its deacon fall again upon his knees, and strain over the rough altar railing. The minister with the worshipers heard every word.

"Lord Father, it is I, thy servant, Ebenezer"— surely you and I should have pronounced him Bedford Pharisee. "Thou knowest I have been a good and faithful servant, Father, and have kept Thy commandments all my life. Laid up for me is a Golden Crown in Heaven. But Lord, I come before Thee to pray that my reward be taken from me and given this dying brother of mine, this son of Thine. Give Thou to him what is mine, O Lord, my portion, my crown and passage to Heaven, And I take the sins of Jeremiah Ritter on my own head. For, O Lord, Thou art Justice, and nothing can be done by Thee but what is righteous and just.

Amen."

The speaker finished. There followed a terrible hush. The church saw Jeremiah Ritter fight to gain his feet. He stared up blindly.

"No, Red! No!" chokingly, he called. "I won't take it. It's too much. No!" For a moment his hard, rasped breathing penetrated to the loft. Then oddly it softened. And a strange voice came out of the silence, a voice curiously relaxed and low.

"Red! It's come! The door is open and I feel Him when I reach. The Lord be praised, for His mercy endureth forever!" The minister and Ebenezer both knew the voice, for they saw a peace that passeth the understanding of you and me come over the dying man's face.

They buried Jerry Ritter in the graveyard behind the church. And everyone went about his business. Quibbling over the last half dollar, the deacon sold his farm. To an astonished Methodist church board went every cent and a few hundred Bedford bank savings. The family of Straint moved to the farm of a married son, but not the father. Alone, pockets empty, with nothing but the clothes on his back, the shoes on his feet and the staff in his hand, the old man struck westward over the mountains. No one tried to restrain him. That was something without the ken of people that knew Ebenezer Straint. Besides, he was going to give the rest of his now twilighted life to lighten in some measure the unpardonable sins on his head. Atonement was hopeless. Both man and people were sure of that.

With the words, "a murderer shall never enter the Kingdom of God," seared deep into his forehead, Ebenezer Straint went up the long mountain side. It was a steep and sandy Allegheny road, a stony, endless road, that has never been traveled by you or me.

GARET GARRETT
"Undergoing a Caesarian"

John Breakspeare sets up
a nail-making monopoly

Time: 1870s   Setting: Pittsburgh

This selection from the novel The Cinder Buggy *touches on a number of business practices usually regarded as evils — monopoly, price-fixing, stock manipulation. Pittsburgh bankers and industrialists of the 1870s are shown hell-bent for profit and more than willing to wink at protocol.*

Nonetheless this chapter and The Cinder Buggy *as a whole present the entrepreneurs of the dawning Steel Age enthusiastically, triumphantly. Looking back from the 1920s, when the novel was written, Garrett can picture the coming of steel as the wave of the future, a cataclysmic event that was sometimes rough and brutal in immediate effects but in the long run creator of a more democratized Land of Plenty.*

It made no difference how far a thing was hauled Transportation was cheap because steel was cheap. Kansas wheat was sold in Minneapolis, Chicago and in Liverpool. Minneapolis made flour and sent it to New York, Europe and back to Kansas.

The great availability of food released people from agriculture. They went to the industrial centers to make more steel and things rising of steel, so that there were more of such goods to sell.

More, more, more of everything.
Sell! Sell! Sell!
That was the voice of the steel age.

What makes The Cinder Buggy *an engaging generally successful novel is the style in which Garrett presents his vision. The thrusting, punching quality of his sentences vibrates with the energy that he attributes to the steel industry. Beyond that, his metaphors stress the godlike, Promethean power of those who bring forth metals from the earth:*

A blast furnace even then was what a blast furnace is,—the most audacious affront man has yet put upon nature. He decoys the elemental forces and gives them handy nicknames. Though he cannot tame them, he may control them through knowledge of their weaknesses. He learns their immutable habits. From the Omnipotent Craftsman he steals the true process. In the scale of his own strength he reproduces in a furnace the conditions under which the earth was made, and extracts from the uproar a lump of iron.

The metaphor of birth central to the chapter reprinted here — "the great mother was undergoing a Caesarian operation" — runs through the book as a whole. As part of the total vision of released energy, it is as though the birth of the Steel Age is generated by some great cosmic sexual act:

Now take it: The iron ore is in the ore bed, embracing those other elements at random, particularly Oxygen. First you oxidize him by roasting. That is, you wed him to Oxygen; you give him Oxygen until he is sick of it. Then you melt him down with coal in a furnace to deoxidize him—to divorce him, that is to say, from his affinity Oxygen. It is the first fiery ordeal. But at the same time you wed him to Carbon. Thus deoxidized and carbonized, divorced and wedded by one stroke, he becomes pig iron.

The primary character in this chapter, John Breakspeare, is descended from an iron-making family of eastern Pennsylvania; Thane is the iron master he brings to Pittsburgh; and Jubal Awns is an associate. The character in the background, Enoch Gib, an enigmatic threat to John's plans, is a long-time rival of the Breakspeare family. In the novel as a whole, Gib represents the tenacity with which the iron men held to the old ways.

Garet Garrett (1878-1954) was a journalist (a financial writer) by trade, though he wrote several other novels in addition to The Cinder Buggy.

"Undergoing a Caesarian"

While Thane was thinking how to set the nail mill in order, John, sitting in the hotel lobby with his feet in the window, gnawing a cigar, was reflecting in another sphere. His problem was the nail industry at large. It was in a parlous way. Although cut iron nails had been made by automatic machines for a long time there had recently appeared a machine that displaced all others, because it made the nail complete, head and all, in one run, and was very fast. This machine coming suddenly into use had caused an overproduction of nails. The price had fallen to a point where there was actually a loss instead of a profit in nail making unless one produced one's own iron and got a profit there. The Twenty-ninth Street plant had to buy its iron. The probability of running it at a profit was nil.

His meditations carried him far into the night. The lights were put out and still he sat with his feet in the window, musing, reflecting, dreaming, with a relaxed and receptive mind. An idea came to him. It will be important to consider what that idea was for it became afterward a classic pattern. It had the audacity of great simplicity. He would combine the whole nail making industry in his North American Manufacturing Company, Ltd. Then production could be suited to demand and the price of nails could be advanced to a paying level.

He took stock of his capital. It was fifteen thousand dollars. Maybe it could be stretched to twenty. In his work with Gib, selling nails, he had acquired a miscellaneous lot of very cheap and highly speculative railroad shares, some of which were beginning to have value. But twenty thousand

dollars would be the outside measurement, and to think of setting out with that amount of capital to acquire control of the nail making industry, worth perhaps half a million dollars, was at a glance fantastic. But one's capital may exist in the idea. John already understood the art of finance.

Leaving the Twenty-ninth Street plant in Thane's hands, with funds for overhauling it, he consulted with Jubal Awns and set out the next morning on his errand.

The nail makers were responsive for an obvious reason. They were all losing money. In a short time John laid before Awns a sheaf of papers.

"There's the child," he said. "Examine it."

He had got options in writing on every important nail mill in the country save one. The owners agreed to sell out to the North American Manufacturing Co., Ltd., taking in payment either cash or preferred shares at their pleasure. The inducement to take preferred shares was that if they did they would receive a bonus of fifty per cent. in common stock.

"But they will take cash in every case," said Awns, "and where will you find it?"

"They won't," said John. "I'll see to that. What have you done with Gib?"

Awns had been to see Enoch. The New Damascus mill produced in its nail department a fifth of all the nails then made. There was no probability of buying him out. John well knew that. Yet his nail output had to be controlled in some way, else the combine would fail. So he had sent Awns to him with alternative propositions. The first was to buy him out of the nail making business. And when he had declined to sell, as of course he would, Awns was to negotiate for his entire output under a long term contract.

"He wouldn't sell his nail business," said Awns.

"I knew that," said John.

"But I've got a contract for all his nails," said Awns, handing over the paper. "The price is stiff, —fifty cents a keg more than nails are worth. It was the best I could do."

"That's all right," said John reading the agreement. "We are going to add a dollar a keg to nails. This phrase—'unless the party of the second part,' (that's Gib), 'wishes to sell nails at a lower price to the trade'—who put that in?"

"He did," said Awns. "I couldn't see any point in objecting to it. No man is going to undersell his own contract."

John handed the agreement back and sat for several minutes musing.

"There's a loose wheel in your scheme, if I'm not mistaken," said Awns. "If you add a dollar a keg to nails won't you bring in a lot of new competition? Anybody can make nails if it pays. These same people who sell out to you may turn around and begin again. You'll be holding the umbrella for everybody else."

"Anybody can't make nails," said John. "I've looked at that."

"Why not?"

"Nail making machines are covered by patents. There are only four firms that make them. I've made air tight contracts with them. We take all their machines at an advance of twenty-five per cent. over present prices and they bind themselves to sell machines to nobody else during the life of the contract. So we've got the bag sewed up top and bottom. They were glad to do it because there isn't any profit in machines either with the nail makers all going busted."

Awns stared at him with doubt and admiration

50

A nineteenth-century bank, corner of Oliver Avenue and Wood Street, Pittsburgh.

mingled.

"Well, that is showing them something," he said. "If you go far with that kind of thing laws will be passed to stop it."

"It's legal, isn't it?"

"There's no law against it," said Awns.

"We're not obliged to be more legal than the law," said John. "Tell me, what do you know about bankers in Pittsburgh? I've got to do some business in that quarter."

Pittsburgh at this time was not a place prepared. It was a sign, a pregnant smudge, a state of phenomena. The great mother was undergoing a Caesarian operation. An event was bringing itself to

pass. The steel age was about to be delivered.

Men performed the office of obstetrics without knowing what they did. They could neither see nor understand it. They struggled blindly, falling down and getting up. Forces possessed them. Their psychic condition was that of men to whom fabulous despair and extravagant expectation were the two ends of one ecstasy. They were hard, shrewd, sentimental, superstitious, romantic in friendship and conscienceless in trade. They named their blast furnaces after their wives and sweethearts, stole each other's secrets, fell out with their partners, knew no law of business but to lay on what the traffic would bear, read Swedenborg and dreamed of Heaven as a thoroughfare resembling Wood Street, Pittsburgh, lined with banks and in the door of each bank a grovelling president, pleading: "Here's money for your payrolls. Please borrow it here. Very fine quality of money. Pay it back when you like."

They were always begging money at the banks. When they made money they used it to build more mills and to fill the mills with automatic monsters that grew stranger and more fantastic. Many of these monsters, like things in nature's own history of trial and error, appeared for a short time and became extinct. When they were not making money they were bankrupt. That was about half the time. Then they came to the banks in Wood Street to implore, beg, wheedle money to meet their payrolls.

There is the legend of a man, afterward one of the great millionaires, who drove one mare so often to Wood Street and from one bank to another in a zig-zag course that the animal came to know the stops by heart, made them automatically, and could not be made to go in a straight line through this lane of money doors.

51

The bankers were a tough minded group. They had to be. Nobody was quite safe. A man with a record for sanity would suddenly lose his balance and cast away the substance of certainty to pursue a vision. The effort to adapt the Bessemer steel process to American conditions was an irresistible road to ruin. That process was producing amazing results in Europe but in this country it was bewitched with perversity and it looked as if the English and German manufacturers would walk away with the steel age. Fortunes were still being swallowed up in snail shaped vessels called converters, not unlike the one Aaron had built at New Damascus twenty-five years before.

Of all the bankers in Wood Street the toughest minded was Lemuel Slaymaker.

"All the same," said Awns, "I should try him first. His name would put it through and he loves a profit."

Awns knew him. They went together to see him. Slaymaker saluted Awns and acknowledged his introduction of Mr. John Breakspeare not otherwise nor more than by turning slowly in his chair and staring at them. He had a large white face, pale blue eyes and red, close-cropped hair. The impression he made was one of total sphericity. There was no way to take hold of him. No thought or feeling projected.

John laid out his plan, producing the papers as exhibits, A, B, C, in the appropriate places. Lastly he produced data on the nail trade, showing the amount of nails consumed in the country and the normal rate of annual increase with the growth of population, together with a carefully developed estimate of the combine's profits at various prices per keg. When he had finished the idea was lucid, complete in every part and self-evident. Therein lay the secret of his extraordinary power of persuasion. He seemed never to argue his case. He expressed no opinion of his own to be combatted. He merely laid down a state of facts with an air of looking at them from the other man's point of view.

"And what you want is a bank to guarantee this scheme," said Slaymaker. "You want a bank to guarantee that if these people want cash instead of stock the cash will be forthcoming."

This was the first word he had spoken. The papers he had not even glanced at. They lay on his desk as John had placed them there.

"That's it," said John. "Guarantee it. Very little cash will be required."

"How do you say that?"

"To make them want stock instead of cash," said John, "you have only to engage brokers to make advance quotations for the stock, here and in Philadelphia at, say, par for the preferred and fifty for the common. If you do not know brokers who can do that I will find them. The scheme is sound. The stock will pay dividends from the start. A bank that had guaranteed it might very well speak a good word for it here and there. The public will want some of the stock."

Slaymaker gazed at a corner of the ceiling and twiggled his foot. Then he turned his back on them.

"Leave the papers," he said, "and see me at this time tomorrow."

When they were in the street again Awns said: "You got him."

And so the infant trust was born,—first of its kind, first of a giant brood. Biologically they were all alike, but with evolution their size increased prodigiously. The swaddling cloths of this one would not have patched the eye of a twentieth century specimen delivered in Wall Street.

MARGARET DELAND
"Oh My Darling"

**A teen-age boy
suffers his first jilting**

Time: 1870s   **Setting: Pittsburgh?**

Margaret Deland's The Iron Woman *tells the story of the developing relations between the characters who figure directly in this passage — Blair Maitland, Elizabeth Ferguson, and David Richie — who are children when the book begins in the late 1860s, young adults when the action ends. Elizabeth and Blair are both headstrong and impetuous, the latter drawn especially by the pursuit of pleasure and the indulgence of an artistic temperament; both are at odds with the dominantly Presbyterian and commercial ethic of the environment in which they are growing up. Their romance, which first comes to public notice in the episode included here, is a basic issue on which the plot of the novel turns.*

By modern standards, The Iron Woman *is to some extent an old-fashioned book about the perils of elopement and the abuses of "honor." But whatever a reader in the 1970s may think about such matters, the novel also achieves a genuine excellence in its delineation of character and its portrayal of personal relationships. "The iron woman" of the title, the novel's central figure, is Mrs. Maitland, Blair's mother. The label as applied to her suggests more than the fact that she owns and runs an iron mill: She is in fact a frigid widow devoted to a Puritanical work ethic that instinctively converts everything into profit and loss. Though she pushes her own view of the world with an aggressiveness that brooks no contradiction, she also feels the indignity of being regarded as sexless and the pain of having her own son tell her more than once that she is "ugly." Late in the novel she must at last face the agony of understanding that her Puritanism has somehow caused her son's*

excessive indulgence and irresponsibility.

Even the fragment printed here reflects the temperamental conflict between mother and son that runs through the novel as a whole. "The awful, ... the damned dinner" that had preceded his "engagement" to Elizabeth was an elaborate teen-age dinner party Blair had planned for the pure fun of it, and Mrs. Maitland had publicly embarrassed him by criticizing his inclination to frills and fripperies.

In contrast to Blair, who stands to inherit a fortune, David Richie, the central character in this excerpt, completes the novel's romantic triangle with a sobriety of character, an overearnestness, that seems born of the sense that he must make his own way up from the bottom if he is to be a social success.

The Iron Woman *is full of local color that is recognizably western Pennsylvanian. The specific location of the action, however, is somewhat disguised. Deland calls the novel's locale "Mercer," but many of the details of setting — including the river scenes of this selection — suggest the Ohio River valley, and possibly Pittsburgh's North Side.*

Margaret Deland was born in 1867, probably in Old Allegheny, and lived as a child near Manchester, on the north side of the Ohio River. Though she left Pittsburgh when she was seventeen and remained in the East for the rest of her life, a number of her many fictional works are set in western Pennsylvania, notably the best-selling Old Chester Tales *and its sequels, which seem specifically placed in the Manchester area. She died in 1945.*

"Oh My Darling"

When the company had gone,—"I thought they never *would* go!" Nannie said—she rushed at her brother. "Blair!"

The boy flung up his head proudly. "She told you, did she?"

"You're engaged!" cried Nannie, ecstatically.

Blair started. "Why!" he said. "So I am! I never thought of it." And when he got his breath, the radiant darkness of his eyes sparkled into laughter. "Yes, *I'm engaged!*" He put his hands into his pockets and strutted the length of the room; a minute later he stopped beside the piano and struck a triumphant chord; then he sat down and began to play uproariously, singing to a crashing accompaniment:

> " '. . . . lived a miner, a forty-niner,
> With his daughter Clementine!
> Oh my darling, oh my *darling*—' "

—the riotous, beautiful voice rang on, the sound overflowing through the long rooms, across the hall, even into the dining-room. Harris, wiping dishes in the pantry, stopped, tea-towel in hand, and listened; Sarah Maitland, at her desk, lifted her head, and the pen slipped from her fingers. Blair, spinning around on the piano-stool, caught his sister about her waist in a hug that made her squeak. Then they both shrieked with laughter.

"But Blair!" Nannie said, getting her breath; "shall you tell Mamma to-night?"

Blair's face dropped. "I guess I won't tell anybody yet," he faltered; "oh, that awful dinner!"

As the mortification of an hour ago surged back upon him, he added to the fear of telling his mother a resentment that would retaliate by secrecy. "I won't tell her at all," he decided; "and don't you, either."

"I!" said Nannie. "Well, I should think not. Gracious!"

But though Blair did not tell his mother, he could not keep the great news to himself; he saw David the next afternoon, and overflowed.

David took it with a gasp of silence, as if he had been suddenly hit below the belt; then in a low voice he said, "You—*kissed* her. Did she kiss you?"

Blair nodded. He held his head high, balancing it a little from side to side; his lips were thrust out, his eyes shone. He was standing with his feet well apart, his hands deep in his pockets; he laughed, reddening to his forehead, but he was not embarrassed. For once David's old look of silent, friendly admiration did not answer him; instead there was half-bewildered dismay. David wanted to protest that it wasn't—well, it wasn't *fair*. He did not say it; and in not saying it he ceased to be a boy.

"I suppose it was when you and she went off after dinner? You needn't have been so darned quiet about it! What's the good of being so—mum about everything? Why didn't you come back and tell? You're not ashamed of it, are you?"

"A man doesn't tell a thing like that," Blair said scornfully.

"Well!" David snorted, "I suppose some time you'll be married?"

Blair nodded again. "Right off."

"Huh!" said David; "your mother won't let you. You are only sixteen. Don't be an ass."

55

"I'll be seventeen next May."

"Seventeen! What's seventeen? I'm pretty near eighteen, and I haven't thought of being married;—at least to anybody in particular."

"You couldn't," Blair said coldly; "you haven't got the cash."

David chewed this bitter fact in silence; then he said, "I thought you and Elizabeth were kind of off at dinner. You didn't talk to each other at all. I thought you were both huffy; and instead of that—" David paused.

"That damned dinner!" Blair said, dropping his love-affair for his grievance. Blair's toga virilis, assumed in that hot moment in the hall, was profanity of sorts. "David, I'm going to clear out. I can't stand this sort of thing. I'll go and live at a hotel till I go to college; I'll—"

"Thought you were going to get married?" David interrupted him viciously.

Blair looked at him, and suddenly understood,—David was jealous! "Gorry!" he said blankly. He was honestly dismayed. "Look here," he began, "I didn't know that *you*—"

"I don't know what you're talking about," David broke in contemptuously; "if you think *I* care, one way or the other, you're mistaken. It's nothing to me. 'By''; and he turned on his heel.

It was a hot July afternoon; the sun-baked street along which they had been walking was deep with black dust and full of the clamor of traffic. Four big gray Flemish horses, straining against their breastplates, were hauling a dray loaded with clattering iron rods; the sound, familiar enough to any Mercer boy, seemed to David at that moment intolerable. "I'll get out of this cursed noise," he said to himself, and turned down a narrow street toward the river. It occurred to him that he would

go over the covered bridge, and maybe stop and get a tumbler of ice-cream at Mrs. Todd's. Then he would strike out into the country and take a walk; he had nothing else to do. This vacation business wasn't all it was cracked up to be; a man had better fun at school; he was sick of Mercer, anyhow.

He had reached Mrs. Todd's saloon by that time, and through the white palings of the fence he had glimpses of happy couples sitting at marble-topped tables among the marigolds and coreopsis, taking slow, delicious spoonfuls of ice-cream, and gazing at each other with languishing eyes. David felt a qualm of disgust; for the first time in his life he had no desire for ice-cream. A boy like Blair might find it pleasant to eat ice-cream with a lot of fellows and girls out in the garden of a toll-house, with people looking in through the palings; but he had outgrown such things. The idea of Blair, at his age, talking about being in love! Blair didn't know what *love* meant. And as for Elizabeth, how could she fall in love with Blair? He was two months younger than she, to begin with. "No woman ought to marry a man younger than she is," David said; he himself, he reflected, was much older than Elizabeth. That was how it ought to be. The girl should always be younger than the fellow. And anyway, Blair wasn't the kind of man for a girl like Elizabeth to marry. "He wouldn't understand her. Elizabeth goes off at half-cock sometimes, and Blair wouldn't know how to handle her. I understand her, perfectly. Besides that, he's too selfish. A woman ought not to marry a selfish man," said David. However, it made no difference to him whom she married. If Elizabeth liked that sort of thing, if she found Blair—who was only a baby anyhow—the kind of man she could love, why then he was disappointed in Elizabeth. That was all. He was not jealous, or anything like that; he was just disappointed; he was sorry that Elizabeth was that kind of girl. "Very, very sorry," David said to himself; and his eyes stung. . . . (Ah, well; one may smile; but the pangs are real enough to the calf! The trouble with us is we have forgotten our own pangs, so we doubt his.). . . .Yes, David was sorry; but the whole darned business was nothing to him, because, unlike Blair, he was not a boy, and he could not waste time over women; he had his future to think of. In fact, he felt that to make the most of himself he must never marry.

Then suddenly these bitter forecastings ceased. He had come upon some boys who were throwing stones at the dust-grimed windows of an unused foundry shed. Along the roof of the big, gaunt building, dilapidated and deserted, was a vast line of lights that had long been a target for every boy who could pick up a pebble. Glass lay in splinters on the slope of sheet-iron below the sashes, and one could look in through yawning holes at silent, shadowy spaces that had once roared with light from swinging ladles and flowing cupolas; but there were a few whole panes left yet. At the sound of crashing glass, David, being a human boy, stopped and looked on, at first with his hands in his pockets; then he picked up a stone himself. A minute later he was yelling and smashing with the rest of them; but when he had broken a couple of lights, curiously enough, desire failed; he felt a sudden distaste for breaking windows,—and for everything else! It was a sort of spiritual nausea, and life was black and bitter on his tongue. He was conscious of an actual sinking below his breast-bone. "I'm probably coming down with brain fever," he told himself; and he had a happy moment of thinking how wretched everybody would be when he died. Eliza-

beth would be *very* wretched! David felt a wave of comfort, and on the impulse of expected death, he turned toward home again. . . . However, if he should by any chance recover, marriage was not for him. It occurred to him that this would be a bitter surprise to Elizabeth, whose engagement would of course be broken as soon as she heard of his illness; and again he felt happier. No, he would never marry. He would give his life to his profession—it had long ago been decided that David was to be a doctor. But it would be a lonely life. He looked ahead and saw himself a great physician—no common doctor, like that old Doctor King who came sometimes to see his mother; but a great man, dying nobly in some awful epidemic. When Elizabeth heard of his magnificent courage, she'd feel pretty badly. Rather different from Blair. How much finer than to be merely looking forward to a lot of money that somebody else had made! But perhaps that was why Elizabeth liked Blair; because he was going to have money? And yet, how could she compare Blair with,—well, *any* fellow who meant to work his own way? Here David

57

touched bottom abruptly. "How can a fellow take money he hasn't earned?" he said to himself. David's feeling about independence was unusual in a boy of his years, and it was not altogether admirable; it was, in fact, one of those qualities that is a virtue, unless it becomes a vice.

When he was half-way across the bridge, he stopped to look down at the slow, turbid river rolling below him. He stood there a long time, leaning on the hand-rail. On the dun surface a sheen of oil gathered, and spread, and gathered again. He could hear the wash of the current, and in the railing under his hand he felt the old wooden structure thrill and quiver in the constant surge of water against the pier below him. The sun, a blood-red disk, was slipping into the deepening haze, and on either side of the river the city was darkening into dusk. All along the shore lights were pricking out of the twilight and sending wavering shafts down into the water. The coiling smoke from furnace chimneys lay level and almost motionless in the still air; sometimes it was shot with sparks, or showed, on its bellying black curves, red gleams from hidden fires below.

David, staring at the river with absent, angry eyes, stopped his miserable thoughts to watch a steamboat coming down the current. Its smoke-stacks were folded back for passing under the bridge, and its great paddle-wheel scarcely moved except to get steerageway. It was pushing a dozen rafts, all lashed together into a spreading sheet. The smell of the fresh planks pierced the acrid odor of soot that was settling down with the night mists. On one of the rafts was a shanty of newly sawed pine boards; it had no windows, but it was evidently a home, for a stove-pipe came through its roof, and there was a woman sitting in its little doorway, nursing her baby. David, looking down, saw the downy head, and a little crumpled fist lying on the white, bare breast. The woman, looking up as they floated below him, caught his eye, and drew her blue cotton dress across her bosom. David suddenly put his hand over his lips to hide their quiver. The abrupt tears were on his cheeks. "Oh—*Elizabeth!*" he said. The revolt, the anger, the jealousy, were all gone. He sobbed under his breath. He had forgotten that he had said it made no difference to him,—"not the slightest difference." It did make a difference! All the difference in the world. . . . "Oh, Elizabeth!" . . . The barges had slid farther and farther under the bridge; the woman and the child were out of sight; the steamboat with its folded smoke-stacks slid after them, leaving a wake of rocking, yellow foam; the water splashed loudly against the piers. It was nearly dark there on the footpath, and quite deserted. David put his head down on his arms on the railing and stood motionless for a long moment.

When he reached home, he found his mother in the twilight, in the little garden behind the house. David, standing behind her, said carelessly, "I have some news for you, Materna."

"Yes?" she said, absorbed in pinching back her lemon verbena.

"Blair is—is spoony over Elizabeth. Here, I'll snip that thing for you."

Mrs. Richie faced him in amazement. "What! Why, but they are both children, and—" she stopped, and looked at him. "Oh—*David!*" she said.

And the boy, forgetting the spying windows of the opposite houses, dropped his head on her shoulder. "Materna — Materna," he said, in a stifled voice.

ELIZABETH MOORHEAD
"A Grand Sight"

Alison Cuddy attends
a production of Shakespeare

Time: 1884   Setting: Pittsburgh

Elizabeth Moorhead's Clouded Hills *follows the career of Alison Cuddy, daughter of a Pittsburgh steel magnate, from her late childhood, around 1880, into the first decade of the twentieth century. This selection indicates the novel's major conflict — Alison's youthful ties to the Pittsburgh scene, the grandeur as well as grimness of its landscape, versus a yearning for a world of culture, art, and romance that will presumably be found in purer form elsewhere. Her Pittsburgh background is complicated by the constraints of a strict Presbyterianism and also by the genuine kindness of an early admirer, Martin Boyce, whose skills are better tuned to mill management than to appreciation of Shakespeare.*

The novel as a whole develops the conflict within Alison through her relation to two other male characters, her husband, Lawrence Reath, and her father, Daniel Cuddy. Lawrence comes from a high-society eastern Pennsylvania family, from "old money" that has been pretty much depleted, although the cultured manners linger on. Lawrence values the things Alison has always wanted — poetry, music, foreign travel, untrammeled nature. By contrast, Daniel Cuddy is "new money" — one of the millionaires created in the rough and tumble of Pittsburgh's industrial development.

Naturally when Alison and Lawrence marry and come to Pittsburgh to live, and when it becomes clear that Lawrence has no money-making career in mind, the tension between him and Daniel is almost intolerable. Alison's problem is to learn sympathy for the weaknesses as well as the strengths of both men, while she simultaneously tries to establish an independent identity of her own.

Though Moorhead modifies some of her place names, Clouded Hills *is clearly set in the Oakland and Shadyside areas of Pittsburgh. Henry Irving and Ellen Terry, with their famous English touring company, stopped several times in Pittsburgh during the late nineteenth century; they performed Shakespeare's* Merchant of Venice *at the Pittsburgh Opera House in 1884.*

Elizabeth Moorhead was born in Pittsburgh in 1866 in a family that dated back to the beginnings of the city. As she relates it in her autobiographic memoir, Whirling Spindle, *her earliest recollections focused on her grandfather's home at 113 Centre Avenue (in the area today called Schenley Farms or the Hill District): "No New England village could have been more tranquil, more respectable, than the locality in which the Moorhead family was settled . . . —high, airy, with comfortable vine-covered houses set back from the streets in shady yards." Later she lived in various locations in Shadyside. When her father's steel business failed in the 1890s, Moorhead had to make her own living, and from 1910 to 1929 she taught literature at Carnegie Tech. In retirement, she turned to writing as a career. During her last years she was a resident of the Schenley Hotel. She died in 1955.*

Like her character Alison Cuddy, Elizabeth Moorhead had an intense interest in the theater from childhood on. In Whirling Spindle *she recalls an instance in which she drove her pony cart out to the intersection of Fifth and Penn Avenues in Point Breeze to present a bouquet to an actress who was staying there at the corner tavern. She comments, "Fifth Avenue then was a quiet country road along which slow horse carts trailed at irregular intervals. No automobiles, no fast driving — a child in a pony cart was safe."*

"A Grand Sight"

Alison was sitting in a theater for the first time in her life. On Martin's overcoat, which he had wadded up into a sort of cushion so that she might see over the rampant feathers on the hat in front of her. People were crowding in, ushers running up and down the aisles, programs rustling. Such a stir of anticipation! Everybody smiling, in holiday mood. She felt reckless, wicked, defiant. Selfishly grasping her own pleasure, disappointing Aunt Alison, who had wanted her to stay in Sherwin. She had consulted her grandfather. He put his hand under her chin and turned up her face to the light for a long searching look before he said: "Go, child. There's no wrong in it. Evil doesn't lie in doing this thing or that. The Christian life is a life of the spirit. We are all full of hungers and desires, but only one thing satisfies. You will find that out for yourself in time. They that hunger and thirst after righteousness, they shall be filled."

A dreadful gloom had settled upon her then.

But now, for good or for evil, she was happy. The curtain hung before her, a picture of a cypress-crowned precipice, a circular temple, a dashing waterfall, and the magic word Tivoli beneath. Tivoli! What visions of beauty in that one word! And beyond the curtain an unknown unimaginable realm of enchantment! Henry Irving and Ellen Terry were there, under this roof, within these walls: to know that was almost enough. She would see them with her own eyes, hear their voices. . . . She was a privileged being; oh, she was glad she was alive! Grandfather didn't understand; he was old; he had forgotten.

When she grew old perhaps she too . . .

The music stopped, the curtain rolled up.

She sat in a breathless hush. She forgot the people about her, forgot Martin. She was in Venice. The elaborate realism of Henry Irving's gorgeous stage-settings created a perfect illusion for her. She had never seen anything so beautiful as these Venetian streets, the blue lagoon in the distance, lordly youths strutting about in their satins and brocades and plumed hats.

Then the halls of Belmont . . .

"By my troth, Nerissa, my little body is aweary of this great world."

These words in that delicious slightly husky voice that was charming audiences the world over. Oh, what a lovely creature! Alison's heart leaped to her. Such grace, such warmth and joy and tenderness! Portia and Ellen Terry were one,—she couldn't separate them, think of them apart. Portia must have been just that,—all white and gold and radiant. She had never imagined a woman so fearless, so noble, and yet so gay. One who treated solemn matters like suitors and a father's will so lightheartedly. And how true she was, serious too when need be—"I remember him well, and I remember him worthy of thy praise."

There was a set of Shakespeare at home behind the glass doors of the walnut bookcase with Dickens and Scott and James Fenimore Cooper. Alison had read the play, knew what was going to happen, but she quivered with excitement throughout the casket scenes, sat on the edge of her seat, could scarcely keep from crying out a hint to Bassanio while he argued with himself. If he should

61

choose wrong!

And Portia's surrender:

"You see me, Lord Bassanio, where I stand,
Such as I am: though for myself alone
I would not be ambitious in my wish,
To wish myself much better; yet for you
I would be trebled twenty times myself,
A thousand times more fair, ten thousand times
    More rich . . ."

What wooing, what royal giving! That was love as it should be. Love. A new feeling, a feeling of utter bliss stirred in her breast,—warm, melting, it ran through her like flame. Her breath came fast. Anything might happen, anything, even to her, in all the wonderful years to come. . . .

Martin looked down at her with a smile. Pleased but a little worried too. She felt it too keenly, he thought; it was only a play, after all.

She wanted to hold the play back; she hated to think that it must come to an end, that these enchanted figures with their lovely speech would pass out of her sight. And the last was the best— that moon-bathed avenue at Belmont, the reunited lovers:

"The moon shines bright: in such a night as this,
When the sweet wind did gently kiss the trees . . ."

The short December afternoon was done when they left the theater. Street-lamps flickered through a rising fog. People went shuffling and teetering over a rough surface of blackened snow packed down hard on the sidewalk, clutching at one another to keep from falling. Alison caught Martin's arm and squeezed it as they pushed through the crowd. She wanted to run, dance, sing. She had found what she had always longed for.

They stood at the corner waiting for the infrequent car to Woodvale. A penetrating chill came up from the Monongahela. The river itself could not be seen from where they stood and the hills on its farther bank seemed to block the very end of the street. Wherever you looked the streets ran against hills. Sometimes a steamboat stretched grotesquely across the foot of Wood Street like a giant toy,—no water visible, only the boat against a hilly background. To-night these outlines were blurred in the darkness and the lights marking the ascent glowed like huge constellations through the mist. Alison often dreamed of the unknown world beyond these barriers. To see the rising and setting of the sun, to follow its whole journey across the sky—what a sense of freedom such wide vision would give! These clouded hills shut her in. Once her father had taken her by the inclined plane up one of the steep cliffs on the South Side, but when she had reached the top there were still hills and more hills stretching beyond,—and the city, as you looked down, was so wrapped in smoke and flame that you shrank from ever sinking back into that fiery pit.

"Did you like it, Ally?" said Martin at last.

"Oh, Martin! I loved it so—I can't bear it!"

"That's a funny way to feel. You'll make me sorry I took you."

"No, no, you mustn't be sorry! It's the best thing I've ever had in my life. . . . Oh, Martin, I—I want so much—so many things!"

"Do you? What sort of things?"

"Oh, how can I tell? I'm shut in—shut in. . . ."

She was jumping up and down, first on one foot then on the other, holding her muff to her face to keep warm in the sodden chill. "I want to go places. To Venice. I want to go everywhere and see

64

Ellen Terry as Portia.

Henry Irving as Shylock.

all the beautiful things in the whole world. And I want—I want—" But no, she couldn't tell. . . .

"Well, you're bound to get it all, Ally, whatever it is. You're the sort of girl to get things."

"Do you really think so?" Again she seemed to catch that glimpse of a dazzling future. Her beautiful eyes looked out over the muff, past Martin, past Martin's round honest face, into the mist. She sighed rapturously. "Oh, I hope that's true!— Martin, it's the play that makes me feel like this. It was too beautiful—it hurt. You know what I mean, don't you?"

"No, I don't believe I do." He hesitated. "Fact is, Ally, that play wasn't just my style. I got sort o' tired now and then with the long speeches. I ain't sure I wouldn't like the Salisbury Troubadours

better, or Oliver Doud Byron in *Across the Continent.*"

"Didn't you think Portia was lovely?"

"A fine girl all right. Pity she had to throw herself away on such a poor excuse of a fellow."

"Oh, I thought he was splendid!"

"That—Bassanio—whatever they call him? Not according to my ideas he wasn't. Borrowing money from a friend so he could go courting a rich girl—expecting to live off of her!"

"I don't think that matters at all," she said stoutly. "And how splendid it was for her—" She stopped.

"What?"

"To give like that, everything she had, to the one she cared for." She flushed. "I think that must be about the happiest thing in the world."

"You do, do you? And him taking it all without a word to say for himself—"

"He couldn't say much, he was too happy. But he understood. What he said was exactly right,—don't you remember?" She repeated softly,

"Madam, you have bereft me of all words,
Only my blood speaks to you in my veins."

Martin eyed her keenly. "You've got a fine memory, Ally. . . . But all that's poetry, it don't work in real life. You better get it out of your head. It's all right when it's the man who does the money giving. A man ought to take care of his wife; that's the right way, and the only right way."

The jingling of the approaching car interrupted them. The car was crowded. A fat woman with a market-basket at her feet good-naturedly moved up and allowed Alison to squeeze in between her and her neighbor. All the ventilators were closed, a coal fire blazed in the stove. The floor was covered with straw to keep out the draughts that came up through cracks in the boards; straw so thickened with mud and filth that it added unsavory smells to the human reek. The air became intolerably heavy. Alison wondered how she could stand it for the long trip out to Woodvale. She grew restless, her legs twitched. She felt annoyed with Martin, too,—hanging from a strap in front of her. His overcoat was worn and shabby, full of creases where she had sat on it, and a button dangled on a loose thread.

She shut her eyes.

"How sweet the moonlight sleeps upon this bank!
Here will we sit and let the sounds of music
Creep in our ears . . ."

She could see phantom shapes—Thisbe fearfully o'er-tripping the dew, and Dido with a willow in her hand, wafting her love to come again to Carthage. . . .

"Sleepy, Ally?"

Martin's cheerful voice roused her. She opened her eyes. He was looking down at her with his wry benevolent smile. Poor Martin. So good and kind, spending his money to give her pleasure. But for all that she didn't want to tell him what she was thinking.

The car was toiling up Soho Hill now. The driver got off and walked along by his steaming mules urging them up the long climb.

"Look behind you, Ally," Martin said.

She turned her head. Below, along the river bank, the furnaces of Loomis and Cuddy flamed in the darkness. Volleys of yellow and orange sparks shot out from the converters, the smoke and steam were like rolling waves of fire.

"Isn't it a grand sight?" Martin murmured, awe in his face.

66

THOMAS BELL
"A Laborer Named Mihal"

Mike Dobrejcak, steelworker,
courts Mary Kracha

Time: 1900   Setting: Braddock

Out of This Furnace *is a "historical" novel that takes as its subject not an imagined world of glamorous heroes and heroines, but a real world of mill-town steelworkers in the Mon Valley. With impressive accuracy and detail, the novel shows the slow process of acculturation and adaptation (from the 1880s to the 1930s) as three generations of a Slovak family learn to master working and living conditions in industrial America.*

Mary Kracha, whose courtship is the subject of this selection, represents the middle generation in the family's evolution. Her father, George Kracha, is the original migrant, and his survival until near the book's end seems to symbolize the toughness, as well as luck, that was necessary to survive the first days in America. Kracha, who arrives in eastern Pennsylvania in 1881 (walking across New Jersey after his New York debarkation), is a rough-and-ready, physical sort of person whose early career is devoted to his work in the mills and running a store, to drinking, and to an extramarital affair when his marriage goes sour.

Mike Dobrejcak, Mary's suitor in the selection, is a half generation younger than Kracha. Born in Slovakia in 1875, he migrates to Braddock as a teen-ager and works (and dies) as a steelworker in the Edgar Thomson Works. Temperamentally more sensitive and intellectual than Kracha, Mike makes more of an effort to understand his new environment — studying English at night school, taking sides in national politics (from an early advocacy of Bryan to a furtive vote for Eugene Debs in 1912). As a native-born citizen and household domestic, Mary Kracha is also acculturated to American ways to a degree her father never had time for. The marriage of these two warm and sensitive people — Mike and Mary — is the subject of the middle third of Out of This Furnace. *It is really the emotional center of the novel as well, since it is Mike and Mary's family that is most harshly victimized by mill-town working and living conditions.*

Overall, Out of This Furnace *unites two memorable themes. One is the gradual evolution of a political consciousness that culminates in the unionizing of the steel mills. Dobie Dobrejcak, Mike and Mary's son, inherits his father's idealism and plays an active role in the successful organizing efforts of the 1930s. On another level, the novel is also a splendid memorial to an ethnic group, to an era, and to a particular place. Riverfront Braddock — now pretty much demolished — is recorded by Bell as it was fifty and seventy-five years ago in the full bustle of life — "the teeming alleys and courtyards and kitchens of the First Ward."*

Thomas Bell (1903-1961) was born in Braddock in the Belejčak family, and Out of This Furnace *uses many autobiographical materials (for instance, the dates of Bell's father, Michael Belejčak, are the same as Mike Dobrejcak's in the novel, 1875-1914, and the burial site of the real-life and fictional figures is the same).*

Bell himself worked for a time in the mills, but shortly after his mother died in 1920 he moved to New York City, where he held various jobs but gradually gave more and more time to writing. At the height of his career, Bell was recognized by both the public and the critics. One novel, All Brides Are Beautiful, *was made into a movie; another,* Till I Come Back to You, *became a Broadway play.*

"A Laborer Named Mihal"

In December of 1900, when people were saying, "Well, the first year of the twentieth century is almost over," and a few were stubbornly reviving the old argument that the twentieth century had yet to begin — "If a century is 100 years, then nineteen centuries are 1900 years and the twentieth doesn't begin until January 1, 1901" — Mike Dobrejcak was twenty-five years old, a quiet, slow-speaking, dry-humored young man whose eyes crinkled before he smiled, who smiled more often than he laughed. He had been in America eleven years, and for ten of them he had worked in the blast furnaces, first as a water boy and then as a laborer. He was still a laborer but Keogh, the furnace keeper on his turn, had taken a liking to him and made him one of his two helpers. Though his wages, fourteen cents an hour, stayed unchanged, he was raised a little out of the anonymity of the labor gangs, he took orders only from Keogh and the work was — comparatively — lighter. Of the two thousand or so men working in the mill a good half were Slovaks or other non-English-speaking foreigners, and of that half not one had a skilled job. Departmental heads did their own hiring, and, whether American, English or Irish, tended to favor their own kind.

The twelve-hour turn left even the very young with little energy to do more than lean against a bar, or sleep, but when an English class for foreigners was started in the schoolhouse on Eleventh Street, Mike attended more faithfully than most. He learned to read and write English and was exposed to those figures and folk tales of American history — Plymouth Rock, the Boston Tea Party and Gettysburg; George Washington and Abraham Lincoln — which his teachers assumed were most potently Americanizing.

Among other matters, Mike learned that Braddock had been named after a General George Braddock. A long time ago, he was told, when all this was still a wilderness, there had been a battle. In this battle General Braddock was killed and George Washington, whose presence was no doubt responsible for Mike's incorrect but persisting impression that the battle was an incident of the Revolution, had several horses shot out from under him. They named a street after Washington, in this exhibiting, it seemed to Mike, a nice sense of proportion.

What the fighting was about Mike had no idea. He knew the Civil War was fought to free the slaves, and that the Revolution started when the British put a tax on postage stamps and tried to make the Pilgrims drink tea with every meal; but what General Braddock and George Washington were doing in these Pennsylvania backwoods was never made clear. Fort Duquesne, which added to the confusion by being in Pittsburgh, was involved somehow, as were the French Army and a horde of Indians, ignorant savages who disregarded the rules of civilized warfare by ambushing General Braddock's troops in a deep ravine and shooting at them from behind rocks and trees, exactly as George Washington had said they would. But General Braddock wouldn't listen to him; and that to Mike was like a sudden flash of light, illuminating the basic, irreconcilable differences between things British and American. George Washington had been so obviously right that perceiving it made Mike feel himself already half an American, and the Revolution inevitable.

The exact site of this battle was obscure. A deep ravine was called for and Braddock itself was anything but a ravine. Set inside a bend of the Monongahela it was flat from the river to Main Street, whence it rose progressively steeper until the streets and back yards of North Braddock raveled out against the treeless, eroded hills. The only likely ravine Mike knew was Dooker's Hollow, an abysmal gorge in the hills to the east of Braddock, up near the foundries — its sewerlike entrance a black tunnel under the Pennsylvania tracks, its single street lined with shabby houses, the bare hills lifting steeply on either side, and, stalking from one height to another, the Bell Avenue bridge, from whose aging timbers fear-rigid boys were periodically rescued by the Fire Department. As a ravine it should have made an ambushing Indian grunt with pleasure.

Historians decided that the Indians had preferred the vicinity of what was now upper Sixth Street but for Mike it was in Dooker's Hollow, a Dooker's Hollow with no houses, no tipsy coal sheds, no forty-five-degree-angle back yards that General Braddock — shaking his fist at the invisible enemy, daring them to come out and fight like eighteenth-century Englishmen — was ingloriously shot, while George Washington leaped acrobatically from one horse to another.

They buried General Braddock on the mountains above Uniontown; George Washington went on to the historically more remunerative business of Valley Forge and crossing the Delaware and posing — apparently in a cloud of steam — for those grim-lipped portraits; and Braddock wasn't mentioned in the history books again.

But, after the soldiers, came the settlers — more and more of them all the time. They cut down the trees and built houses and laid out their dreary, unimaginative pattern of streets and alleys, beginning at the river's edge and working back toward the hills: River Street, Willow Way, Washington Street, Cherry Alley, Talbot. And then, after a long interval, Andrew Carnegie thought there was money in Bessemer steel rails and he bought a hundred acres of riverside farmland from the McKinney brothers and put up two five-ton converters and a three-high, twenty-three-inch hook-and-tong rail mill; and when the prices of blooms and pig iron began to cut into his profits he picked up a secondhand blast furnace in Escanaba and brought it to Braddock in sections: *A Furnace*, this was, with a bricked-in skip hoist, the one the Slovaks called the *mala fana*, the little furnace, with an output of some fifty tons a day. So the mills came to Braddock, stripping the hills bare of vegetation, poisoning the river, blackening heaven and earth and the lungs of the workers, who were in the beginning mostly American and English. When the Irish came the Americans and English, to whom sheer precedence as much as anything else now gave a near monopoly of the skilled jobs and best wages, moved to the streets above Main and into North Braddock. The First Ward was taken over by the Irish. But the forces that had brought the Irish to Braddock were still at work. New mills and furnaces were built, new supplies of labor found. The Slovaks came; and once more there was a general displacement. The Irish began to invade the better parts of town, while those Americans and English who could afford it fled into Pittsburgh's suburbs.

All this was a long time happening, and was not accomplished without bitterness and conflict; but none of it ever got into the history books.

Immigrants continued to pour into the valley, taking over whole sections — invariably the worst sections, nearest the river and the mills — of the steel towns. Braddock got its share of the newcomers; in ten years its population nearly doubled. The First Ward became almost solidly Slovak, though even on Washington Street there were still people who wouldn't rent to foreigners. But the pressure was growing steadily; house by house, street by street, the Slovaks pushed out from center, which might be put at the corner of Eleventh and Washington. Real-estate speculators put up the houses that became so characteristic of the steel towns, long, ugly rows like cell blocks, two rooms high and two deep, without water, gas or conveniences of any kind, nothing but the walls and the roofs: Zeok's Row on Halket, Veroskey's Row along the P. and L. E. railroad, Mullen's double row on Willow Way, were typical. They were filled as soon as they were finished and made no apparent impression on the housing shortage or the rent level.

What few English-speaking people remained in the First Ward clung to its fringes, west of Ninth, above Main. They were for the most part Irish, the common laborer of an earlier day. It was with the Irish that the Slovaks as a whole came into most intimate contact, in town as neighbors and in the mill as pushers and gang foremen, and to this must be ascribed much of the subsequent bitterness between them. The Americans and English were equally contemptuous of the newer immigrants, with an even lordlier air than that they reserved for one another, but there were fewer of them.

71

In the old country the Slovaks had been an oppressed minority from the beginning of time, a simple, religious, unwarlike people, a nation of peasants and shepherds whom the centuries had taught patience and humility. In America they were all this and more, foreigners in a strange land, ignorant of its language and customs, fearful of authority in whatever guise. Arrived in America they were thrust — peasants and shepherds that they were — into the blast furnaces and rolling mills, and many of them paid with their lives for their unfamiliarity with machinery and the English language. Even more bewildering were the hostility and contempt of their neighbors, the men they worked with.

That hostility, that contempt, epitomized in the epithet "Hunky," was the most profound and lasting influence on their personal lives the Slovaks of the steel towns encountered in America. In a large, cosmopolitan city they might perhaps have had an easier time of it, but the steel towns were American small towns, provincial and intolerant. Economically there was no reason why a laborer named, say, Mickey, should dislike a laborer named, say, Mihal; the Mihals did not lower the wage rates of the only kind of jobs they were able to get. Nor did they take others' jobs away from them; the steel industry was in its period of greatest expansion, building new mills and furnaces and hiring new men by the hundred. That the company openly preferred foreigners as laborers, that immigration from western Europe had fallen off, that the hours were long, the work hard and the opportunities for advancement rare, helped explain why the unskilled labor force was predominantly foreign by the beginning of the new century. For the English-speaking peoples' unconcealed racial prejudice, their attitude that it was a disgrace to work on a level with Hunkies, there was no rational excuse. But it was a fact, a large and not pretty fact which marked, stunted and embittered whole generations.

The firstcomers, Kracha's generation, never suffered the full effects of it, partly for the same reason that a prisoner who does not try to escape is not shot at. Few could read or write even their own language; Austria-Hungary had never encouraged, to put it mildly, minority cultures. They lived to themselves of necessity, speaking their own tongue, retaining their old customs. Their lack of curiosity about America, the country, the civilization, was more apparent than real; they had few opportunities to learn and experience taught them that curiosity was not admired. Company men were everywhere, working beside one in the mill, drinking a beer at one's elbow in the saloons, and an interest in politics was almost as suspect as an interest in labor unions. Kracha's advice to Mike on his exciting discovery of American politics during the first Bryan campaign was generally observed: Think what you like but keep your mouth shut.

They had come to America to find work, to make a living. It was their good fortune, perhaps, to come unburdened with many illusions about a land of freedom, a land where all men were equal. They were glad to take whatever jobs were assigned them; they realized that bosses were the same everywhere, and when the epithet Hunky was hurled at them they shrugged. It was hardly pleasant but there was nothing one could do about it. The implied denial of social and racial equality seldom troubled them; as Kracha once said, he had come to America to find work and save money, not to make friends with the Irish.

This ability to shrug, to live to themselves, was the property of that generation and could not be handed on. Their children were born outside the walls, and there was no going back.

When his younger brother, Joe, came to Braddock in the spring of 1901, Mike told him what he could expect. It was quite probable that Joe didn't understand the full implications of what Mike told him, but he learned. They all did.

Years of country living and his service in the Army had made Joe a bigger and heavier man than his brother, but the two were still like enough almost to be twins, with the same broad shoulders, the same fair coloring and regular features and clear gray eyes. Good-looking men. Mike's was the livelier intelligence; he was interested in everything, read newspapers and loved to argue; Joe's was the shorter temper and the drier throat. Joe had left a wife in the old country; Mike was still single.

Joe got a job in the blast furnaces and as a matter of course went to board with Dorta. Mike had been with her so long that many people thought they were close relations, and Dorta's own attitude toward him did much to strengthen that impression. From the time he'd come to her as a boy of fifteen she had seen to it that he got enough sleep, saved his money, went to church and didn't marry the wrong girl. She was passionately interested in his more sentimental adventurings and seemed perpetually torn between a desire to attend his wedding and a conviction that his current girl friend was the last he should even think of taking for a wife.

It was certainly time, she would say, that he was getting married. His best friend, Steve Bodnar, was getting married in a few months. And look at his own brother, two years younger than he and already married over a year. He really should get married. But to a nice girl, one who would make him a good wife, not this Whatever-her-name-was he was going around with now. It was nothing to her, of course, whom he married, whether he married at all or died a lonely old bachelor, doing his own cooking and living like a pig. Why should she worry her head about him? She had enough troubles of her own. But if he expected to get married someday —

And Mike would grin and say, "Sure, when I meet the right girl." He hadn't, he said, met her yet.

As a matter of fact he had known her for years but he really saw her, really looked at her for the first time, that Sunday afternoon in Dorta's kitchen. She had put up her hair and let down her skirts long before he noticed the change. When her

Thomas Bell's parents, Mary and Michael Belejčak, on their wedding day.

father's troubles reached their dismal climax he'd felt sorry for her, even then thinking of her more as a child than as the young woman she was. After she went to work for her American family he seldom saw her; now and then one of her visits to Dorta would find him passing in or out. He would nod to her, noting absently that she was "dressed up," and go on about his business.

During the summer of 1901 he didn't see her at all. The Dexters' cook had left to have a baby or look after her old mother or both, Dorta wasn't sure, and Mary had been installed in her place, her wages raised to two dollars and a half a week. Her younger sister, Alice, a pretty, scatterbrained girl, mad about boys and dancing, took over Mary's duties as upstairs girl and part-time nursemaid. When the Dexters left Braddock for the summer they took Mary with them. Occasionally Dorta would receive a letter or a postcard and pass on to Mike her reports of the wonders of the Atlantic Ocean and Bethany Beach. Mike listened with half an ear and less interest; blast furnaces in July made summers by the sea too unreal even for envy.

That was the summer Carnegie sold his steel company, including the mills in Homestead, Duquesne and Braddock, to J. P. Morgan, who had organized the United States Steel Corporation. In the mill every flat surface — shop walls, crane cabs, ladles — was smeared with stenciled signs proclaiming the birth of America's first billion-dollar corporation. In August about one hundred men were fired in Homestead for trying to revive the union, and the following month sixty were fired in Duquesne for the same reason. The new corporation was giving notice that it planned no innovations in the steel masters' traditional methods of dealing with labor. That was the summer, too, that

McKinley was shot in Buffalo and Anna Kovac, whose father owned a small grocery store on Talbot Avenue, began going around saying that Mike Dobrejcak wanted her to go steady with him.

When Dorta asked him if it was true he didn't deny it, partly because it gave Dorta something to talk about. All he'd said to Anna was, "Would you go steady with me if I asked you?" She had replied coyly that she didn't know. Perhaps she'd expected him to go on and ask her. He hadn't, just then; later on, in spite of Dorta and her stories about the rats on Anna's head and the bugs in her father's flour, he might. He was twenty-seven, long past the age when most Slovak young men married, and Anna was as suitable as most of the girls he knew. She was attractive, young enough to excuse some vanity, and her father did have a nice little business. He could do worse. As it turned out, he might just as well have asked her, for within a week Anna had convinced even her own family that he had.

The Dexters returned to Braddock in September, and the Sunday following, while the country was waiting for McKinley to live or die, Mary came to see Dorta.

It was one of Mike's two Sundays off each month; that is, he had come home from the mill that morning and was off until Monday morning. He slept until midafternoon, then rose and dressed, the clean clothes feeling good against his skin. He could hear Dorta talking in the kitchen. River Street was quiet with heat and the Sabbath; in the mill yard a dinkey screeched like an angry midget. Mike strolled downstairs, rolling up the sleeves of his shirt.

She was sitting by the table, her back to the window that looked out on the railroad tracks and the river. She was all in white. He noticed that first, her white dress with its little ruffles at the throat and spilling down her bosom, the full skirt flowing over her crossed leg, the white buttoned shoes. She had taken off her hat and put it on the table beside her; it was white too, wide-brimmed and trimmed with white flowers. A white parasol leaned against her thigh.

She was quite the prettiest and most splendidly dressed young woman he had ever seen.

"Why," he said, "it's Mary Kracha."

"Who did you think it was?" Dorta asked.

"I hardly knew her."

Mary's face was lightly tanned; her teeth flashed when she smiled. "Have I changed so much in one summer?"

"You don't look the same." He stared at her. "You look more like an American girl now."

"Why shouldn't she look like an American girl?" Dorta demanded. "Wasn't she born here? Didn't she go to school here?"

"I think he means my dress," Mary said. "He never saw me in it before."

"What does he know about dresses?"

Mike wasn't sure what he meant. Here was a girl who looked as though she had stepped out of a magazine advertisement, lovely and cool and strange; and the girl was Mary Kracha, whom he had never before looked at twice. The transformation was bewildering. Common sense and his own dignity urged him to be as casual and lordly as one should be with a neighbor's girl, one of dozens; but what his eyes saw made that impossible. Nor did it help to have Dorta watching him.

"Well," he said at last, "I think I'll have a bottle of beer. Would you like some?"

Dorta said she would, though he hadn't asked her. Mary said, "No, thank you."

He went down to the cellar and fished around in a tub of water for two bottles. Dorta was smiling at Mary when he returned. He opened the bottles and took one with him to the doorstep. "Did you have a good time while you were away?"

Her face brightened. "Oh, the best time I ever had in my life. At first I was homesick and the noise of the ocean kept me awake but that didn't last long. When the time came to come back I hated to leave."

"It's a lot different from Braddock, I bet."

Mary gestured; the difference was too great for words. "I was telling Dorta, you have no idea how hot and dirty Braddock looked when we came back. I never noticed the smoke and dirt so much before. After seeing nothing but the ocean and white sandy beaches all summer, the clean air —" She gestured again.

He stared outside, trying to see the back yard and the railroad tracks and the cinder dump as

they must have looked to her, after that ocean and that white beach. But it was a Sunday afternoon in summer and everything had its resting, Sunday look, no clotheslines, no dirty children, no hucksters yelling in River Street, no freights on the railroad. It looked like Sunday and it looked good to him, as good as it ever could.

He tilted his bottle. "Just the same," he said, "I bet you were glad to get back."

Mary smiled and shrugged.

Dorta belched.

"Good beer," Mike said.

"*Ach!*"

Mary glanced at the clock. "I really must be going, Dorta. They may get back early." She began to gather her things together.

"How do you go, by streetcar?" Mike asked.

"No, I walk. It's not far; to Fifth Street and then up the hill a block."

"That's far enough, especially on a hot day."

"I don't mind it."

"The streetcar would be better."

"Listen to him," Dorta exclaimed. "Instead of telling her how to get there you'd show more politeness if you offered to take her home."

Mary had risen and was putting on her hat, using the little mirror beside the door that the men shaved by. Her skirt brushed Mike's arm. "Oh no," she said. "Why should he walk all that distance?"

"It won't kill him."

"I'd have to put on a collar and tie," Mike said.

"Indeed? I expected you to go in your undershirt."

He ignored Dorta's inexplicable irony and sought Mary's eyes but she was very busy, her hat seemed to be giving her trouble. He had never noticed before how much grace a girl could put into such a simple task. He glanced at Dorta. She was making faces at him, jerking her head urgently, her lips soundlessly forming the words, "Go on, go on!" He stared at her, his mouth open. Dorta sighed hopelessly and rolled her eyes.

"All right, I will." He scrambled to his feet. "I'll be down in a minute."

Walking beside her along Washington he noticed how heads turned as they passed. When they met people he knew he tipped his hat gravely. Two young men leaning against Perovsky's saloon on the corner of Eleventh said, "Hello, Mike," and then stared at Mary. He could tell they were wondering who she was.

When he saw Anna Kovac it was too late to avoid her. She was standing in front of the schoolhouse at Talbot talking with a girl friend. She was dressed for Sunday but not all in white, she had no parasol and her kid brother was pestering her into a temper. As they approached she gave him a push and exclaimed, "If you don't stop bothering me I'll smack you!" And then she saw Mike, with Mary on his arm.

He tipped his hat to her without missing a step. Anna's mouth opened but she didn't say anything; once past her he could feel her eyes burning into his back until they'd crossed the B. and O. tracks. He heard the girl friend say, "Isn't that Mike Dobrejcak?" just as though she didn't know. Anna's reply didn't reach him, but a sudden howl from her kid brother did. Mary apparently hadn't even seen Anna; she'd gone by her like a lady, like a ship under full sail, her parasol dangling from her wrist, a fold of skirt gathered up in one hand.

They made conversation. He said it was a shame about President McKinley, Republican or no Republican, and she thought it was too. He asked her if she'd seen her father or her sisters since her return; she replied that she was going to Munhall on her next Sunday off. She got two Sundays off a month, and one afternoon and evening each week. Thursdays. He said it was hot; she agreed. No, she didn't want any ice cream. Yes, she liked it. She liked sodas better than sundaes. Chocolate sodas.

Even on Main Street people looked at her a second time.

Her street was a street of big houses, striped awnings, tree-shaded lawns, hitching posts, and a woman playing croquet with a small child on cool-looking grass. It was as far and as different from River Street as anything could be, and he was profoundly relieved when she stopped on the corner and said she'd go the rest of the way herself. Even in his Sunday suit, even beside her, he wouldn't have felt comfortable walking down that street.

"Which is your house?" he asked.

"That one there, the red brick one." It was a big, handsome house, probably the biggest and handsomest there. "It's the one you can see from Main Street. You know."

"Oh, that one." He looked at it again. The Dexters' lawn took up half the block but most of it was back of the house, where the ground sloped steeply to a retaining wall along Main Street, here still predominantly residential. Seen from Main Street the house, sitting on the crest of its green hill, was even more handsome and impressive than at close range. He had often wondered who lived in it.

"I bet it's like a palace inside."

"It's very nice."

"How many rooms has it?"

"Twelve. And a big attic."

"And how many people live there?"

"Four, not counting me and Alice."

"Four people in twelve rooms. Dorta has eleven in four, in three if you don't count the kitchen. What it is to have money!"

"Mr. Dexter would laugh if he heard you. He doesn't think of himself as rich. He has cousins in Philadelphia who are millionaires."

"Millionaires?"

She nodded. "Real millionaires. Bankers."

Mike could only shake his head. "I could do without twelve rooms and cousins in Philadelphia, but I'd like to live on a street like this." He sniffed. "By God, when you have money you can even breathe better air than other people."

She smiled; and Mike smiled back and then watched a young man wearing white trousers clamped untidily to his ankles and a girl wearing a white skirt, both on bicycles, wheeling and turning under the trees. He wondered what the young man did for a living and how much money he made.

"Well," Mary said, "I don't want to keep you."

He took out his watch; he wanted her to see it. "It's not half-past four yet."

"They will be back soon, and I have to change my dress and get supper started. It was nice of you to come with me."

"When are you coming to see Dorta again?"

"I don't know. Maybe next week."

He made a face. "I'm working night turn next week. But this week I'm on day turn," he said hopefully.

She lowered her eyes and twirled her parasol and said, "Are you?"

"Are you going anywhere Thursday night?"

"Thursday night? No, I'm not going anywhere. At least I don't think so."

79

"Well if I should be on this corner here, this very spot, at seven or maybe a few minutes after—"

She looked up and smiled and held out her hand. "Maybe. Good-by."

"No maybe. I'll be expecting you. And think how glad Dorta will be to see you."

This time she laughed, her face framed by her hair and the wide-brimmed hat.

"Is it a promise?"

"All right. Anything, if only you'll let me go." She pulled her hand free. "Good-by."

"Till Thursday."

He tipped his hat and she smiled at him and went down the street, a graceful white figure under the big trees. He watched until she had gone through the gate; then he went back to River Street.

Dorta was getting supper ready and packing lunch buckets to be taken into the mill to the men who were working the long turn. "Well," she said, "did you get her home all right?"

"Sure. What did you think, we'd lose the way?"

"You may be interested to know that I have already been asked if that was Mary Kracha you were seen walking with."

He started upstairs. "What of it?"

"I said that it was," Dorta called after him, "and that you were old friends. Which you are."

He halted in mid-flight, came back and stuck his head around the doorjamb. "Dorta, tell me something. Where does she get the money to buy such fine clothes?"

"Oh, you noticed her clothes, did you? Well, don't worry your head about it. They don't cost her a penny. Not a penny. The lady she works for gives her all her old clothes and Mary fixes them up to suit herself. She sews very well. And she must be a good cook," Dorta added somewhat irrelevantly, "or they wouldn't have kept her this long. She's a smart girl; she could get married tomorrow if she liked."

"Is she going steady?"

"Not yet, but they keep asking her."

"Who?"

"How should I remember all their names?"

He frowned at her suspiciously and then went upstairs, leaving Dorta looking highly pleased with herself.

He was waiting on the corner for her Thursday night, not as sure that she'd really meet him as he would have liked to be. The street was quiet, heavy with dusk; he remembered afterward the glow of lamplit windows and the lingering, melancholy fragrance of burning leaves. When she appeared, her coming heralded by the rustle of her feet among the fallen leaves, he almost failed to recognize her. She was wearing a dark dress and coat and he'd got used to thinking of her in white. She said, "Good evening, Mike," and slipped her hand through his arm as though she had been doing it for years. As they fell into step she said, "Did you wait long?" and he knew that everything was going to be all right. "Since Sunday," he said. "I've been waiting since Sunday."

The next Thursday but one he took her for a walk through the First Ward, a public, almost formal, declaration that he and Anna Kovac were finished with each other. Anna's girl friend had prepared the way by spreading word of the little incident in front of the schoolhouse and an accidental encounter with Anna completed the business. Coming out of a Main Street store on a Saturday night he bumped into the Kovacs, mother, daughter and untamed son. Mike tipped his hat, Anna nodded coldly and Mrs. Kovac, a pleasant, dumpy woman, looked bewildered and burst into rapid Slovak as her daughter drew her away.

Walking with Mary he told her that Anna had never meant anything to him, which was hardly true. But Mary didn't seem to care. They took the route favored by young couples of an evening, along Washington to Eleventh, up Eleventh to Halket, along Halket to Thirteenth and down Thirteenth to Washington again. Along Washington there were stores, lights and people; they said "hello" to people they knew, they stopped to gossip, they looked and were looked at. On Halket they kept to the north side of the B. and O. tracks, where there were still some fine houses and old trees, relics of the days when Halket had been a pleasant street in a quiet river town. Here the couples walked more slowly and talked in whispers as they moved through the deep shadows and the smell of grass and trees; and only as they approached Thirteenth did the blast furnaces and rail mills become too insistent to be ignored. It was the nearest thing to a lovers' lane in the First Ward.

They saw each other every other week when Mike was working day turn, on Thursday nights, and for a few hours on Sunday if the Dexters had gone out for the afternoon. Her Sunday off Mary usually spent in Munhall. Anna was still with Francka. Borka had married one of Francka's boarders the year before and was expecting a baby in December. Kracha still boarded in Homestead. Of Zuska there was no word or sign; her sister continued to insist that she didn't know what had become of her. There were vague rumors that she had been seen in Johnstown and that she was living with a storekeeper in Gary.

Mike no longer waited on the corner; Thursday nights he went around to the kitchen door and knocked and was welcomed in. One by one he had met Mrs. Dexter and her husband and Mrs. Hillis, her mother, an old, sickly woman, and the boy whose nursemaid Mary had been. He was seven or eight, a clean, bright boy who asked Mike questions about the mill and liked to display the few Slovak phrases Mary had taught him. Mike was infinitely more impressed by the boy's good manners; he would have given a month of his life to be able to say "I beg your pardon" and "Excuse me" as naturally. His name was Lawrence Allan Dexter but everyone called him Lad, after his initials. Mr. Dexter owned a small factory on Corey Avenue that manufactured electric lamps; Mary said he had about fifteen men working for him.

The Dexters' was the first private house Mike had ever set foot in which was wired for electricity. For that matter it was the first private house he'd ever been in that had a bathroom, a telephone, steam heat, and in the kitchen a magnificent icebox with a back door cut right through the wall of the house so the iceman could fill it without coming into the kitchen at all.

Mary showed him through the house one Sunday afternoon; the Dexters had taken Mrs. Hillis for a buggy ride to Kennywood — as Kenny's Grove, with the embellishments of merry-go-rounds, roller coasters and such devices, was now called. Mike's interest in houses, in house furnishings, was no greater than most young men's; he had used beds, chairs and forks all his life without ever really noticing them. But in the Dexters' dining room, in their parlor and bedrooms, he saw furniture, dishes, silverware which were desirable and beauti-

81

ful in themselves and not merely as articles of use. For the first time he perceived how graceful the business of eating and sleeping and entertaining one's friends could be, and how one could be proud of one's possessions, the way one lived.

Standing in the parlor he said after a long pause, "This is the way a man should live."

"It is beautiful, isn't it?" Mary said proudly, almost as though it were her own.

"When a man has this much what more can he want?"

Unconsciously he had slipped into Slovak, though usually they spoke to each other in English so that Mike could improve his speech.

Mary smiled. "You think so? Well, Mr. Dexter would like to have a bigger factory, and he is always talking about getting an automobile. Mrs. Dexter will stay here as long as her mother lives but she says Braddock is getting too dirty to live in, she would rather live in Squirrel Hill, where it's more stylish. You see? No matter how much you get you always want more."

"I think I could make shift to be satisfied if I had no more than this house just as it stands," Mike said. "But I suppose what I make in a week wouldn't keep it running for even a day." He looked around. "Maybe it would have been better for me if I'd never seen it."

"Now you're talking foolishness."

He grinned. "All right. But what you don't know you don't miss." He put an arm around her waist. "Do you think we'll ever have anything like this?"

"Mihal, where would we get it?"

"Well, who knows what may happen?"

She stared at him, but instead of taking it lightly her mouth had become tremulous, as though she was afraid to think he might be serious; and it occurred to him that she could believe even such feats were not beyond his accomplishing, he, her chosen one.

He sobered. "*Ach!* What would we want with such a fancy house! No one would come to see us; we'd lose all our friends." He smiled at her, squeezing her waist, her corset a stiff fabric under his hand. "But just the same, *mila moja*, we're not going to be like so many others. We're not greenhorns just off the boat. I know English pretty good. I'm still young. I mean to keep my eyes open and use my head. One of these days I'm going to get a good job and then — well, we shall see."

Mary leaned against him, her eyes dreamy. "We'll get it, Mihal. I'll help you all I can."

"Sure you will. We'll work hard, save our money — you watch. You'll never be sorry you married me."

"What a thing to say!"

He smiled into her eyes, and kissed her. "I want a good life for us, Marcha. For you, for me, for our children."

She stayed close to him.

Then they heard hoofbeats in the street and she stooped to glance out the window. It was late autumn in the street. The day's last sunlight, hard and cold, seeped through the bare trees, lay motionless on the dry lawns, on the quiet houses, glinted icily off the clean glass of lace-curtained windows.

They were married in the spring, from Dorta's house. The company was building two new blast furnaces, closer to Thirteenth Street than any of the others, and there were times when the music of the gipsies' beribboned fiddles was drowned out by the riveters' iron clamor. But nobody minded.

MARCIA DAVENPORT
"The Old Man's Presence"

Paul Scott struggles to retain
control of a steel mill

Time: 1901

Setting: Allegheny City

Because of its market success (amplified by a popular movie version) Marcia Davenport's The Valley of Decision *is probably the best-known single novel about the Pittsburgh area. It clearly is also an ambitious, serious piece of fiction. Beginning in 1873 and concluding in 1941, the novel is a generation-by-generation — almost year-by-year — chronicle of the fortunes of the mill-owning Scott family on Pittsburgh's North Side.*

The passage excerpted here focuses on the "middle" generation of Scotts, those whose adult careers are acted out from about 1880 to 1920. Paul Scott is steelmaster and mill manager of the Scott Works, inheritor, along with his brothers and sisters, of the iron foundry developed by his father, William Scott. As the passage indicates, the family has now scattered: Elizabeth and William live on the East Coast, Constance and Edgar have settled in Europe. The brothers and sisters are also divided over the desirability of selling their interest in the mill or retaining family ownership.

The concept of family ownership is, in fact, a central theme in Davenport's novel. The Valley of Decision *is a pro-management book (it never seriously considers, for example, the workers' interest in unionizing), but it has only scorn for managers whose expertise is merely financial, who make their money through wheeling and dealing in mergers and stock-swapping. Instead Davenport preaches an old-time American religion: The "good" Scotts start with the lowliest jobs in the mills and work their way up; they are self-made men with a right to ownership because they have mastered every facet of their business. For Paul Scott, the mill is a symbol of his personal integrity and determination, of his intelligence and creativity. Sale of the mill, in Davenport's vision, would be a sellout to the impersonality of the giant corporation.*

Like the mill, the Scott's house on Western Avenue — there at the start of the novel, still there at the end — comes to represent the strength and endurance of the family. And one of the memorable features of The Valley of Decision *remains its detailed picture of Pittsburgh's North Side and the changes there over three generations.*

Marcia Davenport, born in 1903 in New York City, was the daughter of famous parents — Alma Gluck, the opera singer was her mother; Efrem Zimbalist, the violinist, her stepfather. She lived briefly in Pittsburgh in the early 1920s (first at the corner of Shady Avenue and Howe Street, then on Beeler Street) and visited repeatedly during the two or three years it took to research and write The Valley of Decision. *But her roots were clearly elsewhere. In her autobiography,* Too Strong for Fantasy *(1967), she explains how she came to choose Pittsburgh as setting for her novel:*

The family in which I would place my woman [character] must be an American family concerned in a basic American industry. Perforce this must be somewhere in the industrial heartland of the U.S., somewhere that was most emphatically American and not New York. I had no experience of any such place. Every taproot of my being that was not in New York was in Europe, except — "Pittsburgh!" . . . .

I was off to Pittsburgh. It was the first of many long stays, and I had not been there twenty-four hours before I knew I was on the right track.

"The Old Man's Presence"

William Scott had not been inside the mill for seventeen years. This December afternoon, gray and gloomy and thick with the acrid fumes of soft coal, reminded him startlingly of the day he had last walked from this place. Nothing might have changed, he thought, driving in a livery hack from the Pennsylvania Station across the Manchester Bridge to the mill. He sat silent, quite ignoring his companion who leaned forward from time to time to look up and down the stretch of the many-bridged river and exclaim at the blazing furnaces which trimmed it like devil's jewels. Nothing seemed to have changed here, William thought. But this was the first year of a new century, and the age had shaken itself and come to birth a full-grown giant. This hill-jagged region of belching stacks, bare stripped coal lands, mile upon mile of sprawling, wildly illuminated sheds from which endless trainloads of rails and girders and bridge spans and pigs and sheets and bars and billets and ingots streamed out across the country—this region too had come of age. It was visibly scarred and torn, aged and blackened. Its riches of money and power, vast beyond any kingdom's, were not to be seen among the stacks and cinders and flat-cars and fires. They lay in a different world of banks and offices, where William felt at ease. For years he had watched in wondering admiration while wealth joined with wealth, force with force, to weld and compress these galvanic forces into ruthless bludgeons of financial power.

He looked curiously at the Scott mill as the horse clopped along the cobbled approach to the entrance. It did not seem possible that this tangle of dirty sheds and blackened stacks and the bulky monstrosity of the old Henrietta could comprise anything anybody could want. He had loathed it with every nerve and fibre the first half of his life. But he saw it in a different light today.

He was fifty now, and he looked all of that descending stiffly from the cramped hack and escorting his companion over the bridge to the main entrance. William had not seen this bridge since before the tragedy of his father's death here. He looked curiously at the oft-renewed coal-black planks as if they could hold some trace of the Old Man's presence.

Paul met them at the door of the outer office.

"You remember Selden Middleton, Paul."

They all shook hands gravely and took places around a fumed oak table which replaced the older one of William's bitter memories.

"Well," said Paul tentatively, "this is quite a surprise."

William cleared his throat.

"It's very natural to see you here at the old stand, Paul. How are things?"

"Pretty good. I can't complain." Paul was handing cigars round and filling his pipe. "We've had a busy year. I suppose you know I sent samples of our new rapid-cutting tool steel to the Paris Exhibition last summer, Bill. It seemed to make quite an impression."

"I know about it," Middleton said with a smile. "I was there. It made more than an impression, it was a sensation. Of course," he said gruffly, "I don't understand much about the technicalities of these things, Mr. Scott, but this mill of yours has attracted remarkable attention the past two or three years. Remarkable."

"Well," Paul said, "we work hard."

There was an awkward silence. Then William said, "Paul, I suppose we might as well come to the point. Middleton came out here with me because he has something he wants to talk over with you. It concerns all of us in the family and I—well, I'm deeply interested."

Selden Middleton looked from one of the Scotts to the other, shooting his heavy-browed eyes from William's faded, narrow face to Paul's broad, serious, kindly one. William Scott's high forehead was accentuated by sparse gray hair. Paul's head had a look of abundance and solidity; his blond hair and full moustache were as thick as ever,

though faded in color. He bent his head and stared back at Middleton from lowered eyelids.

"Why don't you start right in and talk?" he asked.

Middleton examined his cigar.

"I suppose you know," he began slowly, "that all these big consolidations in the steel industry in recent years have been moving toward a climax lately."

Paul nodded, quite expressionless. William watched him closely, turning sidewise in his chair to avoid facing his brother directly. Middleton spoke very slowly, choosing his words and keeping his eyes on Paul. He had a feeling already that nothing he was about to say would come as a surprise to this man, or would elicit any spontane-

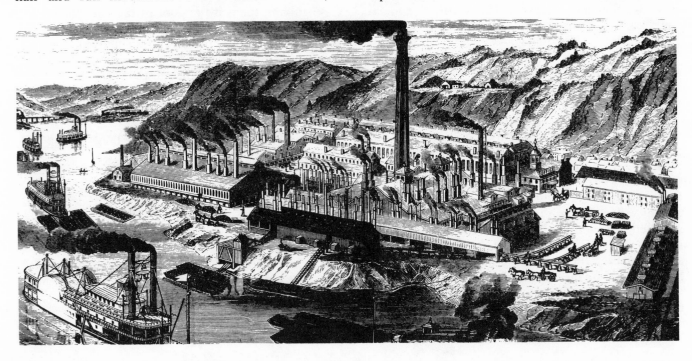

ous reaction. He had come prepared to play his cards very close to his chest; he was a bit nonplussed to find that Paul Scott already gave indications of doing the same thing. Somehow he had sized him up differently at their one meeting in William Scott's house. Perhaps it was the surroundings, grim and noisy, with a freight engine hissing outside the dirty windows, that set him unaccustomedly ill at ease.

"Now you may remember," Middleton continued, "that when we met a few years ago I mentioned to you my interest in the Oliver Iron Mining Company. That was the beginning of a series of moves by which I acquired holdings in the H. C. Frick Coke Company."

He paused. Paul still listened attentively and inscrutably.

"You will forgive my going back into certain personal details," Middleton said with a deprecating gesture, "but I want to give you the background of this whole picture."

"By all means," Paul said.

"Good. Of course you followed the negotiations last winter when the Frick Company was merged with the Carnegie Steel Company. That resulted in the arrangement by which we—I mean the Frick stockholders, who supported Mr. Frick during Carnegie's attempt to oust him—have now acquired stock and bonds of the Carnegie Steel Company in exchange for our previous holdings."

He paused to relight his cigar.

"I have some four hundred and fifty shares of stock in the Carnegie Company," Middleton said slowly, "and approximately an equal holding in bonds."

He stopped speaking as if to allow Paul to calculate the value of these holdings, which Paul promptly did. The Carnegie stock had been issued at par value of a thousand dollars a share; Middleton's interest therefore was about a million altogether. Paul's eyebrows moved slightly. He smiled a little and said, "And the next step is this billion-dollar consolidation they are putting together in New York and calling the United States Steel Corporation."

Now Middleton smiled.

"Correct," he said.

"We watch these things out here," Paul said, "in a kind of a way. That was quite a junket those bankers made to visit Henry Frick here."

"There have been quite a few meetings in New York also," Middleton said.

"Oh yes. Bill here thinks I hate Carnegie so much I don't even notice his existence, but I hear about it when he gives those little dinners for J. P. Morgan and Charlie Schwab. Well, Mr. Middleton, what next?"

Middleton felt more on the defensive than ever. But, imperturbable in his bearded dignity, he took an alligator-skin letter-case from his breast pocket, extracted a memorandum from it, and held it in his hand.

"The plans," he said, "for the prospective steel corporation include some dozen or so companies and mills. Let's just run over them—it would be informative, I think."

He cleared his throat and read from the memo in his hand.

"First, the Carnegie Company. One hundred and sixty million each of capital stock and of bonds."

William swallowed and turned toward Paul.

"Think of it!" he exclaimed. "Think of the size of it!"

"I am thinking," Paul said shortly. "Go on, Mr. Middleton."

"Then comes the Federal Steel Company, with

forty-six million in common stock, fifty-three million preferred. These are round figures, of course. Then the National Tube Company, about forty million each of common and preferred. National Steel Company, around thirty million of common and of preferred. American Bridge Company, thirty million of each. American Steel and Wire Company, forty-nine million common, thirty-nine preferred."

William was leaning forward, fascinated by the recital of astronomical figures. Paul sat back, smoking his pipe.

"Next the American Tin Plate Company, with thirty million common and eighteen preferred. American Steel Hoop Company, nineteen million common, fourteen million preferred. American Sheet Steel Company, twenty-four and twenty-four. The Lake Superior Iron Mines, twenty-nine and a half million common." He paused. Then he said, "As you of course see from this list, Mr. Scott, the basic idea is to put together a corporation which will contain at least one of every kind of major steel producing unit. We have covered the field thoroughly. Ore, coal, coke, transportation both land and water, blast furnaces, plants devoted to Bessemer and open-hearth steels; crucible steels; rail, bridge, sheet, plate, tube, and wire mills—well, I need not bore you with details about which you are infinitely better informed than I. The point is, finally—" he hesitated.

"That you want an alloy and specialty-steel mill," Paul said dryly.

"Precisely." Middleton sat back and smiled. William heaved a sigh as if of relief. He was unexpectedly grateful to Paul for coming out with the thing himself.

Paul champed his pipe-stem reflectively.

"Well, now, Mr. Middleton," he said, "don't you think my—our—mill is a bit smallish in that kind of company?" He pointed to the memo. "We're just a little family concern. This isn't our kind of speed."

William broke in.

"It isn't the size of the mill they care about, Paul, it's the quality. They haven't got a unit where anybody does research like yours."

Paul's lips twitched. He had not looked for anything so obvious from Bill who was, after all, pretty smooth after his years in Boston.

"Well, I'm not going to waste your time," he said to Middleton. "The idea looks ridiculous to me, but what's your offer? I gather you are representing the crowd in New York. Or did Bill think this up?" He smiled at his brother.

"Why—" William had no answer ready.

"Oh—it was—just one of those things," Middleton said, waving his hand. "Your brother and I have had a good many dealings in recent years, what with Laurence Gaylord's estate and one thing or another. I've been interested, naturally, in your mill here. It's quite unique, after all. Those Navy projectiles you made, and that stuff I saw last summer. Quite unique."

"Well, are you making an offer now?" Paul asked.

"Oh, certainly. Now I understand that this is a partnership business. You—ah—have no stock, that is, you are unincorporated?"

"I know Bill has told you all the details," Paul said easily. "You don't have to feel your way, Mr. Middleton. We are a partnership business owned entirely by my brothers and sisters and myself. So any offer would be on the basis of a straight sale, not an exchange of stock or anything of that sort. Bill has also doubtless told you what he thinks the company is worth, and he's probably right about that. What figure did he give you?" Paul asked suddenly, in a sharp changed tone. He leaned forward.

Middleton looked at William, who looked uneasily at Paul.

"Why," William said, looking uncomfortable, "I think I said about two and a half million, didn't I, Selden?"

"Three would be more exact," Paul said, "but it doesn't matter when you're dealing with stuff like that." He pointed again at Middleton's memorandum.

"In that case," said Middleton, visibly making a mental revision of something he had decided before, "I would be instructed to offer you two and a half million in seven per cent cumulative preferred stock of the projected corporation, and a million and a half more in United States Steel common."

He sat back and looked at the ceiling. William looked at Paul.

Paul gave no indication of surprise or any other marked reaction, but he did turn his head and stare for a minute at William.

I bet he's palpitating with eagerness, Paul said to himself.

The silence lasted quite a long time. Then Middleton coughed and said, "Of course this is just a talking proposition so far, Mr. Scott."

"Of course," agreed Paul. He was thinking of his father. If the Old Man were here now the glass would be rattling in the windowpanes and these two chaps would be scurrying around looking for their hats and overcoats. Paul almost laughed at the picture. He was also quite startled to find how calmly he really took this; it must be because he had always expected something of the kind and he had learned long ago not to rush out and meet issues headlong. They caught up with you soon enough.

"I don't want to commit myself too far at this preliminary stage of the matter," Middleton was saying, "but in general you could expect to realize the total book value of your company in preferred stock, and we would about match that in common. In other words—"

"Not quite double our holdings," Paul said.

"Approximately. Of course it would depend on the condition of your property—" Middleton raised his eyes and looked doubtfully around the bare, ugly, dun-colored room as if it had anything to do with the mill's capacity to make steel.

"Of course," Paul said again.

Both men waited for him to say something more. William leaned forward and clasped his thin, perfectly groomed hands on the table before him. He wanted very much to get a real reaction from Paul. He wanted desperately for Middleton to pull this thing off successfully. He wanted beyond endurance the three quarters of a million or more in United States Steel stock that he would get out of this, and he could not conceive that Paul and all the others would not be just as eager to have like amounts themselves. Whether the mill lost its identity and Paul his life work had really never crossed William's mind. He said finally, to break the silence, "How do you feel about it, Paul?"

Paul put his pipe carefully down, balancing it on the edge of the table. For one fleeting instant he looked at William with the full impact of scorn that this whole thing roused in him. Then he resumed his calm good nature and said, "Of course I couldn't possibly give an answer now. For one thing, Mr. Middleton, since Bill told you so much else about the company, did he explain the stipulations of my father's will in respect to partnerships?"

"More or less."

"Then you understand that this sale could only

Marcia Davenport

be consummated through a two-thirds or majority vote of the five partners?"

"Yes, I understand that."

"And it would take a certain amount of time to call a meeting and poll the partners about this."

"Naturally." William said that, with a look of satisfaction. He was relieved at Paul's calm reaction to this offer. He had feared that Paul might make a quick refusal and force him into taking legal action to bring the question to a vote. He murmured something about his gratification that Paul was being so open-minded about it.

"Oh, you can't dismiss an offer to double your property," Paul said. He said it so consideredly that for a minute William felt as if there must be some barb in the remark and he was not quick enough to perceive it.

"So we will consider it very carefully," Paul said, rising from his chair, "and that will take some time. We have a brother and sister in Europe. That takes time. And finally, there is the voting."

William and Selden Middleton exchanged a heavy look. . . .

The meeting was scheduled for three o'clock on the afternoon of February fifteenth. William was to arrive in Pittsburgh at noon and Paul sent Jones to meet him at the station and take him to the Duquesne Club for lunch. . . .

[Later] they chatted desultorily in the carriage driving over to the mill. William still seemed to have something to say which he was holding back. Probably making plans for transferring the assets of the company, Paul thought to himself.

The other men were already seated around the conference table in the outer office when the brothers arrived. They all rose and there was general handshaking. Nobody had ever seen William Scott in such an affable, confident mood in these surroundings. Paul motioned Bill and the bankers to chairs and walked over to the safe with Harry Wilkins. They opened it and took out a heavy manila envelope with thick wax seals.

For the record, Wilkins read aloud a copy of the offer from the projected United States Steel Corporation, as transmitted to the five partners of the Scott Iron Works. He then read the portion of old William Scott's will covering the questions of any sale of the Scott Iron Works or any partnership thereof. Paul gazed out of the window during the reading, his eyes resting on the bridge stretching from the street to the front entrance of the mill. Even today the strong will of his father, expressed in these hard legal words, had the power to hold his closest attention. There was something so immediate about the Old Man in these words; Paul felt as if he were here in the room. Burning with scorn, too.

"Now," said Harry Wilkins, "we are ready to open the votes. Is there any preference as to the order in which we read them?"

Paul listened in complete detachment. He could not feel as if the mill were at stake, though it was still perfectly possible that five minutes from now he might find the whole thing gone, finished, done. He tried to believe that, but he knew perfectly well he was fooling himself. He had had his bad and hopeless moments, but they were over now. He felt completely calm.

Bill was leaning back in his chair with a comfortable smile.

"Why not open them in the order they arrived?" he suggested.

Allegheny City's Western Avenue, circa 1870, the street where the Scott family lived.

90

Everybody nodded.

Wilkins picked up the letter with the Italian stamp. "This came first, didn't it, Paul?"

He slit open the envelope and extracted one thin sheet written in Edgar's hand, and the enclosure, the ballot that had been sent to Edgar to mark.

"Edgar Scott, lay brother of the Order of Saint Benedict, Monte Cassino, Province of Lazio, Rome, Italy, votes against sale of the Scott Iron Works to the projected United States Steel Corporation," Wilkins read. Everybody took that for granted. Wilkins laid down the ballot in the center of the table. "Signature of Edgar Scott duly attested," he said.

Next he picked up the cable, Constance's cable, they all knew. William still sat smiling a little and quite expansive. He knew what this would say. Paul smoked his pipe, perfectly impassive. Wilkins opened the cable.

"I cast my vote," he read aloud, "against sale of Scott Iron Works to projected United States Steel Corporation. Stop. Ballot duly signed witnessed posted London February eleventh nineteen one. Signed Constance, Countess of Melling, born Constance Scott."

William leaned forward, frowning. "What?" he asked, as if he had not heard correctly. Paul's eyebrows twitched. Nobody else spoke. Wilkins handed Constance's cable to William, who read it, his pale gray eyes moving slowly along the lines. He moistened his lips and laughed a little.

"Rather a surprise, isn't it, Paul?" he asked in an artificially easy tone.

"Very much so," said Paul. "What's the next

ballot, Elizabeth's?"

Wilkins picked up the sealed envelope addressed in Elizabeth's handwriting.

"Elizabeth Scott Nicholas of Thirty-six East Thirty-seventh Street, City and County of New York, State of New York, votes to sell the Scott Iron Works to the projected United States Steel Corporation on the terms stated in the notification of January fifteenth. Signature of Elizabeth Scott Nicholas duly attested."

William looked relieved. It made a difference in the atmosphere for the positive votes to appear now. He was really glad that the twins' ballots were opened and finished with; from now on it would be straight sailing. His own ballot lay next on the pile, Paul's on the bottom. William was so sure of Paul that he had urged Selden Middleton to feel out the men who were putting the Corporation together, concerning a highly-paid executive post in one of the Pittsburgh mills for Paul.

"William Campbell Scott of 147 Beacon Street, City and County of Boston, Commonwealth of Massachusetts, votes to sell the Scott Iron Works to the projected United States Steel Corporation on the terms stated in the notification of January fifteenth. Signature of William Campbell Scott duly attested."

There was no comment. Paul's ballot lay alone on the table in its sealed envelope. William was smiling outrightly now; palpably congratulating himself and Paul. The envelope crackled as Wilkins slit it open. He read aloud in his sharp Pittsburgh voice.

"Paul Scott of 1203 Western Avenue, City and County of Allegheny, Commonwealth of Pennsylvania, votes against sale of Scott Iron Works to the projected—"

The rest of his words were drowned in the long,

In 1901, at a rail-shaped table in the Schenley Hotel, a banquet celebrating the creation of the United States Steel Corporation.

93

hoarse gasp that came from William. All the men turned their heads and looked curiously at him. Paul was still perfectly expressionless. William recovered his poise and leaned forward, clutching the table with his long, veined hands.

"There must be some mistake," he said.

Nobody answered.

"Some mistake," he repeated. "Is there not, Paul?"

Wilkins said, "I had better read the last ballot aloud again." He did so.

William was half out of his chair as Harry Wilkins laid down the paper; he leaned over the table towards Paul, with his pale face working. . . .

There was a long silence. The men around the table stirred uncomfortably; the meeting should be dismissed; there could be nothing more to discuss. But just as Paul was about to rise and break up the gathering William said, "You'll regret this to your dying day. This Corporation will get something in place of your piddling mill and crush you out of existence."

"I'll be expecting that," Paul said.

"Well, you needn't have dragged the rest of us down with you!"

"I hope I won't. So far we've made out, I think. Incidentally, Bill—"

The men all looked up expectantly. They sensed what Paul was about to say. William sat glaring at the table.

"—any time you are dissatisfied with my management," Paul continued, "I'll be glad to buy you out."

"I'm sure you'd be," William answered with hate. "I've no intention of selling—to you."

Paul exchanged a glance with Harry Wilkins, who stood up with palpable relief. "This concludes the business before the meeting, I believe," he said.

Paul stood at the head of the table while the men gathered their hats and overcoats and filed out. William was in a hurry to get away. He had quickly accepted Wilkins' invitation to drive him to the station.

"You won't come up for dinner, Bill?" Paul asked. He had been undecided whether this was wise or foolhardy. After all, Bill might come. But his brother only replied curtly, "No, thank you. I hardly think we'd have anything—congenial to talk about." He said good-bye abruptly and followed Harry Wilkins out. When the last of the men had gone Paul went into his private office and shut the door. He sank slowly into his swivel chair, and . . . stared hard at the big framed picture of the Old Man which years ago he had hung on the wall between the windows. . . . Suddenly he jumped to his feet, ripped off his coat, and ploughed into his dungarees which he kept hanging on a hook. He hurried out of his office, ran down the ramp to the open-hearth shed, and went to Number One Furnace. . . . The boss, in purple goggles, was squinting through the fire-door. The gang were waiting near him with their shovels. The boss opened the door and yelled "Shoot!" The crew swung past the open inferno, slinging in their loads of ferro-manganese. Paul grabbed the shovel from the last man, his heart pounding with wild happiness.

"Let me take a turn," he said. "I need a workout."

The Hunky heater protested. "No good, no uset', bad for you."

But Paul swung the shovel anyway. He could have burst for happiness. Down by the yard the big ladle loomed in the entrance, brimful of blazing red soup from the Henrietta. Paul leaned on his shovel and looked at it and thought of the Old Man.

O. HENRY
"Conscience in Art"

Two "gentle grafters" swindle
a millionaire

Time: 1900?   Setting: Pittsburgh

Taken from The Gentle Grafter, one of O. Henry's posthumous volumes, "Conscience in Art" is a comic short story that builds on (and perhaps helped perpetrate) Pittsburgh's turn-of-the-century reputation as a raucous rags-to-riches world full of captains of industry notable for wealth but laughable in education and taste.

Much of the fun of the story derives from the slangy wisecracks of the traveling con men, Jeff Peters and Andy Tucker, especially as they ring them off at the expense of "the Midas Americanus, commonly known as the Pittsburg millionaires": "How are we going to get acquainted with these coke kings and pig iron squeezers?" . . . "Isn't the entree nous into the salons of the stogie smokers going to be harder than you imagined?" . . . "Though their ways are boisterous and unpolished, under it all they have a great deal of impoliteness and discourtesy." . . . "I saw [one who'd] just won a bet of $10,000 with a Steel Corporation man that there'd be four suicides in the Allegheny rolling mills today. So everybody in sight had to walk up and have drinks with him." O. Henry's dialogue is full of the stand-up comic's one-liners.

The real humor of the story, however, grows from a more fundamental satiric perception — that the small-time con men at the bottom of the totem pole are no different from the men who have risen to the top. Jeff Peters shows mock concern for holding his partner to the "legitimate ethics of pure swindling," but he can only explain Andy's lack of scruples by comparing him to high financiers: "He used to devise schemes of money-getting so fraudulent and high-financial that they wouldn't have been allowed in the bylaws of a railroad rebate system." Andy, Jeff makes clear, is a product of the times: "I don't think he could have traced his descent any further back than a corporation."

Beyond the satiric equation of con game and corporate success is the story's final, time-honored joke: The folks at the bottom, with their down-to-earth savvy, turn out to be smarter than the pompously successful. And not only are they smarter, they enjoy themselves more.

O. Henry's Gentle Grafter is full of humor that jabs at the profiteering and display of wealth popularly ascribed to the Gilded Age. In another of the stories, a little exchange between Jeff and Andy perhaps sums up the theme of the whole volume:

"There are two kinds of grafts," said Jeff, "that ought to be wiped out by law. I mean Wall Street speculation and burglary."

"Nearly everybody will agree with you as to one of them," said I, with a laugh.

"Well, burglary ought to be wiped out, too," said Jeff.

O. Henry (1862-1910) undoubtedly remains the single most popularly successful American practitioner of the short story. Born in North Carolina (his real name was William Sidney Porter), he spent the first decades of his life in the South, in Texas, and in Central America. It was not until the turn of the century, when he moved to New York City, that he became a full-time writer. Although he is famous for the very short story, his collected works (including posthumous volumes) fill the best part of two thousand pages. Most of those stories were written in the last decade of his life.

O. Henry lived for several months in Pittsburgh en route to his eventual settlement in New York.

96

"Conscience in Art"

"I never could hold my partner, Andy Tucker, down to legitimate ethics of pure swindling," said Jeff Peters to me one day.

"Andy had too much imagination to be honest. He used to devise schemes of money-getting so fraudulent and high-financial that they wouldn't have been allowed in the bylaws of a railroad rebate system.

"Myself, I never believed in taking any man's dollars unless I gave him something for it—something in the way of rolled gold jewelry, garden seeds, lumbago lotion, stock certificates, stove polish or a crack on the head to show for his money. I guess I must have had New England ancestors away back and inherited some of their stanch and rugged fear of the police.

"But Andy's family tree was in different kind. I don't think he could have traced his descent any further back than a corporation.

"One summer while we was in the middle West, working down the Ohio valley with a line of family albums, headache powders and roach destroyer, Andy takes one of his notions of high and actionable financiering.

" 'Jeff,' says he, 'I've been thinking that we ought to drop these rutabaga fanciers and give our attention to something more nourishing and prolific. If we keep on snapshooting these hinds for their egg money we'll be classed as nature fakers. How about plunging into the fastnesses of the skyscraper country and biting some big bull caribous in the chest?'

" 'Well,' says I, 'you know my idiosyncrasies. I prefer a square, non-illegal style of business such as we are carrying on now. When I take money I want to leave some tangible object in the other fellow's hands for him to gaze at and to distract his attention from my spoor, even if it's only a Komical Kuss Trick Finger Ring for Squirting Perfume in a Friend's Eye. But if you've got a fresh idea, Andy,' says I, 'let's have a look at it. I'm not so wedded to petty graft that I would refuse something better in the way of a subsidy.'

" 'I was thinking,' says Andy, 'of a little hunt without horn, hound or camera among the great herd of the Midas Americanus, commonly known as the Pittsburg millionaires.'

" 'In New York?' I asks.

" 'No, sir,' says Andy, 'in Pittsburg. That's their habitat. They don't like New York. They go there now and then just because it's expected of 'em.'

" 'A Pittsburg millionaire in New York is like a fly in a cup of hot coffee—he attracts attention and comment, but he don't enjoy it. New York ridicules him for "blowing" so much money in that town of sneaks and snobs, and sneers. The truth is, he don't spend anything while he is there. I saw a memorandum of expenses for a ten days trip to Bunkum Town made by a Pittsburg man worth $15,000,000 once. Here's the way he set it down:

R. R. fare to and from	$ 21 00
Cab fare to and from hotel	2 00
Hotel bill @ $5 per day	50 00
Tips	5,750 00
Total	$5,823 00

" 'That's the voice of New York,' goes on Andy. 'The town's nothing but a head waiter. If you tip it too much it'll go and stand by the door and make fun of you to the hat check boy. When a Pittsburger wants to spend money and have a good time he stays at home. That's where we'll go to catch him.'

"Well, to make a dense story more condensed, me and Andy cached our paris green and antipyrine powders and albums in a friend's cellar, and took the trail to Pittsburg. Andy didn't have any especial prospectus of chicanery and violence drawn up, but he always had plenty of confidence that his immoral nature would rise to any occasion that presented itself.

"As a concession to my ideas of self-preservation and rectitude he promised that if I should take an active and incriminating part in any little business venture that we might work up there should be something actual and cognizant to the senses of touch, sight, taste or smell to transfer to the victim for the money so my conscience might rest easy. After that I felt better and entered more cheerfully into the foul play.

" 'Andy,' says I, as we strayed through the smoke along the cinderpath they call Smithfield street, 'had you figured out how we are going to get acquainted with these coke kings and pig iron squeezers? Not that I would decry my own worth or system of drawing room deportment, and work with the olive fork and pie knife,' says I, 'but isn't the entree nous into the salons of the stogie smokers going to be harder than you imagined?'

" 'If there's any handicap at all,' says Andy, 'it's our own refinement and inherent culture. Pittsburg millionaires are a fine body of plain, wholehearted, unassuming, democratic men.

" 'They are rough but uncivil in their manners, and though their ways are boisterous and un-

polished, under it all they have a great deal of impoliteness and discourtesy. Nearly every one of 'em rose from obscurity,' says Andy, 'and they'll live in it till the town gets to using smoke consumers. If we act simple and unaffected and don't go too far from the saloons and keep making a noise like an import duty on steel rails we won't have any trouble in meeting some of 'em socially.'

"Well Andy and me drifted about town three or four days getting our bearings. We got to knowing several millionaires by sight.

"One used to stop his automobile in front of our hotel and have a quart of champagne brought out to him. When the waiter opened it he'd turn it up to his mouth and drink it out of the bottle. That showed he used to be a glassblower before he made his money.

"One evening Andy failed to come to the hotel for dinner. About 11 o'clock he came into my room.

" 'Landed one, Jeff,' says he. 'Twelve millions. Oil, rolling mills, real estate and natural gas. He's a fine man; no airs about him. Made all his money in the last five years. He's got professors posting him up now in education—art and literature and haberdashery and such things.

" 'When I saw him he'd just won a bet of $10,000 with a Steel Corporation man that there'd be four suicides in the Allegheny rolling mills today. So everybody in sight had to walk up and have drinks on him. He took a fancy to me and asked me to dinner with him. We went to a restaurant in Diamond alley and sat on stools and had sparkling Moselle and clam chowder and apple fritters.

" 'Then he wanted to show me his bachelor apartment on Liberty street. He's got ten rooms over a fish market with privilege of the bath on the next floor above. He told me it cost him $18,000 to furnish his apartment, and I believe it.

" 'He's got $40,000 worth of pictures in one room, and $20,000 worth of curios and antiques in another. His name's Scudder, and he's 45, and taking lessons on the piano and 15,000 barrels of oil a day out of his wells.'

" 'All right,' says I. 'Preliminary canter satisfactory. But, kay vooly, voo? What good is the art junk to us? And the oil?'

" 'Now, that man,' says Andy, sitting thoughtfully on the bed, 'ain't what you would call an ordinary scutt. When he was showing me his cabinet of art curios his face lighted up like the door of a coke oven. He says that if some of his big deals go through he'll make J. P. Morgan's collection of sweatshop tapestry and Augusta, Me., beadwork look like the contents of an ostrich's craw thrown on a screen by a magic lantern.

" 'And then he showed me a little carving,' went on Andy, 'that anybody could see was a wonderful thing. It was something like 2,000 years old, he said. It was a lotus flower with a woman's face in it carved out of a solid piece of ivory.

" 'Scudder looks it up in a catalogue and describes it. An Egyptian carver named Khafra made two of 'em for King Rameses II. about the year B. C. The other one can't be found. The junkshops and antique bugs have rubbered all Europe for it, but it seems to be out of stock. Scudder paid $2,000 for the one he has.'

" 'Oh, well,' says I, 'this sounds like the purling of a rill to me. I thought we came here to teach the millionaires business, instead of learning art from 'em?'

" 'Be patient,' says Andy, kindly. 'Maybe we will see a rift in the smoke ere long.'

"All the next morning Andy was out. I didn't see him until about noon. He came to the hotel and called me into his room across the hall. He pulled a roundish bundle about as big as a goose egg out of his pocket and unwrapped it. It was an ivory carving just as he had described the millionaire's to me.

" 'I went in an old second hand store and pawnshop a while ago,' says Andy, 'and I see this half hidden under a lot of old daggers and truck. The pawnbroker said he'd had it several years and thinks it was soaked by some Arabs or Turks or some foreign dubs that used to live down by the river.

" 'I offered him $2 for it, and I must have looked like I wanted it, for he said it would be taking the pumpernickel out of his children's mouths to hold any conversation that did not lead up to a price of $35. I finally got it for $25.

" 'Jeff,' goes on Andy, 'this is the exact counter-

A Pittsburgh hotel interior, circa 1900.

part of Scudder's carving. It's absolutely a dead ringer for it. He'll pay $2,000 for it as quick as he'd tuck a napkin under his chin. And why shouldn't it be the genuine other one, anyhow, that the old gypsy whittled out?'

" 'Why not, indeed?' says I. 'And how shall we go about compelling him to make a voluntary purchase of it?'

"Andy had his plan all ready, and I'll tell you how we carried it out.

"I got a pair of blue spectacles, put on my black frock coat, rumpled my hair up and became Prof. Pickleman. I went to another hotel, registered, and sent a telegram to Scudder to come to see me at once on important art business. The elevator dumped him on me in less than an hour. He was a foggy man with a clarion voice, smelling of Connecticut wrappers and naphtha.

" 'Hello, Profess!' he shouts. 'How's your conduct?'

"I rumpled my hair some more and gave him a blue glass stare.

" 'Sir,' says I. 'Are you Cornelius T. Scudder? Of Pittsburg, Pennsylvania?'

" 'I am,' says he. 'Come out and have a drink.'

" 'I have neither the time nor the desire,' says I, 'for such harmful and deleterious amusements. I have come from New York,' says I, 'on a matter of busi—on a matter of art.

" 'I learned there that you are the owner of an Egyptian ivory carving of the time of Rameses II., representing the head of Queen Isis in a lotus flower. There were only two of such carvings made. One has been lost for many years. I recently discovered and purchased the other in a pawn—in an obscure museum in Vienna. I wish to purchase yours. Name your price.'

" 'Well, the great ice jams, Profess!' says Scudder. 'Have you found the other one? Me sell? No. I don't guess Cornelius Scudder needs to sell anything that he wants to keep. Have you got the carving with you, Profess?'

"I shows it to Scudder. He examines it careful all over.

" 'It's the article,' says he. 'It's a duplicate of mine, every line and curve of it. Tell you what I'll do,' he says. 'I won't sell, but I'll buy. Give you $2,500 for yours.'

" 'Since you won't sell, I will,' says I. 'Large bills, please. I'm a man of few words. I must return to New York to-night. I lecture to-morrow at the aquarium.'

"Scudder sends a check down and the hotel cashes it. He goes off with his piece of antiquity and I hurry back to Andy's hotel, according to arrangement.

"Andy is walking up and down the room looking at his watch.

" 'Well?' he says.

" 'Twenty-five hundred,' says I. 'Cash.'

" 'We've got just eleven minutes,' says Andy, 'to catch the B. & O. westbound. Grab your baggage.'

" 'What's the hurry,' says I. 'It was a square deal. And even if it was only an imitation of the original carving it'll take him some time to find it out. He seemed to be sure it was the genuine article.'

" 'It was,' says Andy. 'It was his own. When I was looking at his curios yesterday he stepped out of the room for a moment and I pocketed it. Now, will you pick up your suit case and hurry?'

" 'Then,' says I, 'why was that story about finding another one in the pawn—'

" 'Oh,' says Andy, 'out of respect for that conscience of yours. Come on.' ''

MARY ROBERTS RINEHART
"Another Flood"

**Mrs. Pitman suspects murder
has been done**

Time: 1904?   Setting: Allegheny City

A spring flood is the setting for the beginning of The Case of Jennie Brice. *An elemental force has been set loose, workday restraints are suddenly irrelevant (in holiday spirit, the men get drunk). The rules are off: Anything, even murder, may happen.*

As Rinehart sets the stage in these two opening chapters, the flood is one of several physical details skillfully introduced as omens of violence to come. At the start of the story a dog's body is discovered in the basement; later a dead kitten is found, then a broken knife; meanwhile a neighborhood boy has drowned. By the time Rinehart closes her second chapter, the reader is ready to shiver with Mrs. Pitman when she gives an innocent household instruction — "You can get the meat at the butcher's." The flood itself has taken on a claustrophobic quality, trapping Mrs. Pitman at what may be the scene of a crime, and with a man who may be a murderer.

102

But for all these sinister elements, the opening chapters of The Case of Jennie Brice *also have a tone of good humor, even amusement, that is already present in the understatement of the very first sentence: "We have just had another flood, bad enough, but only a foot or two of water on the first floor." Clearly someone who can speak so routinely of only a foot or two of water in her living room, who can look at a flood as almost part of a spring ritual — such a person can cope, probably even with murder. As she has done elsewhere (for example,* The Circular Staircase), *Rinehart seems to take amused pleasure in confronting the reader with a heroine who might normally be passed over or not taken seriously — on the surface*

fussy, opinionated, even a little silly, but nonetheless fundamentally tough, resilient, and commonsensical.

Mary Roberts Rinehart (1876-1956) was born in Allegheny City, and in her autobiography, My Story, *recalls the experience of floods during her youth on the North Side:*

Floods were familiar to me from my earliest days. . . .

Floods then were an act of the providence of God. No one referred them to man's criminal folly in deforesting the hills and overgrazing the plains. They came, were lived through, came again. There were warnings, and the people whose homes were near the water front moved upstairs, and tied a skiff to a window sill. Then the rivers came down, the Allegheny, the Monongahela. They swept through the streets, backed up through the sewers, tore up brick pavements. In due time they receded, having deposited their silt in every cellar and many lower floors, and the skiffs were put away until Providence should again elect to send the rivers outside their banks.

One flood, however, was man-made. I was a little older then, but still a child.

I was wakened one early morning and taken to the river bank. Something dreadful had happened; a dam had given way, and my mother's eyes were red and swollen. We stood by the river, on a bit of high land, and saw houses sweeping by and all sorts of strange things. Men were watching too, for now and then a body was salvaged. My mother continued to cry. That was the Johnstown flood, and a very dear friend of hers had been on a railroad train and was lost.

Rinehart was a highly prolific writer, the author of some fifty books. Other novels that use a Pittsburgh setting include The Circular Staircase *and* The Man in Lower Ten.

"Another Flood"

We have just had another flood, bad enough, but only a foot or two of water on the first floor. Yesterday we got the mud shoveled out of the cellar and found Peter, the spaniel Mr. Ladley left when he "went away." The flood, and the fact that it was Mr. Ladley's dog whose body was found half buried in the basement fruit closet, brought back to me the strange events of the other flood five years ago, when the water reached more than half-way to the second story and brought with it to some, mystery and sudden death, and to me the worst case of "shingles" I have ever seen.

My name is Pitman in this narrative. It is not really Pitman, but that does well enough. I belong to an old Pittsburgh family. I was born on Penn Avenue, when that was the best part of town, and I lived until I was fifteen very close to what is now the Pittsburgh Club. It was a dwelling then. I have forgotten who lived there.

I was a girl in 'seventy-seven during the railroad riots, and I recall our driving in the family carriage over to one of the Allegheny hills, and seeing the yards burning and the sound of shooting from across the river. It was the next year that I ran away from school to marry Mr. Pitman, and I have not known my family since. We were never reconciled, although I came back to Pittsburgh after twenty years of wandering. Mr. Pitman was dead. The old city called me, and I came. I had a hundred dollars or so, and I took a house in lower Allegheny where, because they are partly inundated every spring rents are cheap, and I kept boarders. My house was always orderly and clean, and although the neighborhood had a bad name a good many theatrical people stopped with me. Five minutes across the bridge and they were in the theater district. Allegheny at that time was still an independent city. But since then it has allied itself with Pittsburgh. It is now the North Side.

I was glad to get back. I worked hard, but I made my rent and my living, and a little over. Now and then on summer evenings I went to one of the parks and sitting on a bench watched the children playing around, and looked at my sister's house, closed for the summer. It is a very large house; her butler once had his wife boarding with me—a nice little woman.

It is curious to recall that at that time five years ago I had never seen my niece, Lida Harvey, and then to think that only the day before yesterday she came in her car as far as she dared, and then sat there waving to me, while the police patrol brought across in a skiff a basket of provisions she had sent me.

I wonder what she would have thought had she known that the elderly woman in a calico wrapper with an old overcoat over it and wearing a pair of rubber boots was her full aunt!

The flood and the sight of Lida both brought back the case of Jennie Brice. For even then Lida and Mr. Howell were interested in each other.

This is April. The flood I am writing about five years ago was earlier, in March. It had been a long hard winter, with ice gorges in all the upper valley. Then in early March there came a thaw. The gorges broke up and began to come down, filling the rivers with crushing grinding ice.

There are three rivers at Pittsburgh, the Alle-

gheny and the Monongahela uniting there at the Point to form the Ohio. And all three were covered with broken ice, logs, and all sorts of debris from the upper valleys.

A warning was sent out from the weather bureau, and I got my carpets ready to lift that morning. That was on the fourth of March, a Sunday. Mr. Ladley and his wife, Jennie Brice, had the parlor bedroom and the room behind it. Mrs. Ladley, or Miss Brice as she preferred to be known, had a small part at a local theater which kept a permanent stock company. Her husband was in the same business, but he was not working that season. It was the wife who paid the bills, and a lot of quarreling they did about it.

I knocked at the door at ten o'clock, and Mr. Ladley opened it. He was a short man, rather stout and getting bald, and he always had a cigarette in his mouth. Even yet, the parlor smells of them in damp weather.

"What do you want?" he asked sharply, holding the door open about an inch.

"The water's coming up very fast, Mr. Ladley," I said. "It's up to the swinging shelf in the cellar now. I'd like to take up the carpet and move the piano."

"Come back in an hour or so," he snapped, and tried to close the door. But I had got my toe in the crack.

"I'll have to have the piano moved, Mr. Ladley," I said. "You'd better put off what you're doing."

I thought he was probably writing. He spent most of the day writing, using the washstand as a desk, and it kept me busy with oxalic acid taking

ink spots out of the splasher and the towels. He was writing a play, and talked a lot about the Shuberts having promised to star him in it when it was finished.

"Hell!" he said, and turning spoke to somebody in the room.

"We can go into the back room," I heard him say, and he closed the door. When he opened it again the room was empty. I called in Terry, the Irishman who does odd jobs for me now and then, and we both got to work at the tacks in the carpet, Terry working by the window and I by the door in the back parlor, which the Ladleys used as a bedroom.

That was how I happened to hear what I afterward told the police.

Someone, a man but not Mr. Ladley, was talking. Mrs. Ladley broke in. "I won't do it!" she said flatly. "Why should I help him? He doesn't help me. He loafs here all day, smoking and sleeping, and sits up all night drinking and keeping me awake."

The voice went on again, as if in reply to this, and I heard a rattle of glasses as if they were pouring drinks. They always had whisky, even when they were behind with their board.

Exposition Park, Allegheny City, 1901, captioned in a newspaper, "Why the opening game was not played yesterday."

"That's all very well," Mrs. Ladley said. I could always hear her, since she had the theatrical sort of voice which carries. "But what about the prying she-devil that runs the house?"

"Hush, for God's sake!" broke in Mr. Ladley, and after that they spoke in whispers. Even with my ear against the panel I could not catch a word.

The men came just then to move the piano, and by the time we had taken it and the furniture upstairs the water was over the kitchen floor, and creeping forward into the hall. I had never seen the river come up so fast. By noon the yard was full of floating ice, and at three that afternoon the police skiff was on the front street, and I was wading around in rubber boots, taking the pictures off the walls.

I was too busy to see who the Ladleys' visitor was, and he had gone when I remembered him again. The Ladleys took the second-story front, which was empty, and Mr. Reynolds who was in the silk department in a store across the river had the room just behind.

I put up a coal stove in a back room next the bathroom, and managed to cook the dinner there. I was washing up the dishes when Mr. Reynolds came in. As it was Sunday he was in his slippers, and he had the colored supplement of a morning paper in his hand.

"What's the matter with the Ladleys?" he asked. "I can't read for their quarreling."

"Booze, probably," I said. "When you've lived in the flood district as long as I have, Mr. Reynolds, you'll know that the rising of the river is a signal for every man in the vicinity to stop work and get tight. The fuller the river, the fuller the male population."

"Then this flood will likely make 'em drink themselves to death!" he said. "It's a lulu."

"It's the neighborhood's annual debauch. The women are busy keeping the babies from getting drowned in the cellars, or they'd get full too. Since it's come this far I hope it will come farther, so the landlord will have to paper the parlor."

That was at three o'clock. At four Mr. Ladley went down the stairs, and I heard him getting into a skiff in the lower hall. There were boats going back and forth all the time, carrying crowds of curious people, and taking the flood sufferers to the corner grocery, where they were lowering groceries in a basket on a rope from an upper window.

I had been making tea when I heard Mr. Ladley go out. I fixed a tray with a cup of it and some crackers and took it to their door. I had never liked Mrs. Ladley, but it was chilly in the house with the gas shut off and the lower floor full of ice water. And it is hard enough to keep boarders in the flood district.

She did not answer to my knock, so I opened the door and went in. She was at the window, looking after him, and the brown valise which figured in the case later was open on the floor. Over the foot of the bed was the black and white dress with the red collar.

When I spoke to her she turned around quickly. She was a tall woman, about twenty-eight, with very white teeth and yellow hair, which she parted a little to one side and drew down over her ears. She had a sullen face and large well-shaped hands, with her nails long and very pointed.

"The she-devil has brought you some tea," I

Federal Street, Allegheny City, 1907.

said. "Where shall she put it?"

"She-devil!" she repeated, raising her eyebrows. "It's a very thoughtful she-devil. Who called you that?"

But what with the sight of the valise and the fear that they might be leaving, I thought it best not to quarrel. She had left the window, and going to her dressing table had picked up her nail file.

"Never mind," I said. "I hope you are not going away. These floods don't last, and they're really a benefit. Plenty of the people around here rely on them every year to wash out their cellars."

"No, I'm not going away," she replied lazily. "I'm taking that dress to Miss Hope at the theater. She is going to wear it in *Charlie's Aunt* next week. She hasn't half enough of a wardrobe to play leads in stock. Look at this thumbnail, broken to the quick!"

If I had only looked to see which thumb it was! But I was putting the tea tray on the washstand and moving Mr. Ladley's papers to find room for it. Peter, the spaniel, begged for a lump of sugar and I gave it to him.

"Where is Mr. Ladley?" I asked.

"Gone out to see the river."

"I hope he'll be careful. There's a drowning or two every year in these floods."

"Then I hope he won't," she said calmly. "Do you know what I was doing when you came in? I was looking after his boat and hoping it had a hole in it."

"You won't feel that way tomorrow, Mrs. Ladley," I protested, shocked. "You're just nervous and worn out. Most men have their ugly times. Many a time I wished Mr. Pitman was gone—until he went. Then I'd have given a good bit to have him back again."

She was standing in front of the dresser fixing her hair. She turned and looked at me over her shoulder.

"Probably Mr. Pitman was a man," she said. "My husband is a fiend, a devil."

Well, a good many women have said that to me at different times. But just let me say such a thing to them, or repeat their own words to them the next day, and they would fly at me in a fury. So I said nothing, and put the cream into her tea.

I never saw her again.

There is not much sleeping done in the flood district during a spring flood. The gas and electric light were shut off, and I gave Mr. Reynolds and the Ladley's each a lamp. I sat in the back room I had made into a temporary kitchen, with a candle and with a bedquilt around my shoulders. The water rose fast in the lower hall, but by midnight at the seventh step it stopped rising and stood still. I always have a skiff during the flood season, and as the water rose I tied it to one spindle of the staircase after another.

I made myself a cup of tea, and at one o'clock I stretched out on a sofa for a few hours' sleep. I think I had been sleeping only an hour or so when someone touched me on the shoulder and I started up. It was Mr. Reynolds, partly dressed.

"Someone has been in the house, Mrs. Pitman," he said. "They went away just now in the boat."

"Perhaps it was Peter," I suggested drowsily. "That dog is always wandering around at night."

"Not unless Peter can row a boat," said Mr. Reynolds dryly.

I got up, being already fully dressed, and taking the candle we went to the staircase. I noticed it was a minute or so after two o'clock as we left the room. The boat was gone, not untied, but cut loose. The end of the rope was still fastened to the stair rail. I sat down on the stairs and looked at Mr. Reynolds.

"It's gone!" I said. "If the house catches fire we'll have to drown."

"It's rather curious, when you consider it." We both spoke softly, not to disturb the Ladleys. "I've been awake, and I heard no boat come in. Yet, if no one came in a boat, and came from the street, they would have had to swim in."

I felt queer and creepy. The street door was open, of course, and there was some light outside. It gave me a strange feeling to sit there in the darkness on the stairs, with the arch of the front door like the entrance to a cavern, and see now and then a chunk of ice slide into view, turn around in the eddy, and pass on. It was bitter cold too, and the wind was rising.

"I'll go through the house," said Mr. Reynolds. "There's likely nothing worse the matter than some drunken mill hand on a vacation while the mills are underwater. But I'd better look."

He left me, and I sat there alone in the darkness. I had a presentiment of something wrong, but I tried to think it was only discomfort and the cold. The water, driven in by the wind, swirled at my feet. And something dark floated in and lodged on the step below. I reached down and touched it. It was a dead kitten. I had never known a dead cat to bring me anything but bad luck, and here was one washed in at my very feet.

Mr. Reynolds came back soon, and reported the house quiet and in order.

"But I found Peter shut up in one of the third-floor rooms," he said, "and let him out. Did you put him there?"

I had not, and said so; but as the dog went everywhere, and the door might have blown shut, we did not attach much importance to that at the time.

Well, the skiff was gone, and there was no use worrying about it until morning. I went back to the sofa to keep warm, but I left my candle lighted and my door open. I did not sleep. The dead cat was on my mind, and as if it were not bad enough to have it washed in at my feet, about four in the morning Peter, prowling uneasily, discovered it and brought it in and put it on my couch, wet and stiff, poor little thing!

I looked at the clock. It was a quarter after four, and except for the occasional crunch of one ice cake hitting another in the yard everything was quiet. And then I heard the stealthy sound of oars in the lower hall.

I am not a brave woman. I lay there, hoping Mr. Reynolds would hear and open his door. But he was sleeping soundly. Peter snarled and ran out into the hall, and the next moment I heard Mr. Ladley speaking. "Down, Peter," he said. "Down. Go and lie down."

I took my candle and went out into the hall. Mr. Ladley was stooping over the boat, trying to tie it to the staircase. The rope was short, having been cut, and he was having trouble. Perhaps it was the candlelight, but he looked ghost-white and haggard.

"I borrowed your boat, Mrs. Pitman," he said, civilly enough. "Mrs. Ladley was not well, and I went to the drugstore."

"You've been more than two hours going to the drugstore," I said.

He muttered something about not finding any open at first, and went into his room. He closed

109

and locked the door behind him, and although Peter whined and scratched he did not let him in.

He looked so agitated that I thought I had been harsh, and that perhaps she was really ill. I knocked at the door and asked if I could do anything. But he only called "No" curtly through the door, and asked me to take that infernal dog away.

I went back to the sofa and tried to sleep, for the water had dropped an inch or so on the stairs and I knew the danger was over. Peter came shivering at dawn and got on the sofa with me. I put an end of the quilt over him, and he stopped shivering after a time and went to sleep.

The dog was company. I lay there, wide awake, thinking about Mr. Pitman's death; and how I had come, by degrees, to be keeping a cheap boarding-house in the flood district, and to having to take impudence from everybody who chose to rent a room from me, and to being called a she-devil. From that I got to thinking again about the Ladleys, and how she had said he was a fiend, and to doubting about his having gone out for medicine for her. I dozed off again at daylight and being worn out I slept heavily.

At seven o'clock Mr. Reynolds came to the door, dressed for the store. He was a tall man of about fifty, neat and orderly in his habits, and he always remembered that I had seen better days, and treated me as a lady.

"Never mind about breakfast for me this morning, Mrs. Pitman," he said. "I'll get a cup of coffee at the other end of the bridge. I'll take the boat and send it back with Terry."

He turned and went along the hall and down to the boat. I heard him push off from the stairs with an oar and row out into the street. Peter followed him to the stairs.

At a quarter after seven Mr. Ladley came out and called to me: "Just bring in a cup of coffee and some toast," he said. "Enough for one."

He went back and slammed his door, and I made his coffee. I steeped a cup of tea for Mrs. Ladley at the same time. He opened the door just wide enough for the tray, and took it without so much as a "thank you." He had a cigarette in his mouth as usual, and I could see a fire in the grate and smell something like scorching cloth.

"I hope Mrs. Ladley is better," I said, getting my foot in the crack of the door so he could not quite close it. It smelled to me as if he had accidentally set fire to something with his cigarette, and I tried to see into the room.

"What about Mrs. Ladley?" he snapped.

"You said she was ill last night."

"Oh, yes! Well, she wasn't very sick. She's better."

"Shall I bring her some tea?"

"Take your foot away!" he ordered. "No. She doesn't want tea. She's not here."

"Not here!"

"Good heavens!" he snarled. "Is her going away anything to make such a fuss about? The Lord knows I'd be glad to get out of this infernal pig-wallow myself."

"If you mean my house—" I began.

But he had pulled himself together and was more polite when he answered. "I mean the neighborhood. Your house is all that could be desired for the money. If we don't have linen sheets and double cream, at least we're paying muslin and milk prices."

Either my nose was growing accustomed to the odor or it was dying away. I took my foot away from the door. "When did Mrs. Ladley leave?" I asked.

"This morning, very early. I rowed her to Federal Street."

"You couldn't have had much sleep," I said dryly. For he looked horrible. There were lines around his eyes, which were red, and his lips looked dry and cracked.

"She's not in the piece this week at the theater," he said, licking his lips and looking past me, not at me. "She'll be back by Saturday."

I did not believe him. I do not think he imagined I did. He shut the door in my face, and it caught poor Peter by the nose. The dog ran off howling, but although Mr. Ladley had been as fond of the animal as it was in his nature to be fond of anything he paid no attention. As I started down the hall after him, I saw what Peter had been carrying —a slipper of Mrs. Ladley's. It was soaked with water. Evidently Peter had found it floating at the foot of the stairs.

Although the idea of murder had not entered my head at that time, the slipper gave me a turn. I picked it up and looked at it, a black one with a beaded toe, short in the vamp and high heeled, the sort most actresses wear. Then I went back and knocked at the door of the front room again.

"What the devil do you want now?" he called from beyond the door.

"Here's a slipper of Mrs. Ladley's," I said. "Peter found it floating in the lower hall."

He opened the door wide and let me in. The room was in tolerable order, much better than when Mrs. Ladley was about. He looked at the slipper, but he did not touch it. "I don't think that's hers," he said.

"I've seen her wear it a hundred times."

"Well, she'll never wear it again." And then seeing me stare he added: "It's ruined with the water. Throw it out. And by the way I'm sorry, but I set fire to one of the pillow slips—dropped asleep, and my cigarette did the rest. Just put it on the bill."

He pointed to the bed. One of the pillows had no slip, and the ticking cover had a scorch or two on it. I went over and looked at it.

"The pillow will have to be paid for too, Mr. Ladley," I said. "And there's a sign nailed on the door that forbids smoking in bed. If you are going to set fire to things I shall have to charge extra."

"Really!" he jeered, looking at me with his cold fishy eyes. "Is there any sign on the door saying that boarders are charged extra for seven feet of filthy river in the bedrooms?"

I was never a match for him, and I make it a principle never to bandy words with my boarders. I took the pillow and the slipper and went out. The telephone was ringing on the stair landing. It was the theater, asking for Miss Brice.

"She has gone away," I said.

"What do you mean? Moved away?"

"Gone for a few days' vacation," I replied. "She isn't playing this week, is she?"

"Wait a moment," said the voice. There was a hum of conversation from the other end, and then another man came to the telephone.

"Can you find out where Miss Brice has gone?"

"I'll see."

I went to Ladley's door and knocked. Mr. Ladley opened it a crack and answered from just beyond.

"The theater is asking where Mrs. Ladley is."

"Tell them I don't know," he snarled, and shut the door. I took his message to the telephone.

111

Whoever it was swore and hung up the receiver.

All the morning I was uneasy, I hardly knew why. Peter felt it as I did. There was no sound from the Ladleys' room, and the house was quiet, except for the lapping water on the stairs and the police patrol going back and forth.

At eleven o'clock a boy in the neighborhood, paddling on a raft, fell into the water and was drowned. I watched the police boat go past carrying his little cold body, and after that I was good for nothing. I went and sat with Peter on the stairs. The dog's conduct had been strange all morning. He had sat just above the water, looking at it and whimpering. Perhaps he was expecting another kitten, or—

It is hard to say how ideas first enter one's mind. But the notion that Mr. Ladley had killed his wife and thrown her body into the water came to me as I sat there. All at once I seemed to see it all: the quarreling the day before, the night trip in the boat, the water-soaked slipper, his haggard face that morning, even the way the spaniel sat and stared at the flood.

Terry brought the boat back at half past eleven, towing it behind another.

"Well," I said, from the stairs, "I hope you've had a pleasant morning."

"What doing?" he asked, not looking at me.

"Rowing about the streets. You've had that boat for hours."

He tied it up without a word to me, but he spoke to the dog. "Good morning, Peter," he said. "It's nice weather for fishes, ain't it?"

He picked out a bit of floating wood from the water, and showing it to the dog, flung it into the parlor. Peter went after it with a splash. He was pretty fat, and when he came back I heard him wheezing. But what he brought back was not the stick of wood. It was the knife I use for cutting bread. It had been on a shelf in the room where I had slept the night before, and now Peter brought it out of the flood where its wooden handle had kept it afloat. The blade was broken off short.

It is not unusual to find one's household goods floating around during floodtime. More than once I've lost a chair, and seen it after the water had gone down, new scrubbed and painted, in Molly Maguire's kitchen next door. And perhaps now and then a bit of luck would come to me, a dog kennel or a chicken house or a kitchen table, or even as happened once a month-old baby in a wooden cradle which lodged against my back fence and had come forty miles, as it turned out, with no worse mishap than a cold in its head.

But the knife was different. I had put it on the mantel over the stove I was using upstairs the night before, and I hadn't touched it since. As I sat staring at it, Terry took it from Peter and handed it to me.

"Better give me a penny, Mrs. Pitman," he said in his impudent Irish way. "I hate to give you a knife. It may cut our friendship."

I reached over to hit him a clout on the head, but I did not. The sunlight was coming in through the window at the top of the stairs and shining on the rope that was tied to the banister. The end of the rope was covered with stains, brown with a glint of red in them.

I got up shivering. "You can get the meat at the butcher's, Terry," I said, "and come back for me in a half hour." Then I turned and went upstairs, weak in the knees, to put on my hat and coat. I had made up my mind that there had been murder done.

112

AGNES SLIGH TURNBULL
"A Beau at Institute"

Connie Richards attends the
Westmoreland County Teachers' Institute

Time: 1904

Setting: Greensburg

Agnes Sligh Turnbull's The Rolling Years *is a family chronicle that is realistically specific to a time, a place, and a particular ethnic-religious group — Scotch Presbyterians in a small town in Westmoreland County from 1852 to 1910. At the start, the book focuses on a farm couple, Daniel and Sarah McDowell; it then moves to their children, especially David and Jeannie (the former eventually becomes a Pittsburgh judge, the latter marries a local school teacher, James Richards). The Richards' daughter, Connie, is the central figure in the last third of the novel.*

Although The Rolling Years *is narrated with a detail and affection that indicate an autobiographical origin, Turnbull's account also emphasizes the provincialism of her characters, the sometime harshness, sometime pettiness of their rigid Presbyterian code. An early episode dramatizes the congregational uproar created when a farmer in the community works his fields on a Sunday; later passages portray Connie's pangs of conscience for indulging in dancing, and still later she rejects her "beau" when he admits that he cannot believe in the dogma of the Virgin Birth.*

The effect of the novel is neither to support nor to criticize these religious and moral values, but rather to show life "the way it was." Turnbull takes her characters seriously as people, and it is clear that she regards them as "good" people, capable of a flexibility and compassion in their personal relations that may sometimes be belied by the public mores they enforce.

The "rolling years" of the title, suggestive primarily of the family's evolving generations, also point to the larger social and economic changes that influenced life in rural Westmoreland County — the sale of farmland for coal rights, the mobility that makes cities and far-off places available, the encroachment of new standards. Though Connie and her husband decide to build their own home in the Westmoreland countryside, a trip to Greensburg will never be the thrill to their daughter that it was to Connie in 1904:

Sarah was gone, and Jeannie. And age, Connie knew, would someday work its will upon her. The ever-rolling stream moved on. What would the coming years bring to her child? 1912–1914–1918–1920–1930–1935. . . .

So the tale of time would be told again in the life of the new Jeannie, and who could predict how far the experiences of these unborn years would carry her into a new and different world!

Agnes Sligh Turnbull (1888–) is a native of New Alexandria in Westmoreland County and is of Scotch-Irish heritage. She attended the Washington Seminary and Indiana State Normal School, both in western Pennsylvania, and taught English at various schools in the area until her marriage in 1918, when she moved to Maplewood, New Jersey. She has written prolifically about western Pennsylvania. Other novels include Remember the End *(1938),* The King's Orchard *(1963),* The Day Must Dawn *(1942), and* The Midlands *(1975).*

In 1942 Turnbull summed up her allegiances: "I am a Presbyterian and a Republican."

"A Beau at Institute"

When she reached the railroad station next morning, Connie's hands were stiff with cold, and her suitcase decidedly heavy. It was a long walk, all the length of Main Street, past the post office ("Well, Connie, off for Institute, I suppose! Don't get too highfalutin in the big town!"), on down the hill past Galloway's ("So, Connie, this is the big week for the schoolmarms! Don't let anybody run off with you in the county seat!"), and still farther to the long covered wooden bridge over the Loyalhanna, with the muddy waters showing plainly through the wide cracks as she trod with moderate ease the great central beam that divided the bridge floor in half.

Once over the creek, there was a short, brisk upward climb, and the station was reached. There was plenty of stir around it this Monday morning, and Connie thrilled to the excitement of it. She pushed open the door with numb fingers and entered the hot, dusty, smoky, steamy atmosphere of the waiting room. The big iron "egg" stove in the center was red-hot, while the west windows were still white with frost.

Several milk-shipping farmers in cloth caps with fur earlugs, worn overcoats, and felt boots, stood about the stove, warming their hands; and over in the corner stood Huldah with a group of other girls who taught in Ferry and Galen townships, all atingle with the unusual business of travel, and the anticipation of the week to come.

As Connie was turning away from the ticket window, the outer door slammed, and Billy Brown entered the waiting room looking twice as large in his working clothes as in his Sunday suit. He came straight to her while the group of girls stopped talking to watch.

"Well," he said, looking at her in his intent fashion, "I s'pose you're off to the big town this morning! Say!" He lowered his voice. "I might have an errand into Greensburg about Wednesday. How about going along with you to the night lecture?"

"Why, of course," Connie stammered.

"All right then, see you Wednesday."

He spoke to Huldah, and with the full assurance that his position gave him, chaffed the other girls, who blushed with pleasure at his notice, and then, as the noise of the train became apparent, picked up Connie's suitcase (and Huldah's as an afterthought) and helped them get settled in the coach. Just as he was leaving, he leaned nearer Huldah.

"How's Jennie now?" he asked.

Huldah shook her head, and her eyes filled.

"Not very good," she said in a low voice.

"Mother's going over today," Billy answered. Then the train whistled, and with a last look at Constance, Billy ran down the aisle and made what to the girls was a daring jump, from the steps to the platform.

Huldah and Connie sat with their heads close, discussing the excitements of the week. Huldah was full of questions about Billy. How long had it been going on? You could tell by the way he looked at Connie he was serious! Jack McIlvaine was coming in Wednesday night to take her to the lecture. And Billy and Connie! Why, it was perfect! Jack said they might get in by afternoon. If *only* the boys would think of taking them to the hotel

115

for dinner! But she knew they would never do that. They could well afford it, too, but they just didn't know how to do things like city men. But anyway she and Connie would go themselves Thursday night. So there would be two big nights in the week.

Connie felt her heart beating quickly. For the first time she would have a beau at Institute. She had been too quick perhaps to criticize Billy when he was bringing her all this pleasure.

The famous Westmoreland County Teachers' Institute met in the large High School building that crowned one of the Greensburg hills, facing toward its more prominent sister-edifice, the Courthouse, a little farther down. Here each year, the week before Christmas, gathered some eight hundred teachers to drink in culture, absorb new professional methods, eat candy out of paper "pokes" in the back seats, tell stories behind the bulky *Illuminator* programs, and develop new and passionate interests in the opposite sex to such an extent that often before the next year was over many a couple returned to the Courthouse down the hill for a marriage license!

There were experienced teachers amongst the crowds in the halls that first day of registering— mature women a trifle bored with the whole affair, assured in all their actions, dressed in the latest fashion from their comfortably secure incomes; there were young girls of seventeen from remote country districts in poorly fitting suits paid for out of a salary of thirty-five dollars a month, awkward and timid in the unaccustomed crowd, but with eyes shining at the magnificent novelty of it all.

There were men, too, of all types: suave high-school principals and pimply youths fresh from the farm, teaching in little red schoolhouses in distant clearings to earn money for college. Over them all,

like to a god—in the eyes of the lesser folk at least—towered the County Superintendent, going here and there on errands of his own, stopping now and then to speak to a favored few, busy with the heavy responsibilities of the week. It was he, along with his assistants, who held the examinations in scattered schoolhouses each summer which decided who should have the right to teach; and who issued the thin blue paper certificates which represented to many the passport to a heaven of opportunity. He visited the schools during the year, too, driving up in his smart buggy usually, it seemed to fluttered young country teachers, on the days when the stove flue smoked or the children were all coming down with measles!

On Monday afternoon the first session of the Institute got under way, and by Wednesday Connie felt as though she had done nothing all year but attend lectures. She and Huldah took notes assiduously, were entertained by their own small jokes, and watched with avidity the big world of people around them.

Their boarding place was pleasant and presented exciting differences from home: the distant sound of trains constantly coming and going; the odor of gas in their bedroom fireplace and flaring jet; the horses' feet on the paved streets; the bathroom! First, last, and most of all, the bathroom!

On Wednesday afternoon the girls, who had thoughtfully seated themselves near the door, nudged each other sharply. Billy Brown and Jack McIlvaine were standing just inside the wide side entrance to the auditorium, carefully scanning the crowd. Huldah lifted a hand, and in a few minutes the boys had seen them. Huldah and Connie removed their coats from the seats beside them, and the young men edged along the row and seated themselves with a nice enough bit of confusion to

116

center the attention of that whole section upon the two couples.

Billy's face was flushed as he looked at Connie. He leaned closer until his arm pressed hard against hers.

"You don't have to listen to this stuff, do you?" he asked in a loud whisper.

As a matter of fact the lecture under way was of especial interest to Connie. It was given by Dr. Warre, a professor in an eastern college, and dealt with nineteenth-century poets, among whom were her chief gods. But at her other side Huldah whispered back that the speaker was "dull as dishwater," and at once started an animated, noiseless conversation by means of signs and smiles and nods. Billy seemed quite content to lean close to Connie, fingering her purse, her gloves, her program, managing to touch her hands frequently, whispering when he dared—and Connie missed Browning and Tennyson!

At the evening lecture she tried to pretend she was entirely happy. They had excellent seats near the front. Amongst vast billows of unattended young females, she and Huldah had good-looking male escorts. There was a thrill of pride in that. Billy kept his promise, too, as he said good-bye at their boarding house. He didn't ask for a kiss even though it was pretty clear that Jack's evening was crowned in that fashion. And yet—and yet—as Connie lay wakeful in the big walnut bed listening to the muted whistle and roar of the trains, her heart went the rounds of her problem again. In every way Billy was a suitable young man for her to marry. Why couldn't she accept his attentions with satisfaction? Why could she not take life as she found it, like Huldah for instance?

The next day something happened to Huldah. A tall young man with red hair and glasses who had been casting glances in her direction found some one to introduce him to her at the morning recess, and all through the afternoon they sat together. Connie drifted off with some other girls she knew, amused at Huldah's unfailing popularity even in strange places.

The young man was a high-school teacher from Latrobe and was staying at the hotel. All the Latrobe crowd were staying there, Huldah told Connie as they dressed that evening. She had met some of them at dances. They would be sure to see them at dinner.

To Connie the matter of going to the Palace Hotel for dinner (at a cost of seventy-five cents!) was a momentous thing. In all her life she had eaten at a hotel but once before—that was with Uncle David in Pittsburgh. It was the only time she had had the strange and delightful sense of being a part of the great world of wealth and fashion which lay outside her experience.

As to the Palace, here in Greensburg, she had glimpsed its splendors wistfully on many occasions. There were colored waiters in the dining room, and an orchestra half hidden by palms. Just to walk through the hotel lobby would be something. But to eat dinner there!

The girls did not hurry. It was more fashionable, Huldah said, to eat as late as you could. When they reached the hotel at last, they sat for some time in the lobby, watching the people coming and going, enjoying the delicious sensation of knowing that, whenever they wished, they could saunter through the magic doors into the dining room.

At last, Huldah pronounced it time. They moved slowly, acutely conscious of themselves, toward the entrance where the head waiter stood in evening clothes. Beyond him there came a burst of lights and music and the sound of many people

117

dining.

He intercepted them now.

"You wished dinner?" he asked with an accent.

"For two," Huldah said with dignity.

He shook his head and scanned the crowded room.

"I am sorry. You should have made reservations. There are no more places. I cannot seat you until perhaps eight."

"But the lecture begins at eight," the girls cried in one breath, their faces stricken with disappointment.

The waiter was looking over the room again.

"Do you know anyone dining here?" he asked.

Huldah had already seen her rusty-haired swain sitting with a group of young people at one of the largest tables near the middle of the room. She indicated them to the head waiter.

"I might set one more place there," he said, "but only one. So I cannot seat you together. For the other young lady," he added, turning to Connie, "there is one place at the small table for two there by the wall, if you wish. There will be later a young gentleman at the other place. Is that agreeable?"

Connie looked at Huldah. Surely, after all their weeks of planning, Huldah would not do this to her—would not go to the gay center table with the other young people, and leave her *alone*, or even worse, with a stranger, at the small table along the wall!

"Huldah," she began in a small voice, but Huldah was already excitedly cheerful.

"I guess it's the best we can do, isn't it, Connie? I'm awful sorry we can't sit together, but the dinner'll taste the same anyway. It's lucky I know that Latrobe crowd or we wouldn't have got in at all. Well, what do you say, Connie? Will we tell him

to go ahead and fix us up that way?"

"I suppose so," Connie said very low. She bit her lips for a moment and then managed honestly, "I know it's all we can do now, with dinner over at the boarding house. Go on, Huldah, and have a good time."

Huldah's natural kindliness came to the surface then.

"You go to the big table, Connie! Honest, I don't care! You can tell them you're my friend—"

"Huldah, you're sweet. Of course I won't. I don't know a soul there. Go right on and enjoy yourself. I'll be all right!"

The waiter was already signing to her. She walked over to the small table and sat down. She could hear the acclaim with which Huldah was received by the Latrobe crowd. All the gayety of the room seemed to eddy and swirl about the group.

Connie laid aside her coat and sat up very prim and straight in her chair, holding the menu card tightly with cold fingers. It was absurd, she told herself, to feel so bitterly disappointed. But she had looked forward to it so! And seventy-five cents was such an *awful* price to pay for a dinner you weren't going to enjoy.

She sat facing the dining-room entrance and the lobby, so she saw him as he crossed from the elevator to the desk. He was handed a letter which he opened carelessly and read as though letters were common and casual occurrences. He straightened then, putting the envelope in his pocket, and walked toward the dining room. And even as she looked at him, Connie felt a warmth creep over her, as though all the blood in her body had been heated by strange wine. She saw him speak to the head waiter and then come slowly toward the table, his eyes upon her. Connie meant to drop her own, but she could not. So they watched each other with a kind of grave amazement as though they had neither asked nor expected this of life, while he approached and bowed beside his chair.

"I hope you don't mind," he said slowly. "I usually sit here with my uncle, but he's dining with some school men tonight."

"Oh, I am the one who's intruding, really," Connie began as he seated himself. "My friend, Huldah Henderson, and I came late, and this was the only arrangement the head waiter could make. Huldah is over at the center table."

"I suppose I should offer to change places with her at once," the young man said slowly, while Connie's heart missed a beat. "But I'm not going to. You see—it might make too much trouble for our friend the head waiter. And I have suddenly the warmest feeling for him."

And then they both laughed, his gray eyes holding her dark ones strongly to him as though in an embrace.

He happened to be in Greensburg because his uncle, Dr. Warre, was one of the Institute lecturers and was, in fact, the speaker that night. He hadn't been well, so the family hadn't wanted him to come alone. His own name was Ian Donaldson, and he was in his second year at Union Theological. His parents, both dead, had been Scotch, and he himself had been born in Edinburgh but had lived in this country with his uncle since he was twelve.

Connie introduced herself, but the mere particulars of birth and residence were brushed quickly aside. What did it matter who they were or where they had lived? The miracle was that they were here together now, with but the tiny stretch of white cloth between them; hands almost touching, eyes demanding their fill, and then dropping again before the mystery of a revealed and alluring personality.

There was no end to what they found to say to each other. They were deep in Browning when Huldah and her red-haired admirer stopped at the table, Huldah's eyebrows raised in a huge interrogation.

"It's just about time to go, Connie. We can wait

Greensburg railroad station, 1913.

119

in the lobby for you—"

Ian had risen, showing suddenly by comparison how tall he was. He acknowledged the introductions easily, then turned again quickly to Connie.

"May I not take you up to the lecture when we've finished dinner? I should go to it myself, you know. Can't I get some tickets at the door?"

Connie murmured an assent, her cheeks warm under Huldah's interested scrutiny. Then the other two passed on, and she and Ian were once more alone, leaning near across the small table, absorbed again in Browning and in the fresh delights of their own minds.

"Do you know 'A Grammarian's Funeral'?" Ian asked eagerly.

"Oh, yes! I love it!"

"There's meat in that. I keep thinking of the old chap pegging away at his Greek particles even when he was dead from the waist down, sure he'd get a chance to finish up the job and do all the other things he hadn't had time for here."

"I know," Connie answered. " 'Leave Now for dogs and apes, Man has Forever.' "

"That's it! The long look ahead. Doesn't it change things, though? Staking neck or nothing on a life to come! Keeps us from being too fussy over affairs here, I guess."

Then he broke off. Connie's face was shining with what Jeannie would have called her "alabaster lamp look"—a delicate radiance of the spirit. Ian lowered his eyes.

"Forever," he said slowly, as though the idea had taken on a new significance. "I like that word—*forever*."

They were the last to leave the dining room. When Connie brought forth her precious seventy-five cents, Ian demurred earnestly.

"No, please! I want you to be my guest tonight. I won't consider anything else. *Please!*"

Connie watched with admiration the easy, accustomed way in which he paid the bill, left the tip, which she would never have thought of, and then waved the waiter quite definitely aside so that he himself could help her on with her coat. And for the first time her heart bitterly rebelled against a lining that was not silk!

"Will you wait in the lobby till I get my coat and hat?" he asked.

In a few minutes they were out in the frosty air, walking slowly up the long hill. If it had been sweet to face each other across the small table, it was doubly so to be out alone in the darkness, his arm guiding her. They talked on earnestly like old friends who had an absence of many years to bridge quickly. She told him then of Jeannie. It seemed natural to speak of her under the stars. She spoke of Uncle David, and the coal under the old farm, which now had a chance of selling.

Ian was interested in it all, but as they neared the high school building he grew silent.

"We're taking the midnight train back east," he said soberly. "I can't quite express what this evening has been to me. May I write to you, Miss Richards?"

"Oh, I'd like you to," Connie answered quickly.

"And you'll be sure to answer?"

"I promise."

Late that night in their high walnut bed the two girls lay talking. Huldah had had, according to her lights, a great evening. . . . "Wasn't the hotel dinner *grand?*"

And Connie with a queer realization of the significance of the confession, whispered back, "I don't know one thing I ate!"

Huldah pondered this unfathomable mystery till sleep finally overtook her.

120

WILLIAM ATTAWAY
"Crazy-Mad Steel"

Smothers narrates a lost wager
at the rolling tables

Time: 1919

Setting: Mon Valley

Set in an unnamed Monongahela mill town (a good guess might be Donora), Blood on the Forge is a novel told from the workers' point of view, specifically through the experiences of three Black brothers (Chinatown, Melody, and Big Mat) who have migrated from rural Kentucky to work in the mills. This selection, climaxed by the soliloquy of the half-crazed Smothers, another Black from the South, registers the laborers' mixed attitudes toward the awesome machines and hot metal they must confront daily — the sense of challenge, energy, exhilaration, the exhaustion and nightmare terror: "Steel want to git you." Elsewhere in the novel Attaway develops more fully the feeling of "unnaturalness" about steel work, especially for men whose work had originally been tilling the soil. Again the voice is Smothers':

"It's wrong to tear up the ground and melt it up in the furnace. Ground don't like it. It's the hell-and-devil kind of work. Guy ain't satisfied with usin' the stuff that was put here for him to use—stuff on top of the earth. Now he got to git busy and melt up the ground itself. Ground don't like it, I tells you. . . . Listen close now, an' I'm goin' to talk to you so you know something. Steel want to git you. Onliest thing—it ain't gittin' you fast enough."

As a whole, Blood on the Forge *is about the culture shock experienced by people abruptly moved from one environment to another (the three brothers were shipped from Kentucky to the Mon*

*Valley in closed boxcars as steel companies tried to undercut the unions with a supply of cheap labor). If the sheer spectacle of steel-making boggles the mind of the new immigrant, so too does the whole daily environment. The twelve-hour shifts, with twenty-four straight hours every other Sunday, the bunkhouse and shanty slums, the necessary escapes with whiskey and prostitutes — all make civilized life nearly impossible. Even the idea of unionizing (*Blood on the Forge *ends with the violence of the 1919 organizing strike) is beyond the brothers' comprehension. Attaway shows that the pressured circumstances of their lives make them incapable of understanding the issues, choosing a side intelligently, or imagining any form of collective action. For Big Mat, Chinatown, and Melody, the task at hand is not choosing political strategies, but simply staying sane (and by the book's end, only one has really been able to do that).*

Born in Mississippi in 1912, William Attaway moved to Chicago with his family while still a child, went through school there, and got a B.A. from the University of Illinois. His list of published fiction is not long — one other novel, Let Me Breathe Thunder *(1939). Perhaps discouraged by the scant recognition given his work, Attaway turned to writing radio and TV scripts as a career.*

"Crazy-Mad Steel"

Chinatown should have been feeling good that morning. The world had swung back to a familiar pattern. Melody was on his way to get Big Mat out of the jailhouse. He was going to hold down a job at the blast furnaces until Melody was ready to take over. It was like old times—the Moss boys working like a family should work. But there was something wrong that morning. The wrong was not in him—it was in the air about him.

Smothers hobbled at his heels on the way to the mills. He didn't say why he wanted Chinatown's company. Neither of them had anything to say. Both men marked the strangeness of that. They were two whose mouths had always been full of talk.

Once or twice, from the corners of his slant eyes, Chinatown caught Smothers' face. It was a face full of random movement. The corners of the lips were hard and soft in turn; the eyes were big, to show white around the balls, looking inward; the thin nose flared wide at its base, searching the wind.

But Chinatown was glad for Smothers to keep shut. There was his own self to search. He was walking along, feeling like a spring coiled on a hair trigger. He didn't exactly know—his body just felt as if something were going to happen. His body was getting ready for something.

Only once before could he remember feeling like that. A long time ago, down in Kentucky. To get away from what looked like a cottonmouth snake he had dived through a thick bush. He had not known what was on the other side. It seemed a year to think in while he was sailing through that bush. But his mind couldn't tell him anything. It was his body that had talked, had warned him that he was going to land hard. And, sure enough, he had landed in a trap of broken slate. He had broken a leg that time.

Now his body was flashing that same warning, telling him that he was going to land hard.

An icy shiver passed through him when Smothers spoke.

"Keep a sharp lookout! Look sharp, ever'body!"

"How come? How come?" he asked, but he knew.

"I got grief in my bones."

Smothers was in dead earnest. The quake in his voice sent another shiver through Chinatown.

A distance from the mills all sounds softened into one another; up close every sound had its own history. Through the roar of the Bessemers the ear-splitting cries from the plate mills began with a whine and ended in a strangled rasp. Engines panted and struggled with the rails. The ore boats along the river kept up their own noises. Each tin house had its own pulse. And above everything an organ of whistles sighed and bellowed.

These things had not come to be commonplace to Chinatown. The mills would never be his home. His gold tooth was still a token, keeping his mind south of the Mason-Dixon line.

They checked in together. On all sides men were headed for their jobs—not running but, to Chinatown's eyes, making great speed. He had that same feeling of haste when he started for the blast furnaces. To him life in the mills was stepped up. Inside he ran more slowly.

When he passed the open hearth he kept his eyes open for old friends. He could see one of the gangs working like crazy men to draw the heat before turning the furnaces over to the new crew. Now and again, through openings underneath the hearth, he glimpsed the pit men, swinging to get the last cleanup over and done with. A man called out to him from a tin shack. The voice sounded high and off key. But things were different that morning. He was hearing and seeing in fine detail, as a man does in the awareness of danger.

Smothers had separated himself from Chinatown but now he came hobbling back. He pointed toward the blast furnaces.

"Trouble," was what he said.

A little knot of men stood in the yard around one of the blast furnaces. They were hand-rolling cigarettes and chewing cut plug as though this were quitting time instead of the starting hour for the long shift.

Chinatown saw Bo at the water trough. He trotted toward him. Smothers swung along on his sticks.

"What the hell!" hollered Chinatown. "You guys ain't gittin' ready?"

"How many is dead ones?" panted Smothers.

Bo did not glance up. He bit off some rope tobacco. He spoke through the juice when they were close enough for him not to have to raise his voice.

"They jest got a special crew. Tryin' to git that Goddamn number four ready."

One of the Irishmen in Bo's gang came toward them.

"This here rest don't make me mad." He grinned.

"Startin' in is always bad," said the other Irishman. "I can do a shift one handed after I get heated up."

"This here number four a jinx," growled Bo. "I tell you it's a jinx. Yesterday Melody gits hurt. They work all night on it, and now the water cooler burn out. No sooner they git that fixed than the damn thing begin to freeze up. Look like for a while she's goin' up. Took a lot of guys off the other crews. Put everybody behind."

Another of the gang heard what was being said —the Italian stove tender.

"Sure as my name John—sure as pope—sure as anything—furnace gotta devil in him."

"It don't do no good to jest line and half ass fix around a cold blast," argued Bo. "I tell you that a long time ago."

"You sure said so." The hayseed nodded.

Smothers had been trying to get in a word, but the men didn't want to hear his raving. They kept shifting to keep him from latching onto a group. Finally he stopped and cast his eye around to catch every man within hearing distance.

"Ever'body better be on the lookout. Steel liable to git somebody today. I got a deep feelin' in my bones."

Bo hollered, "Maybe steel gonna git you, Smothers."

Smothers was glad of someone to take notice. He hobbled up to Bo.

"It gonna git somebody. I know it's got to git somebody."

Bo laughed. "Well, if it's you, Smothers, we make you up into watch fobs. The boys round the bunkhouse'll wear you across their vests for luck."

Chinatown knew what Smothers was feeling. His body was flashing that same warning right along.

He said, "You say yourself there a jinx, Bo.

Could be, 'cause I been feelin' somethin' ever since I started out this mornin'.''

John, the stove tender, crossed himself and muttered in his own tongue.

One of the Irishmen laughed. "You ain't super-stitious, eh, John?"

"Not me," said John. "I ain't believe nothin'."

"Then what was you sayin' to yourself?"

"Oh, that ain't nothin'." John grinned. "Just old prayer. Lotsa times fella wrong. Better be on safe side."

Smothers broke in, "There ain't no safe side."

The Irishmen laughed.

Smothers grabbed Chinatown by the arm.

"You ain't a bad guy, Chinatown. You know old Smothers talkin' sense."

"Sure, sure," Chinatown tried to pull away.

"Ever'body laugh when I tell 'em what I know," said Smothers.

Chinatown was embarrassed. He pulled away.

"They jest laugh 'cause they scared, I bet." And he laughed.

Smothers grabbed again. He caught the hayseed. The man shoved his shirt back into his pants.

"I know steel and ever'thin' talk to you," he said, "but it's tellin' you wrong when it tells you to tear up my clothes."

Smothers clawed at him.

"Somebody got to believe me. Steel gonna git somebody."

"Shut up, you crazy fool!" hollered the hay-seed. The freckles grew dead white against his flushed face. He whirled on the other men. "Whyn't somebody make this Goddamned nut keep quiet?"

He barely managed to duck from the path of the stick Smothers swung at him. The men laughed.

For an instant the hayseed wavered between anger and the laughter of the men. Then he grinned. Before Smothers could move the hayseed had snatched both of his sticks. Laughing, he held the

125

sticks up for everyone to see.

Smothers started forward. But his legs could not hold up. Spitting curses, he fell to the ground. That made the young hayseed almost split with laughing. Then he stopped his noise. With an innocent gesture he made as though to stop the game. He held the sticks out to the crippled man. Smothers grabbed. The sticks were again drawn out of reach.

That kept up—Smothers dragging himself over the ground toward the sticks, every few feet falling forward on his elbows when he tried to grab.

The men were laughing.

Chinatown recalled Smothers' strange dignity. He did not like to see him in the dirt.

"Sure is a shame to plague a cripple that-a-way," he said to Bo.

"Heard somethin' today," said Bo.

"Aw, make them cut it out!" insisted Chinatown.

"Fella was tellin' me 'bout what happen to a gold tooth in the war."

"Somebody ought to stop it."

"Fella said that after a fight some guys would go over the stiffs with pliers and pull all the gold out'n their heads."

"Damn!" said Chinatown.

"Yeah," said Bo. "Get so the colored boys would pull out their gold ones and throw them away. Ascared of bein' shot in the back."

"Damn!"

Bo's eyes wandered to Smothers.

"If I said anything they think I stickin' up for Smothers jest 'cause he's colored."

"Glad I wasn't in the war," breathed Chinatown.

Bo said, "Naw, I can't mix in. Only one in the mill with micks under him."

The hayseed had gotten tired of pestering. He tossed the sticks into the water trough. Cursing,

Smothers began a slow journey toward the trough.

One Irishman said, "Maybe that'll learn that Smothers not to be a wild man."

The words spurred Smothers. In a convulsion of movement he reached his goal and got his sticks under his armpits. Then he turned toward the men, and his voice went into a scream.

"None of you fellas knows why you's runnin' wild when before you come here you was tame. Ain't none of you got no idea. But I know."

A few men came out of the furnace house to see what was going on. They stood grinning with the rest. The Irishmen laughed outright.

"Listen, and I tell you so you'll know somethin'," screamed Smothers. "I tell you 'bout a fella who been around here a long time. Once he's one of the best catchers they ever put on a roll table. But that's once upon a time. Now he ain't nothin' but a old cripple-leg timekeeper. The boss men jest job him around 'cause they kind of sorry for him. Don't think he don't know that.

"He work a farm down in Texas for a hell of a time before he ever see a rollin' mill. Then he don't really know how he ever got in this here valley. It's jest that one day he find hisself the best catcher along the river. There plenty of frogskins in his pocket, and them greenbacks buy more corn whisky than he kin drink. He kin sleep with women that he git lynched for jest lookin' at back in Texas. So what he do then? He go crazy. He try to make all the money, screw all the gals and drink all the corn whisky in the valley. And one day that same corn tell him he's big as God A-mighty. It's the heat of the steel makin' that corn boil inside him, and he vow to walk the roll tables from one end of the mill to the other. And half the rollers bet he kin, and half bet he can't. There's two

127

thousand dollars say he will and he won't.

"Them roll tables takin' steel full speed, and his corn whisky walks him halfway down the line and leaves him there on his own."

No man was laughing now. They all leaned forward. With this madman they were walking half the length of a big roll table, dodging white-hot steel shuttling full speed across and between the crushing rollers. Men forgot to spit their tobacco, and spit-rolled smokes burned right down to cracked lips.

Smothers was still talking. "I said his corn whisky leave him there, and he ain't able to go on under his own steam. The heat saps him all of a sudden, and his legs give out. Some fellas run to shut off the power, but he's crawlin' on his hands and knees, tryin' like hell to git over the side of that table. He almost make it, too—woulda made it if the fella who was s'posed to stop the table hadn't got fussed and, instead of stoppin' the table, reversed it—reversed it and sent a hot bar 'cross that table-walker's legs."

One of the listeners started a soft chant that was like little explosions in among Smothers' words.

"Goddamn . . . Goddamn . . . Goddamn . . ." went the chant.

"There wasn't no pain," screamed Smothers. "There wasn't nothin' but the steel all over the mill, yellin' an' laughin' fit to kill. Roll steel git him . . . roll steel git him. . . . Yellin' an' laughin'."

Smothers' voice went up into a song. "It was *me* the roll steel git! It was *me!*" Then the high voice slid down the scale to its regular whine, and misery dropped over his face. And that made it as though those steel voices were still yelling and laughing in his ears: *Roll steel git him . . . roll steel git him. . . .*

"All the time in the hospital I kin hear that steel talkin'," said Smothers. "I kin hear that steel laughin' an' talkin' till it fit to bust my head clean open. But I git well. Steel didn't git me that time like it think. I come on back to the mill on two sticks. They give me a job where I can set down most of the time. But, settin' or standin', I kin hear when cold steel whisper all the time and hot roll steel scream like hell. *It's a sin to melt up the ground,* is what steel say. *It's a sin.* Steel bound to git ever'body 'cause o' that sin. They say I crazy, but mills gone crazy 'cause men bringin' trainloads of ground in here and meltin' it up.

"So when I git so I kin hear what steel is sayin' I know jest why I go wild and git drunk and try to walk the roll table. I know why all you guys runnin' wild and goin' crazy of a Monday. It's that crazy-mad steel whisperin' and yellin' all the time, makin' men crazy-mad too."

The men did not say anything. When they went in to work they were still silent. Hours passed before anyone had a word for the shamed hayseed.

The Italian crossed himself again and was not questioned.

That night, when a break came in the long shift, Chinatown walked out of the blast house. He saw the pointed stars of fire along the edge of the Monongahela. He looked up in the sky at the points of fire so much like those along the river. He took his last look at all of these. And he remembered Smothers' words to the green men: "Somethin' dropped right out the sky, blazin' down, lightin' up this old river in the dead of night." A warning out of the sky. That was strange—iron dropping out of the sky. Maybe it was a sin to melt up the ground. He didn't know. He felt now as he had felt before—lost and full of great changing fears that he didn't understand.

JOHN DOS PASSOS
"Very Young and Very Sweet"

Mary French finds a job
with the Amalgamated Workers

Time: 1919   Setting: Pittsburgh

This selection focuses on the labor violence of 1919, when after a generation of union quiescence (since the 1892 Homestead strike) the steelworkers again struck in an effort to have their union recognized. Just as the earlier strike is recalled in the shorthand of popular memory by one episode — the riverfront confrontation with the Pinkertons — so the events of 1919 have come to be summed up in a single violent image — the "Cossacks," the mounted police hired to "keep order" in the mill towns. Both Thomas Bell in Out of This Furnace *and William Attaway in* Blood on the Forge *present versions of the 1919 strike (though the novels are represented in this anthology by other segments of their action). Here the events of 1919 are seen from the point of view of a young woman, Mary French, who stays in Pittsburgh for a few months while traveling across the country looking for a job with political and social significance.*

Mary French is very much an example of a young person seeking a "cause." Her background is middle class — her father was a doctor and she has attended Vassar. But her father set an idealistic and humanitarian example, devoting his Colorado practice to miners and migrant workers. Clearly Mary has adopted her father's values. She has dropped out of college because it seems too remote from real life and has even decided that social work at Chicago's Hull House is too genteel. By the time she arrives in Pittsburgh, she is ready to plunge into political action on the side of the workers.

The Big Money *is the third novel in Dos Passos' famous trilogy,* U.S.A., *a massive work that runs to some fifteen hundred pages and gives Dos Passos' version of the American experience from about 1900 to 1930. Even though this selection is neces-*

sarily a very small sample of the whole, it seems representative. For one thing, there is the distinctive style with its flat, relentless quality that never pauses for dramatic flourishes. If the medium is the message, this style seems to say, "These are the facts, this is the way it was; and no one had the power or wisdom to change events for the better." At the narrative level, the effect is a gritty realism — as though a black-and-white movie camera follows the characters around.

Like the style, the characters too, even glimpsed in a brief passage, seem doomed to a sort of perpetual motion. Mary French's career has already moved her from Colorado to Poughkeepsie to Chicago to Cleveland to Pittsburgh, and it is about to move her back to the East Coast. The other major characters in The Big Money *are also in motion: Charley Anderson moves between Minnesota, New York, Europe, and Florida; Margo Dowling, from New York to the Caribbean to Hollywood. All of this transcontinental motion in* U.S.A. *seems to argue that the famous mobility of Americans is actually random and pointless, a search for success that can never be ended because Americans do not put down roots long enough to master circumstances.*

John Dos Passos (1896-1970) can be bracketed with the likes of Ernest Hemingway, William Faulkner, Willa Cather, and Eugene O'Neill in a generation of major American writers that did much of its significant work during the 1920s and 30s. In The 42nd Parallel, *the first novel of the trilogy, Dos Passos also develops a Pittsburgh subject — J. Ward Moorehouse, PR man for Pittsburgh industry.*

"Very Young and Very Sweet"

For several weeks the announcement of a lecture had caught Mary French's eye as she hurried past the bulletinboard at Hull House: "May 15 G. H. Barrow, Europe: Problems of Postwar Reconstruction." The name teased her memory, but it wasn't until she actually saw him come into the lecturehall that she remembered that he was the nice skinny red-faced lecturer who talked about how it was the workingclass that would keep the country out of war at Vassar that winter. It was the same sincere hesitant voice with a little stutter in the beginning of the sentences sometimes, the same informal way of stalking up and down the lecturehall and sitting on the table beside the waterpitcher with his legs crossed. At the reception afterwards she didn't let on that she'd met him before. When they were introduced she was happy to be able to give him some information he wanted about the chances exsoldiers had of finding jobs in the Chicago area. Next morning Mary French was all of a fluster when she was called to the phone and there was Mr. Barrow's voice asking her if she could spare him an hour that afternoon as he'd been asked by Washington to get some unofficial information for a certain bureau. "You see, I thought you would be able to give me the real truth because you are in daily contact with the actual people." She said she'd be delighted and he said would she meet him in the lobby of the Auditorium at five.

At four she was up in her room curling her hair, wondering what dress to wear, trying to decide whether she'd go without her glasses or not. Mr. Barrow was so nice.

They had such an interesting talk about the employment situation which was not at all a bright picture and when Mr. Barrow asked her to go to supper with him at a little Italian place he knew in the Loop, she found herself saying yes without a quiver in spite of the fact that she hadn't been out to dinner with a man since she left Colorado Springs after her father's death three years ago. She felt somehow that she'd known Mr. Barrow for years.

Still she was a bit surprised at the toughlooking place with sawdust on the floor he took her to, and that they sold liquor there and that he seemed to expect her to drink a cocktail. He drank several cocktails himself and ordered red wine. She turned down the cocktails, but did sip a little of the wine not to seem too oldfashioned. "I admit," he said, "that I'm reaching the age where I have to have a drink to clear the work out of my head and let me relax. . . . That was the great thing about the other side . . . having wine with your meals. . . . They really understand the art of life over there."

After they'd had their spumoni Mr. Barrow ordered himself brandy and she drank the bitter black coffee and they sat in the stuffy noisy restaurant, smelly of garlic and sour wine and tomatosauce and sawdust, and forgot the time and talked. She said she'd taken up socialservice work to be in touch with something real, but now she was beginning to feel coopedup and so institutional that she often wondered if she wouldn't have done better to join the Red Cross overseas or the Friends Reconstruction Unit as so many of the girls had, but she so hated war that she didn't want to do

131

anything to help even in the most peaceful way. If she'd been a man she would have been a C.O., she knew that.

Mr. Barrow frowned and cleared his throat: "Of course I suppose they were sincere, but they were very much mistaken and probably deserved what they got."

"Do you still think so?"

"Yes, dear girl, I do.... Now we can ask for anything; nobody can refuse us, wages, the closed shop, the eighthour day. But it was hard differing with old friends ... my attitude was much misunderstood in certain quarters...."

"But you can't think it's right to give them these dreadful jail sentences."

"That's just to scare the others.... You'll see they'll be getting out as soon as the excitement quiets down.... Debs's pardon is expected any day."

"I should hope so," said Mary.

"Poor Debs," said Mr. Barrow, "one mistake has destroyed the work of a lifetime, but he has a great heart, the greatest heart in the world." Then he went on to tell her about how he'd been a railroadman himself in the old days, a freight agent in South Chicago; they'd made him the business agent of his local and he had worked for the Brotherhood, he'd had a hard time getting an education and suddenly he'd waked up, when he was more than thirty, in New York City writing a set of articles for the *Evening Globe,* to the fact that there was no woman in his life and that he knew nothing of the art of life and the sort of thing that seemed to come natural to them over there and to the Mexicans now. He'd married unwisely and gotten into trouble with a chorusgirl, and a woman had made his life a hell for five years, but now that

he'd broken away from all that, he found himself lonely getting old wanting something more substantial than the little pickups a man traveling on missions to Mexico and Italy and France and England, little international incidents, he called them with a thinlipped grin, that were nice affairs enough at the time but were just dust and ashes. Of course he didn't believe in bourgeois morality, but he wanted understanding and passionate friendship in a woman.

When he talked he showed the tip of his tongue sometimes through the broad gap in the middle of his upper teeth. She could see in his eyes how much he had suffered. "Of course I don't believe in conventional marriage either," said Mary. Then Mr. Barrow broke out that she was so fresh so young so eager so lovely so what he needed in his life and his speech began to get a little thick and she guessed it was time she was getting back to Hull House because she had to get up so early. When he took her home in a taxi, she sat in the furthest corner of the seat, but he was very gentlemanly, although he did seem to stagger a little when they said goodnight.

After that supper the work at Hull House got to be more and more of a chore, particularly as George Barrow, who was making a lecturetour all over the country in defense of the President's policies, wrote her several times a week. She wrote him funny letters back, kidding about the oldmaids at Hull House and saying that she felt it in her bones that she was going to graduate from there soon, the way she had from Vassar. Her friends at Hull House began to say how pretty she was getting to look now that she was curling her hair.

For her vacation that June Mary French had been planning to go up to Michigan with the Cohns, but when the time came she decided she really must make a break; so instead she took the *Northland* around to Cleveland and got herself a job as countergirl in the Eureka Cafeteria on Lakeside Avenue near the depot.

It was pretty tough. The manager was a fat Greek who pinched the girls' bottoms when he passed behind them along the counter. The girls used rouge and lipstick and were mean to Mary, giggling in corners about their dates or making dirty jokes with the busboys. At night she had shooting pains in her insteps from being so long on her feet and her head spun from the faces the asking mouths the probing eyes jerking along in the rush hours in front of her like beads on a string. Back in the rattly brass bed in the big yellowbrick roominghouse a girl she talked to on her boat had sent her to, she couldn't sleep or get the smell of cold grease and dishwashing out of her nose; she lay there scared and lonely listening to the other roomers stirring behind the thin partitions, tramping to the bathroom, slamming doors in the hall.

After she'd worked two weeks at the cafeteria, she decided she couldn't stand it another minute, so she gave up the job and went and got herself a room at the uptown Y.W.C.A. where they were very nice to her when they heard she'd come from Hull House and showed her a list of socialservice jobs she might want to try for, but she said No, she had to do real work in industry for once, and took the train to Pittsburgh where she knew a girl who was an assistant librarian at Carnegie Institute.

She got into Pittsburgh late on a summer afternoon. Crossing the bridge she had a glimpse of the level sunlight blooming pink and orange on a confusion of metalcolored smokes that jetted from a wilderness of chimneys ranked about the huge corrugatediron and girderwork structures along the riverbank. Then right away she was getting out of the daycoach into the brownish dark gloom of the station with her suitcase cutting into her hand. She called up her friend from a dirty phonebooth that smelled of cigarsmoke.

"Mary French, how lovely!" came Lois Speyer's comical burbling voice. "I'll get you a room right here at Mrs. Gansemeyer's, come on out to supper. It's a boardinghouse. Just wait till you see it.... But I just can't imagine anybody coming to Pittsburgh for their vacation."

Mary found herself getting red and nervous right there in the phonebooth. "I wanted to see something different from the socialworker angle."

"Well, it's so nice the idea of having somebody to talk to that I hope it doesn't mean you've lost your mind . . . you know they don't employ Vassar graduates in the openhearth furnaces."

"I'm not a Vassar graduate," Mary French shouted into the receiver, feeling the near tears stinging her eyes. "I'm just like any other workinggirl. . . . You ought to have seen me working in that cafeteria in Cleveland."

"Well, come on out, Mary darling, I'll save some supper for you."

It was a long ride out on the streetcar. Pittsburgh was grim all right.

Next day she went around to the employment offices of several of the steelcompanies. When she said she'd been a socialworker, they looked at her awful funny. Nothing doing; not taking on clerical or secretarial workers now. She spent days with the newspapers answering helpwanted ads.

Lois Speyer certainly laughed in that longfaced sarcastic way she had when Mary had to take a reporting job that Lois had gotten her because Lois knew the girl who wrote the society column on the

John Dos Passos

Times-Sentinel.

As the Pittsburgh summer dragged into August, hot and choky with coalgas and the strangling fumes from blastfurnaces, bloomingmills, rollingmills that clogged the smoky Y where the narrow rivervalleys came together, there began to be talk around the office about how red agitators had gotten into the mills. A certain Mr. Gorman, said to be one of the head operatives for the Sherman Service, was often seen smoking a cigar in the managingeditor's office. The paper began to fill up with news of alien riots and Russian Bolshevists and the nationalization of women and the defeat of Lenin and Trotzky.

Then one afternoon in early September Mr. Healy called Mary French into his private office and asked her to sit down. When he went over and closed the door tight, Mary thought for a second he was going to make indecent proposals to her, but instead he said in his most tired fatherly manner: "Now, Miss French, I have an assignment for you that I don't want you to take unless you really want to. I've got a daughter myself, and I hope when she grows up she'll be a nice simple wellbroughtup girl like you are. So honestly if I thought it was demeaning I wouldn't ask you to do it . . . you know that. We're strictly the family newspaper . . . we let the other fellers pull the rough stuff. . . . You know an item never goes through my desk that I don't think of my own wife and daughters; how would I like to have them read it."

Ted Healy was a large round blackhaired man with a rolling gray eye like a codfish's eye.

"What's the story, Mr. Healy?" asked Mary briskly; she'd made up her mind it must be something about the whiteslave traffic.

"Well, these damned agitators, you know they're trying to start a strike. . . . Well, they've opened a publicity office downtown. I'm scared to send one of the boys down . . . might get into some trouble with those gorillas. . . . I don't want a dead reporter on my front page. . . . But sending you down. . . . You know you're not working for a paper, you're a socialservice worker, want to get both sides of the story. . . . A sweet innocentlooking girl can't possibly come to any harm. . . . Well, I want to get the lowdown on the people working there . . . what part of Russia they were born in, how they got into this country in the first place . . . where the money comes from . . . prisonrecords, you know. . . . Get all the dope you can. It'll make a magnificent Sunday feature."

"I'm very much interested in industrial relations . . . it's a wonderful assignment. . . . But, Mr. Healy, aren't conditions pretty bad in the mills?"

Mr. Healy jumped to his feet and began striding up and down the office. "I've got all the dope on that. . . . Those damn guineas are making more money than they ever made in their lives, they buy stocks, they buy washingmachines and silk stockings for their women and they send money back to the old folks. While our boys were risking their lives in the trenches, they held down all the good jobs and most of 'em are enemy aliens at that. Those guineas are welloff, don't you forget it. The one thing they can't buy is brains. That's how those agitators get at 'em. They talk their language and fill 'em up with a lot of notions about how all they need to do is stop working and they can take possession of this country that we've built up into the greatest country in the world. . . . I don't hold it against the poor devils of guineas, they're just ignorant; but those reds who accept the hospitality

of our country and then go around spreading their devilish propaganda . . . My God, if they were sincere I could forgive 'em, but they're just in it for the money like anybody else. We have absolute proof that they're paid by Russian reds with money and jewels they've stole over there; and they're not content with that, they go around shaking down those poor ignorant guineas . . . Well, all I can say is shooting's too good for 'em." Ted Healy was red in the face. A boy in a green eyeshade burst in with a big bunch of flimsy.

Mary French got to her feet. "I'll get right after it, Mr. Healy," she said.

She got off the car at the wrong corner and stumbled up the uneven pavement of a steep broad cobbled street of little gimcrack stores poolrooms barbershops and Italian spaghettiparlors. A gusty wind whirled dust and excelsior and old papers. Outside an unpainted doorway foreignlooking men stood talking in low voices in knots of three or four. Before she could get up her nerve to go up the long steep dirty narrow stairs, she looked for a minute into the photographer's window below at the tinted enlargements of babies with toopink cheeks and the family groups and the ramrodstiff bridal couples. Upstairs she paused in the littered hall. From offices on both sides came a sound of typing and arguing voices.

In the dark she ran into a young man. "Hello," he said in a gruff voice she liked, "are you the lady from New York?"

"Not exactly. I'm from Colorado."

"There was a lady from New York comin' to help us with some publicity. I thought maybe you was her."

"That's just what I came for."

"Come in, I'm just Gus Moscowski. I'm kinder the officeboy." He opened one of the closed doors for her into a small dusty office piled with stacked-up papers and filled up with a large table covered with clippings at which two young men in glasses sat in their shirtsleeves. "Here are the regular guys." All the time she was talking to the others she couldn't keep her eyes off him. He had blond closecropped hair and very blue eyes and a big bearcub look in his cheap serge suit shiny at the elbows and knees. The young men answered her questions so politely that she couldn't help telling them she was trying to do a feature story for the *Times-Sentinel.* They laughed their heads off.

"But Mr. Healy said he wanted a fair well-rounded picture. He just thinks the men are being

misled." Mary found herself laughing too.

"Gus," said the older man, "you take this young lady around and show her some of the sights. . . . After all, Ted Healy may have lost his mind. First here's what Ted Healy's friends did to Fanny Sellers."

She couldn't look at the photograph that he poked under her nose. "What had she done?"

"Tried to organize the workingclass; that's the worst crime you can commit in this man's country."

It was a relief to be out on the street again, hurrying along while Gus Moscowski shambled grinning beside her. "Well, I guess I'd better take you first to see how folks live on fortytwo cents an hour. Too bad you can't talk Polish. I'm a Polack myself."

"You must have been born in this country."

"Sure, highschool graduate. If I can get the dough I want to take engineering at Carnegie Tech. . . . I dunno why I string along with these damn Polacks." He looked her straight in the face and grinned when he said that.

She smiled back at him. "I understand why," she said.

He made a gesture with his elbow as they turned a corner past a group of ragged kids making mudpies; they were pale flabby filthy little kids with pouches under their eyes. Mary turned her eyes away, but she'd seen them, as she'd seen the photograph of the dead woman with her head caved in.

"Git an eyeful of cesspool alley the land of opportunity," Gus Moscowski said way down in his throat.

That night when she got off the streetcar at the corner nearest Mrs. Gansemeyer's, her legs were trembling and the small of her back ached. She went right up to her room and hurried into bed. She was too tired to eat or to sit up listening to Lois Speyer's line of sarcastic gossip. She couldn't sleep. She lay in her sagging bed listening to the voices of the boarders rocking on the porch below and to the hooting of engines and the clank of shunted freightcars down in the valley, seeing again the shapeless broken shoes and the worn hands folded over dirty aprons and the sharp anxious beadiness of women's eyes, feeling the quake underfoot of the crazy stairways zigzagging up and down the hills black and bare as slagpiles where the steelworkers lived in jumbled shanties and big black rows of smokegnawed clapboarded houses, in her nose the stench of cranky backhouses and kitchens with cabbage cooking and clothes boiling and unwashed children and drying diapers. She slept by fits and starts, and would wake up with Gus Moscowski's warm tough voice in her head, and her whole body tingling with the hard fuzzy bearcub feel of him when his arm brushed against her arm or he put out his big hand to steady her at a place where the boardwalk had broken through and she'd started to slip in the loose shaly slide underneath. When she fell solidly asleep she went on dreaming about him. She woke up early feeling happy because she was going to meet him again right after breakfast.

That afternoon she went back to the office to write the piece. Just the way Ted Healy had said, she put in all she could find out about the boys running the publicity bureau. The nearest to Russia any of them came from was Canarsie, Long Island. She tried to get in both sides of the question, even called them "possibly misguided."

About a minute after she'd sent it in to the Sunday editor, she was called to the city desk. Ted

Healy had on a green eyeshade and was bent over a swirl of galleys. Mary could see her copy on top of the pile of papers under his elbow. Somebody had scrawled across the top of it in red pencil: "Why wish this on me?"

"Well, young lady," he said, without looking up, "you've written a firstrate propaganda piece for the *Nation* or some other parlorpink sheet in New York, but what the devil do you think we can do with it? This is Pittsburgh." He got to his feet and held out his hand. "Goodbye, Miss French, I wish I had some way of using you because you're a mighty smart girl . . . and smart girl reporters are rare. . . . I've sent your slip to the cashier. . . ." Before Mary French could get her breath, she was out on the pavement with an extra week's salary in her pocketbook, which after all was pretty white of old Ted Healy.

That night Lois Speyer looked aghast when Mary told her she'd been fired, but when Mary told Lois that she'd gone down and gotten a job doing publicity for the Amalgamated, Lois burst into tears. "I said you'd lost your mind and it's true. . . . Either I'll have to move out of this boardinghouse or you will . . . and I won't be able to go around with you like I've been doing."

"How ridiculous, Lois."

"Darling, you don't know Pittsburgh. I don't care about those miserable strikers, but I absolutely have got to hold on to my job. . . . You know I just have to send money home. . . . Oh, we were just beginning to have such fun and now you have to go and spoil everything."

"If you'd seen what I've seen you'd talk differently," said Mary French coldly. They were never very good friends again after that.

Gus Moscowski found her a room with heavy lace curtains in the windows in the house of a Polish storekeeper who was a cousin of his father's. He escorted her solemnly back there from the office nights when they worked late, and they always did work late.

Mary French had never worked so hard in her life. She wrote releases, got up statistics on t.b., undernourishment of children, sanitary conditions, crime, took trips on interurban trolleys and slow locals to Rankin and Braddock and Homestead and Bessemer and as far as Youngstown and Steubenville and Gary, took notes on speeches of Foster and Fitzpatrick, saw meetings broken up and the troopers in their darkgray uniforms moving in a line down the unpaved alleys of company patches, beating up men and women with their clubs, kicking children out of their way, chasing old men off their front stoops. "And to think," said Gus of the troopers, "that the sonsabitches are lousy Polacks themselves most of 'em. Now ain't that just like a Polack?"

She interviewed metropolitan newspapermen, spent hours trying to wheedle A.P. and U.P. men into sending straight stories, smoothed out the grammar in the Englishlanguage leaflets. The fall flew by before she knew it. The Amalgamated could only pay the barest expenses, her clothes were in awful shape, there was no curl in her hair, at night she couldn't sleep for the memory of the things she'd seen, the jailings, the bloody heads, the wreck of some family's parlor, sofa cut open, chairs smashed, chinacloset hacked to pieces with an axe, after the troopers had been through looking for "literature." She hardly knew herself when she looked at her face in the greenspotted gilt-framed mirror over the washstand as she hurriedly dressed in the morning. She had a haggard desper-

139

ate look. She was beginning to look like a striker herself.

She hardly knew herself either when Gus's voice gave her cold shivers or when whether she felt good or not that day depended on how often he smiled when he spoke to her; it didn't seem like herself at all the way that, whenever her mind was free for a moment, she began to imagine him coming close to her, putting his arms around her, his lips his big hard hands. When that feeling came on, she would have to close her eyes and would feel herself dizzily reeling. Then she'd force her eyes open and fly at her typing and after a while would feel cool and clear again.

The day Mary French admitted to herself for the first time that the highpaid workers weren't coming out and that the lowpaid workers were going to lose their strike, she hardly dared look Gus in the face when he called for her to take her home. It was a muggy drizzly outofseason November night. As they walked along the street without saying anything, the fog suddenly glowed red in the direction of the mills.

"There they go," said Gus. The glow grew and grew, first pink then orange. Mary nodded and said nothing. "What can you do when the woikin'class won't stick together! Every kind of damn foreigner thinks the others is bums and the 'Mericans they think everybody's a bum 'cept you an' me. Wasn't so long ago we was all foreigners in this man's country. Christ, I dunno why I string along wid 'em."

"Gus, what would you do if we lost the strike? I mean you personally."

"I'll be on the black books all right. Means I couldn't get me another job in the metaltrades, not if I was the last guy on earth.... Hell, I dunno.

Take a false name an' join the Navy, I guess. They say a guy kin get a real good eddication in the Navy."

"I guess we oughtn't to talk about it.... Me, I don't know what I'll do."

"You kin go anywheres and git a job on a paper like you had.... I wish I had your schoolin'.... I bet you'll be glad to be quit of this bunch of hunkies."

"They are the workingclass, Gus."

"Sure, if we could only git more sense into our damn heads.... You know I've got an own brother scabbin' right to this day."

"He's probably worried about his wife and family."

"I'd worry him if I could git my hands on him.... A woikin'man ain't got no right to have a wife and family."

"He can have a girl...." Her voice failed. She felt her heart beating so hard as she walked along beside him over the uneven pavement she was afraid he'd hear it.

"Girls aplenty," Gus laughed. "They're free and easy, Polish girls are. That's one good thing."

"I wish..." Mary heard her voice saying.

"Well, goodnight. Rest good, you look all in." He'd given her a pat on the shoulder and he'd turned and gone off with his long shambling stride. She was at the door of her house. When she got in her room she threw herself on the bed and cried.

It was several weeks later that Gus Moscowski was arrested distributing leaflets in Braddock. She saw him brought up before the squire, in the dirty courtroom packed close with the gray uniforms of statetroopers, and sentenced to five years. His arm was in a sling and there was a scab of clotted blood on the towy stubble on the back of his head. His blue eyes caught hers in the crowd and he grinned and gave her a jaunty wave of a big hand.

"So that's how it is, is it?" snarled a voice beside her. "Well, you've had the last piece of c——k you get outa dat baby."

There was a hulking gray trooper on either side of her. They hustled her out of court and marched her down to the interurban trolleystop. She didn't say anything, but she couldn't keep back the tears. She hadn't known men could talk to women like that. "Come on now, loosen up, me an' Steve here we're twice the men . . . You ought to have better sense than to be spreadin' your legs for that punk."

At last the Pittsburgh trolley came and they put her on it with a warning that if they ever saw her around again they'd have her up for soliciting. As the car pulled out she saw them turn away slapping each other on the back and laughing. She sat there hunched up in the seat in the back of the car with her stomach churning and her face set. Back at the office all she said was that the cossacks had run her out of the courthouse.

When she heard that George Barrow was in town with the Senatorial Investigating Commission, she went to him at once. She waited for him in the lobby of the Schenley. The still winter evening was one block of black iron cold. She was shivering in her thin coat. She was deadtired. It seemed weeks since she'd slept. It was warm in the big quiet hotel lobby, through her thin paper soles she could feel the thick nap of the carpet. There must have been a bridgeparty somewhere in the hotel because groups of welldressed middleaged women that reminded her of her mother kept going through the lobby. She let herself drop into a deep chair by a radiator and started at once to drowse off.

"You poor little girl, I can see you've been working. . . . This is different from socialservice work, I'll bet." She opened her eyes. George had on a furlined coat with a furcollar out of which his thin neck and long knobby face stuck out comically like the head of a marabou stork.

She got up. "Oh, Mr. Barrow . . . I mean George." He took her hand in his left hand and patted it gently with his right. "Now I know what the frontline trenches are like," she said, laughing at his kind comical look.

"You're laughing at my furcoat. . . . Wouldn't help the Amalgamated if I got pneumonia, would it? . . . Why haven't you got a warm coat? . . . Sweet little Mary French. . . . Just exactly the person I wanted to see. . . . Do you mind if we go up to the room? I don't like to talk here, too many eavesdroppers."

Upstairs in his square warm room with pink hangings and pink lights he helped her off with her coat. He stood there frowning and weighing it in his hand. "You've got to get a warm coat," he said. After he'd ordered tea for her from the waiter, he rather ostentatiously left the door into the hall open. They settled down on either side of a little table at the foot of the bed that was littered with newspapers and typewritten sheets. "Well, well well," he said. "This is a great pleasure for a lonely old codger like me. What would you think of having dinner with the Senator? . . . To see how the other half lives."

They talked and talked. Now and then he slipped a little whiskey in her tea. He was very kind, said he was sure all the boys could be gotten out of jail as soon as the strike was settled and that it virtually was settled. He'd just been over in Youngstown talking to Fitzpatrick. He thought he'd just about convinced him that the only thing

141

to do was to get the men back to work. He had Judge Gary's own private assurance that nobody would be discriminated against and that experts were working on the problem of an eighthour day. As soon as the technical difficulties could be overcome, the whole picture of the steelworker's life would change radically for the better. Then and there he offered to put Mary French on the payroll as his secretary. He said her actual experiences with conditions would be invaluable in influencing legislation. If the great effort of the underpaid steelworkers wasn't to be lost, it would have to be incorporated in legislation. The center of the fight was moving to Washington. He felt the time was ripe in the Senate. She said her first obligation was to the strike committee. "But, my dear sweet child," George Barrow said, gently patting the back of her hand, "in a few days there won't be any strikecommittee."

The Senator was a Southerner with irongray hair and white spats who looked at Mary French when he first came in the room as if he thought she was going to plant a bomb under the big bulge of his creamcolored vest, but his fatherly respectful delicate flowerofwomanhood manner was soothing. They ordered dinner brought up to George's room. The Senator kidded George in a heavy rotund way about his dangerous Bolsheviki friends. They'd been putting away a good deal of rye and the smoky air of George's room was rich with whiskey. When she left them to go down to the office again, they were talking about taking in a burlesque show.

The bunch down at the office looked haggard and sour. When she told them about G. H. Barrow's offer, they told her to jump at it; of course it would be wonderful to have her working for them

in Washington and besides they wouldn't be able to pay even her expenses any more. She finished her release and glumly said goodnight. That night she slept better than she had for weeks, though all the way home she was haunted by Gus Moscowski's blue eyes and his fair head with the blood clotted on it and his jaunty grin when his eyes met hers in the courtroom. She had decided that the best way to get the boys out of jail was to go to Washington with George.

Next morning George called her up at the office first thing and asked her what about the job. She said she'd take it. He said would fifty a week be all right; maybe he could raise it to seventyfive later. She said it was more than she'd ever made in her life. He said he wanted her to come right around to the Schenley; he had something important for her to do. When she got there he met her in the lobby with a hundreddollar bill in his hand. "The first thing I want you to do, sweet girl, is to go buy yourself a warm overcoat. Here's two weeks' salary in advance.... You won't be any good to me as a secretary if you catch your death of pneumonia the first day."

On the parlorcar going to Washington he handed over to her two big square black suitcases full of testimony.

"Don't think for a moment there's no work concerned with this job," he said, fishing out manila envelope after manila envelope full of closely typed stenographers' notes on onionskin paper. "The other stuff was more romantic," he said, sharpening a pencil, "but this in the longrange view is more useful."

"I wonder," said Mary.

"Mary dear, you are very young ... and very sweet."

WILLA CATHER
"Double Birthday"

The Engelhardts recall the old days
in Allegheny City

Time: 1920s   Setting: Pittsburgh

Set in the 1920s, with allusions back to the late nineteenth century, "Double Birthday" deals centrally with the passage of time. The simultaneous birthdays of Albert Engelhardt and his uncle, plus their renewed contact with old acquaintances Judge Hammersley and his daughter, set the stage for a review of the past: the loss of the Engelhardt family fortune, the tragic outcome (narrated in section 3) of Uncle Albert's efforts years earlier to supervise a young woman's musical career. But despite the erosions of time, the surviving Engelhardts are not unhappy men. Taking up a theme very typical of her fiction, Cather points out a contrast between their personalized, cultured lifestyle and that of Judge Hammersley, who values "success in the world."

This contrast between the Engelhardts and Hammersley points to another time-connected theme in "Double Birthday" — the changes thirty or forty years bring to a city. The opening paragraph of the story states, "Even in American cities, which seem so much alike, . . . there are still survivals of a past more loosely woven, there are disconcerting beginnings of a future yet unforeseen." The past in "Double Birthday" is Pittsburgh's North Side at the turn of the century, when it was Allegheny City. Cather presents the older city as a community in which people of different classes mingled in friendly intimacy, in which the round of daily errands performed on foot created a neighborhood familiarity — "The Allegheny market was one of the best in the world. Mrs. Engelhardt went to market every morning of her life; such vegetables and poultry, such cheeses and sausages and smoked and pickled fish as one could buy there! Soon after she made her rounds, boys in white aprons would come running across the park with her purchases."

By the 1920s all this has changed. Though the Engelhardts themselves still live comfortably with their working-class neighbors, their South Side location is not respectable in the eyes of such a man as Judge Hammersley. The "good" neighborhoods are now three or four miles out along the trolley lines, in Squirrel Hill, or on Ellsworth Avenue. And for his part, Albert doesn't care for the new neighborhoods. As he climbs the hill to Judge Hammersley's house, he thinks, "This solid comfort, this iron-bound security, didn't appeal to him much. These massive houses, after all, held nothing but the heavy domestic routine; all the frictions and jealousies and discontents of family life." As pictured in "Double Birthday," the suburbs seem to cater to neurotic privacy, to affluent selfishness. The process of dispersion is killing an earlier vitality in the city.

Willa Cather (1873-1947) wrote six short stories set in the Pittsburgh area. Besides "Double Birthday," they are: "Paul's Case" (Oakland, East Liberty), "Uncle Valentine" (Sewickley), "The Namesake" (Monongahela Valley?), "The Professor's Commencement" (lower Hill District), and "A Gold Slipper" (Oakland, East Liberty).

Cather came to Pittsburgh in 1896 to work on a family magazine, the Home Monthly (her first job after graduating from the University of Nebraska), and stayed for ten years, working later as a newspaper reporter and a high-school teacher. When she left for New York in 1906, the novels (O Pioneers!, My Antonia, etc.) that were to make Willa Cather probably the most famous writer to have lived and worked in Pittsburgh still lay in the future.

"Double Birthday"

I

Even in American cities, which seem so much alike, where people seem all to be living the same lives, striving for the same things, thinking the same thoughts, there are still individuals a little out of tune with the times—there are still survivals of a past more loosely woven, there are disconcerting beginnings of a future yet unforeseen.

Coming out of the gray stone Court House in Pittsburgh on a dark November afternoon, Judge Hammersley encountered one of these men whom one does not readily place, whom one is, indeed, a little embarrassed to meet, because they have not got on as they should. The Judge saw him mounting the steps outside, leaning against the wind, holding his soft felt hat on with his hand, his head thrust forward—hurrying with a light, quick step, and so intent upon his own purposes that the Judge could have gone out by a side door and avoided the meeting. But that was against his principles.

"Good day, Albert," he muttered, seeming to feel, himself, all the embarrassment of the encounter, for the other snatched off his hat with a smile of very evident pleasure, and something like pride. His gesture bared an attractive head—small, well-set, definite and smooth, one of those heads that look as if they had been turned out of some hard, rich wood by a workman deft with the lathe. His smooth-shaven face was dark—a warm coffee color—and his hazel eyes were warm and lively. He was not young, but his features had a kind of quick-silver mobility. His manner toward the stiff, frowning Judge was respectful and admiring—not

in the least self-conscious.

The Judge inquired after his health and that of his uncle.

"Uncle Albert is splendidly preserved for his age. Frail, and can't stand any strain, but perfectly all right if he keeps to his routine. He's going to have a birthday soon. He will be eighty on the first day of December, and I shall be fifty-five on the same day. I was named after him because I was born on his twenty-fifth birthday."

"Umph." The Judge glanced from left to right as if this announcement were in bad taste, but he put a good face on it and said with a kind of testy heartiness, "That will be an—occasion. I'd like to remember it in some way. Is there anything your uncle would like, any—recognition?" He stammered and coughed.

Young Albert Engelhardt, as he was called, laughed apologetically, but with confidence. "I think there is, Judge Hammersley. Indeed, I'd thought of coming to you to ask a favor. I am going to have a little supper for him, and you know he likes good wine. In these dirty bootlegging times, it's hard to get."

"Certainly, certainly." The Judge spoke up quickly and for the first time looked Albert squarely in the eye. "Don't give him any of that bootleg stuff. I can find something in my cellar. Come out tomorrow night after eight, with a gripsack of some sort. Very glad to help you out, Albert. Glad the old fellow holds up so well. Thank'ee, Albert," as Engelhardt swung the heavy door open and held it for him to pass.

Judge Hammersley's car was waiting for him,

145

and on the ride home to Squirrel Hill he thought with vexation about the Engelhardts. He was really a sympathetic man, and though so stern of manner, he had deep affections; was fiercely loyal to old friends, old families, and old ideals. He didn't think highly of what is called success in the world today, but such as it was he wanted his friends to have it, and was vexed with them when they missed it. He was vexed with Albert for unblushingly, almost proudly, declaring that he was fifty-five years old, when he had nothing whatever to show for it. He was the last of the Engelhardt boys, and they had none of them had anything to show. They all died much worse off in the world than they began. They began with a flourishing glass factory up the river, a comfortable fortune, a fine old house on the park in Allegheny, a good standing in the community; and it was all gone, melted away.

Old August Engelhardt was a thrifty, energetic man, though pig-headed—Judge Hammersley's friend and one of his first clients. August's five sons had sold the factory and wasted the money in fantastic individual enterprises, lost the big house, and now they were all dead except Albert. They ought all to be alive, with estates and factories and families. To be sure, they had that queer German streak in them; but so had old August, and it hadn't prevented his amounting to something. Their bringing-up was wrong; August had too free a hand, he was too proud of his five handsome boys, and too conceited. Too much tennis, Rhine wine punch, music, and silliness. They were always running over to New York, like this Albert. Somebody, when asked what in the world young Albert had ever done with his inheritance, had laughingly replied that he had spent it on the Pennsylvania Railroad.

Judge Hammersley didn't see how Albert could hold his head up. He had some small job in the County Clerk's office, was dependent upon it, had nothing else but the poor little house on the South Side where he lived with his old uncle. The county took care of him for the sake of his father, who had been a gallant officer in the Civil War, and afterward a public-spirited citizen and a generous employer of labor. But, as Judge Hammersley had bitterly remarked to Judge Merriman when Albert's name happened to come up, "If it weren't for his father's old friends seeing that he got something, that fellow wouldn't be able to make a living." Next to a charge of dishonesty, this was the worst that could be said of any man.

Judge Hammersley's house out on Squirrel Hill sat under a grove of very old oak trees. He lived alone, with his daughter, Margaret Parmenter, who was a widow. She had a great many engagements, but she usually managed to dine at home with her father, and that was about as much society as he cared for. His house was comfortable in an old-fashioned way, well appointed—especially the library, the room in which he lived when he was not in bed or at the Court House. Tonight, when he came down to dinner, Mrs. Parmenter was already at the table, dressed for an evening party. She was tall, handsome, with a fine, easy carriage, and her face was both hard and sympathetic, like her father's. She had not, however, his stiffness of manner, that contraction of the muscles which was his unconscious protest at any irregularity in the machinery of life. She accepted blunders and accidents smoothly if not indifferently.

As the old colored man pulled back the Judge's chair for him, he glanced at his daughter from under his eyebrows.

"I saw that son of old Gus Engelhardt's this afternoon," he said in an angry, challenging tone.

As a young girl his daughter had used to take up the challenge and hotly defend the person who had displeased or disappointed her father. But as she grew older she was conscious of that same feeling in herself when people fell short of what she expected; and she understood now that when her father spoke as if he were savagely attacking someone, it merely meant that he was disappointed or sorry for them; he never spoke thus of persons for whom he had no feeling. So she said calmly:

"Oh, did you really? I haven't seen him for years, not since the war. How was he looking? Shabby?"

"Not so shabby as he ought to. That fellow's likely to be in want one of these days."

"I'm afraid so," Mrs. Parmenter sighed. "But I believe he would be rather plucky about it."

The Judge shrugged. "He's coming out here tomorrow night, on some business for his uncle."

"Then I'll have a chance to see for myself. He must look much older. I can't imagine his ever looking really old and settled, though."

"See that you don't ask him to stay. I don't want the fellow hanging around. He'll transact his business and get it over. He had the face to admit to me that he'll be fifty-five years old on the first of December. He's giving some sort of birthday party for old Albert, a-hem." The Judge coughed formally but was unable to check a smile; his lips sarcastic, but his eyes full of sly humor.

"Can he be as old as that? Yes, I suppose so. When we were both at Mrs. Sterrett's, in Rome, I was fifteen, and he must have been about thirty."

Her father coughed. "He'd better have been in Homestead!"

Mrs. Parmenter looked up; that was rather commonplace, for her father. "Oh, I don't know. Albert would never have been much use in Homestead, and he was very useful to Mrs. Sterrett in Rome."

"What did she want the fellow hanging round for? All the men of her family amounted to something."

"To too much! There must be some butterflies if one is going to give house parties, and the Sterretts and Dents were all heavyweights. He was in Rome a long while; three years, I think. He had a gorgeous time. Anyway, he learned to speak Italian very well, and that helps him out now, doesn't it? You still send for him at the Court House when you need an interpreter?"

"That's not often. He picks up a few dollars. Nice business for his father's son."

After dinner the Judge retired to his library, where the gas fire was lit, and his book at hand, with a paper-knife inserted to mark the place where he had left off reading last night at exactly ten-thirty. On his way he went to the front door, opened it, turned on the porch light, and looked at the thermometer, making an entry in a little notebook. In a few moments his daughter, in an evening cloak, stopped at the library door to wish him good night and went down the hall. He listened for the closing of the front door; it was a reassuring sound to him. He liked the feeling of an orderly house, empty for himself and his books all evening. He was deeply read in divinity, philosophy, and in the early history of North America.

II

While Judge Hammersley was settling down to his book, Albert Engelhardt was sitting at home in

147

a garnet velvet smoking-jacket, at an upright piano, playing Schumann's *Kreisleriana* for his old uncle. They lived, certainly, in a queer part of the city, on one of the dingy streets that run uphill off noisy Carson Street, in a little two-story brick house, a workingman's house, that Albert's father had taken over long ago in satisfaction of a bad debt. When his father had acquired this building, it was a mere nothing—the Engelhardts were then living in their big, many-gabled, so-German house on the Park, in Allegheny; and they owned many other buildings, besides the glass factory up the river. After the father's death, when the sons converted houses and lands into cash, this forgotten little house on the South Side had somehow never been sold or mortgaged. A day came when Albert, the last surviving son, found this piece of property the only thing he owned in the world besides his personal effects. His uncle, having had a crushing disappointment, wanted at that time to retire from the practice of medicine, so Albert settled in the South Side house and took his uncle with him.

He had not gone there in any mood of despair. His impoverishment had come about gradually, and before he took possession of these quarters he had been living in a boarding house; the change seemed going up instead of going down in the world. He was delighted to have a home again, to unpack his own furniture and his books and pictures—the most valuable in the world to him, because they were full of his own history and that of his family, were like part of his own personality. All the years and the youth which had slipped away from him still clung to these things.

At his piano, under his Degas drawing in black and red—three ballet girls at the bar—or seated at his beautiful inlaid writing table, he was still the elegant young man who sat there long ago. His rugs were fine ones, his collection of books was large and very personal. It was full of works which, though so recent, were already immensely far away and diminished. The glad, rebellious excitement they had once caused in the world he could recapture only in memory. Their power to seduce and stimulate the young, the living, was utterly gone. There was a complete file of the *Yellow Book*, for instance; who could extract sweet poison from those volumes now? A portfolio of the drawings of Aubrey Beardsley—decadent, had they been called? A slender, padded volume—the complete works of a great new poet, Ernest Dowson. Oscar Wilde, whose wickedness was now so outdone that he looked like the poor old hat of some Victorian belle, wired and feathered and garlanded and faded.

Albert and his uncle occupied only the upper floor of their house. The ground floor was let to an old German glass engraver who had once been a workman in August Engelhardt's factory. His wife was a good cook, and every night sent their dinner up hot on the dumb-waiter. The house opened directly upon the street, and to reach Albert's apartment one went down a narrow paved alley at the side of the building and mounted an outside flight of wooden stairs at the back. They had only four rooms—two bedrooms, a snug sitting room in which they dined, and a small kitchen where Albert got breakfast every morning. After he had gone to work, Mrs. Rudder came up from downstairs to wash the dishes and do the cleaning, and to cheer up old Doctor Engelhardt.

At dinner this evening Albert had told his uncle about meeting Judge Hammersley, and of his particular inquiries after his health. The old man was very proud and received this intelligence as his due, but could not conceal a certain gratification.

"The daughter, she still lives with him? A damned fine-looking woman!" he muttered between his teeth. Uncle Albert, a bachelor, had been a professed connoisseur of ladies in his day.

Immediately after dinner, unless he were going somewhere, Albert always played for his uncle for an hour. He played extremely well. Doctor Albert sat by the fire smoking his cigar. While he listened, the look of wisdom and professional authority faded, and many changes went over his face, as if he were playing a little drama to himself; moods of scorn and contempt, of rakish vanity, sentimental melancholy . . . and something remote and lonely. The Doctor had always flattered himself that he resembled a satyr, because the tops of his ears were slightly pointed; and he used to hint to his nephews that his large pendulous nose was the index of an excessively amorous disposition. His mouth was full of long, yellowish teeth, all crowded irregularly, which he snapped and ground together when he uttered denunciations of modern art or the Eighteenth Amendment. He wore his mustache short and twisted up at the corners. His thick gray hair was cut close and upright, in the bristling French fashion. His hands were small and fastidious, high-knuckled, quite elegant in shape.

Across the Doctor's throat ran a long, jagged scar. He used to mutter to his young nephews that it had been justly inflicted by an outraged husband—a pistol shot in the dark. But his brother August always said that he had been cut by glass, when, wandering about in the garden one night after drinking too much punch, he had fallen into the cold-frames.

After playing Schumann for some time, Albert,

without stopping, went into Stravinsky.

Doctor Engelhardt by the gas fire stirred uneasily, turned his important head toward his nephew, and snapped his teeth. "Br-r-r, that stuff! Poverty of imagination, poverty of musical invention; *fin-de-siècle!*"

Albert laughed. "I thought you were asleep. Why will you use that phrase? It shows your vintage. Like this any better?" He began the second act of *Pélleas et Mélisande.*

The Doctor nodded. "Yes, that is better, though I'm not fooled by it." He wrinkled his nose as if he were smelling out something, and squinted with superior discernment. "To this *canaille* that is all very new; but to me it goes back to Bach."

"Yes, if you like."

Albert, like Judge Hammersley, was jealous of his solitude—liked a few hours with his books. It was time for Uncle Doctor to be turning in. He ended the music by playing half a dozen old German songs which the old fellow always wanted but never asked for. The Doctor's chin sank into his shirt front. His face took on a look of deep, resigned sadness; his features, losing their conscious importance, seemed to shrink a good deal. His nephew knew that this was the mood in which he would most patiently turn to rest and darkness. Doctor Engelhardt had had a heavy loss late in life. Indeed, he had suffered the same loss twice.

As Albert left the piano, the Doctor rose and walked a little stiffly across the room. At the door of his chamber he paused, brought his hand up in a kind of military salute and gravely bowed, so low that one saw only the square up-standing gray brush on the top of his head and the long pear-shaped nose. After this he closed the door behind him. Albert sat down to his book. Very soon he

149

heard the bath water running. Having taken his bath, the Doctor would get into bed immediately to avoid catching cold. Luckily, he usually slept well. Perhaps he dreamed of that unfortunate young singer whom he sometimes called, to his nephew and himself, "the lost Lenore."

III

Long years ago, when the Engelhardt boys were still living in the old house in Allegheny with their mother, after their father's death, Doctor Engelhardt was practising medicine, and had an office on the Park, five minutes' walk from his sister-in-law. He usually lunched with the family, after his morning office hours were over. They always had a good cook, and the Allegheny market was one of the best in the world. Mrs. Engelhardt went to market every morning of her life; such vegetables and poultry, such cheeses and sausages and smoked and pickled fish as one could buy there! Soon after she had made her rounds, boys in white aprons would come running across the Park with her purchases. Everyone knew the Engelhardt house, built of many-colored bricks, with gables and turrets, and on the west a large stained-glass window representing a scene on the Grand Canal in Venice, the Church of Santa Maria della Salute in the background, in the foreground a gondola with a slender gondolier. People said August and Mrs. Engelhardt should be solidly seated in the prow to make the picture complete.

Doctor Engelhardt's especial interest was the throat, preferably the singing throat. He had studied every scrap of manuscript that Manuel Garcia had left behind him, every reported conversation with him. He had doctored many singers, and imagined he had saved many voices. Pittsburgh

air is not good for the throat, and traveling artists often had need of medical assistance. Conductors of orchestras and singing societies recommended Doctor Engelhardt because he was very lax about collecting fees from professionals, especially if they sent him a photograph floridly inscribed. He had been a medical student in New York while Patti was still singing; his biography fell into chapters of great voices as a turfman's falls into chapters of fast horses. This passion for the voice had given him the feeling of distinction, of being unique in his profession, which had made him all his life a well-satisfied and happy man, and had left him a poor one.

One morning when the Doctor was taking his customary walk about the Park before office hours, he stopped in front of the Allegheny High School building because he heard singing—a chorus of young voices. It was June, and the chapel windows were open. The Doctor listened for a few moments, then tilted his head on one side and laid his forefinger on his pear-shaped nose with an anxious, inquiring squint. Among the voices he certainly heard one Voice. The final bang of the piano was followed by laughter and buzzing. A boy ran down the steps. The Doctor stopped him and learned that this was a rehearsal for Class Day exercises. Just then the piano began again, and in a moment he heard the same voice, alone:

"Still wie die Nacht, tief wie das Meer."

No, he was not mistaken; a full, rich soprano voice, so easy, so sure; a golden warmth, even in the high notes. Before the second verse was over he went softly into the building, into the chapel, and for the first time laid eyes on Marguerite Thiesinger. He saw a sturdy, blooming German girl standing beside the piano; good-natured one knew at a glance, glowing with health. She looked like a big peony just burst into bloom and full of sunshine—sunshine in her auburn hair, in her rather small hazel eyes. When she finished the song, she began waltzing on the platform with one of the boys.

Doctor Albert waited by the door, and accosted her as she came out carrying her coat and school-books. He introduced himself and asked her if she would go over to Mrs. Engelhardt's for lunch and sing for him.

Oh, yes! she knew one of the Engelhardt boys, and she'd always wanted to see that beautiful window from the inside.

She went over at noon and sang for them before lunch, and the family took stock of her. She spoke a very ordinary German and her English was still worse; her people were very ordinary. Her flat, slangy speech was somehow not vulgar because it was so naive—she knew no other way. The boys were delighted with her because she was so jolly and interested in everything. She told them about the glorious good times she had going to dances in suburban Turner halls, and to picnics in the damp, smoke-smeared woods up the Allegheny. The boys roared with laughter at the unpromising places she mentioned. But she had the warm bubble in her blood that makes everything fair; even being a junior in the Allegheny High School was "glorious," she told them!

She came to lunch with them again and again, because she liked the boys, and she thought the house magnificent. The Doctor observed her narrowly all the while. Clearly she had no ambition, no purpose; she sang to be agreeable. She was not very intelligent, but she had a kind of personal warmth that, to his way of thinking, was much

better than brains. He took her over to his office and poked and pounded her. When he had finished his examination, he stood before the foolish, happy young thing and inclined his head in his peculiar fashion.

"Miss Thiesinger, I have the honor to announce to you that you are on the threshold of a brilliant, possibly a great career."

She laughed her fresh, ringing laugh. "Aren't you nice, though, to take so much trouble about me!"

The Doctor lifted a forefinger. "But for that you must turn your back on this childishness, these sniveling sapheads you play marbles with. You must uproot this triviality." He made a gesture as if he were wringing a chicken's neck, and Marguerite was thankful she was able to keep back a giggle.

Doctor Engelhardt wanted her to go to New York with him at once, and begin her studies. He was quite ready to finance her. He had made up his mind to stake everything upon this voice.

But not at all. She thought it was lovely of him, but she was very fond of her classmates, and she wanted to graduate with her class next year. Moreover, she had just been given a choir position in one of the biggest churches in Pittsburgh, though she was still a schoolgirl; she was going to have money and pretty clothes for the first time in her life and wouldn't miss it all for anything.

All through the next school year Doctor Albert went regularly to the church where she sang, watched and cherished her, expostulated and lectured, trying to awaken fierce ambition in his big peony flower. She was very much interested in other things just then, but she was patient with him; accepted his devotion with good nature, respected his wisdom, and bore with his "stagey"

151

manners as she called them. She graduated in June, and immediately after Commencement, when she was not quite nineteen, she eloped with an insurance agent and went to Chicago to live. She wrote Doctor Albert: "I do appreciate all your kindness to me, but I guess I will let my voice rest for the present."

He took it hard. He burned her photographs and the foolish little scrawls she had written to thank him for presents. His life would have been dull and empty if he hadn't had so many reproaches to heap upon her in his solitude. How often and how bitterly he arraigned her for the betrayal of so beautiful a gift. Where did she keep it hidden now, that jewel, in the sordid life she had chosen?

Three years after her elopement, suddenly, without warning, Marguerite Thiesinger walked into his office on Arch Street one morning and told him she had come back to study! Her husband's "affairs were involved"; he was now quite willing that she should make as much as possible of her voice—and out of it.

"My voice is better than it was," she said, looking at him out of her rather small eyes—greenish yellow, with a glint of gold in them. He believed her. He suddenly realized how uncommonly truthful she had always been. Rather stupid, unimaginative, but carried joyously along on a flood of warm vitality, and truthful to a degree he had hardly known in any woman or in any man. And now she was a woman.

He took her over to his sister-in-law's. Albert, who chanced to be at home, was sent to the piano. She was not mistaken. The Doctor kept averting his head to conceal his delight, to conceal, once or twice, a tear—the moisture that excitement and pleasure brought to his eyes. The voice, after all, he told himself, is a physical thing. She had been growing and ripening like fruit in the sun, and the voice with the body. Doctor Engelhardt stepped softly out of the music room into the conservatory and addressed a potted palm, his lips curling back from his teeth: "So we get that out of you, *Monsieur le commis voyageur,* and now we throw you away like a squeezed lemon."

When he returned to his singer, she addressed him very earnestly from under her spring hat covered with lilacs: "Before my marriage, Doctor Engelhardt, you offered to take me to New York to a teacher, and lend me money to start on. If you still feel like doing it, I'm sure I could repay you before very long. I'll follow your instructions. What was it you used to tell me I must have—application and ambition?"

He glared at her; "Take note, Gretchen, that I change the prescription. There is something vulgar about ambition. Now we will play for higher stakes; for ambition read aspiration!" His index finger shot upward.

In New York he had no trouble in awakening the interest of his friends and acquaintances. Within a week he had got his protégée to a very fine artist, just then retiring from the Opera, a woman who had been a pupil of Pauline Garcia Viardot. In short, Doctor Engelhardt had realized the dream of a lifetime: he had discovered a glorious voice, backed by a rich vitality. Within a year Marguerite had one of the best church positions in New York; she insisted upon repaying her benefactor before she went abroad to complete her studies. Doctor Engelhardt went often to New York to counsel and advise, to gloat over his treasure. He often shivered as he crossed the Jersey ferry; he was afraid of Fate. He would tell over her assets on his fingers to reassure himself. You might have seen a small, self-important man of about fifty, standing by the rail of the ferry boat, his head impressively inclined as if he were addressing an amphitheatre full of students, gravely counting upon his fingers.

But Fate struck, and from the quarter least under suspicion—through that blooming, rounded, generously molded young body, from that abundant, glowing health which the Doctor proudly called peasant vigor. Marguerite's success had brought to his office many mothers of singing daughters. He was not insensible to the compliment, but he usually dismissed them by dusting his fingers delicately in the air and growling; "Yes, she can sing a little, she has a voice; *aber kleine, kleine!*" He exulted in the opulence of his cabbage rose. To his nephews he used to match her possibilities with the singers of that period. Emma Eames he called *die Puritan,* Geraldine Farrar *la voix blanche,* another was *trop raffinée.*

Marguerite had been in New York two years, her path one of uninterrupted progress, when she wrote the Doctor about a swelling of some sort; the surgeons wanted to operate. Doctor Albert took the next train for New York. An operation revealed that things were very bad indeed; a malignant growth, so far advanced that the knife could not check it. Her mother and grandmother had died of the same disease.

Poor Marguerite lived a year in a hospital for incurables. Every weekend when Doctor Albert went over to see her he found great changes—it was rapid and terrible. That winter and spring he lived like a man lost in a dark morass, the Slave in the Dismal Swamp. He suffered more than his Gretchen, for she was singularly calm and hopeful to the very end, never doubting that she would get well.

The last time he saw her she had given up. But she was noble and sweet in mood, and so piteously apologetic for disappointing him—like a child who has broken something precious and is sorry. She was wasted, indeed, until she was scarcely larger than a child, her beautiful hair cut short, her hands like shadows, but still a stain of color in her cheeks.

"I'm so sorry I didn't do as you wanted instead of running off with Phil," she said. "I see now how little he cared about me—and you've just done everything. If I had my twenty-six years to live over, I'd live them very differently."

Doctor Albert dropped her hand and walked to the window, the tears running down his face. "*Pourquoi, pourquoi?*" he muttered, staring blindly at that brutal square of glass. When he could control himself and came back to the chair at her bedside, she put her poor little sheared head out on his knee and lay smiling and breathing softly.

"I expect you don't believe in the hereafter," she murmured. "Scientific people hardly ever do. But if there is one, I'll not forget you. I'll love to remember you."

When the nurse came to give her her hypodermic, Doctor Albert went out into Central Park and wandered about without knowing where or why, until he smelled something sweet which suddenly stopped his breath, and he sat down under a flowering linden tree. He dropped his face in his hands and cried like a woman. Youth, art, love, dreams, trueheartedness—why must they go out of the summer world into darkness? *Warum, warum?* He thought he had already suffered all that man

153

could, but never had it come down on him like this. He sat on that bench like a drunken man or like a dying man, muttering Heine's words, "God is a grimmer humorist than I. Nobody but God could have perpetrated anything so cruel." She was ashamed, he remembered it afresh and struck his bony head with his clenched fist—ashamed at having been used like this; she was apologetic for the power, whatever it was, that had tricked her. "Yes, by God, she apologized for God!"

The tortured man looked up through the linden branches at the blue arch that never answers. As he looked, his face relaxed, his breathing grew regular. His eyes were caught by puffy white clouds like the cherub-heads in Raphael's pictures, and something within him seemed to rise and travel with those clouds. The moment had come when he could bear no more. . . . When he went back to the hospital that evening, he learned that she had died very quietly between eleven and twelve, the hour when he was sitting on the bench in the park.

Uncle Doctor now sometimes spoke to Albert out of a long silence: "Anyway, I died for her; that was given to me. She never knew a death-struggle— she went to sleep. That struggle took place in my body. Her dissolution occurred within me."

IV

Old Doctor Engelhardt walked abroad very little now. Sometimes on a fine Sunday, his nephew would put him aboard a street car that climbs the hills beyond Mount Oliver and take him to visit an old German graveyard and a monastery. Every afternoon, in good weather, he walked along the pavement which ran past the front door, as far as the first corner, where he bought his paper and cigarettes. If Elsa, the pretty little granddaughter

of his housekeeper, ran out to join him and see him over the crossings, he would go a little farther. In the morning, while Mrs. Rudder did the sweeping and dusting, the Doctor took the air on an upstairs back porch, overhanging the court.

The court was bricked, and had an old-fashioned cistern and hydrant, and three ailanthus trees—the last growing things left to the Engelhardts, whose flowering shrubs and greenhouses had once been so well known in Allegheny. In these trees, which he called *les Chinoises,* the Doctor took a great interest. The clothes line ran about their trunks in a triangle, and on Mondays he looked down upon the washing. He was too near-sighted to be distressed by the sooty flakes descending from neighboring chimneys upon the white sheets. He enjoyed the dull green leaves of his *Chinoises* in summer, scarcely moving on breathless, sticky nights, when the moon came up red over roofs and smokestacks. In autumn he watched the yellow fronds drop down upon the brick pavement like great ferns. Now, when his birthday was approaching, the trees were bare; and he thought he liked them best so, especially when all the knotty, curly twigs were outlined by a scurf of snow.

As he sat there, wrapped up in rugs, a stiff felt hat on his head—he would never hear to a cap—and woolen gloves on his hands, Elsa, the granddaughter, would bring her cross-stitch and chatter to him. Of late she had been sewing on her trousseau, and that amused the Doctor highly—though it meant she would soon go to live in lower Allegheny, and he would lose her. Her young man, Carl Abberbock, had now a half-interest in a butcher

The old Allegheny Market.

154

stall in the Allegheny market, and was in a hurry to marry.

When Mrs. Rudder had quite finished her work and made the place neat, she would come and lift the rug from his knees and say, "Time to go in, Herr Doctor."

V

The next evening after dinner Albert left the house with a suitcase, the bag that used to make so many trips to New York in the opera season. He stopped downstairs to ask Elsa to carry her sewing up and sit with his uncle for a while, then he took the street car across the Twenty-second Street Bridge by the blazing steel mills. As he waited on Soho Hill to catch a Fifth Avenue car, the heavy, frosty air suddenly began to descend in snow flakes. He wished he had worn his old overcoat; didn't like to get this one wet. He had to consider such things now. He was hesitating about a taxi when his car came, bound for the East End.

He got off at the foot of one of the streets running up Squirrel Hill, and slowly mounted. Everything was white with the softly-falling snow. Albert knew all the places; old school friends lived in many of them. Big, turreted stone houses, set in ample grounds with fine trees and shrubbery and driveways. He stepped aside now and then to avoid a car, rolling from the gravel drives on to the stone-block pavement. If the occupants had recognized Albert, they would have felt sorry for him. But he did not feel sorry for himself. He looked up at the lighted windows, the red gleam on the snowy rhododendron bushes, and shrugged. His old schoolfellows went to New York now as often as he had done in his youth; but they went to consult doctors, to put children in school, or to pay the bills of incorrigible sons.

He thought he had had the best of it; he had gone a-Maying while it was May. This solid comfort, this iron-bound security, didn't appeal to him much. These massive houses, after all, held nothing but the heavy domestic routine; all the frictions and jealousies and discontents of family life. Albert felt light and free, going up the hill in his thin overcoat. He believed he had had a more interesting life than most of his friends who owned real estate. He could still amuse himself, and he had lived to the full all the revolutions in art and music that his period covered. He wouldn't at this moment exchange his life and his memories—his memories of his teacher, Rafael Joseffy, for instance—for any one of these massive houses and the life of the man who paid the upkeep. If Mephistopheles were to emerge from the rhododendrons and stand behind his shoulder with such an offer, he wouldn't hesitate. Money? Oh, yes, he would like to have some, but not what went with it.

He turned in under Judge Hammersley's fine oak trees. A car was waiting in the driveway, near the steps by which he mounted to the door. The colored man admitted him, and just as he entered the hall Mrs. Parmenter came down the stairs.

"Ah, it's you, Albert! Father said you were coming in this evening, and I've kept the car waiting, to have a glimpse of you."

Albert had dropped his hat and bag, and stood holding her hand with the special grace and appreciation she remembered in him.

"What a pleasure to see you!" he exclaimed, and she knew from his eyes it was. "It doesn't happen often, but it's always such a surprise and pleasure." He held her hand as if he wanted to keep her there.

"It's a long while since the Villa Scipione, isn't it?"

They stood for a moment in the shrouded hall light. Mrs. Parmenter was looking very handsome, and Albert was thinking that she had all her father's authority, with much more sweep and freedom. She was impulsive and careless, where he was strong and shrinking—a powerful man terribly afraid of little annoyances. His daughter, Albert believed, was not afraid of anything. She had proved more than once that if you aren't afraid of gossip, it is harmless. She did as she pleased. People took it. Even Parmenter had taken it, and he was rather a stiff sort.

Mrs. Parmenter laughed at his allusion to their summer at Mrs. Sterrett's, in Rome, and gave him her coat to hold.

"You remember, Albert, how you and I used to get up early on fete days, and go down to the garden gate to see the young king come riding in from the country at the head of the horse guards? How the sun flashed on his helmet! Heavens, I saw him last summer! So grizzled and battered."

"And we were always going to run away to Russia together, and now there is no Russia. Everything has changed but you, Mrs. Parmenter."

"Wish I could think so. But you don't know any Mrs. Parmenter. I'm Marjorie, please. How often I think of those gay afternoons I had with you and your brothers in the garden behind your old Allegheny house. There's such a lot I want to talk to you about. And this birthday—when is it? May I send your uncle some flowers? I always remember his goodness to poor Marguerite Thiesinger. He never got over that, did he? But I'm late, and father is waiting. Good-night, you'll have a message from me."

Albert bent and kissed her hand in the old-fashioned way, keeping it a moment and breathing in softly the fragrance of her clothes, her furs, her person, the fragrance of that other world to which he had once belonged and out of which he had slipped so gradually that he scarcely realized it, unless suddenly brought face to face with something in it that was charming. Releasing her, he caught up his hat and opened the door to follow her, but she pushed him back with her arm and smiled over her shoulder. "No, no, father is waiting for you in the library. Good-night."

Judge Hammersley stood in the doorway, fingering a bunch of keys and blinking with impatience to render his service and have done with it. The library opened directly into the hall; he couldn't help overhearing his daughter, and he disliked her free and unreproachful tone with this man who was young when he should be old, single when he should be married, and penniless when he should be well-fixed.

Later, as Albert came down the hill with two bottles of the Judge's best champagne in his bag, he was thinking that the greatest disadvantage of being poor and dropping out of the world was that he didn't meet attractive women any more. The men he could do without, Heaven knew! But the women, the ones like Marjorie Hammersley, were always grouped where the big fires burned—money and success and big houses and fast boats and French cars; it was natural.

Mrs. Parmenter, as she drove off, resolved that she would see more of Albert and his uncle— wondered why she had let an old friendship lapse for so long. When she was a little girl, she used often to spend a week with her aunt in Allegheny. She was fond of the aunt, but not of her cousins, and she used to escape whenever she could to the

157

Engelhardts' garden only a few doors away. No grass in that garden—in Allegheny grass was always dirty—but glittering gravel, and lilac hedges beautiful in spring, and barberry hedges red in the fall, and flowers and bird cages and striped awnings, boys lying about in tennis clothes, making mint juleps before lunch, having coffee under the sycamore trees after dinner. The Engelhardt boys were different, like people in a book or a play. All the young men in her set were scornful of girls until they wanted one; then they grabbed her rather brutally, and it was over. She had felt that the Engelhardt boys admired her without in the least wanting to grab her, that they enjoyed her aesthetically, so to speak, and it pleased her to be liked in that way.

VI

On the afternoon of the first of December, Albert left his desk in the County Clerk's office at four o'clock, feeling very much as he used to when school was dismissed in the middle of the afternoon just before the Christmas holidays. It was his uncle's birthday that was in his mind; his own, of course, gave him no particular pleasure. If one stopped to think of that, there was a shiver waiting round the corner. He walked over the Smithfield Street Bridge. A thick brown fog made everything dark, and there was a feeling of snow in the air. The lights along the sheer cliffs of Mount Washington, high above the river, were already lighted. When Albert was a boy, those cliffs, with the row of lights far up against the sky, always made him think of some far-away, cloud-set city in Asia; the forbidden city, he used to call it. Well, that was a long time ago; a lot of water had run under this bridge since then, and kingdoms and empires had

fallen. Meanwhile, Uncle Doctor was still hanging on, and things were not so bad with them as they might be. Better not reflect too much. He hopped on board a street car, and old women with market baskets shifted to make room for him.

When he reached home, the table was already set in the living room. Beautiful table linen had been one of his mother's extravagances (he had boxes of it, meant to give some to Elsa on her marriage), and Mrs. Rudder laundered it with pious care. She had put out the best silver. He had forgotten to order flowers, but the old woman had brought up one of her blooming geraniums for a centerpiece. Uncle Albert was dozing by the fire in his old smoking jacket, a volume of Schiller on his knee.

"I'll put the studs in your shirt for you. Time to dress, Uncle Doctor."

The old man blinked and smiled drolly. "So? *Die* claw-hammer?"

"Of course *die* claw-hammer! Elsa is going to a masquerade with Carl, and they are coming up to see us before they go. I promised her you would dress."

"Albert," the Doctor called him back, beckoned with a mysterious smile; "where did you get that wine now?"

"Oh, you found it when she put it on ice, did you? That's Judge Hammersley's, the best he had. He insisted on sending it to you, with his compliments and good wishes."

Uncle Albert rose and drew up his shoulders somewhat pompously. "From my own kind I still command recognition." Then dropping into homely vulgarity he added, with a sidelong squint at his nephew, "By God, some of that will feel good, running down the gullet."

"You'll have all you want for once. It's a great

occasion. Did you shave carefully? I'll take my bath, and then you must be ready for me."

In half an hour Albert came out in his dress clothes and found his uncle still reading his favorite poet. "The trousers are too big," the Doctor complained. "Why not *die* claw-hammer and my old trousers? Elsa wouldn't notice."

"Oh yes, she would! She's seen these every day for five years. Quick change!"

Doctor Engelhardt submitted, and when he was dressed, surveyed himself in his mirror with satisfaction, though he slyly slipped a cotton handkerchief into his pocket instead of the linen one Albert had laid out. When they came back to the sitting room, Mrs. Rudder had been up again and had put on the wine glasses. There was still half an hour before dinner, and Albert sat down to play for his uncle. He was beginning to feel that it was all much ado about nothing, after all.

A gentle tap at the door, and Elsa came in with her young man. She was dressed as a Polish maiden, and Carl Abberbock was in a Highlander's kilt.

"Congratulations on your birthday, Herr Doctor, and I've brought you some flowers." She went to his chair and bent down to be kissed, putting a bunch of violets in his hand.

The Doctor rose and stood looking down at the violets. "Hey, you take me for a Bonapartist? What is Mussolini's flower, Albert? Advise your friends in Rome that a Supreme Dictator should always have a flower." He turned the young girl around in the light and teased her about her thin arms—such an old joke, but she laughed for him.

"But that's the style now, Herr Doctor. Everybody wants to be as thin as possible."

"Bah, there are no styles in such things! A man

will always want something to take hold of, till Hell freezes over! Is dat so, Carl?"

Carl, a very broad-faced, smiling young man with outstanding ears, was suddenly frightened into silence by the entrance of a fine lady, and made for the door to get his knotty knees into the shadow. Elsa, too, caught her breath and shrank

The house at the top of Murrayhill Avenue in Pittsburgh's Squirrel Hill where Willa Cather lived for a time.

159

away.

Without knocking, Mrs. Parmenter, her arms full of roses, appeared in the doorway, and just behind her was her chauffeur, carrying a package. "Put it down there and wait for me," she said to him, then swept into the room and lightly embraced Doctor Engelhardt without waiting to drop the flowers or take off her furs. "I wanted to congratulate you in person. They told me below that you were receiving. Please take these flowers, Albert. I want a moment's chat with Doctor Engelhardt."

The Doctor stood with singular gravity, like someone in a play, the violets still in his hand. "To what," he muttered with his best bow, "to what am I indebted for such distinguished consideration?"

"To your own distinction, my dear sir—always one of the most distinguished men I ever knew."

The Doctor, to whom flattery was thrice dearer than to ordinary men, flushed deeply. But he was not so exalted that he did not notice his little friend of many lonely hours slipping out of the entry-way—the bare-kneed Highland chief had already got down the wooden stairs. "Elsa," he called commandingly, "come here and kiss me good-night." He pulled her forward. "This is Elsa Rudder, Mrs. Parmenter, and my very particular friend. You should have seen her beautiful hair before she cut it off." Elsa reddened and glanced up to see whether the lady understood. Uncle Doctor kissed her on the forehead and ran his hand over her shingled head. "Nineteen years," he said softly. "If the next nineteen are as happy, we won't bother about the rest. *Behüt' dich, Gott!*"

"Thank you, Uncle Doctor. Good-night."

After she fluttered out, he turned to Mrs. Parmenter. "That little girl," he said impressively, "is the rose in winter. She is my heir. Everything I have, I leave to her."

"Everything but my birthday present, please! You must drink that. I've brought you a bottle of champagne."

Both Alberts began to laugh. "But your father has already given us two!"

Mrs. Parmenter looked from one to the other. "My father? Well, that is a compliment! It's unheard of. Of course he and I have different lockers. We could never agree when to open them. I don't think he's opened his since the Chief Justice dined with him. Now I must leave you. Be as jolly as the night is long; with three bottles you ought to do very well! The good woman downstairs said your dinner would be served in half an hour."

Both men started toward her. "Don't go. Please, please, stay and dine with us! It's the one thing we needed." Albert began to entreat her in Italian, a language his uncle did not understand. He confessed that he had been freezing up for the last hour, couldn't go on with it alone. "One can't do such things without a woman—a beautiful woman."

"Thank you, Albert. But I've a dinner engagement; I ought to be at the far end of Ellsworth Avenue this minute."

"But this is once in a lifetime—for him! Still, if your friends are waiting for you, you can't. Certainly not." He took up her coat and held it for her. But how the light had gone out of his face; he looked so different, so worn, as he stood holding her coat at just the right height. She slipped her arms into it, then pulled them out. "I can't, but I just will! Let me write a note, please. I'll send Henry on with it and tell them I'll drop in after dinner." Albert pressed her hand gratefully and took her to his desk. "Oh, Albert, your Italian writing table, and all the lovely things on it, just as it stood in your room at the Villa Scipione! You used to let me write letters at it. You had the nicest way with young girls. If I had a daughter, I'd want you to do it all over again."

She scratched a note, and Albert put a third place at the table. He noticed Uncle Doctor slip away, and come back with his necktie set straight, attended by a wave of *eau de cologne*. While he was lighting the candles and bringing in the wine cooler, Mrs. Parmenter sat down beside the Doctor, accepted one of his cigarettes, and began to talk to him simply and naturally about Marguerite Thiesinger. Nothing could have been more tactful, Albert knew; nothing could give the old man more pleasure on his birthday. Albert himself couldn't do it any more; he had worn out his power of going over that sad story. He tried to make up for it by playing the songs she had sung.

"Albert," said Mrs. Parmenter when they sat down to dinner, "this is the only spot I know in the world that is before-the-war. You've got a period shut up in here; the last ten years of one century, and the first ten of another. Sitting here, I don't believe in aeroplanes, or jazz, or Cubists. My father is nearly as old as Doctor Engelhardt, and we never buy anything new; yet we haven't kept it out. How do you manage?"

Albert smiled a little ruefully. "I suppose it's because we never have any young people about. They bring it in."

"Elsa," murmured the Doctor. "But I see; she is only a child."

"I'm sorry for the young people now," Mrs. Parmenter went on. "They seem to me coarse and bitter. There's nothing wonderful left for them, poor things; the war destroyed it all. Where could

any girl find such a place to escape to as your mother's house, full of chests of linen like this? All houses now are like hotels; nothing left to cherish. Your house was wonderful! And what music we used to have. Do you remember the time you took me to hear Joseffy play the second Brahms, with Gericke? It was the last time I ever heard him. What did happen to him, Albert? Went to pieces in some way, didn't he?"

Albert sighed and shook his head; wine was apt to plunge him into pleasant, poetic melancholy. "I don't know if anyone knows. I stayed in Rome too long to know, myself. Before I went abroad, I'd been taking lessons with him right along—I saw no change in him, though he gave fewer and fewer concerts. When I got back, I wrote him the day I landed in New York—he was living up the Hudson then. I got a reply from his housekeeper, saying that he was not giving lessons, was ill and was seeing nobody. I went out to his place at once. I wasn't asked to come into the house. I was told to wait in the garden. I waited a long while. At last he came out, wearing white clothes, as he often did, a panama hat, carrying a little cane. He shook hands with me, asked me about Mrs. Sterrett—but he was another man, that's all. He was gone; he wasn't there. I was talking to his picture."

"Drugs!" muttered the Doctor out of one corner of his mouth.

"Nonsense!" Albert shrugged in derision. "Or if he did, that was secondary; a result, not a cause. He'd seen the other side of things; he'd let go. Something had happened in his brain that was not paresis."

Mrs. Parmenter leaned forward. "Did he *look* the same? Surely, he had the handsomest head in the world. Remember his forehead? Was he gray?

His hair was a reddish chestnut, as I remember."

"A little gray; not much. There was no change in his face, except his eyes. The bright spark had gone out, and his body had a sort of trailing languor when he moved."

"Would he give you a lesson?"

"No. Said he wasn't giving any. Said he was sorry, but he wasn't seeing people at all any more. I remember he sat making patterns in the gravel with his cane. He frowned and said he simply couldn't see people; said the human face had become hateful to him—and the human voice! 'I am sorry,' he said, 'but that is the truth.' I looked at his left hand, lying on his knee. I wonder, Marjorie, that I had the strength to get up and go away. I felt as if everything had been drawn out of me. He got up and took my hand. I understood that I must leave. In desperation I asked him whether music didn't mean anything to him still. 'Music,' he said slowly, with just a ghost of his old smile, 'yes— some music.' He went back into the house. Those were the last words I ever heard him speak."

"Oh dear! And he had everything that is beautiful—and the name of an angel! But we're making the Doctor melancholy. Open another bottle, Albert—father did very well by you. We've not drunk a single toast. Many returns, we take for granted. Why not each drink a toast of our own, to something we care for." She glanced at Doctor Engelhardt, who lifted the bunch of violets by his plate and smelled them absently. "Now, Doctor Engelhardt, a toast!"

The Doctor put down his flowers, delicately took up his glass and held it directly in front of him; everything he did with his hands was deft and sure. A beautiful, a wonderful look came over his face as she watched him.

"I drink," he said slowly, "to a memory; to the lost Lenore."

"And I," said young Albert softly, "to my youth, to my beautiful youth!"

Tears flashed into Mrs. Parmenter's eyes. "Ah," she thought, "that's what liking people amounts to; it's liking their silliness and absurdities. That's what it really is."

"And I," she said aloud, "will drink to the future; to our renewed friendship, and many dinners together. I like you two better than anyone I know."

When Albert came back from seeing Mrs. Parmenter down to her car, he found his uncle standing by the fire, his elbows on the mantle, thoughtfully rolling a cigarette. "Albert," he said in a deeply confidential tone, "good wine, good music, beautiful women; that is all there is worth turning over the hand for."

Albert began to laugh. The old man wasn't often banal. "Why Uncle, you and Martin Luther—"

The Doctor lifted a hand imperiously to stop him, and flushed darkly. He evidently hadn't been aware that he was quoting—it came from the heart. "Martin Luther," he snapped, "was a vulgarian of the first water; cabbage soup!" He paused a moment to light his cigarette. "But don't fool yourself; one like her always knows when a man has had success with women!"

Albert poured a last glass from the bottle and sipped it critically. "Well, you had success tonight, certainly. I could see that Marjorie was impressed. She's coming to take you for a ride tomorrow, after your nap, so you must be ready."

The Doctor passed his flexible, nervous hand lightly over the thick bristles of his French haircut. "*Even in our ashes*," he muttered haughtily.

162

MICHAEL A. MUSMANNO
"The Young Violinist"

Ivan Gunthers is introduced
to work in a coal mine

Time: 1920s   Setting: Allegheny County

"The Young Violinist" (Musmanno's title for the chapter from which this selection comes) narrates the first descent into the mines of a boy who at seventeen is starting out as a miner. Much of the impact of the piece stems from the deadpan style that seems to echo both the inevitability of the boy's career choice and the harsh pressures of work in the mines. The episode, of course, gains added poignancy — a touch of melodrama — because Ivan Gunthers wants, more than anything, to be a violinist, and the "gnarled talons and alligator-hide palms and corrugated wrists" that result from long work in the mines will mean the death of his wishes.

As a novel, Black Fury is an intriguing blend of realism and melodrama. Drafted in the 1930s, the story was originally conceived by Musmanno as a propaganda piece to insure the civil (and organizing) rights of miners. In its first form it was a film script on which actor Paul Muni and others collaborated with Musmanno; produced by Warner Brothers and starring Muni, the movie had its premiere in Pittsburgh in 1935. Musmanno himself describes his purpose:

I traveled with the film—which was to fulfill the powerful purpose of wiping out the shame of the Coal and Iron Police—all over Pennsylvania, delivering speeches from the stage at the beginning or conclusion of each showing. I called upon the audience to wire or to write to their state senators and representatives, urging them to vote in favor of the elimination of the Coal and Iron Police. There was no city or large town in the state in which I did not appear with Black Fury and speak.

The propagandistic intent of Black Fury is reflected in the novel version that Musmanno published in 1966. The main character is Jan Volkanik, a "superman" miner (in fact the mining variant of Joe Magarac or Paul Bunyan), and at the novel's climax Volkanik single-handedly holds off the "coalandiron" forces by threatening to dynamite the mine unless the union is recognized.

But despite (and sometimes, because of) its melodramatic elements the novel is good reading. Overall, its exaggerated moments are balanced by a starker realism that seems content (as in this passage) to let the facts speak for themselves. It is this realistic style that, later in the book, registers the brutal murder of miner John Barneski, a novelistic rendering of an actual murder in 1929 that was the specific impetus for Black Fury.

For all its vehement denunciation of the "coalandirons" and of exploitative mine owners, Black Fury is far from a "radical" novel. The book finds equally villainous the Communist efforts to enlist workers in the National Miners Union, and Musmanno's version of the unionizing struggle in the twenties shows the owners and Communists both manipulating the miners for their own purposes. Black Fury argues that in the United Mine Workers of America can be found the strength and solidarity to make the mining economy work within the traditional American system.

Michael Musmanno (1897-1968) was born in Stowe Township of immigrant parents. Among various jobs, his father worked as a miner, and for a time at age fourteen Musmanno himself was a coal loader. Musmanno's adult career — as state representative, state supreme court justice, presiding justice at the Nuremberg trials, and an outspoken commentator on many issues — is well remembered in western Pennsylvania.

"The Young Violinist"

Steve Gunthers lived next door to the Barneskis. He was a short, stocky man with a huge head and a short, thick neck. Twenty years of mine work had turned his hands into lobster claws. His eyes, somehow, didn't match his body—they were brooding eyes, sensitive and still touched with wonder.

The wonder was boyish and out of key with the rest of him. And every time he looked at his son Ivan, the eyes widened in awe and disbelief. Because out of this background, out of this grim and brutal world, he had a son who was able to create magic with a cheap violin that had been given to him as a boy. Ivan played at weddings and christenings and children's parties. He was invited to play at nearly every social function in the town, and he always went, because he loved playing his violin. He dreamed of taking lessons someday, to do honor to the gentlest and noblest of all instruments.

Those dreams, Steve thought, were remote right now—just as remote as his own, nursed through the sunless years; to buy a farm and work in the sun all day and leave coal mining behind, with its dangers, worries and hardships.

The day seemed no nearer now. And Ivan's dream was almost out of sight, because the boy had finally reached the age when, in a mining community, he went to work in the mines as inevitably as a two-year-old thoroughbred horse goes to the post.

Steve stood outside his house and took a fresh look at the world he was about to bequeath to his son. It was a dismal world—doubly so for a gifted musician in need of training that a miner could not afford.

Steve stared around him. Coaltown, in this year of 1925, was a bleak and huddled landscape of some six or seven hundred two-story frame houses that he knew so well, four rooms in each. Many of them had leaky gutters, sagging porches, and damp cellars, but each was home to every miner because sentiment gradually attaches to any place man lives in long enough. Dirt streets separated the rows of houses. Arc lamps at intersections seemed to contribute more gloom than light to the surrounding area.

All the houses were owned by Coaltown Enterprises, Inc., which collected the rent by withholding it from the paycheck. It also deducted the bill for goods bought at the company store. Not just groceries, hardware, window glass, and everything else needed in the house. Such purchases didn't rankle quite so much, but other things did: working equipment, explosives—everything the miner used, helped the company make a profit.

Steve remembered how many times he, and all his friends in the mines, had found that at the end of the two-week work period there was not a nickel in pay to collect. House rent, work expenses, groceries—these sometimes ate it all up. You came away from the paymaster's office with nothing to show for those two back-breaking weeks in the blackness below except a statement listing debits and credits—black-and-white totals to prove there was no money coming to you.

Steve again studied his world. In addition to the company dwelling houses, there were the inevitable neighborhood drug store, a small motion-picture theater, a dirty and soot-stained railroad station, a

165

post office, six or seven shoe-repair shops—because a coal miner's shoes were short-lived, a doctor's office, a pool parlor, two or three tobacco stores, and some other little mercantile shops. Railroad tracks cut into the town like strokes of a knife cutting a large pie. Freight cars rumbled and grumbled over the rails, whether empty as they came in or filled to the brim on their way out.

The pride of the town was Union Hall, a two-story warehouse of a building capable of seating twelve hundred people. When some big decision was pending, the full membership of the local, numbering sixteen hundred, could crowd into its cavernous dimensions. The second floor of the building was partitioned off into a large recreation room almost gymnasium size and various union offices. Coaltown No. 6 was the largest bituminous mine in Pennsylvania, and the union local equally enjoyed the largest enrollment of members.

Although Union Hall was the most prominent place in the community because of its size and its importance to the population, the most conspicuous structure was the coal tipple, a tall and ungainly steel structure that kept chattering and muttering throughout the day as it lifted the coal cars from the mine beneath. When the cars reached the crest, a mechanical contrivance released the endgates and the coal cascaded into conveyors that shook and vibrated like popcorn skillets. The coal passed over holes of so many different dimensions that there was not a lump, no matter how oddly shaped, that did not find its own size. The small pieces moved on to a washery where the specific gravity of the water and chemical solution therein sent the coal to the surface. The impurities sank to the bottom.

Those impurities were later dumped on the ground. In time they formed a slag pile that looked like a small mountain on fire—a stunted Vesuvius enveloped in a red aura rising from the fire in its entrails. In the dawn, Steve Gunthers often heard the smoldering embers hiss in the dew-drenched air.

A little volcano, Steve thought, with an ominous suggestion in it of physical ruin, economic and social eruption.

He never failed to feel dismayed as he watched all vegetation in Coaltown being destroyed by the dragon in its midst, a dragon whose nostrils breathed out locomotive flame-shot smoke, slag mountain fumes, and dirt and dust of the mine. The farmer in him made him picture the other side of the clay hills which surrounded the town. Beyond those hills nature still smiled in fragrant meadows, murmuring brooks, hills cloaked with bright, live foliage.

Steve had come to think of Coaltown as a desert oasis in reverse. Whereas an oasis is a little touch of heaven in a desert land of hell, Coaltown was a neatly packaged inferno grafted into the middle of nature's paradise.

He glanced down at his gnarled talons and alligator-hide palms and corrugated wrists that stuck grotesquely out of his sleeves. If Ivan had ever studied them, as they grasped his dinner bucket or held on to his corncob pipe, he would know that after enough years his own hands would no longer be able to bow and finger the delicate strings of a violin.

It was the bitterness of gall to Steve that this delicate son of his had to go down into the brutalizing mine, but he comforted himself with the thought that perhaps, after a couple of years, Ivan might earn enough to study at a conservatory of music. He wished this with real passion. He had never got over the horror which seized him the day when Ivan had said in a sudden blurt: "Dad, do you think coal mining will hurt my hands for—for the violin?"

"No, son," he had replied, as honestly as he could. "Not if you don't stay at it too long—as long as I have." And he had shoved his hands deep inside his pockets.

Now, he walked inside the house and called his son.

"Ivan, let's go over and talk to Jan Volkanik. I'd like you to work with him tomorrow—that first day will be important. Jan can help you more than any miner I know. Even more than I can."

They walked out together. Steve believed—as others did—that Volkanik was the most competent miner in Coaltown. It wasn't only Jan's enormous physical vigor that was so impressive. Jan knew the practical skills and tricks of mining probably better than most technical engineers.

He had a firsthand knowledge of the machinery in the mine. Others called upon him to make small repairs in electrical connections when the regular experts were not around. He came by his abilities naturally. He had a remarkable capacity for learning quickly whatever was once shown him in practical fashion. Steve had observed Volkanik in action for several years. He was confident that under his supervision Ivan would suffer no harm in learning how to use his musician's hands to attack the heavy, body-breaking work of mining.

They found Volkanik at the Barneskis'. Steve told him why he had come. "I'd like you to be a big brother to my Ivan tomorrow," he said as one good friend talks to another.

"Sure, Steve! That's fine! I be glad to take care from Ivan. You know, he's playin' my weddin'." Volkanik made mock motions of an imaginary bow sawing across a fiddle. "Got to take care of Ivan or I never marry Nora," he said, grinning.

"I'll be mighty pleased to play for you, Mr. Volkanik," Ivan added, shyly.

"And don't you worry from the coal mining. I will take care from you, Ivan."

And Steve knew Volkanik would. He felt much better when they left.

It was six o'clock the next morning when Volkanik and Ivan reached the shaft, ready to descend into the mines. They entered the elevator cage with twenty others.

Ivan felt as strange as he knew he looked. Where the others were big and rugged and heavy-set, he had a pale young face and a slim body. There were no calluses on his hands and his fingers were long and tapered. He felt himself tremble as the bell rang. The gate clanged shut and the wooden floor beneath his feet gave way so suddenly it filled him with the shocked sense that someone had cut the supporting cable.

The cage plunged downward. Ivan froze with the feeling that the descent was not regulated. A glimmer of light penetrating into the shaft revealed the walls streaking upward with horrifying speed. A fierce gust of wind from below ballooned his trousers. . . . He heard water dripping. He tried to study Volkanik's expression to see how he was reacting to all this, but the light was too dim. His friend's face was only a dark blur that told him nothing.

It was all a bad dream to Ivan—diving, tumbling, pitching, falling down, down, down. . . .

167

He felt the humidity creep over him. His skin seemed to sense the chill of suddenly lowered temperature. The cage bounced in its unrelenting drop. Through the cracks of the floor he thought he detected a lessening of the darkness—a faint glow of illumination of some kind. The speed of the fall was checked. He felt a straining and tightening above—the cable was not cut after all. Then a flood of light fell on them. They had reached the shaft bottom.

Volkanik playfully tilted up the boy's chin and looked into his pallid face.

"So you was scared?" Volkanik asked, in a voice gentle for such a brawny man. "That make no difference, Ivan. I scared myself." He twisted his face into a picture of mock terror. Ivan smiled weakly. He looked around at this new world, six hundred feet below the surface.

"Before we start work I show you coal mine. You think you like?"

"Oh yes, Mr. Volkanik. I'd like that very much."

They left the shaft bottom and walked into the haulageway. It was twelve feet wide, five feet six inches high. Electric lights had brightened the shaft bottom but there were none here. All that Ivan could make out, squinting his eyes, were bobbing tiny incandescences—the electric cap lamps worn by the miners. He couldn't see much else.

"Mr. Volkanik, is my light turned on? I can't see so well."

"Yes, you light on. But you eyes not used to coal mine. No worry, Ivan—soon you see just like rats."

Ivan recoiled. Were there really rats down here? Or was Mr. Volkanik joking again? Just then they reached a string of small cars. All Ivan could think of were the cars of a roller coaster in an amuse-

ment park. Volkanik climbed into one of them while he warned Ivan to watch out for the trolley wire from which the electric locomotive that pulled the cars got its power. Ivan was startled to see the live wire was only five feet above the floor—mere inches above the heads of the passengers.

About two hundred other men got into the twenty cars, along with them.

"Now," Volkanik told him, "you on what we call 'mantrip.' "

169

Ivan made a mental note of the term. The underground mine train leaped forward like a horizontal rocket, bowling along at forty miles an hour. Ivan winced again and again as he saw miners along the track suddenly leap to the side, flatten against a rib of coal to avoid being hit by the train. It whizzed along on its narrow-gauge tracks—they looked no bigger and not much more solid than toy Christmas electric train tracks.

Unequipped with springs or upholstery of any kind the mantrip gave Ivan as teeth-chattering and bumpy a ride as he had ever experienced. After ten or fifteen minutes the train ground to a stop, the passengers clambered out and quickly disappeared into the several entries which converged at this point. Then the train vanished with a rumble into the darkness.

Ivan slid to the ground and sat there, trying to shake off the effects of the severe jolting. Volkanik laughed.

"You ride rolly coaster, Ivan, and you get sick!"

Ivan felt too shaken to answer. He looked around, mystified. Where was everybody? It was a strange business, down here in the mine. You saw hundreds of men descend into the shaft and then minutes later you saw nobody. An oppressive sense of desolation crept over him. Finally he spoke his thought aloud.

"Where is everybody, Mr. Volkanik?"

Volkanik spread his hands. "This mine cover maybe thirty square mile. They go away fast, huh, Ivan?"

Ivan managed to get to his feet. Volkanik started to walk and Ivan followed him as well as he could. The passageway had such a low ceiling, he couldn't straighten up. Ivan guessed that the average height was about five feet, but for long stretches it was less, nearer four feet. Then sometimes it lifted to seven or eight feet, but he knew from hearing his father talk that this meant danger—the roof was not secure. All that height had come about because the overhead strata had fallen away.

Off to the side of the entry he saw two men in a pocket of coal, hemmed in on all sides. They were bent over, almost at right angles, as if their hip joints had hardened and set. They were hacking away with desperate energy, and gave the impression of men engaged in the hopeless task of digging themselves out of a pit into which they had fallen.

Volkanik suddenly raised his hand. "Stop! Listen!"

Ivan froze in apprehension. Only ten feet away he heard a noise that sounded like he thought a rattlesnake warning would sound. Then the ceiling gave way. It crashed down—tons of slate and rock filling the entry. Ivan choked a little inside. His heart pumped hard. Ten more feet and they would have been buried under the avalanche. Ten short feet!

Ivan felt sweat pour over him, but Volkanik gave him a reassuring pat on the shoulder and bade him continue. The youthful miner felt a deep sense of physical relief each time the low ceiling ended and they came to a straightaway where he could walk without stooping. The hump in his back melted away as he became an erect human being again. But it was a dangerous luxury, he knew. Fear gripped him each time he heard a cracking sound above. Usually the cracking sound came from his own head, bumping against a projection. He was grateful for the hard cap on his head, which probably saved him from being knocked senseless.

Every so often they reached accumulated waters, too wide and deep to be called puddles.

They waded through them, ankle-deep. Mr. Volkanik called over his shoulder:

"Water always coming into mine. We got pumps. Don't worry."

Little shock piled on little shock as Ivan walked. In one of the working entries the ceiling dipped so sharply that the miner underneath it had a space of only three to four feet in which to work. Then he saw something crawling, something as big as a man. A shudder trembled through him when he saw it was actually a man—a shirtless miner with face, neck, arms, back and waist crusted with a layer of coal dust. The crust was so thick he looked more like an animal than a human being.

Ivan thought of his own pink-and-white complexion. The mirror had told him youth and health glowed in it. How long would it last now? Would it become coated, scaly with coal shavings, like this man's? Would he become permanently tatooed with coal dust? Volkanik was watching him. He seemed to guess what Ivan was thinking.

"No worry, Ivan, no worry! Plenty of water in crick and we buy lots soap!"

Suddenly, shooting fragments of light like Fourth of July sparklers punctured the clammy darkness.

"What's that, Mr. Volkanik?"

"Come, Ivan. I show you something."

Mr. Volkanik led him several hundred feet along the corridor. They stopped before a metal monster that looked more fearsome than any dragon he had seen in pictures or dreamed up in his imagination. A gigantic iron-and-steel turtle of prehistoric shape was belligerently leaving the track on which it had traveled. It grumbled and snorted. It emitted flashes and sparks, as if impatient to attack the wall of coal toward which it lumbered. Then utter-ing ominous, rumbling sounds, this underground demon finally faced its enemy, the wall. It thrust forward a ramlike snout with sharp spikes that reminded Ivan of the attacking front prongs of a swordfish which had awed him in a picture book about the sea.

Two men tried to control the monster but it seemed to have a will of its own, needing no urging and wanting no harness. Striking the wall head-on, the turtle-swordfish began to work in earnest.

Ivan studied the monster as it worked: an endless chain holding the spikes, or blades, revolved around the entire length of the projecting ram, pulverizing the iron-like coal into tiny particles. In a matter of minutes it had undercut the coal for a depth of six feet, leaving a slot about eight inches thick at the bottom of the "face."

Mr. Volkanik explained that this machine made mining coal a lot easier. The miner bored a hole into the upper surface and inserted dynamite. The explosion that followed forced a downward pressure; and since there was now space to accommodate the force of the detonation, the coal would break into larger lumps than if it had no room to expand.

Soon the traveling miners started for Butt 40. Ivan was bewildered. How did Mr. Volkanik know his way around in this maze of tunnels, this baffling network of black alleys? They would walk perhaps five hundred feet in one direction, then Mr. Volkanik would turn right or left, open a door—and there would be another apparently endless tunnel. They would move on several hundred feet farther in this passageway and then turn into a similar corridor that had no end in sight. *Clid . . . clop . . . clid . . . clop. . . .* They moved along. All this happened in darkness. They met no one. What

171

a mystery a mine was, Ivan thought. Packed with the furious activity of hundreds of men—and yet it constantly seemed deserted!

More stunned astonishment swept over him as he suddenly smelled stable odors. He had spent several summers on a farm and he knew stable smells. But where were the horses down here? In another moment they looked into a long cave built into the coal—an underground stable with twenty stalls, empty except for five. Two horses and three mules stood motionless. Joyfully Ivan ran forward to stroke the animals. He felt like a man who had landed on another planet and found fellow human beings after a dark, eerie search. "But where are the others?" he asked Volkanik.

"They out workin', Ivan, where we go pretty soon."

"Oh no!" Ivan pleaded. "Let's stay here awhile." The horses responded with gentle neighing to Ivan's soft stroking, but the mules resented Ivan's attentions. Mules seemed to have a grudge against the world. Ivan knew why. He remembered that at the farm he had been told how mules were brought into existence by a special arrangement between male donkeys and mares. It was an arrangement, Ivan had always felt, which revealed man's abject selfishness, because the only purpose of the union was to create animal slaves. This did not mean, however, that the owner didn't realize the worth of a mule. His father had told a true miner's story that Ivan never forgot.

A mine superintendent had received a message from inside the shaft which read: "Cave-in Section 57, Left 42. Five men and two mules killed." The superintendent clapped his hand to his head and groaned: "My God! Two mules killed!"

That was no joke. It was easy to get miners, his father had said, but it cost money to produce a mule. And yet, despite its commercial value, no one ever spoke affectionately to a mule. Its lot was to be addressed with curses, worked to the limit and beaten. And when it could work no more it was discarded.

Yet the mule, Ivan had heard, did not need to worry that its offspring would have the same agonizing life—having no offspring. It was the one way the mule outsmarted man.

Mine horses weren't much better off, his father had told him. And now Ivan noticed that although they responded to a friendly gesture, that delightful muscular shiver of the healthy horse on the farm was missing. He said: "Mr. Volkanik, are these horses taken to the surface at night?"

The big man slowly, sadly shook his head.

"Aren't they *ever* taken up?"

"No, Ivan."

The tragic fact hit Ivan almost like a physical blow. These animals, he thought, had once been frisky, playful colts. They had galloped joyously over green, sweet-smelling pastures, their handsome manes streaming in the wind. Now they were the condemned, in the deep galleys of unrelenting slavehood and unending darkness. They were exiles, sentenced to a life of hard labor and imprisonment. They would never again breathe the fragrance of the meadow, never again enjoy the cool waters of a brook or creek about their feet, never again whinny joyously to the caress of an affectionate hand.

As usual, Ivan saw that his friend instinctively knew what he was thinking about. The boy felt his hand taken in a huge, work-hardened one. "Let's go, Ivan," he said. And then they walked on, to Mr. Volkanik's working place.

EDWARD FENTON

"The Great World of Timothy Francis Brennan"

Timothy Francis Brennan goes
sightseeing in the big city

Time: 1930s   Setting: McKees Rocks?/ Pittsburgh

Timothy Francis Brennan, fourteen years old, lives with his grandmother in a mill town named *Duffy's Rocks* (Pittsburgh-area readers may decide the setting is McKees Rocks). Timothy's mother is dead and his father, Bart Brennan, has not lived in *Duffy's Rocks*, or even returned for a visit, in years. Presumably Timothy's father is working in exotic, distant places as an engineer — at least that's what the boy's grandmother tells him.

Duffy's Rocks is centrally concerned with Timothy's desire to be reunited with his father, or at least to find out the truth about him — since it is clear that his grandmother does not want to talk about the matter. The mysterious career of Bart Brennan becomes a painful subject that threatens to destroy the love between Timothy and his grandmother: She is bent on protecting the image of her son Bart, while Timothy, just as stubbornly, must know where his father is. The pinched, drab circumstances of life in a milltown during the Great Depression make Bart's life seem even more romantic, and the Saturday trip to downtown Pittsburgh narrated in this selection suggests Timothy's desire to escape Duffy's Rocks, as well as forecasting his efforts toward the end of the book to search out his father on his own.

But if the central plot of the novel is about a young boy's quest, *Duffy's Rocks* touches on many themes relative to the social topography of western Pennsylvania. There is the perennial ethnic mix and the awareness of class differences —

174

Timothy is befriended by a wealthy Shadyside woman, only to discover later the awkwardness of explaining to her what life in Duffy's Rocks is like. Since some of the Brennan family has moved out to Stowe Township, another conflict is introduced, and Timothy's grandmother is allowed to speak for an older generation that refuses to be lured from the neighborhood that is "home":

"What's the sense of staying in Duffy's Rocks," Uncle Matt went on, "when there's practically no IRISH left on the street, all your old friends are moved away, and we can't get over to see you as often as Anna'd like? . . ."

Gran had been listening to him with an odd thin smile on her face. Now she held up her hand.

"I'm not leaving," she said in a sharp determined voice, "not until they carry me out. This is my house and I'm staying here. . . . Your father and I bought this house in Duffy's Rocks when we were married; we worked hard to pay for it; we never owed anybody a penny on it. . . . It may be a little old-fashioned like you say, Matthew, but I'm a little old-fashioned too. . . . And while I live, Duffy's Rocks and this house, please God, is where I'll live."

Though *Duffy's Rocks* is classified in libraries as a "juvenile" book, it is totally free from condescension, sentimentality, and moralizing. It is, quite simply, a good novel.

Born in New York City, Edward Fenton was moved to write *Duffy's Rocks* by a visit to the Pittsburgh area. He currently lives in Athens, Greece.

"The Great World of Timothy Francis Brennan"

The first and only time that he took Mary Agnes with him on one of his Saturdays, Timothy began to regret it almost from the moment he set out. . . .

It had not turned out at all the way that Mary Agnes had expected it to, either.

For one thing, she had known that Timothy was itching to be on his own. That only made her all the more determined to make him take her along.

It was their grandmother who settled the matter in the end.

"Ah," she had snapped, "I've had enough of your wrangling. Wouldn't the walls just crack around our heads from the racket of it! Outside, now, with the both of yous. Mr. Kinsella and I will be the better for it if we're shet of yous for the day." She turned to Timothy, her pale eyes reproachful behind her rimless glasses. "As for you, Timothy Francis, I don't know where it is you find to go, all on your own, but it's not going to kill you if you take Mary Agnes with you, just once. If I know boys, you'll be on your knees to a lot worse in a few years' time, begging to do you the honor of hanging on your arm. Mary Agnes is not a person to be ashamed of."

Little did Gran know, Timothy thought bitterly while Mary Agnes performed a little wriggle of triumph behind Gran's back.

"He hates me because I'm his cousin!" Mary Agnes cried.

Gran pursed her lips. "I won't listen to such talk." Her eyes remained fixed on Timothy's sullen face. "What would your father think if I was to write him such a thing?" She beckoned him to her side. Then she reached for her worn, black, leather-ette snap purse, which hung from the back of the kitchen chair. She opened it. "Here," she said quietly. "You'll be needing some extra carfare, since you have a lady along to pay for."

Timothy glanced down at his palm. There was a quarter in it. "The times is bad and the flesh is weak, so take it and use it before I change my mind," she said. "And now," she added, before he could even thank her for it, "out!"

Their grandmother's front door was less than a block behind them when, "Where are we going?" Mary Agnes demanded.

"I'm not sure yet," he told her.

Her face turned mean with suspicion.

"What do you mean you're not sure?"

The savage excitement that seized him every Saturday morning now, whenever it was time for him to go off on his expedition, had begun to boil in his veins. Grinning jauntily he said, "I never know where I'm going until I get there."

"Timothy Francis Brennan!" she exclaimed. "That's stupid."

His face clouded. It was almost a year that he had been going down to Pittsburgh to explore, every Saturday. Saturdays were his own property now. They were private. Wasn't it bad enough that she had forced him to take her along this time without her deliberately trying to spoil it for him? After all, she was a big girl now, practically thirteen, only less than a year younger than he was. He couldn't see why Mary Agnes couldn't go off on adventures of her own, with her girl friends, instead of having to barge in on his personal, private arrangements.

He kicked out at a ridge of ice turned to black lace at its edge, all that was left of the snowfall of the week before. "Why is that so stupid?" he asked.

But Mary Agnes was too busy to reply. She was tugging at her long ribbed stockings. She had stopped right there on the sidewalk in front of Lesniak's grocery store to do it.

He stared disapprovingly at her until she had finished.

"Well," he persisted. "Why is it so stupid?"

Mary Agnes tried to look superior, as though those stockings were not still clinging to her thin shins in lumpy brown wrinkles.

"I always like to know where I'm going," she declared.

"Don't you like surprises?"

She pressed her lips together. "Only when I know what they're going to be," she said.

Looking at her small, set, pointed face, suspicious and already dark with disappointment, Timothy knew that it would be hopeless to explain to her that this was what he always did. He just went. And then, once he got there, he let things happen.

He called out, "Here comes the streetcar now!" and started to sprint to the car stop. Mary Agnes forgot about her stockings and panted after him. The rear door clattered open. All the seats were already taken, so they had to stand on the rear platform, holding onto the poles.

They rode in silence. Mary Agnes looked resentfully at Timothy, while Timothy looked out through the soot-streaked glass. He stared at the small frame houses, all exactly like his grandmother's, with their gritty curtains stretched across the front windows. He stared at the skimpy bare trees, at the grime-layered store fronts, at the shabby beer parlors on every corner, their entrance doors clotted with unemployed men. In the center of almost every block there stood a church with its blackened brick parochial school, exactly like St. Bridget's where he and Mary Agnes went. They all flashed past as the streetcar clanged downhill.

They were like a rosary strung across the town with each bead in a different language. There was a German church, Holy Trinity; then St. Margaret of Hungary; St. Ladislaus, which was Slovak; St. Jan Nepomuk's (Czech; Mrs. Sevchick from next door went there). After that came St. Sava's, for the Serbians; the Croatian church; Sts. Cyril and Methodius, the Slovene church; the Lithuanian church with a saint's name that he couldn't pronounce; St. Josaphat's Ukrainian Catholic Church; Our Lady of Czestochowa, which was Polish; and St. Catherine of Genoa, faced all over with gaudy Italian stonework.

As the neighborhood receded, Timothy's heart bounded higher. Soon they had even left behind them Kolb's Used Car Lot where, week after week, the same automobiles stood. None of them ever seemed to get sold, in spite of the huge banners that stretched across the entrance: *No Reasonable Offer Refused! Easy Terms Arranged on the Spot!*

After that, the railroad tracks cut across the street. Now the faces of the unemployed men on the sidewalk were black. He looked out for the mysterious store front which had all its windows painted over in yellow and purple and red, with a sign over the doorway: *African Church of the Pentecostal Brotherhood. Come to the Refreshing Spring and Be Saved!*

Once past the Colored church, Timothy knew

McKees Rocks a few years before the action of the story.

that he was really on his way. There was still more than half an hour's ride ahead of him, uphill and downhill, winding through a grubby string of industrial towns exactly like Duffy's Rocks, all grown together into a shapeless suburb. Each had its rows of gaunt, gray, company houses like dingy wash on a line, and stores whose shabby windows denied the hope that prosperity was just around the corner, and more churches.

He smiled to himself now. He glanced down at his feet. He hadn't managed to save up for the boots with the knife in the side, but his old shoes shone. He had polished them himself in the kitchen the night before. His hair was combed, stiff and dark with water, and carefully parted. His white shirt crackled with starch, and although his tie was an old one, he had spent a long time getting the knot just right. His blue serge suit was shiny only where it didn't show. And if his overcoat was too small for him, that didn't matter because he could feel the money waiting in its pocket. He had his weekly dollar that he earned from carting out the ashes from Mrs. Sevchick's furnace.

He was on his way: off to the adventure that waited for him. The whole week, to him, was a trough between his Saturdays. It was the thought of them that made it possible to endure all those dreary weekdays which led up to them. For the moment he even forgot that this time Mary Agnes was with him, secured to his side like a block of cement.

Soon he would be able to see the river. Then the bulk of the skyscrapers would loom ahead of him, shining through the grit-filled air. And after that he would be downtown.

He pressed closer to the window, but just then some broad Slovak ladies got up. They clutched black oilcloth shopping bags in their chapped hands, and their faces under their shawls were steamy and red. They surrounded him, blocking the view. He could only tell when the streetcar was crossing the river from the way it lurched and from the sound of the wheels rattling on the bridge. After that the car began to empty. But there was no sense in sitting down now.

Suddenly, he grabbed Mary Agnes by the sleeve. "Come on. We're getting off here!"

"Where?"

"Oh, come on!"

She jumped down, plunging after him into the crowds that clogged the intersection.

The great world, Timothy thought: this was it! He turned, lifting his face eagerly toward it, ignoring the people who had to jostle him in order to pass. There was not much smoke today. Everything was clear in the cold winter air. His eyes drank in the wide streets filled with traffic and lined with vast office buildings. He knew the name of every single one of the glittering granite buildings of downtown Pittsburgh. All around him, in every direction, they stretched: banks, department stores with their enormous crystal display windows, theatres. A sea of preoccupied faces milled in and out of them. Every Saturday he felt the same surge of wild exhilaration. It was all there. And it was all his!

Mary Agnes, at his shoulder, said, "What are we going to do now?"

He blinked at her. "I just like to mingle with the crowd."

It was a phrase which he especially liked that year. He had found it in a book.

Mary Agnes was not impressed by it.

"And?" she persisted.

He could have smacked her, but he only said, "And that's enough for right now. Later on, we'll see."

She trailed after him as he made his way to Smithfield Street. He walked along, oblivious of the cindery grit under his shoes, gazing hungrily into the shop windows. Even though there weren't many customers in the stores, and half the windows had big stickers pasted across them with signs like *Sale, All Prices Slashed!* or *Going Out of Business, Everything Must Be Sold!* they were filled with wonderful objects.

"We can't buy anything," Mary Agnes said. "So what's the sense of looking?"

He said loftily, "I'm just playing my game."

She gave him a sharp, dubious look.

"What game?"

"I always play it when I'm by myself. From every window I pick the one thing I'd take."

"That's easy," she said in a decisive voice. "I'd look at the prices and then I'd just take what costs the most."

"You can't do that," he explained patiently. "It has to be something you really want for yourself. How much it costs doesn't count."

She reflected for a moment.

"Supposing it's, well, a store with nothing I could use? Then what?"

"Then you have to pick a present to give somebody. But you have to say who it's for."

"All right. I'll take that evening bag, the one with the gold chain and the red sequins all over it."

"Who for?"

She gave him a withering look. "For myself," she said.

Slowly they proceeded up Smithfield Street. They hardly ever agreed on what they picked. Timothy was convinced that most of Mary Agnes' choices were silly, and Mary Agnes said she couldn't imagine what he would ever do with most

of the things he took. Then, halfway down the other side of Smithfield, right under the Kaufmann's Department Store clock, Mary Agnes suddenly stopped.

"I don't want to look anymore," she said.

179

"Why not?"

"I'm cold."

He glowered at her.

"Cold?"

She chattered her teeth at him. "Yes. C.O.L.D," she said.

"Well, that makes us even. You wanted to come, didn't you? You pestered me to come along."

"That was because you really didn't want me to. And now all we're doing is just walking around the streets looking in store windows at stuff we can't really have anyway. And I'm freezing." She sniffed. "And what are you going to do about it?"

"But we really haven't done anything yet, Mary Agnes. Come on, you'll like it. You'll see."

"I don't want to just walk around anymore. I want to go home now if we're not going to do anything warm."

Timothy stared at her. She was an infuriating sight. Her fists were crammed into the pockets of her windbreaker. Under her big, knitted green cap with its frayed white pompom her peaked gypsy face looked smaller than ever, and her lips were turning blue. Her skirt, he realized for the first time, was too short for her skinny legs. She looked angry and lost.

Then he remembered that Mary Agnes was not really used to downtown the way he was. His face softened.

He said, "Don't you like just looking at things?"

"Not when I can't have them," she retorted fiercely. "And not when I'm freezing all over."

He stood there for a moment. Then he made a sudden decision.

"All right," he said. "Come with me."

"Can't you even tell me, Timothy, where we're going?"

"You'll see in a minute."

She had to take running steps to keep up with him. And then he vanished. He had been swallowed up by the vast building in front of them. When she read the name of it she hung back, rooted to the sidewalk. She stared after him in unbelief.

He waved to her through the revolving doors to follow him.

Mary Agnes refused to budge.

He had to go around again and pull her in after him.

"We can't go inside," she said in a shocked voice. "It's the William Penn Hotel!"

"Shut up, Mary Agnes!" he told her between his clenched teeth. "Who says we can't come inside?"

"But we don't know anyone here!"

"We don't have to. It's a public place, isn't it?"

She gaped at him.

"But—"

"Stop making such a fuss, Mary Agnes. Do you want people to start looking? You said you were cold, didn't you? Well. Come on, then."

He pulled her after him across the lobby. She proceeded across the thick carpeting as though it had been woven out of eggshells.

Timothy went ahead confidently, but Mary Agnes glanced nervously at the line of bellboys with their tight uniforms and polished buttons. "They'll put us out!" she whispered.

"Not if you act like you belong here," he said sharply.

"But I don't belong here."

He ignored her.

She scooted after him past the lordly gentleman who stood behind the reception desk.

"What are you going to do now, Timothy?" she asked. Her voice shook, but it was no longer because of the cold.

"Nothing," he said firmly. "I'm just going to

find a place where we can sit down.''

He strode ahead of her, eyeing the bulky leather davenports that were lined up against the tall potted plants. "There's an empty one," he said.

"You can't do that!" squeaked Mary Agnes.

"Why not?" He plumped himself calmly down at one end of it. "Now you sit down too," he commanded.

Gingerly, Mary Agnes lowered herself onto it at the opposite end. The cushion slowly sank, and she sank with it.

"Don't bounce!" he warned. "Just sit there as though you were waiting for somebody."

"It's so big," she said in a loud whisper. "It's the biggest sofa I ever sat on." She giggled. "You're so far away, Timothy." She waggled her hand at him. "Yoo-hoo!" she called.

Timothy frowned.

She hastily stuffed her hand back into her pocket. Then she settled back, keeping her knees pressed closely together. "Is this all right?"

He nodded and gave her a tight smile. After that he turned to watch all the people who were moving through the warm lobby.

Mary Agnes glanced around her in awe. Two ladies in fur coats and feathered hats were talking animatedly on the sofa across from theirs. One of the ladies held a little dog on her lap. The dog had on a red woollen sweater.

After a moment Mary Agnes said, "You want to know something, Timothy?"

"What?"

"You look different."

"How, different?"

"I don't know." She considered. "You look almost like somebody who was staying here, like some rich kid from out of town." She giggled again. "I can't help it," she said. "If all those

people at the desk knew, they'd throw us right out of here and chase us home."

He glanced at her with annoyance. "They wouldn't do any such thing," he said firmly. All the time, his eyes flickered in the direction of the gods at the reception desk, just to be sure.

Mary Agnes' eyes wandered cautiously around the lobby, taking in the groups of chatting ladies, the men in felt hats and heavy overcoats dashing off to important appointments, the porters pushing their way behind carts piled with sumptuous luggage, the small whirlpools of activity around the elevator doors. The cigar counter was not far from where they sat. "You don't even have to go outside to buy a newspaper!" she exclaimed.

"I bet there are people here from every single city in the world," Timothy told her. . . .

"Can't you tell me now," she pleaded, "what you really do when you come downtown? I know you don't spend the whole day walking around. If you tell me, Timothy, I won't tell a single solitary soul, not even Gran."

"I don't care if you tell her," he said. "I just go to different places, that's all."

"Like where?" She leaned forward, licking her lips. "Like the movies?"

"Sometimes. But the movies aren't all that special. You don't have to come downtown for that." He paused. Then he said, "I went to a symphony concert once."

"Timothy, you didn't!"

"I was standing outside watching the people go in, and a lady gave me a ticket."

"You mean she just gave it to you, like that?"

"She said she had an extra one. It was right down in the orchestra."

"Honestly!" Mary Agnes' eyes glittered. "How was it, Timothy? It must have been terribly loud."

181

Before he could answer, she went on, "I don't know if I'd have cared so much for it, listening to all that classical music. I mean, all those notes, and it never seems to go anywhere, does it? I'd have liked it better if it was a movie. Still, it was free, wasn't it?"

It had been a lot of notes, Timothy reflected. But how was he to explain to her what it was like, sitting in the hushed atmosphere of the Syria Mosque with everyone around him in their best clothes, and the seat he sat in soft and comfortable, and the music surging around him?

"What else?"

"Well, I go to Schenley Park sometimes, but it's too cold for that now. And sometimes I go to the Institute."

"That's a museum, like, isn't it? What can you do there?"

"I look around. It has paintings."

Mary Agnes reflected. Then, "That's too much like church," she decided. She slid over closer to him and squinted into his face. "What else do you do?"

"Oh," he told her, "I just go around, like I said." He paused. "And I have lunch."

"Where, Timothy? In a cafeteria?"

He looked scornful. "No," he said. "In a restaurant."

"One with real waiters?"

"Of course."

"Honestly!" Mary Agnes exclaimed again. She thought about it for a moment. "Don't you get embarrassed?"

"No. Why should I?"

"I would, if I was to go all by myself."

"There's nothing to it," he assured her. He glanced up at the bronze clock over the bank of elevators. Its hands already pointed to one. He felt

in his pocket. The money was still there.

He turned to Mary Agnes.

"Are you hungry?"

"Not specially," she said, but her tongue stole out furtively and traveled across her upper lip.

"I'll tell you what," he said, breaking into a smile. "We'll eat in a restaurant today. I'll take you."

"Do you mean that, Timothy? Really?" Her face was suffused with excitement. Then it fell. "I only have fifteen cents. It's all I saved this week."

"I'll treat you, Mary Agnes," he told her expansively.

She scanned his face.

"If I say I will, I will," he said.

"I only mean," she told him humbly, "are you sure you have enough money, Timothy?"

"That's my business." He grinned at her. "All right," he said. "Are you ready to go now?"

She nodded.

"Then come on. And no more being cold."

"I won't say a word, I promise, even if my nose freezes! Anyway," she added, scurrying after him toward the revolving doors, "it was getting terribly hot in here."

Out on the windy sidewalk, the two ladies with the dog were getting into an automobile.

"Well," said Mary Agnes, in a patronizing voice, loud enough for them to hear, "I think it's a very nice little hotel, considering." Then she raced down the street after Timothy.

They went on in silence, not bothering to stop in front of windows anymore. But then, on one corner, there was a store with an enormous expanse of polished stone facade in which were set three tiny display windows. They were lit up like miniature theatres.

"We have to look in here!" Mary Agnes said. She

pressed her forehead against the cold pane. "Ooh," she cried. "Look, Timothy. It's all gold and diamonds."

"What did you expect? It's a jewelry store."

"Let's choose something."

Their eyes raked the display.

Timothy joggled her elbow. "How about that necklace?"

"Do you think all those diamonds and rubies could be real?"

"Of course they are."

Her mouth curved in disdain. "Well, I think it's awfully gaudy."

"Gaudy? It must be worth thousands and thousands of dollars!"

"I don't care. I'd never wear anything like that. It looks like glass."

They abandoned the diamond-and-ruby necklace and moved on to the second window. It was lined with white satin, against which had been arranged three gold cigarette cases. "Wouldn't you think they'd have more to show than that?" Mary Agnes remarked contemptuously as she tugged at her stockings.

The last window held crystal and silver tableware.

Mary Agnes let out a little gasp. In the corner of the display stood a tiny silver vase with a single rose in it.

Timothy had seen it at the same time.

They stared at it.

"I wonder how much something like that costs?" Mary Agnes said at last.

"We can find out."

Her jaw went slack. "Timothy Francis Brennan, you wouldn't have the nerve to walk in there and ask them. Never!"

"Wouldn't I?"

She shook her head.

"Then you just stand there and watch me."

He moved toward the massive, bronze-barred door.

"Timothy!" she wailed. "Come back! You'll get arrested!"

He disregarded her and went inside. After a while she saw a man's manicured hand reach into the window through the little curtain behind it and remove the vase. A few minutes later the same hand carefully replaced it. And then Timothy was out there on the street beside her.

Mary Agnes' eyes were as big and as round as coat buttons. "Did they really let you hold it?"

He nodded.

"And? Well, what did they say?"

"They said it costs fifteen dollars. It's sterling silver. And they called me *sir.*"

"Honestly!"

"And if I had fifteen dollars," he added, as they charged across the street before the green light changed, "I would have bought it."

"I bet you would, too, Timothy!" Mary Agnes' eyes were swimmy with admiration.

He only smiled.

When they reached the opposite curb, he had an idea. "I know a short cut to the restaurant," he said.

"All right. Anything you say, Timothy."

"It's nothing great. We can just walk through Gimbels and out the other side. That way you won't be so cold."

"Cold!" She sniffed. "Who's cold? And we can go down in the basement. That's where Mama shops."

They made slow progress through Gimbels basement because there were so many things which she had to stop and finger, and every other minute she had to run on so as not to lose Timothy. One of the very last counters had a little sign: *Genuine Mosaic Brooches Imported from Florence, Italy.* It was Timothy who lingered to inspect them.

"What do you think of that?" he said. "Look, Mary Agnes. They're all made of little bits of colored glass stuck together."

"They look like flowers!"

Together they pored over them. "I like the one you're holding," Mary Agnes said.

"Wouldn't it be nice for Gran, though!"

The big blonde lady behind the counter leaned over toward them. "Pretty, aren't they?" she remarked. "They're a special. And a real bargain, too. Only fifty-nine cents."

They stared at her. Mary Agnes was fascinated by her red earrings and bleached hair.

The saleslady's red fingernails plucked the brooch from Timothy's hand and held it against her blouse. "This one's very classy. Forget-me-nots it's supposed to be. It would make a very gorgeous present for somebody."

Timothy wavered.

The saleslady flashed a smile at him. "I could wrap it for you real nice," she said. "In a gift box with a lining."

"Timothy!" Mary Agnes exclaimed. "You're not going to buy it!"

"Why not?" he said grandly. "It would look nice on Gran." He hauled some money out of his pocket. "I'll take it," he told the saleslady.

"You picked the best one," she assured him. "You got lovely taste."

"He's my cousin," Mary Agnes told her.

When they left the counter the forget-me-not brooch was nested in yellow cotton inside a little box which had "Made in Italy" stamped on the cover.

"Can't you just see Gran's face when she opens it!" said Mary Agnes. "She'll die!"

A few yards away something else drew Mary Agnes' eye. "Hey, Timothy. Look at this!" A small, brown, burlap object dangled from her hand.

"What's that?"

"It's supposed to be a catnip mouse. Anyway, that's what it says on the label."

"I bet Mr. Kinsella would like that," he said.

She looked dubious. "Mr. Kinsella's too old."

Timothy looked at the price tag. "It's only a nickel, marked down from nineteen cents. I'll get it. We can see what Mr. Kinsella does with it."

Mary Agnes cast her eyes quickly around her. Then she lowered her voice. "You go on ahead. I'll hook it."

"What are you talking about, Mary Agnes?"

"Ah, it's easy. Nobody's looking."

"Are you crazy? Here, in Gimbels? They have detectives all over the place."

He fished out a nickel and paid for it. Then, with the pin for their grandmother and the mouse for Mr. Kinsella safely stuffed into his overcoat pocket, they floated up to the main floor on the escalator and made their way out onto the street.

"All the same," said Mary Agnes, "if I hadn't said anything to you I could have swiped it easy."

They walked briskly now. Timothy was hungry. He had been too excited at the prospect of going downtown to eat much breakfast, and now he found himself wishing he hadn't spurned the bowl of oatmeal Gran had set down for him. "It's only a few blocks from here, where we're going," he announced. Mary Agnes didn't mind how far it was. Her eyes were bright, and she didn't seem to feel the cold anymore.

And then, around a corner, there it was.

"Is *that* the place?" she asked.

"It's the one I like best. What's the matter? Don't you like it?"

"It doesn't look like what I imagined. *'Mario's Continentale. Italian and French Cuisine,'*" she read aloud from the sign across the front of it. She wrinkled her nose. "It's foreign," she said.

"But that's the whole point!"

The menu, mimeographed in runny purple ink, was stuck on the inside of the window. "See?" Timothy said. "'Special five-course table d'hote luncheon, 45¢, glass of wine included.'"

"Wine?" she said, scandalized. "Honestly!" She bent to read the menu. "'Choice of entre.'... It's all French and Italian. How do you know what to order?"

"If you don't know, you just ask the waiter and he explains what it is."

"And show him I don't know? I'd never!"

"Oh, come on, Mary Agnes. I'm starving. You can have spaghetti. You like that, don't you?"

"Only when it's out of a can." She pressed her face against the steamy glass and peered through it at the tables set with red-checked cloths and baskets of breadsticks.

"Oh, all right," she agreed. "But I'm not drinking any of that wine!"

Timothy started to sail ahead of her through the door. Then, suddenly, he stopped. He pulled his money out of his pockets and began to count it.

"What's the matter?" Mary Agnes asked.

He looked up at her in dismay. "I didn't think about it when I bought the pin for Gran. We don't have enough."

"Not even with my fifteen cents?"

He calculated. Then he shook his head. "There's the tip, too. You have to leave a dime each."

"Couldn't we just get up when the waiter wasn't looking and walk away very quickly?"

"No," he said. "Anyway, even without the tip there's not enough left."

Mary Agnes had an inspiration. "Look, we could just order one lunch. You could eat half and I'd eat the rest."

He shook his head impatiently. "They don't let you do that."

She reflected. "Maybe they'd take the pin back at Gimbels. We could say it wasn't the right color or something. Mama's always doing that."

Timothy thought about it.

"I don't think the saleslady would mind," Mary Agnes put in. "She looked real kind."

"No," Timothy said at last. "I wouldn't like to disappoint Gran."

"But if she doesn't know we bought it for her, how can she be disappointed?"

"I wouldn't feel right taking it back once we bought it for her," he said slowly.

The door of Mario's Continentale swung open. Two men walked out, releasing a hot whiff of food from the restaurant. Timothy and Mary Agnes looked at the people inside, sitting at the little tables, working their way through the five-course table d'hote.

"Well, Timothy, what are we going to do?"

"We can't just stand here," he said.

She tugged at his arm. "Let's go," she said.

"I'm sorry for your disappointment, Mary Agnes," he said, swallowing his own.

"It doesn't matter, really," she lied. "I'm glad we got the pin for Gran."

Reluctantly, they moved away.

"We'll have to eat something," Timothy told her.

"Don't worry, we'll find a place," she said. "How much do we have left?"

He counted it all again.

"Sixty-eight cents, but that's counting your fifteen and what we have to leave out for carfare home."

"Oh, we're rich!" she said. "Let's start looking."

In the end they settled for Woolworth's. Baked beans were ten cents at the lunch counter.

"They're very filling," Timothy admitted. "But the hot franks are only ten cents too, and you can pile on all the mustard and relish you want."

So they had the frankfurters, and on the way out they paused at the candy department. Peanut brittle was twenty-seven cents a pound.

"We can afford a whole pound," Mary Agnes announced, "and we'll still have enough left over for carfare and a penny change."

Then they were out on the streets again, munching as they passed the bag of peanut brittle back and forth between them. "I like the pecan crunch better, but it costs more," Mary Agnes said, with her mouth full.

They walked without any plan. They stood outside all the movie theatres, inspecting the still photographs in the outer lobbies. "I wish I had a name like Merle Oberon or Miriam Hopkins," Mary Agnes said dreamily as she scanned the display of Coming Attractions, "instead of"—she made a face—"Mary Agnes Doyle."

"There's nothing to stop you from calling yourself Merle or Miriam if you wanted."

She smiled at the thought. The next moment her rapturous expression turned into a sour grimace.

"I'd never. They'd all laugh. Can't you just hear Uncle Matt and Aunt Anna when I told them to call me Merle? And Gran?"

Timothy remembered his grandmother's mocking laughter the day he had announced he was going to call himself T. Frank Brennan.

"Maybe you're right," he said slowly. Then he thought about being an actor. You could be anybody you wanted to be, then. You could be a thousand different people. Aloud, he said, "Of course if you were an actor nobody could say anything about it if you changed your name. They do it all the time."

"I wouldn't want to be an actress," Mary Agnes said. "There's all that kissing they have to do. I wonder how they manage. Don't their teeth ever get in the way?"

The bright theatre facade faded behind them as they moved off.

"I wonder what time it is?" Timothy said. He looked around until he found a clock in a bank window. "I guess we ought to be heading back."

"All right, Timothy," she said in a quiet voice. "There isn't anything else to see. We've seen just about everything there is, haven't we? And anyway, my feet are starting to hurt."

Timothy's feet were tired too, but he didn't say so.

A hard wind rose. It whipped at their legs as they stood on the corner waiting for a streetcar.

"I'm sorry about the lunch, Mary Agnes," he said.

"Oh, ish-kabibble!"

The streetcar came rushing toward them. They climbed in, found seats, and settled themselves.

Mary Agnes pressed his arm.

"You want to know something, Timothy?"

"What?"

"I think you can do anything," she said. Her dark pointed face shone with admiration. "Just anything!"

But Timothy was not really listening to her. His gaze was fixed on the tall buildings of downtown, brilliant in the sharp light of the sinking winter sun, as he prepared himself for the long ride home.

CHESTER AARON
"That Polack Anti-Semite Toadstool Expert"

An argument over toadstools
causes a confrontation

Time: 1930s   Setting: Near Slippery Rock

Set in the coal town of "Sundown" between 1932 and 1944, About Us *chronicles events that befall a Jewish family who run a small general store. Although the central character is Benny Kahn, eight years old when the book begins, each chapter is "about" a different figure within, or involved with, the Kahn family. More than in most novels, many of these chapters (like the one here) stand autonomously, almost in short-story fashion.*

As this selection amply illustrates, About Us *has strong comic moments that convey a depth of family affection. Overall, however, the novel is far from funny, for its theme is the decline and dispersion of the Kahn family. By the book's end, a tragic sense predominates. Anti-Semitic attitudes (real and imagined) are a backdrop to the family's problems, but the effect of the action is to argue, paradoxically, that the relative absence of anti-Semitism is also damaging. As much as anything it is the social and geographic mobility available to the Kahn children that destroys the family, as they go to college, move to town, or date shiksas.*

Before the Great Depression, before the gradual obsolescence of smalltown economies, the Kahns had once had a prosperous, if modest, business. Reuben, Benny's oldest brother, can look back to the 1920s as the good old days:

In [those] days there is no reason for Poppa to admit that he could fail in any task he might attempt. . . . The shelves and counters in the store and the kegs behind the counters are filled with any item anyone can want to buy. . . . (Sitting in the store now you'd never believe that in those days Rachel and I often had to help Momma and Poppa take care of the customers. Sometimes we had to hire four or five kids to help Jacob and Max deliver the orders.)

In those early days, religious faith and ritual were strong in the parents. Momma would sing:

> Torah studies by light
> And sound sleep by eve
> And you'll be a *koehn*
> That I with pride love.

Reuben sat "in Poppa's lap while he studies. . . . Poppa, chanting as he reads, rocks back and forth as he prays." But in America, far from the ghettos of Europe, and in a small town "so far away from the synagogue and other Jews," the old faith unravels: "The rituals of orthodox Judaism . . . transplanted to this world are meaningless and useless. It is as if a different God reigns here, an alien God, a God who scorns and mocks the Jew." Even the faith of Momma and Poppa erodes.

Benny stays at home into the 1940s, after events have long since taken the other children away. He watches the family die and is finally "free," free from the rancor that had soured the past few years, but also in the lonely position of having to build his own set of values.

Chester Aaron, who was raised in North Butler, Pennsylvania, has lived for the past twenty years in California, where he now teaches college. In addition to About Us, *he has published two "young adult" novels and a number of short stories. Among his current works in progress is a sequel to* About Us *that will be titled* About Them; *its action will be set in the same locale as the first novel's.*

188

"That Polack Anti-Semite Toadstool Expert"

For Poppa the entire population of the world has been machined by a cynical God into two classes: Jews and anti-Semites.

We are the only Jews in Sundown, Pennsylvania. Most of the men who work (that is, most of the men who have jobs) are miners. Some are railroad men. A few walk the three miles through the woods to Summer, where they catch a bus to the northern edge of the city, a section called Lyndy, where the steel mills are located.

Though Poppa has a very discerning eye when it comes to evaluating things like wild mushrooms or chickens or tomato plants, he has difficulty distinguishing one man from another in Sundown. He thinks he helps himself by applying additional characteristics to each of his enemies. For example, there is *that fat, goose-lipped anti-Semite* (Milo Yerkovich, the truant-officer); *that pimply-nosed anti-Semite with one ear* (Noyes, the old Welshman who's worked in the mines since he was twelve); *that thieving anti-Semite who sold me the truck* (Oscar Tilko, from whom Poppa bought an ancient truck, with which he now makes his deliveries). And there is *that Polack anti-Semite of a toadstool-expert.*

Like most of the men in Sundown, *that Polack anti-Semite of a toadstool-expert,* George Chupek, works, when there is work, in the mines.

Except for their ages George and Poppa have very little in common. George is, as Poppa pronounces it, a *Cadillac.* George's tiny china-blue eyes and square pink cheeks—despite a sand-colored walrus mustache—convey an impression of irrepressible adolescence. Poppa's dark-brown eyes are flecked with green and always serious, and a perpetual crust of beard exaggerates the roundness of his face. He also has a mustache but, like his hair, it is a collection of shaggy black curls. To my father's Slavic ancestors, I'm sure, there would be something of the ferocious Cossack about George's mustache, and to George's Slavic ancestors there would probably be something of the peddler, the moneylender, the ghetto, about my father's mustache.

George smokes a corncob pipe, using as fill the tobacco he chewed several days before and which, ever since, has lain in the sun to dry. Poppa does not smoke. He used to, thirty or forty a day, all of which he rolled himself. When he started to play the numbers he decided to save all his spare cash for that.

Perhaps because of the traditional conflicts between Pole and Russian in the Old Country, perhaps because of the legendary Polish pogroms and ghettos, Poppa, in his more charitable moments, announces George Chupek to be a liar, a thief, an idiot and a braggart. As well as an anti-Semite. He delights in challenging George's claims each autumn that he, George, has the finest little garden in the state. No matter what George selects as evidence, Poppa always manages to produce redder and firmer and larger tomatoes, sweeter corn, more succulent apples and pears. Poppa's Rhode Island Reds are always heavier than George's Plymouth Rocks and no pullet George selects can out-lay Poppa's prize White Leghorns.

Though the people in Sundown, men and women and children, admit Poppa's superiority in garden and poultry knowledge they all continue a special respect for George's knowledge of mushrooms. That anyone can consider George his superior in anything, and especially in the knowledge of mushrooms, fills Poppa with terrible resentment. That Momma and Rachel and all my brothers secretly and cautiously agree with the enemy helps keep that resentment aflame. Once, when he learned that Momma had me take some mushrooms he picked to George Chupek for analysis, Poppa notified all of us that if he was ever again so humiliated he would take his belt to whoever carried the mushrooms, even if it was me—his favorite.

After a cold and dreary winter the spring's crop of mushrooms promises a tonic for the people in Sundown. Normally, they wait for Saturday nights for excitement, and then they have to journey three miles through the woods to Summer to collect it. But here will be excitement at home, due any hour.

The men who lounge on the store porch or around the coal stove when it rains (even though the stove, several weeks ago, burned its last lump of coal until next fall) conceive elaborate tactics to bring the crisis to a head. Mixing their instincts for profit and fun, they establish a pool, a kitty, into which any gambler may contribute fifty cents. The one who selects the date closest to that on which the explosion comes will receive all of the cash. Smiley, the bookie for the numbers racket, holds the kitty.

The men write abusive notes to George and sign them with Poppa's name. Similar notes to Poppa are signed with George's name. They pick mushrooms along the tracks or in the fields around the mines and they bring them to Poppa. When he

judges certain ones safe to eat and others dangerous the men, with mock surprise, exclaim isn't it odd, George says just the contrary. Momma and Rachel and my brothers know, of course, that the men are being equally deceitful with George. When they try to convince Poppa that he is being victimized he refuses to listen. He charges everyone in the family not only with betrayal but with cowardice. They can sell their family pride, he rages—a father expects that—but the least they can do is respect a Jew, regardless of who he is, in his wars with the anti-Semites.

His own faith unshaken, Poppa continues his early-morning trips to the woods, to those secret caches that have supplied him so faithfully for thirty years or more. Occasionally he returns emptyhanded but more often his basket is filled with hemispheres of red and brown and pink, their blue and gray gilled undersides whispering aromatically of moist and shaded glades in the woods.

I am the only person he ever asks to go with him. At my age—I am ten—I am old enough to be fair company but not yet old enough to be a distraction. On those mornings when he decides to take me he comes to my room at dawn. It is usually a Sunday morning. His breath warm on my cheek and smelling of creamed coffee, he shakes my shoulders and whispers, so as not to wake Max, with whom I sleep, "Hey, mushrooms. Want to go for mushrooms?" I leap out of bed. I carry my clothes downstairs and dress in the kitchen.

In the blue light seeping through the windows I pull on my socks and shoes and then, at the sink, I dash cold water on my face. If Momma were up I'd have to use soap but Poppa does not take notice. I gulp down my steaming coffee and two or three slices of home-made bread spread with butter and jam. Poppa, in the meantime, has made several cheese or jam sandwiches, which he packs in a bag and places in his basket.

Though Poppa feels no special affection for Yenta, our mustard-colored mongrel (who weighs as much as I do and whose only role in life, so far as Poppa's concerned, is to guard the chickens and the garden and our house and store), he never refuses my request to bring the dog along.

About two weeks after Momma threw out those mushrooms that George Chupek condemned, Poppa asks me if I want to go with him again.

As we walk across the fields and along the Connequenessing Creek, Yenta, barking and howling, darts after the ghostly figures and voices in the cattails and the elderberry bushes. Each time a rooster crows I wonder if it might not be some secret and dangerous signal from one of those apparitions Yenta is challenging. I fall behind to collect Yenta and then hurry after Poppa, shouting to him to wait. But Poppa hurries on, his trouser legs wet to the knees from the dew and his mind fixed only on the distant woods.

He has long ago learned to pace his travel so that the sun rises above the horizon almost at the exact moment we enter the woods. This morning, within twenty minutes after we pass the first outpost of birches and willows, it is light enough to distinguish grass from ground and stump from rock. While Poppa goes swiftly to work I go just as swiftly to play.

Yenta chases rabbits and quail and I chase Yenta. Under crabapple and chokecherry trees, through huckleberry bushes and groves of elm and maple and birch and up and down mud paths carved, so the old men of Sundown say, by tribes of Algonquins and Delawares two hundred years before.

I find the tallest birch and climb it. Fifty or sixty feet above the ground I lean into the wind. I sway back and forth, picking out the creek, the railroad tracks, the highway going to Slippery Rock, the Kearnsey farm and the Gornick farm and the Chernik farm, the mouths of Number One mine and Number Three mine, the slag dumps, the reservoir, the woods nearer home and then the few houses in Sundown that I can see. I pick out our store. There is my world. And high above it I lie in the wind that has just passed over it on the way to the other parts of other worlds I'll someday see just as now I see my own. This is how it must feel to be God.

Searching below the tree, I finally locate Poppa moving in and out among the trees and patches of sunlight and shade, bending or kneeling at stump or stone or log, holding his specimens to the sun or to his nose. When, all too soon, he finds my tree and waves me down I obey.

We walk down one of the paths to Indian Springs, a small pool surrounded by dark, dank and mossy boulders. It has the clearest and coldest and sweetest water I will ever taste. There is a house-sized rock with steps cut in its walls. We help each other to the top. The flat surface there is covered with deep pockmarks in which humus has collected and which now sprout a dozen different shapes and sizes and colors of wildflowers. We eat our sandwiches. We climb down to drink the water and then climb up again. We toss pieces of sandwich to Yenta now and then and in between bites she too drinks from the spring. The robins and blue jays and catbirds and wild canaries flash in the trees and call to each other and the flies begin to appear, buzzing in the few rare pockets of sunlight high above our heads. Poppa lies back and motions me close. I lie beside him. With a sly grin on his face he

191

draws a May apple from his basket. I slide it into my mouth, popping the cold sweet fruit out of its skin and letting it glide down my throat. One after one my father draws ten more from his basket. He eats a few but I gladly and gratefully eat most of them. Then we lie on our backs, watching the birds and the already lazy flies. Poppa reaches out his hand, almost absently, and squeezes my fingers. A sudden surge of love nearly bursts my heart.

We return the way we came. Yenta darts in and out among the cattails and elderberry bushes. I wait for her and then the two of us run to catch up with Poppa.

We arrive home before anyone else is stirring. Anyone except George Chupek.

George, too, knows that dawn is the ideal time to gather mushrooms, before the sun can destroy them. He has his own secret sources. This day, certain of his good fortune, he has returned home before Poppa and waits on the store porch, disappointed, probably, that there is no one else on the porch to witness his victory. He sits on a wooden milk crate, his basket, uncovered, at his side. As we come onto the porch, George, his pipe belching smoke, bends to the right, presses a finger to the side of his nose and squirts a pearl into the dust a few inches from Poppa's feet. He looks at Poppa's basket, which is covered, and chuckles.

Poppa, though he can be an impulsive and terrible-tempered man, chooses this morning to be charitable. He lifts the basket lid, as if by accident, just enough to disclose his fine collection, and then somehow manages to spill from his mouth a fart sound that would do justice to an elephant fed a month-long diet of nothing but beans.

George, as astonished as I am at the power of the sound, sits stiffly upright, clamps his teeth, and

snaps the stem of his pipe. Poppa laughs and goes into the store and I follow him, very proud.

I was too involved in play to notice that Poppa had collected a basketful of the very same mushrooms Momma sent to George Chupek for analysis. The mushrooms George claimed to be such deadly toadstools were bright orange lumps ripped from the undersides of rotten logs. Three slices carved from one such lump fill a skillet.

The first time Poppa brought them home (when George had condemned them and Momma had thrown them away), Poppa announced with great ceremony that he'd not seen such mushrooms since his boyhood in the Kafkhaz. Because they had the density and texture of steak and because he had not even the most elementary knowledge of Latin terminology, he referred to them simply as *beefsteak mushrooms.*

Momma recognizes them immediately, but this time she says nothing. She agrees to serve them this evening. But the moment Poppa leaves the kitchen to open the store (which composes the front half of our home), Momma gathers Max and Jacob and me around her. She explains her predicament. I can't help feeling it all some sort of conspiracy against Poppa. My memories of our trip are too fresh in my mind. I don't want to be a part of this plan. But something in my mother's voice alarms me. I linger in the doorway that opens from the kitchen into the store.

Max, who is sixteen, volunteers to take one of the mushrooms to George Chupek. When he returns with the grim information that the mushrooms are exactly the same as those George warned us about before, Momma bursts into tears. Jacob pulls me into the kitchen and closes the door so Poppa won't hear the commotion.

Momma rocks back and forth at the table, won-

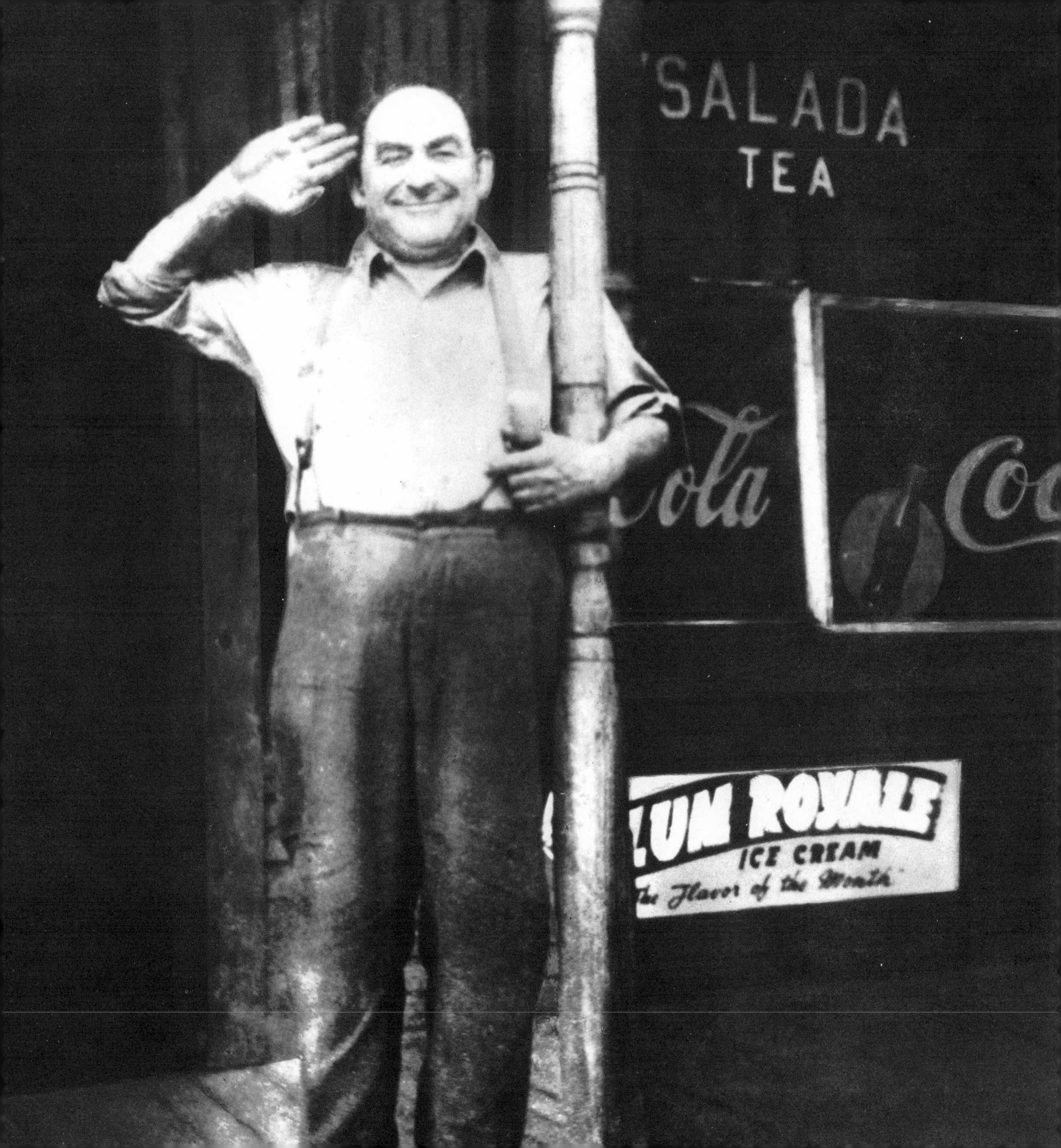
'SALADA
TEA
Cola
LUM ROYALE
ICE CREAM
"The Flavor of the Month"

dering if she shouldn't call Rachel, who's working at Fleischman's Meat Market in Summer. Or maybe we should even call Reuben, at college. "What can I do? What can I do?" Momma chants.

Jacob and Max, like myself, aware of the dangers, are horrified. But we are children. What can we do? We sit in silence, waiting for Momma to direct us.

We know that we can not tell Poppa that we took the mushrooms to George Chupek again. But, obviously, we can not let him eat the mushrooms, which he will certainly insist on doing once he learns that he's been betrayed by us. Remembering his threats to use the belt, Max sits in his chair, trembling.

Momma rushes to the phone, which hangs on the wall near the sink. She calls Fleischman's Market. She tells Rachel everything. Rachel, as upset as Momma, says she'll come right home. We should not do anything until she gets there. She'll have her boy friend, Naty, drive her home. She'll be here in ten minutes. In the meantime, she'll ask Mr. Fleischman for advice.

We sit. The ten minutes pass as if each minute is an hour. Then it's eleven minutes. Twelve. Fifteen. Momma, at the kitchen table, covers her mouth with her hands, covers her eyes, covers her mouth. A half hour after the phone call Rachel comes onto the back porch. When she opens the door Yenta races in before her. I run to Rachel, weeping, but she tells me to be quiet. When Momma begs her for advice she says she talked to Mr. Fleischman and also to the three butchers. Desperate, she'd also called Reuben. Mr. Fleischman said she should use the store phone, he'd pay for it.

Fortunately, Reuben was in his room. He . . . as usual, only he . . . had a plan. Everyone sighs, relieved. If it's Reuben's plan, no worry, it's bound to work.

"What . . . what?" Momma begs. "What's the plan?"

Rachel points at Yenta, who is stretched out at my feet, her chin on my shoes.

"Now listen," Rachel says. "We serve some of the mushrooms to Yenta. She'll die and it will be sad but then Poppa can't argue. He'll have to admit they're poisonous."

Max and Jacob, though never as fond of Yenta as I am, can't help but look stricken. Momma, wringing her hands in desperation, says George Chupek and everyone else in Sundown will laugh and things will be worse than ever. Rachel asks what they're to do then. Are they to let Poppa eat? Should they sit by and let him kill himself?

Only now do I understand what is being planned. I start to howl. Max pushes me, telling me to stop being a cry-baby. Momma comes to me and kneels on the floor in front of me. She says she hates to see Yenta die too and I tell her she never liked Yenta. She's glad to see her die. She hugs me, sobbing, but I pull away and try to run into the store. Rachel holds me. She hugs me to her. "Benny," she says, "it's the only way. Isn't it better to sacrifice Yenta, a dog, than have Poppa killed? Don't you trust Reuben? Reuben says this is the only way."

I return to Yenta and sit on the floor at her side, clutching her head, shocked and sick at such cruelty, and trying hard to resist admitting to myself that what Reuben and Rachel say is the truth.

Jacob, trying to solace me, puts an arm around my shoulders. "We have to do it," he says.

"We'll get another dog, as soon as this is all over," Rachel says. "A puppy. You can pick it out yourself."

I go to a corner of the kitchen and throw myself

195

on a pile of clothes gathered there for the next day's washing. Yenta trots after me, and lies beside me, her muzzle at my ear.

Jacob asks how we can feed Yenta mushrooms, since she will eat nothing but bones and Sweet's Dog Biscuits. Rachel says, "Don't you remember what Yenta loves? And almost never gets?"

"Salami. Kosher salami."

Rachel nods, trying hard not to look at me. "We can wrap a chunk of toadstool in a slice of kosher salami. Come on, Benny, please. Let Yenta go."

I wrap my arms about Yenta but Momma, in a sudden burst of determination to get this over with, jumps up and jerks me away from Yenta. "Come," she says, hauling Yenta to the center of the room. "Come, Yentila."

For the next hour all four of them feed slices of kosher salami to Yenta. Inside each of the slices is a chunk of toadstool as large as my thumb. Yenta accepts it, greedily, but each time she swallows the salami and then spits out the toadstool. She consumes a quarter of a roll of salami before they admit they're failing.

Next, they chop the chunk of toadstool into small pieces and fold the salami slice over the toadstool filling, but Yenta manages somehow to separate the salami and swallow it and then to spit out every piece of the toadstool. Ears sharp, eyes alert, her muzzle wet, she sits and licks her chops, baffled by Max's and Jacob's unusual generosity. But willing and eager to profit by it.

They try feeding her the toadstool alone, they try holding her jaws closed, they try petting her, caressing her, they try scolding her, but they can't get so much as a tiny fragment of toadstool to stay down her throat. Jacob lies on the floor and holds Yenta between his thighs in a scissors grip and Max bends her head back and Rachel pries her jaws apart and Momma shoves her fist down Yenta's throat. Yenta gags, struggles to her feet, and spills out over all of them and all over the floor, everything she's succeeded in getting down until now. Max and Jacob and Rachel and Momma are soaking wet. So is the floor. They, and Yenta, slip and slide. Yenta tries to escape and Max falls back against a wall and Jacob releases his legs and Rachel drops in a chair and Momma sits on the floor, her face in her hands, her loose and tangled hair spotted with bits of salami and toadstools.

"What in hell's goin on?"

Poppa looms in the doorway. When he sees the floor and Momma and Rachel and Jacob and Max, he knows what has been going on. Outraged, he marches to the table and grabs the knife that has been used to cut the toadstools. His heavy black brows form a solid line of anger across his forehead. His dark skin is almost black. The mustachios seem to bristle, erect, like the fur of a cornered, crazed animal.

Momma screams as Poppa grips the knife. "No . . . no . . . they're poison! . . . George Chupek swears . . ."

The house is adrift in a sea of forbidding silence. Poppa gasps. He looks at each of us, trying to identify the traitor. He fingers his belt. Max sits, trembling, expectant. Momma stands, her smooth dark chin jutting out. "I took them. He told me. They're toadstools."

Max and Jacob, in a gesture more of fear than chivalry, manage to stand erect on the slippery floor and go to stand with Momma. Yenta, released, leaps at the back door. She knocks it open and races out of the house.

For one horrible moment it seems to me and to all the others that Poppa is about to rip off his belt and whip Momma. I run to her, pushing myself between Max and Jacob and against her legs, burying my face in her skirt. Rachel takes Momma's hand and stares at Poppa. Momma never moves, but she seems to tower above us all in her courage. She is the only one now who is not trembling or sobbing or whining.

Never has Poppa been confronted with such unified rebellion. It's not fear of us that motivates him now . . . he could lift all four of us at once and throw us out of the house . . . but whatever it is grants him the power to behave as if we were merely an audience of strangers.

Poppa carries what's left of the toadstools to the sink. He washes them. At the stove he shifts a large skillet over a burner and drops a piece of butter onto the iron. He then places three thick slices of the toadstool into the skillet, sprinkles them with salt and pepper and, hand on hip, a spatula between his fingers, he waits.

Rachel goes to him, pleading with him. Momma does the same. He ignores them. Sneering, he brushes Momma's hand away. Jacob tries to grab the skillet but Poppa, with a roar, whirls on him and Jacob retreats.

A customer who's been waiting for service in the store comes into the kitchen to complain but Momma ushers him back through the store and onto the porch. She locks the store door.

Within minutes the word has spread. Every man, woman and child in Sundown arrives at the store, crowding onto the porch, pushing at the windows. They wait, murmuring, with solemn faces. Someone suggests that someone ought to call Brick Shiptick and the township police and someone else runs to comply.

Momma, weeping, kneels on the floor, her head on the seat of a chair. Jacob sits across the table from her. Max stands with his face against the wall, crying softly. Rachel is on the phone, begging the student with whom Reuben shares a room at college to find Reuben immediately and have him call home.

Jacob steps behind Poppa. "Poppa," he begs, "don't eat them. Please don't eat them. We love you, Poppa."

Poppa ignores him and continues frying the toadstools.

The telephone rings.

"Poppa," Rachel shouts, "it's Reuben. It's Reuben. Talk to him, Poppa. Please."

Poppa ignores her.

Reuben's voice can be heard calling all the way from Chicago. He is shouting, screaming, cursing. Rachel holds out the telephone as far as the cord will permit. Poppa does not even look at it. We all hear Reuben say, "Goddamn it, if he wants to kill himself, let him. Stubborn . . . vengeful . . . let him. . . ."

I sit with Momma, thinking that this is the last day we will all be together. After today, Poppa will be gone.

Several people have come onto the back porch. They offer advice to us and even try to convince Poppa that he's being foolish, that they meant no harm, that they all know he's a better man than George Chupek.

Rachel has put up the phone and sits at the table, weeping. I go to her and she takes me on her lap.

More people gather on the porch. There's a larger commotion and George Chupek himself appears. He pushes his way through the crowd and into the kitchen. He talks to Poppa in Polish, pleading with him. Poppa says nothing but reaches

197

a plate down from the shelf above the stove and empties the contents of the skillet onto the plate. He lifts one slice with his fingers, bites, chews, tastes and then shoves the entire slice into his mouth. Momma screams and topples backward to the floor. Max and Jacob, in a fit of tears and screams, rush to Momma's side. Poppa continues eating.

George Chupek, spouting Polish, stomping his feet, his cheeks not pink now but flaming red, calls out "Schtop! Schtop!" It is the only time he's ever been known to try an English word.

The people on the porch surge toward Poppa, who's now well through his second slice of toadstool. He sets the skillet down and raises a chair above his head. The crowd pauses. He swallows what he has in his mouth and with one hand grabs and stuffs the third and final piece into his mouth. His face is covered with grease. The juices running down his cheeks and jowls have stained his shirt. He puts down the chair and sits on it. George Chupek falls back against the sink, his hand making the sign of the cross, over and over.

"Not in this house!" Poppa bellows. He stands, ready to fight should George describe the sign again. But George, meek and mild, submits. He nods his head and folds his hands at his chest and mutters. "And no Cadillac prayers!" Poppa orders. George's muttering stops.

Rachel and Jacob and a few men lift Momma and carry her to a chair at the table. Jacob supports her while Rachel forces water between her lips. She groans, opens her eyes, closes them again, groans again and then sits erect, conscious. "You!" she says, pointing at Poppa.

Poppa nods. "Me," he says. He looks at her and then at every single face in the room. He sits back and crosses his arms on his chest. Everyone in the kitchen stands now and waits.

By the time the police arrive it is obvious that Poppa is going to suffer nothing more serious than indigestion from having eaten so rapidly.

The police move everyone off the porch and drive back to town. Rachel does not return to work. She sits with the rest of us in the kitchen, humble and penitent. When Reuben calls she tells him that Poppa ate the toadstools, and they turned out to be mushrooms. Poppa, sitting at the table and drinking coffee, says, "Tell him *beefsteak* mushrooms. He should look up in one of his fancy books. Tell me them in Latin."

That night at supper, we are all very quiet. Poppa does not lord it over us. In fact he cracks jokes. When Yenta returns he lets her in the house and pats her head. "You didn't believe either, huh?" He playfully pushes Yenta away.

After supper, in the store, all the men sitting on the benches confide their pity for poor old George Chupek, who's brooding away at home, unable to understand how he could have made such a mistake.

Poppa enjoys it all. "All these years," he says, "he sees beefsteak mushrooms and don't pick them. Oy, and such a delicacy. I pity him, too." Then he turns to Smiley, the bookie for the numbers racket, and with whom Poppa bets a dollar or two every day. "Give me my money," Poppa says.

Smiley nods. He takes $15.50 out of his pocket and hands the money to Poppa. Smiley turns to the other men. He shrugs. "He put fifty cents in the kitty, too. He picked today."

Poppa counts the money, nods at Smiley and puts the money in his pocket. Except for a dime, which he tosses at me. "For Saturday," he says. "Go buy a double feature."

198

LESTER GORAN
"The Story of My Life"

Maria Light seeks diversion in
Carnegie Library and Schenley Park

Time: 1940s   Setting: Pittsburgh

As this selection indicates, Maria Light *is a novel whose action is set in Pittsburgh during World War II. The title character is a widow in her late thirties who lives in Addison Terrace (a housing project on the hills above Oakland). Economically, Maria inhabits a twilight zone of underemployment and poverty, working at menial jobs in a bakery and a pawnshop to provide her three children and her elderly father-in-law with some semblance of a stable home. Physically, psychologically, she yearns for a husband, for a man who can give her the warmth and love she once knew with Ben Light.*

She and Ben had lived in "Minertown," not far from Pittsburgh, where he prospered briefly in the business of illegal whiskey during Prohibition. As seen through Maria's memories, Ben was a strong and good-humored man; his grand schemes kept alive her romantic illusions. Ben's death seemed to confirm the fact that Maria's fate is to be trapped by circumstances, for even though she can move to Pittsburgh, she cannot outrun the hard luck bred more than anything by poverty. Events dramatize to Maria time and again that she cannot escape her lot. The novel opens (in a flashback) with the fourteen-year-old Maria sneaking out of her father's Minertown shack to meet a lover, only to be hauled back and beaten, and it ends with an aborted decision to leave Pittsburgh and family behind and start all over again. There's no easy route out of Minertown or Addison Terrace.

But despite its grimness, Maria Light *is not really pessimistic. Goran draws Maria as a compassionate, sensible, and strong woman whose fundamental optimism is, in the end, uncrushable. She is faithful to her family and to a personal sense of her own worth and dignity. At the novel's close, as she returns to Pittsburgh to carry on with her responsibilities, she affirms her determination:*

It was frightening . . . that about her as she walked to the railroad station there were a million people asleep and none of them knew her name. The train station was brightly lit. "My name is Maria Light," she said to the man in the railroad ticket window, not caring a fig that he did not give a damn. "I have a little boy named Georgie and a beautiful little baby girl named Esther."

And at the book's end, she is still expecting to find a good man.

Lester Goran, born and raised in Pittsburgh, attended Schenley High School and the University of Pittsburgh; he now teaches at the University of Miami in Florida. In addition to Maria Light, *Goran has published three other novels that use Pittsburgh settings —* The Paratrooper of Mechanic Avenue, *1960 (the lower Hill District during the Renaissance demolition),* The Candy Butcher's Farewell, *1964 (Homestead), and* The Stranger in the Snow, *1966 (South Oakland). Though Goran fictionalizes some of his specific details (is "Mechanic Avenue" modeled on Centre Avenue?), the general characterization of Pittsburgh districts is clear.*

"The Story of My Life"

"I'd like a book," Maria said, "something that's interesting but without too much description. I don't like books that go on and on about the garden or what the maid's room looked like. I'd like a love story if you have a good one."

The librarian behind her counter and desk moved her chair back, the sound grating sharp on the sleepy summer air. It was hot outside and the same heat leaped up the long stairs outside and into the library. The heat was disturbed only by the electric fans; a small circle would be cool while the heat in the rest of the room remained hot and flat. In desperation Maria had come down to the hall of statuary at night but found it changed somehow, with too many people looking at the statues. She had decided to walk the corridor over to the library. Without even Danny in the apartment, none of the movies in Oakland interesting her, she had fled into the Carnegie Museum.

The hot summer night sat heavily on the iron city, drifted all through the early Schenley Park evening. Tree leaves and grass shone as if they were metal and not soft. The sun was gone, but the feeling of light blue space was good to Maria after the long cramped day in the bakery shop.

Mrs. Cochran had kindly agreed to stay with the old man and the kids. Maria strolled down leisurely from Addison Terrace, not thinking of herself but admiring the pale blue evening. It was a disappointment to find people crowding each other among the statues.

"I'm sure we'd have something for you," the librarian said.

She brought back a book, and said, "Here's a fairly new one. *King's Row*."

Maria looked at the book. "Is it true to life?" she asked.

The librarian said it was very realistic. "It's about people in a small town," she added.

Maria smiled, and weighed the book in her hand. "I come from a small town," she said proudly. "I'm not originally from Pittsburgh."

The librarian adjusted her glasses. She seemed too tired to talk. She was busier with the things on her desk than she had to be on the hot evening. "You'll like that book, I think," the librarian said. "It's a sad story, but it has a kind of happy ending." Someone came to the desk and asked a question; the librarian seemed delighted to turn away from Maria to answer.

The librarian's face was painted heavily with rouge, her cheeks dabbed red like an Indian's mask. Maria thought she saw loneliness smeared on the face of the woman behind the desk, fright in the rimless glasses, long nights in the plump white hands too perfectly manicured. Maria waited until the librarian was alone behind the desk, thinking here was a person needing cheering as badly as she did herself.

"I wish somebody would write the story of my life," Maria said. She hoped that by her great charm and ability to poke fun at herself she could make the other woman feel better.

The woman smiled vaguely, looked away, and adjusted her watch. It was eight-twelve and still light outside. "Is it possible," Maria asked, "for a book not to have an end, I mean, just to go on and on or maybe not to even start."

The librarian looked very busy. "I don't know what you mean," she said.

"I mean," Maria said, "if a book was written about my life nothing would ever happen in the book. Nothing ever happens in my life. My life didn't start nowhere, like you know in a Chapter One and all, and it's going to end the same way. If somebody was to write a book about my life all the pages—" she thought about it, "—no, say, half the pages in the book would have to be blank."

The librarian smiled politely. "Was there anything else I can help you with?" she asked. She tapped a pencil.

Maria leaned forward on the counter and handed the book back to the librarian. "I don't want this book," Maria said, "I know I'm not going to like it. The small town in this book isn't going to be like the place I come from."

Maria pointed with her hand to the library shelves piled with hot, leathery books. "There ain't a true word in this whole place," she said. "There ain't one book in this place with every other page blank. Even if the writer was truthful and didn't want to gyp people who had paid good money to read his book he should write, 'Sorry, but nothing happened for ten years or twenty years.' "

"I'm sorry," the librarian said. She stood and walked behind a stack of books.

"Please," Maria called, "I didn't mean anything personal. I was just trying to cheer you up—I was only making talk. Miss, I didn't mean to start an argument." Fortunately (or Maria would have run out), the library was empty except for an old man who sat sleeping in a chair, his hands folded on his stomach. "Miss!" Maria called. "—I'm sorry."

Maria thought that the poor girl in the library would never believe she had not meant anything personal, that she had only meant that every other page in everybody's life should be blank. Especially mine, she thought. She sat outside on a park bench, recovering.

The air itself danced with a nervous summer life of its own. The war was in the park air. Couples clawed at each other wherever a person looked, on benches, on the grass, even standing and walking they held each other closely as though their grips were what held them together. Maria sighed—a serviceman, a corporal, hot and red and with a bad complexion, had seated himself on the other end of her bench as if unaware of her.

Maria sighed deeply, wishing for something and not knowing what to call it.

"Excuse me," the soldier said, "my name is Herbert Brownstone. Are you from around here?"

Maria did not seem to look at him. "I don't talk to strangers," she said.

Maria ached once again with loss and summer. She wished she could wear a frilly dress, cool with her bra straps showing through and her neck sunburned; she wished she could walk hand in hand with a soldier.

The night was warm and the face of the corporal on the other end of the bench glistened. "I'm not one of these kids going to school here," he said. "I'm in charge of one of the barracks up at Tech. I'm regular army."

Mrs. Maria Light said she thought he looked more mature than most of the soldiers she saw around.

He offered her a cigarette, and she said, "No, thank you."

They sat silent for a few minutes, then the soldier told her it was a funny thing but Schenley Park was one of the best parks in the country—he had seen them all—and a darned shame that the people in Pittsburgh didn't appreciate such a swell place. He stood and stretched, tall and yellow in his suntans, but stiff too, watching her.

"There's a particular place I know in this park," he said. "I'd bet there's not one out of fifty people comes here knows about it." He looked at her like a dog on suntanned hind legs, begging for a scrap from the table. "I go there myself often, there's a little stream runs through—it's right near the roadway."

She let him hold her hand while they walked. She wondered was she doing the right thing.

It was in the air, the comradeship and the love and good-bye and the war. Maria felt like waving at other couples, walking too on their evening in the park. They walked past Flagstaff Hill where fat men in undershirts lay snoring under the night sky. Sounds of laughter drifted on the dark, heavy air. The park bridges were islands above worry; she walked quicker, lighter. The soldier and Maria Light did not talk.

He led Maria past the conservatory, lit for the night like a fairy-tale glass house where all light was gathered once and for all.

"I'd like to go in there some time," Maria said, "and see the flowers."

From the way the soldier said "A person shouldn't miss something like that," she knew he had not been there.

They walked around the Westinghouse Lagoon and stood before the stiff statue of the schoolboy wearing knickers and with his cap in his hand. It was too dark to see the emblazoned trains and carvings on the big marble shell that was at the end of the lagoon. Couples sat on all the marble benches; Maria and the soldier crossed the narrow street. "They call this Lover's Lane," the soldier said.

They walked on grass toward a dark opening and walked through bent trees down dark stone steps toward the Hollow.

"There's not one person in fifty knows this

203

place," the soldier said.

The grass and trees sighed of its being everybody's war. In the grotto a stream ran and the air was cool. The soldier sat with her on the grass and put his arm around her waist. "People would never know this place was here," the soldier said.

He seized her violently and threw her back. His hands grasped her breasts and pulled. He made small animal sounds. "Let me," he blubbered.

His desperation woke her from her dream of love and belonging. She angrily pushed him away, and said, "Sit there," and sat five feet away from him.

"Don't come no closer," she said. "I mean it."

The soldier looked at her but not from the few feet that separated them, from miles away with hollow, scared eyes. "What—what's the matter?" he asked. "I didn't do nothing wrong, did I?"

"I'm a respectable widow," Maria said. "I don't go in for that kind of stuff."

He looked at her blankly. He started to move closer, then changed his mind and sat dumbly looking at her.

Maria stood and dusted off her skirt. "You better find somebody else for that kind of stuff," she said. "I have a son in the army and a baby at home. I'm not some floozie you find sailing around the park."

The soldier sat mutely staring at the place where Maria had been.

"Are you going to walk back with me like a gentleman?" she asked. "I'll walk back myself if that's the way you want it."

The soldier looked down at the ground, still sitting. "I knew it would be like this," he said. "This ain't the first time this has happened to me."

"You didn't know nothing of the sort."

The soldier cried. He sat with his hands clenched between his knees and with his head bent wept loud and fearlessly like a child. "I don't blame you," he sobbed. "I don't blame you one bit." His shoulders shook with his gasps. "There's plenty of good-looking young fellows around, with clear skin and everything—I'm past forty and I'm still a corporal. They call me 'Corporal Ugly,' the young guys. They say I was behind the door when looks was passed out."

"You poor man," Maria said, and sat and stroked his coarse reddish hair. He lay in her arms with his eyes closed, cool August night sounds around them, branches breaking and falling, insect cries.

He let himself be held, not touching her. Had he moved, turned and pushed her back into the grassy sod, run his hands gently over her body, he could have had her. She wished him to turn and kiss her tenderly.

He leaned, however, dreamlike in her arms, not moving, wanting only someone soft to lean against. She held him until she was tired and then walked with him back to the park entrance, past the library up Forbes Street. "I feel real good," the soldier said. "I feel as good as if you let me, Mrs. Light, good like when it happens. Mrs. Light, forgive me for thinking you were a bad woman."

She agreed to meet him again the next night, knowing for a certainty she would not be there and he would weep like a child somewhere alone later. On one of the blank pages in the book of my life, she thought angrily, glaring back at the library building and the librarian who sat inside, you can mark one more time in big, black letters—One more night as usual nothing happened to Maria Light.

MICHAEL O'MALLEY
"Irish Picnic"

The Rileys set out
for Irish Day at Kennywood

Time: 1940s   Setting: Braddock

Miners Hill is a coming-of-age novel. The central character of the story, Pat Riley, in his early teens, is trying to decide how much he really wishes to become a priest and whether he should leave home to attend a seminary high school.

The adults in Pat's family are relatively recent immigrants, having come to this country after the "Troubles" in Ireland during the 1920s, and they have settled in the Braddock area because work is available in the mills. As this selection shows, Pat's father is a fun-loving and tolerant man, usually ready to forgive and forget; the priesthood is too rarified and unphysical to appeal to him entirely as a vocation for his son. It is Mrs. Riley who rules the family, with a heavy hand and sharp (even cruel) tongue; she sees the priesthood for Pat as a route to family prestige as well as an escape for him from the harshness of mill-town life. The conflict between his parents makes Pat's year of decision a continuing crisis.

Pat's choices, however, are played out on a stage larger than life with his family. A major character is Leila, a Protestant girl who has just recently moved into the neighborhood. Although she never forms an explicit sexual liaison with Pat, Leila does come to represent, in the book's religious context, the virtues of human love, the value of personal relationships. Leila loves beauty, and she and Pat share their pleasure in music, poetry, and nature. She has an outgoing warmth and interest in other people that Pat, victim of his mother's pressures, cannot develop.

In a still larger context, the setting of Miners Hill *also plays a thematic role. The environment of the novel conveys the allure of the sensual world — its*

colors, textures, tastes. O'Malley's dense poetic style underscores this. For Pittsburgh-area readers, this sensuous registration of the novel's setting becomes an especially memorable quality because the topography is undeniably that of Braddock and North Braddock, from run-down riverfront to the green graveyards on the hills above (which Pat and his peers use as playgrounds):

[He walked] . . . past the historical monument, lumpy and anonymous beneath its coat of pigeon shit. Past the bridge and up Miners Hill while the town spread out slowly behind him and the long silver of the river appeared across the valley. He turned at the top and paused there, still, breathing the air in through hungry eyes. His heart quickened as the lights flicked on across the curven towering breasts of the city like a necklace, and he felt his life bound up in the long strong line of the river and the town below him. And all its myriad streets and twinkling glitter were in him and part of him, and he returned home as he had left it, as always, full of wonder.

Though O'Malley disguises specific street names in the neighborhood of the novel's action, readers familiar with North Braddock will not doubt that "Miners Hill" is reached in real life by climbing Coalmont Street and that the novel's "Sudden Avenue" (where the Rileys live) is Seddon Avenue fictionally revisited.

There can be no doubt at all that this selection describes a trip to Kennywood for "Irish Day."

Michael O'Malley was born in North Braddock and now works for an insurance company in Wausau, Wisconsin. He has published one other novel, Every Day by Storm *(1967).*

"Irish Picnic"

The morning was bright, white-lit, shot with melon-colored gold light, like all good picnic mornings. Something in the air, all sorts of things in the air: the gaiety of expectation, a happy tense jiggling nervousness, a sky that promised glory and a green-cool afternoon. There was the wild anxiety to be off, to clank off rocking in a big rattling orange trolleycar, grinning importantly from the window because of the sign that said *Chartered*. There was the opulence of that *Chartered* sign, and the shouting crush of passengers—the portly Irish housewives and their picnic baskets bulging, and the huge men, broadbacked, the Irishmen, laughing and greeting each other, roughly touching their big tender callous hands, surprised and embarrassed by their joy, by their desire to embrace one another. There was awkward masculine laughter, deep-throated and sincere, and the self-conscious, halting conversations of the men in rusting Gaelic, the childlike glow of pleasure in their faces as they turned inward speaking their own secret language here in this strange country, under these smoke-wreathed hills. There was the shrill talking of the women as they settled into the creaking, straw-woven seats, the chantlike, keening rhythm of their speech, and the loud joy of children, and—Oh, all of this was as a promise in the picnic-morning air, all this and more, the joy more immediate: the quickening dark feel of early sunrise roaring-on-a-hilltop, a strength that made the chest swell, the rollicking sweep of laughter—all in the picnic morning.

And in the air at home, as the house stirred early, the thronging picnic smells, thick and pun-gent. Bridie thumped about the kitchen preparing the huge wicker picnic basket. Quart after quart of rich loamy yellow potato salad, crisscrossed with crescent slices of hard-boiled egg whites and golden with their yolks, big chunks of mealy flaking potato, nuggets of crisp celery, tiny orange strips of carrot and slices of tart green pepper, and all mixed in the creamy mayonnaise. She packed the salad tight in glistening Mason jars, scooping it from the vast earthenware crock in which she had mixed it, and the savory lush smell filled the house. For the sandwiches she had a huge mound of fresh pink chipped ham wrapped in white butcher's paper, ham laced and tender with little snowy veins of fat, and dozens of heavy round sandwich rolls. She worked amid the yeasty sugar-smell of home-made sweet buns, great puffy crowns on them, buns which had been put into the oven before dawn, and a big jar of crisp warty sweet pickles, and the ferny smell of steak tomatoes for the sandwiches, tart-red and firm and beaded with moist coolness, and there were two royal heads of lettuce, and more mayonnaise to be slathered on the sandwiches, and a pint jar containing butter for the children and one with oleomargarine for the adults, and two jars of dark homemade grape jelly topped with slabs of gray paraffin, and a brown-crowned swelling loaf of fresh-baked bread, and on the window sill three pies cooling, two of apple and one lemon meringue (with the brown-singed beaten egg whites over an inch thick on top), and a little heap of red radishes, and india relish, and stacks of paper plates and cups, wooden forks and spoons . . . And as Bridie stuffed firm cold hard-boiled eggs, peeled and slippery as olives, into another pint jar, a blackened pot of strong tea brewed on the stove, sending a whiff of light lemony fragrance through the heavier smells. The kitchen was running over with the teeming profusion of food for the picnic. Through it all Bridie moved, red-faced and sweating with purpose, not dressed yet, still in a shapeless wrapper with her hair pinned up and bound in an old blue scarf, with the pink glow of anticipation in her lips and cheeks, assembling and packing this mountain of provender.

Knowing how Pat loved his sleep, she called him last.

"C'mon up there, yer majesty!" she shouted, knocking briskly on the wall, "get up an' get yer breakfast an' hurry up about it!" When he entered the kitchen she had cleared a corner of the table for him.

"Get an orange outa the icebox and a bowl o' cereal an' that's all ye'll need. We wanna get outa here to the streetcar so's we can get a decent table in the park."

She had everything packed when he finished eating. "Out with ye now an' tell them all we're goin' in fifteen minutes. Send Kathleen in to put her good dress on."

Outside the sun already had a lusty strength, cutting through the morning's light-aired coolness —a pleasant day, with a gentle stirring breeze and in the breeze the smell of smoke and of a warm and mellow August day, tokening triumph, promising a soft black evening full of stars.

It never rained on the Irish Picnic: the Hibernians had an agreement with God. . . .

The Rileys arrived early at the schoolyard on Main Street where they were to board the char-tered trolleys. Mick and Miles went off to get the identification tags. . . . The rest of the family sat down with Bridie on the stone steps of the school, near the heavy black wrought-iron gates, to await the coming of the cars.

Other families were entering the yard now. Bright clothes, loose clothes, a belly-forward happy look to them all, a softness in them, feeling the picnic mood, hair combed not very neatly on the men and curled elaborately on the women, big smiles on all, expectation in the clattering voices, swarms of children dressed for fun, for hard knocks, wear-and-tear, the men leaning against the weight of the picnic baskets, and shopping bags, bundles, everyone carrying something, the families ambling slowly into the flat gray concrete yard through the side gate and meandering through the crowds, the many little clumps of people, and the small children madly dashing from their parents when they entered the yard, fanning out like multi-colored buckshot, crawling underfoot on a hundred little quests of their own amid the towering corduroy-clad legs. Voices grew jagged, happy, quietly excited—the men in their barked greetings, gruff and eager: "Why, how are ye, Miles," leaping to shake hands with him, to grasp his arm affectionately, "and how've ye been? Aw, yer lookin' grand, grand. We never see ye atall now since ye went on night-turn at the mill." And the women chattering eagerly, heads close together, glancing sideways from their eyes, busily gossiping, and hugging one another, kissing the air over the shoulders of the newly arrived as they embraced them, catching up on all the news: "Oh, *that* one won't be comin', don't worry yersel' about *her*. She thinks she's a regular *queen*, God fergimme, since they bought that house. But ye don't see their name on the Dollar-a-Sunday list at the church—small chance o' that! Her majesty will be comin' in style, I imagine, in a taxicab or somethin'!'' And the others affirming: "That's the God's truth!—Aw, it goes without sayin' . . .''

The yard filled up, and more desperate voices were heard, trying loudly to get things organized: "C'mon now, folks. The streetcars will be comin' now. C'mon, make a kinda line, like, over by the gate. C'mon, folks, let's get movin' . . .''

After a brief foray to check the new arrivals, Bridie returned to the children. "Where's yer father and Uncle Miles?" she asked Pat.

"I dunno," he said. "They ain't back yet."

"Did ye see where they went?"

"Nope."

"Aw, *grand!* That's just *grand.* They just scamper off without worryin' about a thing, do they? Well, if they ain't here when the streetcars come, I'm gonna leave all this stuff right on the steps an' get on the cars without it. They can come all the way back an' get it—if it's still here. An' God help them if it ain't!—Mick!" she called, "Mick!"

"Aw, Mom, please don't holler," Pat said. "They'll be here." The people nearby looked curiously at Bridie, but she paid no heed to their glances.

One man, safely hidden within a cluster of people, called out with mischief in his voice: "Aw, I think the poor man is just takin' a little walk to the other side of the street, Mrs. Riley."

"To the saloon!" Bridie said bitterly. "God fergive him, before I get my foot on the streetcar he's off like a streak o' lightnin' to the saloon. An' Miles with him! How in God's name I'm supposed to manage all this stuff an' all you pack o' kids by myself is beyond me!" Her eyes darted over the yard again, and she nibbled at her lip. "—Where's

Tony, now? Jesus, Mary, an' Joseph! He's just like his father; that's what's killin' me, he's just like himself. He's run off again now an' he'll be gettin' into somethin' or fallin' offa somethin' or breakin' his neck on somethin', an' he don't care who's worryin' about him, neither! He don't care about no one but himself an' it's very poor care of himself he takes, too. Just like yer father—they're two peas in a pod. That's what gets me so mad at the two o' them. Tony!" she shouted, "Tony! Come here!—One's as bad as the other, God help us all!"

Pat crouched back on the gray stone steps, gritting his teeth, rubbing his hand furiously through his hair. His eyes rolled about in desperation. She was intentionally exciting herself, he thought, intentionally getting all worked up to raise hell with everyone, so that the rest of the day would go her way. "I'll go and find him, Mom," he said, rising. "Just try not to get so excited about it. He's around here somewheres. So is Daddy, I bet."

She turned on him, jerking her head like a fierce bird. "Ye'll stay right here, mister! I'm gonna keep my eye on you today, don't worry yer pretty head about *that!* If ye think yer gonna go sneakin' around today with no one to say boo to ye, ye got another think comin'. Ha! Yer gallivantin' is over now, boyo. Ye'll be back to school an' I won't have to worry mysel' about where yer hangin' around—" she simpered ominously, and the boy felt a sharp catch in his belly and wondered if she knew, "—an' *who* yer hangin' around *with.*—Oh, God Almighty, where's that Tony? Tony!" she called again, lifting her head high, well back, her voice ringing over the heads of the crowd.

The long line of chartered trolleycars, bells clanging exuberantly, hove into view on Main

209

Street, and the children around them began to clap and shout. *"Yay! Yaaay!"* As the cars approached, Bridie's anxiety increased. "Tony! Where's that child? Oh, Holy Mother o' God, every time I go on one o' these picnics I swear I'll never set foot on another. Ye know," she said to Pat, "he gets it from yer father—yer father don't worry himsel' about nothin' atall, so Tony don't either. I could throttle the both o' them!"

"I see him, Momma," Kathleen shrieked. "He's over there climbin' on the fence."

"Good fer you, Kathleen. Yer the only one o' the bunch has any sense. G'wan over there an' get him now an' tell him to get back here before I break his neck." She caught sight of Mick ap-

proaching on the sidewalk below in jovial conversation with Miles and a few burly Hibernians and yelled out to him, with no thought of the crowd: "Ah, *there* ye are, yer lordship! An' here I was thinkin' ye were goin' to spend the rest o' the day in the saloon over there an' let *me* haul this load an' this pack o' kids over to the park myself. Get a move on ye now, the two o' ye—those cars will be here in no time."

"Fer God's sake, Bridie!" Mick whispered as he hurried up to her. "Ye don't have to be shoutin' at the top o' yer lungs!"

"Ha! Why don't ye stay around an' gimme a hand, then, instead o' sneakin' off to yer saloon as soon as I turn my back? I ain't gonna do every-

210

thing myself an' watch all this stuff an' these kids. And *this* one—" she said, grabbing Tony as he came up to them in Kathleen's tow, sweaty and disheveled, his hands already black with dirt "—this one is just like ye, runnin' away the minute I take my eye off him, the little monkey!" She gave him a cuff on the ear.

"Aw, leave him alone," said Mick. "He's all right."

"All right, is he? Look at him—he's nothin' atall, just bones, an' half o' them broken at that!"

"O.K.," Mick said. "Ye don't have to holler."

"Now, now, Mick," said Miles with resignation, "Bridie just don't feel a picnic is any good unless it starts off with a nice public floggin' of somebody."

"My own brother," Bridie said in disgust, "an' talkin' like that . . . C'mon, let's be goin'."

The first of the trolleys had drawn up opposite the gate, almost throbbing on the tracks in its eagerness to be off, the other cars lined impatient behind it, and the Irish poured down the steps and into the street and up the high steel steps, past the smiling motorman, and in the car they rushed to be seated, threw open the windows, shouted to each other and the crowd outside, and heard the hiss as the doors clumped shut, the gong clanged twice, and they were off in a great surge of cheering, the huge steel wheels of the car rumbling smoothly louder on the rails, the trolley above flashing sparks from the wire, and inside the smell of sweat and of the old straw seats and the acrid sharp oily smell of the motors below.

Mary, Tony, and Kathleen had run to the rear of the car, to the big curved seat and window there. Mick sat down listlessly beside Bridie, Pat and Uncle Miles in the seat behind. Pat, making himself as small as possible, pressed his nose against the window, held his breath, and prayed: Oh, please, God, don't let them fight, not on the picnic . . .

"Dammit, Bridie," Mick began, "don't ye know ye shouldn't be hollerin' like that when we're out in public?"

"Ha! I don't care *where—*"

"I know! I know!" Mick said vehemently. "That's the whole trouble with ye."

"When I go to all the trouble that one o' these picnics is," Bridie told him, "I expect I'm gonna get some help. An' I'll tell ye this—I'm gonna get help, or you're gonna hear about it, public place or not!"

Beside Pat, Miles stirred uneasily. "Aw, Bridie," he said in a coaxing voice, "now, why don't ye—"

"An' you're no better!" she said to him over her shoulder. "Ye toddled right off after his heels, like a couple o' drunken sailors as soon as ye caught the smell o' the saloon!"

"Aw be quiet," Mick said.

"I will not be quiet!" she barked. "Who d'ye think ye are, anyways? Don't tell me to be quiet! I'll say whatever I please an' I don't care *who* hears me! I'm gonna have a bit of enjoyment at this picnic, too. An' you're gonna *help* me!"

Mick shook his head in despair. "Jesus!—As long as every little thing is just yer own way, yer all right. But you don't worry about anybody else enjoyin' himself. Ye knew we'd come back to carry the baskets when we heard the cars comin'. Ye knew we wouldn't miss the car, that we'd be there. But just because we wasn't there every minute at yer beck an' call, ye started carryin' on . . ."

Bridie's head came around stiffly from the window, and she looked Mick full in the face. Her jaw was trembling a little and her eyes widened, and glowed, much weary knowledge in them, the ancient bitter knowledge of women, seeming to

211

pour this naked knowing into Mick's eyes—and yet, strangely, it seemed to the boy as though she were also taking something, hungrily, from his father's eyes, as though she were at the essence, the secret heart of a man, and was looking out from, as well as into it. When she spoke, she sounded very sure of what she said: "D'ye know, Mick, what's killin' ye? I'm an anchor round yer neck, ain't I, a regular anchor? Yer a real wild Irishman, Mick—or ye were *once*—an' ye still can't figger out what happened to ye. Ye still think ye can go out drinkin' an' carryin' on whenever ye have a mind to, or that ye should be able to go chasin' off after any cute little behind that comes twitchin' along. Oh, I've seen ye lookin' at them," she said, as Mick started to protest, "—I don't think ye've done any actual chasin' of them, though it's not that ye wouldn't like to, or raise whatever other hell comes into yer head. But ye *can't,* Mick. I wish to God ye'd get used to that idea. Ye can't. Them days are over and gone. Yer a family man now, an' these four kids are yours. Ye gotta feed them, an' put clothes on their backs, and bring 'em up right. If I'm gonna kill myself workin' fer them, always bein' too tired to ever go out an' see anybody, wearin' the same old rags year after year—well, then, *you're* gonna help, too. Ye know, this ain't Ireland—"

"No, it ain't," Mick said mournfully, shaking his head, "an' sometimes I think it was a cold sad day I left Ireland."

"Sure it was!" Bridie said in disgust. "Ye have no right to be in this country. Ye should be back there in the rain, scratchin' at the rocks in that miserable piece o' land yer father was goin' to give ye. Well, let me tell yer honor, I learned somethin' since I come out here. When I was workin' fer the Shuttleworths, in their big mansion, servin' their meals, washin' their dishes, cleanin' up their dirt

after them, even though I was green I kept my eyes open. An' I saw that most o' the rich are the poorest excuse fer people on the face o' the earth. Except fer old man Shuttleworth, God rest his soul, I was worth six o' them—an' it was himself told me that. I learned from him that in this country—not like the dear ol' sod yer always blubberin' about—if ye had some brains an' worked hard, ye could go a long long ways. An' I made up my mind that my kids would be just as good or better than theirs was, if there was anything on God's earth I could do to get it, an' I just might do it, if I ain't forever trippin' over your big lazy behind in the meantime! Paddy's got more brains than any o' the Shuttleworth kids, and he's gonna be a priest, an' the rest o' them will amount to somethin', too, if God spares me. None o' them will ever work in that lousy mill, that's fer sure!"

"Take care, lady," said Mick. "Don't bite off more than ye can chew. There's nothin' wrong with an honest day's work, mill or no mill, an' the rich'll be rich till Judgment Day. The way yer bringin' them up, they're afraid to get their lily-white hands dirty. Tony's the only one with any fire in him."

"Ha! Ye like that one, don't ye?" she said. "Because he's a wild one like yersel'. Don't worry, boyo, I'll get that outa him."

"Ah, ye will that, I guess," Mick said. "It's not enough he breaks his bones—ye wanna break his back, too."

"Oooh," she said appreciatively, smiling, "ye still got the blarney, don't ye? I don't want him to need his back as much as you need yours. Brains is the thing in this country."

"Aw, ye got a lot of crazy ideas when ye was workin' fer them Shuttleworths. Ye should let kids grow up to be themselves, without tryin' to make millionaires out of them."

"Ha! That'll never happen on what you bring home."

"Aw, why don't ye keep quiet instead of always harpin' about that?"

"Ye watch how ye talk to me, Mick Riley," she said, "or I'll get offa this car right now an' go home."

"I wish ye would," he said, "fer all the good wishin' does."

"I bet ye do. Ye'd go wild over there by yerself."

In the taut silence that followed the argument, a stillness humming with the hostility that arched between Mick and Bridie, a tension outlined in the curve of their shoulders as they strained apart trembling in the same small seat, the boy sat slouched, crouched down, trying to hide from all of this, his forehead pressed against the cold wet glass of the window, vibrating, aching with the rattling of the car, head thrumming with the angry rhythm, trying to escape, to run from this familiar bitterness, to return into the dawn's now-lost glow, the warmth of the picnic mood that had seemed so close upon them all. Through the fogged glass his eyes stared blindly, welling with a moist protest, a rending inability to help or speak to them. He looked at his father's big shaggy head, the thick black hair with random strokes of gray like scratches from a paw, the head bent forward now in sullen thought, and his father's neck, corded and sinewy, strong, stubborn, rising solid like an old Celtic tower from the hillside of his shoulders . . .

There's a back for ye, man, a back to move mountains. There's a back to swing a shovel or a pick, a back with meat on it. To hell with the Yankee narrowback! Here's a back for a slab-sided mountain of a man who'll dig a roadbed, ford a river, lay your railroads down—rock, crushed rock, gravel, more rock, tie, spike, and wheel-burnished silver rail—lay them all down, lay himself down, for your transcontinental railroad, for your long hooting freight train in the night, for your green-plushed glowing windows whizzing by in the Illinois night. Here's a back for the mean job, the dirty job, the rough and dangerous job: the big, top-heavy hod up on the creaking scaffold, or the sand-slogging mud-clogged titans under your rivers, pushing your tunnels through. Here's a back for building, for moving in the bowels of the earth; here's a back to pit against the earth, to pit against huge quivering walls of clay, thick seams of coal; a back to stand on the lip of the roaring furnace and shovel nourishment into its white-hot throat—yes, here's a back for steel, equal to steel, deserving of steel: for the tall hungry glory of the blast furnace belching red-gold light high into the smoky midnight sky; for the furnace's glowing scarlet maw, to keep it spewing steel; for the dark, never-lighted country of the big ladles, under the great sheet-iron sheds of the mills, the great black sheds with their broken windows like battered mouths, where the cranes screech and the huge squat ladles tilt fiery steel out like hot white soup in the darkness. Here's the back for raw steel, to shovel the ore and the slag, to move the coke from the towering gondolas, the back to tap the ominous teeth of the furnace and let the smoking steel river spew out, the back to stack the big pig ingots. Here's a man's back for you, gentlemen, a back fit to contest with the earth . . .

But perhaps Bridie had glimpsed a truth, in a way. Perhaps for the Irish the day of the back was fading. Society drove on, ruthless as ever, the Irish in one wave, and the Italians, also evolving now, coming into a new climate, behind them the Negro

213

Michael O'Malley

stepping in, the black back now bending into the deep traces, moving the ponderous earth-bound wheels of the nation, and behind him surely others, as a nation flowers . . . Perhaps necessity dictated to the Irish that a new day come, that the back straighten up now, that the eye seek more subtle horizons. But if Bridie saw this, Mick did not.

The boy bit at his lip. His hand stole out toward his father's back but paused in the air, hung there a moment, returned to his lap. How to comfort one without hurting the other? How to speak the word for both? The word—what was the word? He wanted to shout: Why don't they comfort each other? Why don't they talk nice?

—What can I say? The word? The word was *love*. Why can't there be love? He addressed himself, in a new and dispassionate way, to God. *Well, God, why? Why do they fight like that all the time?* But at once he regretted the ferocity of his tone. *I'm sorry, God. But, I mean, why can't we love each other? Loving is easier than fighting, isn't it?*— Nobody but ourselves cares whether we live or die, only we're all so busy fighting and hollering at each other that we don't even have a minute for caring. *God, why do we have to keep on picking at each other like the meat on some old bones?*

The boy waited, but he did not hear the answer . . .

They were high on the side of the valley now, having crossed the river, rocketing along, the car swaying from side to side, the trolley hissing and sparking as it skipped beneath the overhead wire. Far below at the foot of the hill was the river, the Monongahela, big and brown and muddy, with little wavelets running across it diagonally to lap at the concrete shoreline. The slop from the mills gushed out of the sewer pipes in a white-brown

tide, fell thickly, making no splash. The hillside opposite sloped gently at first from the riverbank, then soared up, green-crowned, as high as the one they were on though not as steep, with the mills and smaller factories and the grimy little houses slewed across the lap of the valley, rolling up the sides.

"I'm gonna talk to Mrs. Kelly up in the front," Bridie said. "Keep an eye on the kids an' the stuff." As she walked forward in the swaying car, Miles moved up into her place, giving Mick a compassionate grasp of the arm as he sat.

"Better days are comin'," he said.

"Le's hope," said Mick fervently.

At that point the trees and wild bushes beside the tracks fell away, and the car seemed to be soaring free, traveling almost on the lip of the roadbed. The whole smoky panorama of the city was sprawled before them.

"Jesus Christ Almighty!" Miles said very softly. "Did ye ever see such a smokin' stinkin' cesspool of a place?"

"Yeah, look at it," said Mick. "Look at that river."

"A truly inspirin' sight, ain't it?" said Miles. "All fulla shit and garbage."

"Aw, now, it ain't *that* bad," Mick said. "Some days it don't look too dirty. But it never gets rid o' that brown color. They say it's from all the mud up the river, an' then all that what-ye-call they dump in it, chemicals, an' stuff from the mills. Look at them big pipes there with all that crap sloshin' out."

"I see it. Ain't it great how them buggers from the mill takes care o' the landscape? Oh, they write up in the company magazine about the interest they take in improvin' things, an' 'Make Pittsburgh Beautiful' an' so on, an' then all day long the bastards have those smokestacks throwin' out all that soot in big dirty clouds an' those sewers pourin' that shit into the river. Not that I mind the mills goin', mind ye—I'm all fer work. But I was readin' in a magazine how they could put a what-ye-ma'-call in those smokestacks, a filter, an' cut that soot down. Or at least they think they got one now that'll be cheap enough to tempt these stingy bastards to spend a little o' their money on it, with all they're makin' on this war, which—don't let anybody tell ye different, Mick—they are makin' a pot, a goddam *tub* full o' money on, bless their greedy souls. I hope Paddy back there ain't listenin' or I'll have to watch my language." He glanced over his shoulder and the boy looked studiously out the window, trying to subdue the blush that leaped up. "Don't be lookin' so forlorn, Paddy," Miles said. "Ye'd swear ye was goin' to a funeral instead of a picnic." . . .

Below them now in the river a battered towboat was shoving a long string of empty coal barges, angling over toward the Braddock locks on the far side of the river. The shrill hooting of the pilot's lock whistle drifted up, and the boat as it labored, looking heroically small beside the deep gaping barges, belched forth a cloud of soot and rusty smoke. From the lock the long low line of the dam stretched out across the river, and the water made a broad yellow-white band of foam as it slid across.

"Maybe we should take a ride up the river on one o' them paddleboats," Mick said, "an' see if it looks any better up in the coal country."

Miles shook his head. "Sweet Jesus," he said, "see how that water looks goin' over the dam—all white an' foamy like it was fulla piss or somethin', which it probably is, God knows, the state o' this poor river bein' what it is. Fresh water looks differ-ent—it just kinda slides over a little dam like that, kinda smooth like, ye know."

"Yeah. I remember," said Mick.

"An' as fer goin' anywheres on that boat, God ferbid! Why, the mill is pretty dirty but it's a sweet garden o' roses compared with the looks o' *that* tub. Look how filthy it is."

The boy smiled then and shook his head in dissent. That old coal boat was going up the river. His heart quickened as he watched it flail its way toward the locks. Upriver—to all the grimy cities he had never seen, their names familiar, towns he longed to see, coal towns, coal mines, the wry tumble of coal tipples, mountains of coal, big rolling hills, more mills, red and roaring, tall cities, strange sights—Clairton, and Elizabeth, Monessen and Donora, Brownsville—and then down into West Virginia, a magic name, bringing to his mind wild hills and mountaineers and stills smoking in the piney backwoods. And finally, to turn and come back down the river, shoving the deep barges heaped with coal, he could see it all, the swift trip down, and pushing past Brasston and Braddock and into the Braddock lock and then coasting down easy on to Pittsburgh where the river seemed more urgent, more alive, and shoving out into the current of the mighty Ohio, and with the coal trains coming down too, racing along the riverbank past the towboat, their blackened gondolas bulging with coal and long gray streamers of smoke whipping out from the engine and sliding down in the fierce wind beside the cars and fading off to the side as the train hurtles on . . . It was good beyond dreaming: to stand up there in that little shack of a pilothouse and wave at the fast freight, at the winking red caboose as it whizzed by; and to sleep on the boat as it cut through the waters in the night, and to say whatever you wanted to say, and

215

go wherever you wanted to go . . . His eyes opened wide and he grinned foolishly.

". . . D'ye remember how the rivers was at home?" his father was saying to Miles. "D'ye recall that little river over near Cashel, where the water was so green all the time, an' quick an' strong the way it flowed, with just a kind of low rushin' sound to it?"

"Only the once I was there. They called it Donnelly's Brook."

"That's the place. We used to go over on a Sunday, after Mass. Aw, lyin' out there in the sun with a little poteen to keep the chill o' the earth off ye, ye could catch the loveliest fish, Miles, trout big as yer arm there was. Sure, it was tough at home, but we had some grand times, Miles. I haven't been fishin' even once since I come to this country."

"Not even once?" Miles said morosely.

"Naw! God Almighty, there ain't no time here fer anything like that. Ye know? A man don't have a minute's peace in this country. An' where would ye go, anyways?" he said, waving his arm at the sight before them. "I bet there ain't been a fish in that river fer a hundred years. . . . Now, back in Ireland we was never what ye might call rich, Miles, but we had a damn sight more enjoyment outa things." He was silent for a moment. "Well, as Bridie says, it's all in the hands o' God."

Miles looked up at Bridie and lowered his voice. "Ah, she's a great one fer gettin' God into the conversation," he said irreverently, "but she never lets Him bother *her* none. Ye know? She'll tell ye the Good Lord wants this an' that outa ye, but herself'll do exackly what she wants to do. She figures the Good Lord is around to keep the likes o' you an' me in line."

"Ah, but it's a hard job she's got, Miles, raisin' a family. It's no picnic fer anybody—"

"That goes without sayin'," Miles agreed. "But she's *made* fer it, Mick, she's made fer it. She loves to work. She's just like that damn foreman o' mine in the mill: if ye help her finish the job she got scheduled fer the day, she finds sixteen other things to do. . . . It's you an' me ain't made fer it, Mick. I never yet seen Irishman that was."

"Made fer what?"

"Why, fer a nice quiet home life an' raisin' a family."

"But we do raise families," Mick protested indignantly.

"*They* raise 'em," Miles explained, nodding toward the women in front. "They raise 'em, an' they just try to keep a man's itchy foot in the house as much as they can. But as ye just made clear to yerself, I believe, none o' the men thinks it's a big steamin' platter o' bacon an' eggs, an' a little buttered toast on the side, please, if ye know what I mean."

"God only knows . . ." said Mick. "There's no doubt we had some grand times back there at home, Miles, with the fishin' an' boats, and all."

"Sure. If we was home, we could be off to a dance, or down to the bog, perhaps, to make a little poteen just to pass the time . . ." And with sudden derisive bitterness he added: "O' course, we'd probably be half freezin' to death in old raggedy coats in the wintertime, an' hungry as hell half o' the time. God knows, we was when we left!"

Mick, silent now, nodded forlornly in assent.

Then the trolley was grinding to a stop, and the motorman shouted, "Here we are folks! The end of the line!"

"Let's hurry now an' get a good table," Mick said, "or Mom will eat us alive."

GLADYS SCHMITT
"The Persistent Image"

At an art show opening,
Johnnie Reiber recalls Helen Cameron

Time: 1950s   Setting: Pittsburgh

The Persistent Image *is a love story — a story of reawakened love. As this selection indicates, Johnnie Reiber had met and fallen in love with Helen Cameron more than five years earlier. They had planned to marry, but then, apparently under pressure from her family, Helen had instead married Harold Beales and moved away with him. In the intervening years, Reiber — now, in 1953, thirty-three years old — has given up thoughts of a career in professional music, bought into a record store, and settled down rather glumly to bachelorhood and the routine of being a small-time merchant. Though Reiber knows that Helen's marriage did not work out, that she has been divorced, he has done his best to put her and her family out of his mind forever.*

But then in the first chapter of The Persistent Image *Helen's mother has unexpectedly appeared in Reiber's shop to ask him to install a hi-fi set in her home. When she starts talking about what "we" would like, irresistibly Johnnie thinks of Helen — Is she living with her mother? Must he see her again? The past starts flooding back, its persistent images overwhelming him when later that day he visits the Art Center (the section printed here from chapter 2).*

As befits a romance of reawakened memories, much of Schmitt's novel is a mood piece in which details of setting, as often as not architectural details, trigger mental association. Thus the exterior of the Art Center suggests Reiber's melancholy: "The great grey rectangle of the building . . . was set far back on a terrace yellowing to
218
autumn." Later he visits the museum where Helen works as editor of the Monthly Bulletin, *and still trapped in the past, still unable to recommit himself to a renewed love in the present, he waits in the Gallery of Ancient Sculpture, where "the light came down . . . watery through a greenish glass skylight, so that the rows of square white marble pillars and the plaster statues set between them and the cold marble benches placed at discreet intervals all had the shimmering, abandoned look of wreckage at the bottom of the sea."*

Though Schmitt does not use real place names in The Persistent Image, *the Gallery of Ancient Sculpture is clearly Pittsburgh's Carnegie Museum; the Art Center suggests the Arts and Crafts Center at Fifth and Shady avenues; and most of the action seems set in Oakland and Shadyside.*

Gladys Schmitt (1909-1972) was born on Osceola Street in Bloomfield, lived later on Howe Street in Shadyside, and then for many years on Wilkins Avenue, in Squirrel Hill. From 1942 until her death she taught at Carnegie-Mellon University, where her renown as a writer of national stature may have been surpassed by the affection and respect stimulated by her teaching.

Although Schmitt's national reputation came largely from her historical novels (David the King, Rembrandt, etc.), she did write three novels in addition to The Persistent Image *that use Pittsburgh as a setting —* The Gates of Aulus *(1942),* Alexandra *(1947), and* A Small Fire *(1957).*

"The Persistent Image"

The Center—he drove to it through a twilight in which the yellow sky and the newly lighted street lamps dazzled his vision—was a big stone house, willed to the Community by a declining First Family. Whether their interest in supporting the cultural life of the City had been as decisive as their need to disencumber themselves of taxes and upkeep was anybody's guess. The great grey rectangle of the building, relieved by pseudo-Moorish iron grille-work, was set far back on a terrace yellowing to autumn; here, from the grass and from the close-crowded branches of poplars, the urgency of the cicadas sounded again, annoying now. As he parked the car and went in at the rear entrance—to go by the back way was for him a means of denying he had any part in the self-congratulatory spirit of these occasions—he thought how in a crowd like this it would be impossible to think much of anything, which was all to the good: he didn't want to think of Helen Cameron.

Without looking for her among the fifty or sixty people who were jammed into the main gallery to honor their own Arthur McCullough for his lovely work, he remembered how it had been to look for her in the past. For a year after her marriage—not knowing that she had gone away, that she was with *him* at an Army Camp in Alabama all the time—at every concert, every play, every exhibition he had looked for her, until the usual posture of his spirit on public occasions was the posture of a starving cat, crouching and waiting—a shameful business, he couldn't remember it without a warm and weakening surge of shame. And yet—he thought of it while he moved carefully between damp bodies, past powdered necks and beads and ostentatiously sober ties—and yet in that year when he had come to such events only to watch and wait, the stuff of those events, unwanted, unattended-to, had broken upon him with more power than ever before. A school production of Chekov's *Three Sisters* had so undone him that he had to sit through intermission surreptitiously wiping the tears from his face. A little canvas of towers and clouds in the International Exhibition had made him as lightheaded as wine at a wedding breakfast. And the insistent, unfolding splendor of the St. Anne Fugue had actually entered into his person—it seemed to him that the organ notes were multiplying inside him, crowding his vitals, shaking his heart.

It was years now since he had experienced anything as intensely as that. Going past the table with the cookies and the punch, edging toward the outer limits of the crowd so that he could seem to be examining the pictures, he knew how much he had changed and he smiled disparagingly at that lost and excessive capacity for pleasure—and pain. The watercolors—now and again he could catch sight of them between clusters of talking faces—struck him as being at once inoffensive and unimpressive, pale landscapes and seascapes melting in the Marin manner into planes and lines; though for all he knew they might be very good: if a real Marin had been hung against the tan monkscloth by mistake he doubted that he could have singled it out from the rest. People he knew—customers, old acquaintances from the Orchestra, an English teacher who had taught him in the College of Fine

Arts—nodded and smiled at him, and there was something exasperating in this particular brand of nod and smile. It was as if they were urging him to participate in the general enthusiasm over mediocrity, in the City's provincial complacency over the way it was fostering the Arts.

He saw the artist, a tweedy man with white hair and a black moustache, backed up by women against a plush drape and looking ashamed of himself. The artist didn't see him, which was a pity: now he would have to stay around until the embarrassed eyes lighted on him—otherwise how would it ever be known he had been there? A newspaper critic moved through the crush, smoking against the rules and maintaining a deliberately noncommittal face. Four music students from the College of Fine Arts settled themselves with music stands on the landing that separated the two curved upward sweeps of the staircase and began to play a Beethoven quartet—as might have been expected, one of the brashly stupid early quartets.

He had played in a quartet once, and it was queer—he crushed the pack of Chesterfields in his pocket, horribly wanting a cigarette—it was queer and troubling to think how, if he hadn't played in that quartet he would probably never have laid eyes on Helen Cameron. He hadn't belonged in it either; it had been gotten together by the glamor boys of the Symphony: the concertmaster and the first cellist, a lady-charmer from Peru; and it was only the fact that the concertmaster loathed the first violist which accounted for his being asked. He had played with them—and gone with them that February evening to perform at a birthday party at the house of some people named Cameron—chiefly because a person didn't say "No" to the concertmaster if he needed his orches-

tra job . . . The bright lights over the paintings, the scratchy instruments, and the conversation of the crowd, grown shriller to compete with the music, were suddenly oppressive, and he moved toward the front door. The air, dank with a breath of drenched and dying foliage in it, came cool to his face as soon as he crossed the threshold. The broad, roofless porch was littered with leaves; they looked metallic in the light from the street-lamp—some of them dull and rusty, the wetter ones bright gold. He walked upon them, back and forth, lighting his cigarette and drawing on it deep, and let himself remember that first evening in the house on Parkman Road—the dozens of florist's roses and the candlelight and the yellow satin drapes and the men in black tie and the women in evening gowns. Everybody done up in honor of the twenty-third birthday of the daughter of the house—and where was she?

She was standing, slender and dark-haired—he caught a glimpse of her while he was tuning his viola—in front of a very bright lamp at the other end of the music room, some thirty feet away from him. She wore one of those gathered cocktail skirts made of some crimson stuff so stiff that it revealed nothing but the faintest suggestion of a pair of long and rather boyish thighs. Her blouse was silvery, thin-spun, and almost transparent in the white glare of the lamp; but the body which was shadowed forth in the cloudiness of the cloth was slight enough to make him feel a little ashamed of his stare. The small bosom scarcely lifted the tucked and fragile material; and the upper arms, showing through the voluminous balloon-shaped sleeves, were pale and thin and straight like the arms of a ten-year-old.

She was not the sort of girl who usually caught

his eye, and yet he had almost lost his place glancing up during a rest because she had turned and he wanted to see the back of her—the narrowness of her haunches and the long upward sweep of her back and the nape of her neck, thin, with a little hollow between the tendons—a very slight neck overshadowed as it was by an almost too luxuriant growth of glossy brown hair. His interest had an obvious enough explanation: it was *her* party, and her mother in yards of black satin was doing everything possible to show her off and draw her out, and people came over to see her as soon as they walked in and went to her again to take her hand and say good-night, so that she seemed to be—officially at least—the center of everything. But, looking back on it now—remembering it while the talk floated out of the huge open windows of the Art Center and the crickets and beetles on the lawn made a sound like hundreds of distant bells—looking back on it he knew that his awareness of her presence had been acute, almost painful; he had been tightened up inside with worry for her as if he had somehow doubted her ability to get through the occasion. Why, instead of gushing all over her, didn't they let her finish just one of her sentences? Didn't she know any young, easy-going people at all—why was everybody there so polished and punctilious and old?

Young people *had* come to that party, but later, well on toward the end of it. Six or seven of them had walked in together, just as the music was finished and the guests began to move toward the dining room; it was as if they had come on the order of their parents, unwillingly, from some livelier place, but ready to console themselves with such a spread as they would be unlikely to find anywhere else. He waited with the other members of the quartet for an invitation to the table. The lady of the house swept up and drew them into the social sphere with a fine show of ease and good fellowship, talking learnedly about the beautiful Siciliano variation in the Schumann, finding a safe place for their instruments, taking the concertmaster by the elbow with one hand and patting the sleeve of the glamorous Peruvian with the other. They came into the dining room just in time to witness the ceremony of blowing out the candles on the birthday cake. He saw the daughter's face distinctly for the first time when she thrust it into the light of the circle of little flames: it was a pale face, beautifully spare, with a wide mouth and very large bright eyes. The eyes looked straight into the candles and were so dark, so quiet, so fixed on the cake in front of them to the exclusion of everything else that they made him think of a spaniel's eyes.

After that, he thought of her very little. Like the young people that had come so tardily and quieted down so soon, he thought about the spread. Four or five times before, he had walked around such a table with plate and napkin and silver in hand, and every time he had made a pig of himself. There were meat-balls steaming away in a sour-sweet sauce under the heavy lid of a silver chafing dish; there were canapes of egg and cheese and anchovy cut in circles and crescents and stars. There was a whole poached salmon and a huge mound of shredded crabmeat dotted with capers. There was a flaming baked Alaska which, when it was put out and sliced down, turned out to contain an ingenious insertion of raspberry ice, so that every cut of it was marked with a purple "23." He heaped his plate as usual, and as usual he despised himself for heaping his plate. Anybody might think he was

221

undernourished, the way he took whatever he could lay his hands on; and he suspected himself of an even baser reason: he suspected himself of wanting to eat up their status, of wanting to incorporate physically their splendor and their elegance. Nor could he comfort himself with the usual observation that, wealthy as they were, they showed themselves in their talk to be a crowd of ignorant fools. Wherever he went, he found himself on the outskirts of a clever conversation. They talked about Henry James; they talked about Utrillo; they talked about English bishops and Parisian restaurants and Norwegian springs. Everywhere he stopped they were talking about something beyond his experience, and every time he turned away he was drawn back to this platter or that chafing dish and took another helping and was still more furious with himself. So furious that, when he finally lighted upon a subject that he could understand and bear a creditable part in, he was in no mood to do it with restraint.

That conversation . . . Flicking his cigarette over the porch balustrade and watching it disappear in a shower of sparks on the black lawn, he saw himself carry his heaped plate toward the end of the table and stop by the Peruvian and a female member of the Symphony Board who were having an earnest exchange near the ruins of the birthday cake. They were talking about another glamor boy, the young San Franciscan who had just finished a three-week stint as Guest Conductor with the Orchestra. He knew it because the woman—one of those old, thin, rapturous women whose faces are ready on the least provocation to produce an expression of reverent exaltation—was imitating the most controversial of the young Maestro's gestures, the right hand against the heart, the left extended palm

upward in supplication. "I love the way he does that," she said, half veiling her look in wrinkled eyelids. "I know, I've heard people say that it's all put on for effect, but I've never seen anything so touching, so completely sincere as the way he pleads with the strings."

"Oh, I'm sure he's sincere enough," said the Peruvian, looking at the roast beef in order to avoid the fervent eyes. He hated the San Franciscan, who was three years his junior and had been given a feature article in *Time* Magazine. "It's only that we're all inclined to be a little dramatic—affected, shall I say?—when we're young."

"Ah, you can't make me believe that . . ." She had dropped her hands and was shaking her silvery head. She looked at the circle around her—some others, including the daughter of the house, had been drawn by the magnetic subject and were ready to join in. "But here's Mr. . . . Mr. . . . here's the young violist who gave us all so much pleasure tonight. We were just talking about the way your visiting conductor holds his hands when he appeals to the strings. You played under him—don't you think he's sincere when he does that?"

"What difference does it make what he does with his hands?" His voice came out of him louder and harsher than he had meant it to be.

"What difference? I don't understand you."

"All I mean is this: when you have a real conductor, maybe there's some point in discussing whether he's beautiful to watch or not. But in a case like this, when the fellow can't even get a decent ensemble tone, who cares what he does with his hands?"

Oh, well, said the Peruvian, he wouldn't go as far as that. Neither would a fat little lady energetically polishing a pair of rimless spectacles. Neither would one of the supercilious youngsters who had wandered over from the portable bar, smelling blood. But the daughter of the house, the Birthday Girl—*she* raised her voice, and for once they let her finish. "Mr. Reiber's perfectly right—he doesn't get any tone out of them no matter what he does," she

said, crossing her childish arms over her chest and pressing her long, rather blunt fingers into the voluminous folds of her sleeves. "I know because I kept my eyes closed all through the Brahms, and the tone was coarse—it was just the way Mr. Reiber said."

"Maybe I'm no expert," said the spectacle-polisher, "but I have his recording of the Brahms Second, and it always sounded very beautiful to me."

All of them had taken it up now, but he could not follow. He knew only that she was fixing him with that bright, close, spaniel's gaze of hers, as if the rest of the room had receded out of the range of her vision, as if there were nothing there for her except his face.

What had he done, with whom had he talked during the remainder of that evening? He couldn't remember now; he could remember only that he had rejected coffee and brandy because he was certain he couldn't manage both of them at once, and that he felt a disproportionate regret while he was putting his viola back into its case, as if this evening, which had been a mere chore for him, had failed to fulfill some vast expectation, as if these people, whose good opinion would not have been of the slightest use to him, should have known him better and liked him more. He was among the last to leave—the concertmaster had become involved in Viennese recollections with a consumptive look-ing gentleman on a yellow damask sofa; and he had the impression that the concertmaster was some-what uncertain about his role in the house and would rather not have the last of his fellow-performers desert him.

It was in the reception hall that he had spent the last fifteen or twenty minutes of the evening, in

the conviction that if he seemed to be on the point of leaving nobody would wonder why he hadn't attached himself to one of the few little groups that remained inside. *She* was out there too, in her capacity as hostess, to say goodnight; there was a considerable amount of coming and going, and she was standing, with her shoulders drawn in a little, determined not to shiver in recurrent blasts from the front door. She caught sight of him where he was sitting on a needlepoint bench with his coat on and the concertmaster's coat beside him. Twice she looked over at him and smiled. And, when the procession of departure came to a temporary stop, she walked up to him with a long, determined, boyish stride, and stood before him, plainly ex-pecting him to say something.

"It was a very pleasant party, Miss Cameron," he said, getting onto his feet.

"Oh, thank you. I'm glad you liked it. To tell the truth, it was a little bit too big for me—"

"Everybody was absolutely quiet during the music—"

"Oh, yes, they loved the music. We often have musical evenings, but I like them better when they're smaller than this. Maybe you'll come some time again."

He couldn't imagine a possibility more remote. "Thank you," he said, and smiled a quick, point-less smile.

"Oh, but she really means it." It was the mother, speaking to him over the daughter's shoulder. In the light from the immense prism chandelier that hung in the middle of the reception hall, he noticed Emily Cameron's face for the first time, so handsome in its clean lines and flawless planes that it could afford to dispense with make-up—there was nothing but the faintest tinge of coral painted on the thin lips. The eyes looked at him with slate-colored serenity, as if he were part of some spectacle, remote but interesting nevertheless. "She really means it, and so do I."

"Thank you," he said.

"We'll be having another musical evening as soon as my husband gets back from Boston. Suppose you call here, say, Monday or Tuesday of next week, and we'll tell you when."

He had been so startled to see airy politeness transforming itself into a real invitation that he had not answered at once, but had stood staring like a fool at the woman's veined, ringed, quiet hands.

"We'll keep it smaller this time," said the daughter, shivering in spite of herself.

"Thanks very much. I'll call. I'd like to come."

"We'll be looking forward to seeing you then. Helen, for heaven's sake go get yourself a stole or something. You'll catch your death of cold."

Had she given him her hand that evening? He couldn't remember. He remembered those straight, childish arms of hers, saw them again in the balloon-shaped sleeves of her silvery blouse, and then started out of his recollection because somebody had come out of Art McCullough's exhibit onto the front porch, shattering quiet with the bang of the screen door. A youngish woman was walking away from him up the other side of the long porch, keeping close to the balustrade, swaying a little, sometimes putting out her hand to steady herself. Could she be drunk? Certainly not on the watery punch they served in there—they never put anything in to spike it, only a couple of bottles of Rhine wine. Then it occurred to him that maybe she was crippled: as she passed through a swath of light from the street lamp, he could see that her whole narrow back was laboring to pro-

duce every step of the peculiar, swinging gait. She stopped at the far end of the porch, not smoking, only leaning against the railing and staring out over the lawn; and, since he had no wish to encounter her, he went back inside.

It was years since he had remembered any of that, and he had remembered it tonight only because Emily Cameron had come into his shop this morning, wanting God knows what. What was there for anybody to want at this stage of the game? While he looked at the watercolors—the crowd was beginning to thin and it was possible to look at the watercolors—he repeated to himself the hard, unchangeable formula with which he had taught himself to live: I met Helen Cameron, I loved Helen Cameron, I was given reasons—or so I imagined—to think that she loved me, and then all of a sudden it turned out that she was marrying somebody else. And he got on well enough with it, almost as well as if he hadn't been foolish enough to remember: he managed to put some conviction into the congratulatory handshake that he offered to Art McCullough, and he listened with forbearance to the inanities that Mrs. Elliott had thought up to say about the show. It was late, the punchbowl was almost empty and the musicians on the landing were folding up their music stands. Now that there was no other music to cover it, the first line of the *Winterreise* came to the surface again: *A stranger came I hither, a stranger I depart.* He started for the back entrance, thinking how maybe tomorrow he would telephone Sandie. Even if a person had to force himself to it, *that* always came off more or less; and if it came off at all, it was a temporary cure like a couple of aspirins: you came out of the night's sleep cleansed of unprofitable longings and recollections, willing to be satisfied

225

with the divided day and the promise of another night of dreamless sleep.

Somebody—in fact it was the strangely misshapen young woman who had been out on the porch—blocked him by laboring across his path. She wasn't drunk, and she wasn't crippled either. It was only that she was in the last stages of pregnancy. The child—he knew about such things because Sandie was a nurse and his friend George was a resident at Saint Elizabeth's—the child had come down into its final position, and the young woman's body, under the tent-like gathers of a greenish India print, was pear-shaped: flat above and shockingly, unbelievably swollen out below. The face—she went so slowly that there was plenty of time for him to see the face—was beautiful, bony, and haggard: all the softness had been devoured, all the buoyancy had been dragged out of it by the intolerable bulk of the child. Her eyes met his—not deliberately, she was staring at nothing—and were black and beseeching, but he rejected the look. Why didn't she stay home where she belonged? What was she doing walking around in a public place in a state like that? He crossed the parking lot, kicking up the gravel all along the way in an incomprehensible fit of rage.

But he knew the source of his fury as soon as he had closed himself up in the familiar smoke-and-gasoline-scented air of his own car. Helen, my Helen—that's what he had thought when the young woman had lurched past him in the gallery. Helen, my Helen—in some Army post in Alabama, in the thick heat, one summer five years ago *she* went around like that, and the child moved down to its final position so that her body was shaped like a pear, and her cheeks and her temples looked ravaged, eaten up, fallen in, and without knowing what she did she stared into the face of some stranger with beseeching eyes. Oh, he had known she was pregnant—there was always somebody around to tell a person something like that. He had known that she had given birth, had looked for it and read it on the society page of the local newspaper: "Born to Captain and Mrs. Beales, in Somewhere, Alabama, a girl, Cecilia Emily, July Something, 1949." But the actuality of that pregnancy and that birth, like the inescapable fact of the seed sown in darkness, had never entered into him like this, had waited all those years at the edges of his consciousness—he knew it now, wiping the sweat from his forehead—to spring upon him and tear at him and leave him drenched and undone, so that he did not dare to drive.

Helen, my Helen . . . But he had no Helen. The one who had stared at him so fixedly and earnestly near the ruins of the birthday cake, the one who had put her mouth against his so that the shape of her lips had seemed to be pressed there forever like a seal or a brand—she was beyond all conjuring now. No memory that he could summon up for himself while he sat in the smell of smoke and gasoline and listened to the faraway talk and the crickets had any power to materialize or any semblance of reality. The only thing that was real was what he had never seen: Helen Beales, the wife of Captain Harold Beales, the unfortunate, mistreated wife of Captain Harold Beales—for they said the trouble had started early, even before the child was born—Helen, some other Helen who belonged entirely to somebody else, going heavy and ugly with child over the caked mud paths of some Army post, lurching, putting out one hand to steady herself, staring at strangers with terrified and unseeing eyes.

K. C. CONSTANTINE
"Confirming the Obvious"

A call from headquarters spoils
Chief Mario Balzic's Friday night

Time: 1970   Setting: A small town near Pittsburgh

This selection is the opening dozen pages from a detective novel whose interest very much centers on the character of its protagonist, Chief of Police Mario Balzic. In this emphasis on the life-style of his investigator, K. C. Constantine follows in a tradition of crime novels that has produced such memorable figures as Mike Hammer and Sherlock Holmes, Inspector Maigret and Philip Marlowe. Balzic is deliberately conceived as an unheroic figure — a middle-aged cop, a family man, who lives and works in a run-down mining town not far from Pittsburgh. The reader watches Balzic discipline his teen-age daughters, drink beer at the local taverns and deal with neighborhood complaints over the desk at city hall. Rather than unusual mental or muscular prowess, Balzic's professional virtues are common sense, conscientiousness, and the fact that, raised in a small town, he seems to know almost everyone.

The Rocksburg Railroad Murders is rich in regional local color and in details that record its early 1970s setting. One aspect of this is the conglomeration of ethnic types — Slavs, Poles, Italians, and Blacks — presented in the story. Himself of mixed background (though dominantly Italian), Balzic can casually swap ethnic insults with the best of them. After he has told his sergeant that he can be found at Muscotti's, a tavern, this exchange occurs:

"Ah, for the life of a chief," Stramsky said.

Balzic turned back at the door. "You say something?"

"Me? I didn't say nothing."

"You lying Polack. I heard what you said, and I'm going to tell you right now why you'll never be chief. You eat too much kolbassi, and it's starting to affect your brain."

"How 'bout that ginzo crap you eat—what's 'at doing to yours?"

"Making me smarter and smarter. And better looking, too. Hell, just the other day I looked in the mirror, and I said to myself, Balzic, be grateful you weren't born a Polack. Your face would be a mess today. Just like Stramsky's."

"Hey, that reminds me," Stramsky said, reaching in his back pocket for a book of raffle tickets. "Next Sunday's the big day. You want a couple of chances on a bushel of booze?"

"You talking about the corn roast at the Falcons?"

"Yeah. Corn, kolbassi, holupki, kapusta—all for the benefit of the building fund. Two o'clock until."

"I'll take a couple, but I'm damned if I'm going to that thing. Last year I had the runs for a week."

"Buck a chance," Stramsky said, holding out the book of tickets and a ballpoint pen.

"A buck? Last year it was fifty cents."

"So? That's inflation for you. Blame it on Nixon."

Though The Rocksburg Railroad Murders *makes good reading just as a crime novel, its sights and sounds are those of western Pennsylvania.*

In addition to The Rocksburg Railroad Murders, *K. C. Constantine has written two other crime novels,* The Blank Page *(1973), and* The Man Who Liked to Look at Himself *(1974).*

"Confirming the Obvious"

Even with the hand-talkies, it took Chief Mario Balzic a half hour after the game to get the auxiliary police coordinated. Maybe more people were coming to high school football games, or maybe more were coming to Rocksburg High's games, or maybe Rocksburg's narrow streets were never intended to handle this kind of traffic, or maybe there were just too damn many saloons too near the high school field.

Whichever it was, it left Balzic surly, distracted, and thirsting for a beer. He stepped into Evanko's Bar and Grille, hoping for a quick draught, and walked instead into a fist fight between two drunks whose high school football careers had ended at least twenty years earlier and who had started out reminiscing and ended up swinging over the cause of Rocksburg's forty-to-six loss. It took Balzic a half hour to get that straightened out, doing it by buying drinks all around to pacify Mike Evanko to keep him from pressing charges, and by seeing to it that friends of the fist fighters got some coffee into them and gave their word that they'd drive them home.

Back out on the street, traffic seemed worse than before Balzic had gone into Evanko's. Then the auxiliary at the corner of Amelia Street and Eurania Avenue quit communicating and it took Balzic fifteen minutes to get there to find out why.

"Something's wrong with it," Henry Adamchik, the auxiliary, said, holding the radio up to Balzic's ear and shaking it.

Balzic jerked it out of his hand and fiddled with it. "Here, take mine," he said after an exasperating minute trying to make the other one work. "I'll go back and use my car radio."

On the way back to his cruiser, Balzic looked up at the clear black sky and said, "Bad enough you let somebody invent football, but you weren't satisfied with that. No, you had to let somebody go and invent cars, and then radios, and then, Jeezus Christ Almighty, you had to stick me with auxiliaries yet. . . ."

It was eleven-fifteen before the flow of cars approached the usual level of traffic for that time of night on a Friday, and eleven-twenty before Balzic told the auxiliaries to pack it in. He headed his cruiser down Bencho's Alley and threaded his way through a half dozen more alleys before turning onto Delmont Street to his home. Once inside, he headed straight for the refrigerator and a beer.

On the kitchen table was a note from his wife, Ruth, telling him that she'd given the girls permission to go to Valleta's Drug Store after the game, but that they were to be in no later than midnight. The note also said his mother had had a good time at the Eagles' bingo and won a set of dish towels.

Balzic opened the beer and set out a plate. He cut up some provolone and quartered a banana pepper, filled the plate with them, and went into the living room, taking a long drink of beer before setting the dish on the coffee table and turning on the television. With a little luck he thought he might be able to catch the last inning of the Pirates' game out of Saint Louis.

There was another note on the coffee table with a snapshot beside it. The note said: "Hey, Mario, big shot. What you think this? Next time you holler hippeys, you think this over. You look pretty funny. No?" It was his mother's barely legible script.

The snapshot was of himself. There he stood, grinning with the arrogance only being eighteen can muster, thirty pounds lighter, hair slicked back in a duck's tail, wearing a one-button jacket down to his knees and trousers pulled up by inch-wide suspenders to a point just below where his ribs joined and then ballooning out at the knees and coming to rest in a tight circle on his spade, suede shoes. Completing the outfit were a floppy, polka-dotted bow tie and a key chain that nearly touched his shoe.

"Brother, if I wasn't a mess," he said.

He turned the faded snapshot over and looked closely at the smudged date: June 4, 1942, the date of his senior class picnic. He remembered the date very well. The next day he had enlisted in the marines.

He chuckled ruefully and, tossing the snapshot on the table, drank some more beer, and mused for a moment about taking his mother to the court-house to give a lecture to District Attorney Milt Weigh about social customs, particularly in matters of dress. Weigh needed somebody to lecture him about that at least as much as Balzic needed to be reminded of it; to Milt Weigh, anybody who didn't wear four-dollar ties and calf-high socks had to be doing something suspicious.

Balzic chuckled again, thinking about all the things Weigh didn't know and about how Weigh managed to sustain the impression that anything he didn't know wasn't worth knowing.

The sound of the television interrupted his thoughts. He got up to adjust the set and then settled back in the recliner the girls had bought him last Christmas to watch the Pirates and the

Cards. Instead of the game, he got the last minute of a post-game interview and the beginning of what would have been the eleven o'clock news.

He had just kicked off his shoes and put his feet on the coffee table when the phone rang. He swore in Italian and Serbian and was still swearing as he hustled into the kitchen to lift the receiver before it woke either his wife or mother.

"Balzic."

"Royer, Chief."

"Yeah, Joe—oh, wait. Don't tell me you're sick or something and can't make it tonight. Please don't tell me that."

"What do you mean sick? Where the hell you think I'm calling from?"

"You at the station?"

"Hell yes, I'm at the station."

"Jesus, is it after twelve already?"

"Five minutes after."

"Oh boy," Balzic said, sighing. "I just got back from that damn football game. You never saw such a mess. So what's up?"

"Angelo just called in."

"So? Angelo's always calling in. Angelo can't find straight up without calling in."

"He got a reason this time," Royer said. "He found a guy up on the train station platform with his head caved in. Dead."

"Did he get hit by a train, or what?"

"No. Angelo wasn't making too much sense, but from what I gather, somebody beat the shit out of him."

"I'll be right down. You call Weigh's office?"

"Not yet."

"Well, call him, for crissake. I'll be down the train station."

Balzic gulped down a piece of cheese and some

of the pepper as he was putting his shoes back on. He took another gulp of beer, grabbed another piece of provolone to eat on the way, and was starting out the door when his daughters came up on the porch.

"Hi," he said as he hurried past them. "You have a good time? And what are you doing coming in this late? You know you got school tomorrow."

"Tomorrow's Saturday, Daddy," Emily, the fourteen-year-old, said.

"Besides, Mother said it was okay," Marie, the fifteen-year-old, said.

"I'll talk to her about that tomorrow," Balzic said, getting in his car. He got back out to say, "Hey, put that plate of cheese and peppers back in the ice box, will you? And turn the TV off, okay?"

"It's a refrigerator, Daddy," Emily said.

"You know what I mean. And if your mother wakes up tell her I had to go out. Urgent, got it?"

"Yeah, we got it," Marie said with a sidelong glance at her sister.

"Good night, kids," Balzic said, spinning the wheels backing out of the drive.

"Talk about hot-rodders," Marie said.

"Hey, come on," Emily said. "We can watch Humphrey Bogart. He's on channel four."

Balzic had parked his Chevrolet on the State Street side of the Pennsylvania Station when he spotted Angelo Seretti's cruiser. The ticket office was deserted, and he went through the tunnel and up the steps to the platform. Patrolman Angelo Seretti was trying his best to look professional, but the color of his face gave him away. Frank Ben-

nett, the station master, stood beside Seretti, his face more ashen than Seretti's.

"Where?" Balzic said when he approached them.

"Over there," Seretti said. "Under the bench."

Balzic hustled to the bench and went down on one knee. For a second he thought he was going to lose the little beer and cheese he'd gotten down. "Good Christ," he said. He stood up and walked back to Seretti and Bennett. "Get on the horn, Angelo, and tell Royer to get the coroner and the state boys."

"The D.A.'s office, too?"

"He already called them. They should've been here by now. Go on, Angelo."

Angelo, flushing over his hesitation, turned quickly and broke into a run toward the steps.

"Did you know him, Mr. Bennett?"

Bennett nodded, a lock of his gray hair falling over his eye. "So did you," he said, his voice barely above a whisper.

"Who was it?"

"John Andrasko."

"You're—you sure?"

"Yes, I'm sure. John's been riding the eleven-thirty-eight to Knox every night for eight, ten years. I've sold him enough passes. He just bought a new one tonight, as a matter of fact."

Balzic walked back over to the body lying half under the bench. "Good Christ, John, I'm sorry." He was almost going to say he was sorry he hadn't recognized him, but the beer and cheese started coming up, and he just got his face over the edge of the platform in time. He coughed and gagged a couple more times before he wiped his mouth with his hanky. Spitting didn't get rid of the taste.

He was going back to Bennett to ask some other questions when he heard the shoes on the steps coming up.

Milt Weigh, the district attorney, came up, his breath heavy with the smell of gin. He was followed by Sam Carraza, his chief of detectives, and by John Dillman, another county detective. Carraza and Dillman both were raw-eyed and breathing heavily.

"Hello, Milt," Balzic said, nodding to Carraza and Dillman. "I think I ought to warn you guys, be ready to lose all that high-price stuff you been drinking."

"Balzic," Weigh said by way of greeting. "An ugly one?"

"Ugliest one I've seen since Tarawa. Over there. Under the bench."

Weigh, Carraza, and Dillman set off toward the body. The two detectives took a long look, but Weigh recoiled. "My God," he said and immediately turned away and came back to Balzic. "My God," he said again.

"Yeah," Balzic said. "I lost about half a beer, so if you're thinking you're going to lose your gin, don't hold it in on my account."

Weigh took a couple of deep breaths. "What do you have?"

"Just a name so far. John Andrasko. I've known him since I was a kid. Mr. Bennett here had to tell me, though. Says he just bought a pass from him tonight. But I'm really taking his word for it. I haven't gone through his pockets yet."

"Dillman?" Weigh called out.

"Yeah?"

"Check his pockets."

"I'm doing that."

"What's the station man say?" Weigh said.

"Just what I told you. Says he sold John a pass tonight and that he's been riding the eleven-thirty-

233

something every night to Knox for eight, ten years."

"He didn't say anything else?"

"I didn't get a chance to ask him."

"Well, let's go ask him."

They walked back to where Frank Bennett was sitting and kneading his palms.

"Mr. Bennett," Balzic said, "this is Mr. Weigh, the district attorney."

"How do you do, sir," Bennett said.

Weigh extended his hand and Bennett shook it feebly.

"I'd like to ask you some questions, Mr. Bennett."

"Go ahead. I doubt that I can tell you much, though," Bennett said.

"How did you learn about this?"

"Fireman from the eleven-thirty-eight came down and told me."

"What time—I mean, was this fellow Andrasko a regular?"

"Yessir. The only one. Been riding for years. Ever since he took the job over at Knox Steel. Eight, ten years at least. Longer, maybe."

"Did you see anybody else?"

"Nossir. Nobody. Of course that doesn't mean anything. There are lots of ways to get on this platform. You can come down State Street Extension from the other side over there, or you could walk up the tracks from either direction. Going past me is only one of the ways. But nobody went past me since eleven tonight except John. He bought his pass and we talked a bit."

"What time was that?"

"Well, on nights when John just comes in, he gets here about eleven-thirty, but on nights when he buys his pass, he generally comes in about

eleven-twenty and we shoot the breeze. Nothing important. We just talk. He was a nice fellow."

"How does he usually get here?"

"He walks. John doesn't like to drive. Never has. I guess that's why he's one of the few people left who still ride the trains."

John Dillman walked up then, holding everything he'd found in John Andrasko's pockets: a thin billfold, a ring of keys, a package of chewing tobacco, a pack of twisted Italian cigars, and four dollar bills and three dimes. "This is it," he said.

"Mr. Bennett," Weigh said, "you said he bought a pass tonight. How much money, if you know, would you say he might've had?"

"Well, he paid me with a twenty-dollar bill, as he always does. That money you're holding there is the change I gave him. Should be four dollars and thirty cents. Month pass to Knox costs fifteen-seventy."

"Mario," Weigh said, "I assume your people have contacted the state police."

Balzic nodded. "They should've been here by now."

"Mr. Bennett, are you positive nobody else went past you tonight?"

Bennett nodded slowly. "Yessir. But I've already told you that doesn't mean anything. I mean—no disrespect, Mr. Weigh—but somebody had to get up here tonight, and they didn't come by me."

"Here come the state boys," Dillman said. "Looks like they brought half the barracks."

Lieutenant Phil Moyer, in plain clothes, followed by Sergeant Ralph Stallcup, led a contingent of seven troopers up the steps onto the platform. One of them carried a camera and immediately began photographing the body of John Andrasko from a variety of angles. The rest of them, with no

234

direction from either Lieutenant Moyer or Sergeant Stallcup, fanned out over the platform and began examining it. Moyer ordered them off the platform after about ten minutes, and they started to make their way up and down the three sets of tracks.

Moyer and Stallcup listened as Frank Bennett repeated what little he knew about John Andrasko and the events leading up to the discovery of the body by the fireman from the eleven-thirty-eight to Knox. Moyer went through the effects found by Dillman, verifying the amount of money with the amounts Frank Bennett gave as the price of the pass and the change given.

"Mario," Moyer said, "what's it look like to you?"

"Looks to me probably what it looks like to you. Somebody either had a grudge or else that somebody's off his rocker. Nobody does that kind of job for any other reason that I know of. It sure wasn't for money, unless he was carrying a wad nobody knew about. But a guy like John, well, he was too steady. Too regular."

"You knew him?" Moyer said.

"Ever since I was a kid. Went all through school with him. We were in the same room most of the time."

"Wasn't there anything irregular about him?"

"Not that I knew about. He married a little late, I suppose. No. I can't even say that. He just didn't get married as early as the rest of us is what I meant to say."

"Gambler?"

"Not that I know of. No. He watched his money pretty close even when he was a kid."

"What did he do for a living?"

"He was a millwright over at Knox Steel. Before that I think he worked for one of the big steel outfits down the river. I'm not really sure."

"Ever in trouble?"

"Hell no. John was as straight a guy as everybody ought to be. If everybody was like him, you and me'd be looking for sensible work."

"From what you say, it looks like we can rule out a grudge job."

"Oh, I wouldn't do that. Not just yet anyway."

"Why not?"

"Well, as far as I know, John was a straight, regular guy. But that doesn't mean there wasn't somebody around who thought he was a prick. I just said I've known him most of my life, but I wasn't a drinking buddy of his or anything like that. He may have had a side to him he never showed me. For one thing, I've never even seen his wife. He kept pretty much to himself."

"Where'd he live?"

"He bought a small farm years ago about three miles out of town. North, on 986."

"And you say he rode the train every night to get to work?"

"That's what Mr. Bennett says."

"So how'd he get from his place to here every night?"

"I think I can answer that for you," Frank Bennett said. "John walked. He was a great believer in the virtue of walking."

"Why?"

"Said it kept him in shape."

"He had a driver's license. It's right here," Moyer said, pulling it out of Andrasko's thin, black wallet.

"Oh, he could drive all right," Bennett said. "But he hated to. Never drove unless he absolutely had to. Just to go shopping for groceries and for

235

things he needed for the farm."

"So he walked in here every night? More than three miles? In bad weather, too?"

"Yessir. Every night. Rain, snow, whatever. He walked."

"Well, hell," Moyer said. "Look here. He's got two vehicle registration cards. One for a Ford pickup and this one's for a Ford sedan. Why the hell's a guy who hates driving have two vehicles?"

"He said he needed them," Bennett replied. "Many's the time he wished he didn't need them, but then he'd just shrug and say what's the use. America was car-crazy, he used to say."

"Lieutenant?" one of the troopers walking the tracks called out. "Think you better come have a look at this."

Except for Frank Bennett, everybody on the platform set off toward the trooper. He was standing under the State Street bridge, and when they got to him, he flashed his lamp on the gravel near one of the rails between two ties. The light reflected off the fragments of a Coke bottle. Moyer squatted and took a pen from his inside pocket and lifted the neck of the bottle. It was the largest piece.

"Looks like we got the weapon."

"Which means that whoever did it went across the tracks and up the steps to State Street and then dropped it. Or threw it. Must've been thrown. I doubt it would've broken from that height, just being dropped."

"And I'll just bet if somebody took the trouble to throw it, he also took the trouble to wipe it clean," Moyer said.

"One thing's sure," Stallcup said, "he had to have a lot of blood on him."

"Well," Moyer said, standing, "get everything measured off and get the photographer. And get the plastic bags. I want as much of this bottle as we can get."

"Beaten to death with a Coke bottle," Milt Weigh said. "My God."

"Hell of a thought, ain't it?" Balzic said.

"Well," Moyer said, "I think that's about all we can do until we get some daylight. The coroner showed yet?"

"That's probably him now," Balzic said. "Behind the ambulance."

"That only leaves one thing," Moyer said. "Who wants the pleasure?"

"What are you talking about?" Milt Weigh said.

"The next of kin, Mr. Weigh. You want to give them the good news?"

"I'll pass that if you don't mind."

"How about you, Mario?"

"Yeah. I guess I'm up for this one. Rather do it alone."

"Hell, be my guest. And see what you can find out."

"Well, I'm not going to ask any questions. I'll nose around, but tonight ain't the night for asking questions."

"Why not?" Milt Weigh said.

"Well, if you want to ask them, Milt, you're welcome to come along and do the asking."

Weigh thrust his hands into his coat pockets. "I'll take your word for it."

"You'll let me know. Right, Mario?" Moyer said.

"Yeah, sure," Balzic replied, clearing his throat and spitting. "See you, gentlemen." He turned to leave the platform as the county coroner, Dr. Wallace Grimes, was placing a stethoscope on John Andrasko's chest, confirming what was obvious.

HANIEL LONG
"How Pittsburgh Returned to the Jungle"

Pittsburgh becomes a mecca
for sightseers, botanists, and newly-weds

Time: The future   Setting: Pittsburgh

"How Pittsburgh Returned to the Jungle" is a fantasy that builds on a couple of time-honored comic devices. One of them is the game of reversing expectation. If Pittsburgh is renowned for its mammoth technology and air pollution, why not imagine its opposite — a Pittsburgh known for infinite greenery and horticultural perfume? Part of the comic strategy also involves applying literally the cliches of conventional wisdom. Are people advised "Beautify your cities" or "Keep America green"? Long's fantasy takes these maxims the whole route, returning Pittsburgh to a state of nature.

Like much comedy, "How Pittsburgh Returned to the Jungle" finally manages to raise questions that are not as easily answered as the light tone of the piece might imply. Is this strange floral flourishing of Pittsburgh any less bizarre a civic image than the real-life one? Would a jungle of vines and flowers clogging the streets be any less productive than a tangle of traffic? Would a worldwide reputation for flora provide fewer jobs than fame in "basic industry"?

Bizarre as its scenario is, "How Pittsburgh Returned to the Jungle" succeeds in posing the question, Why not? Why not give it a try? But then Long also implies that it will not be up to the citizenry to make that decision: A bright entrepreneur will have to come up with the idea and maneuver it through the state legislature.

Haniel Long's own roots were deep in Pittsburgh. Though he was born abroad in 1888, the son of a missionary, he came to Pittsburgh as a young child and was to remain for some forty years. He begins his prose poem "Homestead, 1892" with his childhood recollection:

Homestead is almost my first memory.
A July morning of early childhood. I bring in the
  milk bottles and the morning paper, and across the
  paper is big black type.
My father starts when he sees the headlines and says
  to my mother,
"Some anarchist has stabbed Clay Frick."

As a local minister, Long's father used his church as a relief station for striking workers.

Most of Long's adult career in Pittsburgh (from 1910 to 1929) was spent teaching English literature at Carnegie Tech, where he was a colleague of Elizabeth Moorhead (who is also represented in this anthology). In 1929 Long retired and moved to the Southwest; he died in 1956.

In Pittsburgh Portraits, *Elizabeth Moorhead describes Haniel Long in his years at Carnegie Tech:*

He had the bewildered look of one who is caught unawares in a great humming hive of alien endeavor. . . . Carnegie Tech was instituted for practical purposes leading to what is called "success." . . . Would Long be able to lift his teaching into the realm of imagination beyond the mere mechanics of paragraphing and punctuation?

As this selection indicates, Long also had ambivalent feelings about Pittsburgh itself, a fascination that drew him to it for literary subjects (for example, his volume Pittsburgh Memoranda), *a revulsion at its harshness. In the end, the natural beauty of the Southwest won out.*

"How Pittsburgh Returned to the Jungle"

The story of how Pittsburgh returned to the jungle may or may not have a moral, but it is a curious example of the effect of legislation on a modern city. One spring a millionaire nurseryman, lobbying for his private gain, and in league with a manufacturer of window boxes, was clever enough to attach to a piece of legislation, a rider which had nothing to do with the measure in question and which favored abundantly his own business. This rider made it compulsory for every Pittsburgher who owned or rented a window to have a window box, to have a window box indeed for every window. In the confusion which prevails at the close of a tiresome session, the state legislature passed the bill—a popular one—without noticing the rider, and in due course it became law.

The millionaire nurseryman, who had a monopoly of the sale of seeds and flowers in his city, saw to it that the officers enforced the law. At once there was a loud outcry. The owners of skyscrapers protested. They were joined by the owners of factories and by the private corporations. The governor sent a special representative to take charge of the situation, and a number of property owners were arrested. Their friends brought the case into court, but they were defeated. The judge, it was whispered, had a private fondness for flowers; and he was known to have said that the law was no more unreasonable than most laws. The property owners appealed the case.

Meanwhile the nurseryman and the box maker were busy spreading propaganda. Naturalists and platform orators of note appeared mysteriously in the city to lecture on behalf of flowers. A great musician publicly praised the law. So did a well-known evangelist. The national association of women's clubs hired an investigator, and on the strength of his report came out flatly in the cause of window boxes. Here and there in down-town windows flowers began to appear. An instinctive liking for their color and fragrance, in the hearts of stenographers, abetted the design. It introduced a new interest and source of rivalry, and also a new reason for looking out of the window.

The supreme court upheld the law, and the manufacturer of window boxes quadrupled his plant and operated it day and night. The face of the skyscrapers began to turn green. Bittersweet, honeysuckle, climbing hydrangea, and even grapevines crawled along the surfaces of white tile and red brick, and ran up and down on little trellises. The presence in their season of jonquils and anemones, of pansies, larkspur and iris, of peonies and dahlias, of asters and chrysanthemums, wrought an indescribable change in the deep canyons. This change was not in color only; the flowers attracted insects, especially bees, and many varieties of birds. Every traffic policeman put a neat little bird-box on his Stop-and-Go signal, for purple martins. Stone valleys, where hitherto had sounded only the noise of vehicles, were now filled with birdcries and the humming of tiny insects.

The vines grew longer year by year, and hung in the air, or were shorn close about the windows. Flowers flared in many new varieties. Visitors were struck by the novelty of the sight, and reports of a new wonder filled the world. Pictures of Pittsburgh in wistaria time or in the season of gladiolus ap-

239

peared in the movies everywhere, and were marvelled at by millions. The city hitherto notorious as being devoted to naked industry was now featured on all American tours for its beauty, and became the mecca of the recently married, of sightseers disappointed in Niagara, of ornithologists, botanists, and searchers for the exotic.

A great new revenue came thus to the city. That portion of humanity which makes its living on the traveler began to influence the business life of the town of steel. Hotels of mammoth proportions went up on tier after tier of leisurely gardens to heights of over sixty stories. It was well known how wonderful were the hanging gardens of Pittsburgh; they contained trees and lakes, and paths which wound for miles over green chasms. Awnings of white and orange covered the wide roofs, and all winter long the sun flashed on glass walls which protected flowers.

In the meantime, though not altogether from the invasion of the window boxes, the city lost its industrial prestige. It had a bitter struggle with competitors younger than itself and more favorably situated for manufacturing. Gary, Pueblo, and Birmingham were like young Titans who proved too strong for their giant father. When the time came that it was no longer expedient to maintain the larger furnaces, Pittsburgh awoke to find its beauty its source of livelihood.

Certain skyscrapers, now without tenants, were given over unreservedly to horticulture. Then in deadly earnest did the jungle set out to conquer the city of ravines and gulches. Little by little its tide ran up the river valleys and across the abandoned mills, softening angular roofs and turning

cupolas into amazing sights. The bridges across the five rivers became fairer than the bridges of vision.

The air grew clearer. No smoke was permitted; only electric locomotives penetrated the city. The roads and highways were banked with shrubs and blossoms. If the wind blew in the right direction, the citizens of Youngstown, or Morgantown, or Cleveland could smell the fragrance of Pittsburgh from afar. It seemed to them strange and fabulous as it overpowered the sulphur dioxide to which they were accustomed, and they would say to one another, "Oh to be in Pittsburgh, in beautiful Pittsburgh!"

The population of the city changed its nature. Anglo-Saxons, being unhandy with flowers, decreased. But thousands and thousands of gardeners were needed to produce those floral effects which men talked of from Cape Town to Thibet; and the children of immigrants found Pittsburgh much to their taste. As to the millionaire nurseryman who was the unwitting cause of so complete a transformation, his was a singular fate. The unforgiving corporations pursued him relentlessly; and though they found themselves powerless to check the movement he had started, they had their revenge, for they convicted him of bribery and corrupt practices. Rather than go to prison he committed suicide, clasping to his bosom a bouquet of lilies. The passing of years changed him into a symbolic figure, a martyr and a saint. The visitor to Pittsburgh may now see his beautiful memorial down at the Point, where two sky-blue rivers, mingling under his unseeing eyes, form the Ohio, that stream which, as the poets of Louisiana say, flows south to them from a city of unfading flowers.

ART DIRECTION: William Ackley, Mellon Bank, N.A.
GRAPHIC DESIGN: Caropresi Associates, Inc., Pittsburgh, Pa.
Artists: Susan Paulus, Gary Geyer, and Kit Ford
PAPER: P. H. Glatfelter Company, Spring Grove, Pa.
PRINTING: Deeds Associates, Inc., Pittsburgh, Pa.
EDITION BINDING: Lake Book Bindery, Inc., Cicero, Ill.